Susan's Story

by

John P. Palmer

Copyright 2020
London, Ontario Canada

Susan's Story is a companion novel to **2605**. Each novel stands on its own, and while they can be read in either order, it is probably helpful know that **2605** was written first.

Susan's Story is divided into four parts:

    Part One..............Getting the News
    Part Two..............New Beginnings
    Part Three..........The World of Politics
    Part Four............Senator Susan Young

Other books by John P. Palmer available on Amazon:
- **2605**
- **Three Murder Mysteries**
- **Murder at the Office Christmas Party**

Copyright John P. Palmer, London, Ontario, 2020
Rev. 01

Chapter 1 – Getting the News

We didn't usually need an alarm because Fred always woke up at 6:30, but he was out of town on business, and so I set the alarm as a precaution.

The alarm went off at 6:30am ... right after I woke up.

I showered and dressed, and on my way downstairs to the kitchen I stopped to wake the children for school. We had two children, Timothy (15) and Liz (13). Like most teenagers, they liked to sleep in, and so I didn't just call to them; I woke them individually to make sure they would actually get up and be ready for school on time.

I started my coffee, set out the cereal and milk, and poured juice for each of us. Then I checked the laptop we kept in the kitchen. As I hoped and expected, there was a message from Fred:

> 'morning, Love. Looking forward to meeting with Jordan Singer. I guess he's the point man for our project with Cantor Fitzgerald. I'll let you know how things go. Love to you and the kids.

Fred was a managing partner for the agricultural finance firm, Klein-Staily. He usually worked at his office here in Omaha, Nebraska, but that morning he was in New York to work on a deal with Cantor-Fitzgerald. It was an important meeting for Fred; he'd been having some difficulties at work, and he was expecting that this meeting would help make things less bad or maybe even a little better.

I hoped Fred's meeting would help him get back on a more even keel and we could become closer as a family again. We had drifted apart a bit while Fred was involved in the go-go world of finance, and that concerned me; but it looked as if we could maybe regroup now – before it was too late for Fred and me, and before it was too late for the children.

I replied:

> Hope it goes well! Call me when you're done.
> Love you!
> ~~Susan~~

As the children sat down for breakfast, I mused, "I'm thinking of trying to make chicken lasagna for supper tonight," and I took a package of boneless chicken thighs out of the freezer.

"Well..." said Liz with a hint of doubt. "I like lasagna; that might be okay."

"Do you have a recipe for it?" asked Timothy. "Or will this be another 'experiment'?"

He actually used air quotes and was grinning devilishly as he asked.

"We eat too much red meat," I pronounced. "I thought we might try having more chicken. Chicken lasagna sounds good."

As we ate our breakfasts I asked, "What's on after school today?" I didn't really have to ask them – I knew their schedules. I didn't want to nag them; I only wanted to make sure they knew what they had to do, and I wanted them to let me know what they were doing.

"I have soccer," answered Timothy. "I probably won't be home until after five-thirty.

"And I have Spanish choir," said Liz. "It's only half an hour or so, though. I should be home by quarter-to-five."

"Everyone have their homework? Textbooks? Library books? Snacks?" It was my standard set of questions before they set off for school.

Liz had to walk farther to get to school, but her school started later than Timothy's so the two of them left the house together most days. Timothy was in 10th grade at Burke High School, and Liz was in 8th grade at Beveridge Middle School.

I loved seeing them walk off to school together. Timothy was tall, like his father – already over six feet tall, but Liz was only about five-feet, four inches tall, about an inch shorter than me, and it looked as if she wasn't going to get much taller. The Mutt-and-Jeff contrast between them as they walked up the street together always made me smile.

They left the house about 7:45, and I opened the morning paper to do the word jumble and crossword.

On Sunday mornings, Fred and I always sat across the kitchen counter from each other with our coffee and tried to do the New York Times crossword together. That was one reason we had the laptop in the kitchen: to look up answers for the crossword! I missed Fred when he was out of town, and even though it was only Tuesday, not Sunday, I enjoyed pretending he was there with me, doing the word jumble and then the crossword. I was eager for him to come home, and my doing the word puzzles, pretending he was there with me, was comforting.

That was the last time I would feel comfortable for a long time.

I was jarred from my contentment when the telephone rang. It was Thelma Hazelton, our neighbor two doors up and across the street.

"Susan, do you have the news on?"

"No, why?"

"Go put CNN on. Someone just flew a big plane into one of the World Trade Center Towers in New York City."

My heart skipped a beat. I knew Fred was in New York, and I thought maybe his appointment was at the World Trade Center.

"Oh no," I murmured softly. "Fred may be there."

I turned on CNN, and sure enough they were talking about how a big jetliner had flown right into one of the World Trade Center Towers.

"I'll be right over," and Thelma hung up the phone.

I took out my cell phone and called Fred.

No answer. "The person you are calling is out of cellular range," an anonymous-sounding recorded message told me.

I tried two more times and heard the same message repeated.

I was trembling as Thelma rang the doorbell and then just came on in without waiting for me to answer. She must have sensed something – she had never done that before.

I set my phone down and began crying uncontrollably as she came over and held me.

I must have been crying for more than a minute when our land line and my cellphone both began ringing.

"I'll answer your home phone if you like," Thelma offered. "You take the cell phone."

"He'll be ok," I said out loud. "The area must be pure chaos. The plane must have hit at least ten minutes before his appointment."

I began crying again, but tried to control myself as I answered my cell phone. It was Ben Gruvel, Fred's closest friend and colleague at Klein-Staily.

"Susan, it's Ben. Have you heard from Fred?"

"Nooooo," I started sobbing again. "Have you? I can't get an answer on his cell phone."

"We can't get through to him either. Susan, his appointment was with Cantor-Fitz in the World Trade Center. Have you been following the news this morning?" he asked in very calm, measured tones.

"Yes, I have CNN on now. I'm so scared, Ben. What happened? What's happening? How can I get through to Fred?"

"We've tried calling Singer, the man he had an appointment with at Cantor, but we can't reach him. We can't get an answer from the main reception number for them either. So all we know is what we're seeing on television and OH MY GOD!! Another plane just flew into the other tower."

"I know!!! I just saw it. Ben! Tell me he'll be okay."

Ben hesitated almost imperceptibly. I knew he was trying to think of something positive to say.

"He might not have gotten to his appointment yet when the plane hit... And maybe Singer's office is on the opposite side of the building from where the plane hit. Hold on.... They're saying the plane hit about the 100th floor of the north tower. Singer's office is on the 101st floor. So maybe Fred was able to get out down a different staircase and the cell towers there just aren't working right now. ...."

I knew Ben was trying to think of every possibility that might mean Fred was okay. But I was crying anyway.

"Thanks, Ben."

And then a thought hit me.

"The children!" I shouted. "I have to get the children! Call me the minute you hear anything. ANYTHING!!" I yelled into the phone and hung up.

Thelma had already answered two calls for me on our home phone.

"Susan, I'll need something to take notes with. I have a feeling you're going to get a lot of calls this morning, asking about Fred."

As I got a pad and pen for her, I hurriedly said, "I have to get the children. I can't leave them in school to hear about this before I can talk with them. And…" I started crying again… "and I need them here, with me."

As I rushed to the car, I heard Thelma answer the phone. "Young residence… No, I'm sorry she can't come to the phone right now. May I take your name, phone number, and a message?"

Meanwhile I had my cell phone out and was dialing Timothy's school.

"Burke High," said the voice at the other end.

"Hello," I started, trying to be calm. "This is Susan Young, Timothy Young's mother. He's in tenth grade there. We've just had a serious family emergency, and I'm on my way to the school to pick up Timothy. Could you please have him bring things and meet me in the parking lot?"

"Just a minute, please, Mrs. Young."

There was a pause. It was probably only about five seconds, but it felt like five minutes.

"Hello, Mrs. Young," said a different voice. "We sometimes get prank calls, and so we need some more information. I see you have a password set up with the school. What is your password for Timothy?"

"Celebrate! Can you please send him out with his things now?!!" and I hung up. I was borderline hysterical and I knew it. I was doing my best to try to control my emotions.

I pulled into the school parking lot just as Timothy was coming out. I wiped my eyes, blew my nose, and got out of the car to greet him. I wanted to hug him, not tell him the news across the console in the car where we couldn't comfort each other.

My getting out of the car signaled Timothy that something was wrong. He had no idea what was going on, but he was worried.

"What's wrong, Mom?"

I held him tight. "You know your father is in New York on business? He had an appointment with someone in one of the World Trade Center towers, and two planes have been flown into those towers, one hit right about where your father's appointment was."

I tried to maintain my composure, but Timothy was losing his. Suddenly, he yelled louder than I had ever heard him yell, "NOOOOOOOOO," and went over to the car and started pounding on the fender. "No! No! No!"

I put my arm around him as we stood next to the car.

"I've tried calling him and can't get an answer. Uncle Ben has tried, too. There's a chance he wasn't at his appointment yet, or that maybe he was on the other side of the building and managed to get out. We just don't know."

Timothy stood straight up. "Mom, what are we going to do?" and he started crying again.

I became very matter-of-fact and said, "I don't want you children subjected to all sorts of questions until we know what's happening. Also, I want you both with me, at home. I need to call Liz's school now so we can pick her up. Do you have everything you'll need from school?"

"Yeah, I guess…. I don't know."

I dialed Beveridge Middle School, where we went through the password routine again.

And then the voice asked, "May I ask the nature of the family emergency?"

"I want to talk to Liz about it before discussing it with anyone else," I replied. "It's serious, and I hope you'll understand. If necessary, I can call you back in a couple of hours to let you know."

"Oh." The voice seemed surprised. "Of course. I'll send her out now."

"Prying busybodies!" I said under my breath as I hung up.

When we pulled up to the drop-off station at Beveridge Middle School, Liz was already outside waiting for us. I left the engine running, and both Timothy and I jumped out and hurried over to Liz.

When she saw our faces, she said a low "No," shaking her head. And again "No…. Noooooo." I hugged her tight, and then Timothy joined in and the three of us hugged each other all at once.

"Mom?" Liz asked.

"Liz, have you heard any news about what's happening in New York?"

"Only that some dumb pilots flew planes, like, into the World Trade Center. Why?"

"Your father had an appointment up in one of the towers."

Liz started crying, and I hurried on.

"I've tried calling him and so has Uncle Ben, but we can't get an answer. We don't know where he is or what happened."

"Try again!" Liz urged. "Mom! Try again!"

I hit redial and held the phone out for us all to hear.

"The person you are calling is out of cellular range," the recording said.

"Uncle Ben thinks there's a chance the first plane hit near where your father's appointment was, but that maybe it hit before your father got there or maybe your father was able to get out on the other side of the building.

As we drove back home, Timothy took my phone and kept redialing his father's cell phone number, but there was still no answer.

The radio was filled with news and speculation about what had happened. President Bush had been spirited out of the classroom he'd been visiting and was being kept safe somewhere. The general consensus was that terrorists had coordinated hijacking the planes, flying them into the World Trade Center towers on some spectacular suicide mission.

As we pulled into the driveway, I stopped short of going into the garage.

"Why?" I asked, trying to remain calm, but I was horribly unsuccessful. I slammed my fists against the steering wheel, "And why today, when Fred was there?"

As we got out of the car, I put my arms around the children and held them tight, one on each side of me as we hobbled up the front walk in an awkward threesome, wanting to be close.

Thelma opened the door before we got to it, and gave each of the children a big hug and then she hugged me again. The four of us tried mightily to hold back our tears, but we still cried a bit in the process.

"Any news?" I asked.

Thelma just shook her head and turned to go back in.

The children went to the back family room and turned on the TV. They plunked their backpacks down onto the floor and plunked themselves onto the easy chairs that had somehow become "theirs". Timothy kept dialing his father's number every two or three minutes.

He never got an answer.

"Thelma, there might be some coffee left," I half-stammered as we made our way to the kitchen. "Would you like some, or should I make a fresh pot?"

"Let's make a fresh pot," Thelma said, but before she could dump out the old coffee, I grabbed the pot and poured a cup for myself. I held up the pot toward her in a gesture that asked if she would like some of the old coffee before we made a new pot, but she scowled and wrinkled her nose. I smiled and said, "I just can't waste it."

"You had eight more calls while you were out. One from a company that wants to clean your ductwork...." And we both rolled our eyes.

"There were six from various friends of yours, or so they said, who knew Fred was in New York and wanted to know if you had heard from him. And there was one from a reporter who somehow found out that Fred was there. I just told them all you couldn't come to the phone and that I'd be happy to take a message."

The phone rang again.

"Hello. Young residence…… No, I'm sorry she can't come to the phone. If you'd like I can take a message……. Okay. Cindy Gruvel…" and she started to write down a number.

I held my hand up to Thelma and took the phone from her.

"Cindy! Thanks for calling."

"Susan, I'm so concerned for you and your kids. Ben called and told me what's going on … or actually that nobody knows for sure what's going on. Would you like us to come over to be with you?

"I'd love that, Cindy. Our neighbor Thelma Hazelton is here now; she's the woman who answered the phone. I think we might need quite a bit of help until we find out what's happening …"

And then it registered with me. "Us? Both you and Ben?"

"Yes, Ben suggested it. He'll bring his laptop and cell phone so he can stay in touch with the office while we're there."

It was only a little after eight-thirty, and already so much had happened.

Chapter 2 – A Sinking Feeling

Thelma showed me the message pad she had started.

"Thelma, would you mind answering the phone for a while longer? I don't think I can answer all the questions right now, especially since nobody knows what's happening."

"Of course."

The phone rang again. "Young residence. May I take a message? ... No, she isn't able to come to the phone. I told you that before," and she hung up.

"It's that pushy reporter from the Herald," Thelma sighed. "I'm sure he's just doing his job, but he sounds pretty obnoxious."

"Well, let's hope he doesn't decide to stop by and harass us."

"Mom?" asked Timothy. "Why don't we turn the ringer off? It's not going to stop ringing until a long time after we find out how Dad is."

"You're right, Timothy. He'll call my cell phone the minute he can..."

"People can just leave a message," I told Thelma as I reached under the phone and moved the ringer lever to 'OFF'. "The ringing will drive us crazy if we don't turn this off."

Timothy ran upstairs to turn off the ringer on the bedroom phone, and then the children sat with me on the sofa. Timothy controlled the TV remote, switching randomly between CNN and the four major networks.

"What's going on, Mom?" asked Liz. "Why would people do this? Like, what did we ever do to them?"

I just shook my head and squeezed her a bit. "I don't know, Liz, but I'm guessing some people somewhere are really angry with our government, and this is the only way they know to show it."

When the doorbell rang, Thelma jumped up and said, "I'll get it. No one will bother you today." She had fire in her eyes, as if she was preparing to do battle with just about anyone.

Thelma and I had known each other ever since Fred and I moved onto the block sixteen years earlier. We'd had coffee together, done aerobics or walked together regularly, and we had jointly shepherded our children through the three Ss: scouts, schools, and sports. We were both committed to our nurturing roles, and we frequently compared stories about the trials and tribulations of suburban motherhood.

It was Ben and Cindy at the door. As they came into the family room, I started crying again. Cindy hugged me and then Ben hugged me, both of them giving me meaningless reassurances that nevertheless comforted me.

Cindy sat on the sofa between the children while Ben motioned me to the kitchen.

Ben was over six-feet tall and fit as a fiddle. He was smart, and with his tanned good looks he had a commanding presence, both in the office and socially. He had been like a surrogate father for Fred and father-in-law for me.

"We've all been trying to reach Fred," he said in a low voice, "But we haven't been able to get through to him yet."

"Ben, it hasn't even been an hour since the plane hit that building. I'm guessing he either got out but hasn't been able to get through to us yet, or he is up there injured, waiting to be rescued when the emergency crews can get to him. I *have* to think that."

And then I turned toward the counter to hide more tears and asked, "Would you like a cup of coffee? Thelma just made this pot…"

"Sure. Black."

"OH NO!!" shouted Thelma, pointing at the TV. "One of the towers just collapsed!"

I nearly did too. I staggered to one of the easy chairs, where Thelma and Ben half-caught me as they helped me down into it.

The children got up and came over to the armchair and each of them sat on an arm of the chair, leaning their heads against mine. We were all too shocked to cry.

"Which tower was it," Ben asked. "Did anyone catch that?"

Just then the announcer said, "The south tower has collapsed, and they are trying to evacuate everyone they can from the north tower. The south tower took a bigger, more devastating direct hit, and so authorities are hoping the north tower won't collapse. But as a precaution all emergency personnel have been told to evacuate the north tower. ..."

Ben breathed a tiny sigh of relief and scratched his left eyebrow. "Well, Fred's appointment was in the north tower. Let's hope he got out already or is well on his way out."

The children and I just sat there stunned while Ben stepped back into the kitchen to talk with someone at Klein-Staily. A minute later, he came back to the family room and announced, "We have both Lucy and Murph assigned to the phones, trying to call anyone they can in New York to find out about Fred, but they can't get through. Everybody and his uncle is trying to call in or out of New York City, and the phone lines are completely clogged up. They'll keep trying, though, and they'll let us know as soon as there is any news."

Ben placed another call to the office. I didn't hear everything, but at one point he said, "Get some people on the ground there to help as soon as you can. Check rescue centers and hospitals. And send someone to his hotel…"

When the north tower collapsed a few minutes later, I moaned. I didn't know where Fred was. I didn't know whether he was there, whether he had escaped, or whether he had even gotten there. I wanted to scream, but I couldn't; it came out as a guttural moan.

"Mom?" Timothy looked at me questioningly. "Mom?... Mom? … …Mom!"

He finally got my attention. His look showed more concern than fear.

"Mom? Are you okay? Can I get you anything?"

I had been moaning a low "Noooooo".

I looked up at him and said. "Let's hope what Uncle Ben says is right. Let's hope your father got out in time but can't get through to us."

But the waiting and the uncertainty were killing us all.

Just then the doorbell rang again. Thelma started to get up from the sofa, but Ben held up his hand and answered it himself. We heard an unfamiliar voice saying something, and then Ben very loudly and slowly said, "No, you may not have just a quick word with her. We'll let everyone know as soon as we know anything."

The voice said something else, and then Ben exploded, "'No' means 'no'. Get the hell out of here. If you come back uninvited, you'll be wearing this hot coffee." And he slammed the door.

As he came back to the family room, I detected a hint of a smile.

"It was Jeremy Hall from the Herald," he said. "He has a way of dramatizing and exploiting human tragedy. Don't anyone talk to him until we know what's happening. Okay?" He paused. "Okay?"

We all nodded.

"Thanks, Ben. Fred and I don't much care for that man. I know he gets stories that sell newspapers, but he really does squeeze every ounce of drama out of human-interest stories."

I choked up again as I realized I was speaking about Fred and me in the present tense. I was still hoping we would hear from him any minute.

"What should we tell people who come to the door," Thelma asked.

I thought for a few moments. "If it's our neighbors, please tell them we appreciate their concern but that we know absolutely nothing. We'll let people know as soon as we find out anything. Also please tell them that I'm in shock and have some friends looking after me. Tell them the children are here with me and are fine but we are really puzzled, concerned, and worried."

That felt weird. The way I said that made me feel as if I was acting like a press secretary for a politician or something. I had done some media work off and on for Arkero Foods over the past twenty years, but it sounded strange, the way I said that.

And then I remembered how all the neighbors sent food to a family whenever there was a death in the family, and so I added, "Thelma, I don't know if it will come to this, but if any of the neighbors sends food over, let's make sure we thank them and write it down on a separate sheet of paper."

I knew I wouldn't need food from the neighbors right then; I would want to cook supper, just to take my mind off the uncertainty.

I was happy Thelma and the Gruvels were with us, and I was glad Ben would be answering the door for us. I didn't like the idea of being home alone, without someone there to help, and I was dreading the evening and nighttime, if it came to that.

But I was way ahead of myself. "Think in the present. Think in the present tense." I repeated to myself.

The doorbell rang again. Ben refilled his cup with hot coffee and went to answer it.

It was a television crew wanting to capture our moods and reactions as the news unfolded! I already resented the intrusions into people's lives by various members of the media, but I hated them all that day. Some news company actually kept a reporter with a portable video camera posted near our home for the next twelve hours.

I smiled at Ben gratefully when he returned to the family room. "And don't let any self-appointed so-called 'grief counselors' or church ministers in, either," I said. "We need to know what's happening. Fred may be perfectly okay. We just don't know." I was determined to hold out hope.

It was nearly ten o'clock Omaha time. It had been two hours since the plane hit the north tower. I kept reassuring the children and myself, "He'll be okay. He's fine. He just can't reach us yet."

Ben said, "Susan. I have my laptop with me. If it's okay with you, I'll just set up a bit in the dining room. But mostly for now Cindy and I are here to do whatever needs doing."

We knew there was nothing that "needed doing", but I was grateful for the emotional support they were providing for the children and me.

The rest of the day, Ben answered the door for us, and when we turned the ringer back on, Thelma handled the phone calls. I'd have been a total wreck if they hadn't been there with me.

Chapter 3 – **Afternoon Uncertainty**

For the next hour or so, I sat with the children, watching the news, holding hands or touching them somehow the entire time. Timothy kept checking my cellphone, dialing his father's number, but to no avail.

I knew in my heart that the odds were not high that Fred had survived, but I wouldn't allow anyone to give up hope.

Around eleven, we were all getting antsy. We wanted news of Fred, but we hated watching the rehashing of rehashings on the news. At one point Ben came in to tell us they had people in New York City stationed at nearly every possible hospital and emergency clinic, looking for Fred or, failing that, looking for any information they could find about Fred.

I was a total wreck, but I suggested to the children that they help me put together the chicken lasagna for supper. That got us all going.

"Cindy and Thelma, I think there's enough bread, cheese, lunch meat, and other food around. Let's put out sandwich makings for lunch, okay?"

Once the sandwich makings were on the kitchen table, Timothy broke off from helping with the lasagna, but before he made his own sandwich, he asked us, "What would you like, Mom? Liz?"

He was offering to make sandwiches for us. I didn't remember his ever having done that before. He could see that things needed doing, not so much to get them done but to show his care and concern for his sister and me. I smiled at him and melted inside.

"Maybe just some lettuce, cheese, and tomato? And you know I like just a hint of mayo."

While he got started on the sandwiches, I turned to his sister. "Liz, why don't you ask people what they would like to drink?"

We pulled some chairs into the eating area, and Ben joined us when the food was ready.

"We don't usually pray before meals," I said, "but can we please each pray silently for Fred's safe return?" The six of us reached out and held each other's hands around the table before we sat down.

That afternoon, the local radio stations and television stations carried the news that maybe Fred was at the World Trade Center when the planes hit. Maybe. The result was more media at our doorstep, more phone calls from friends and neighbors, and more neighbors stopping by to see if they could do anything.

Meanwhile, there was nothing we could do but wait, and every minute was excruciating.

"Anything!" I said to the television. "Anything. Tell us something!"

Ben was on the phone much of the afternoon, calling people in New York, making sure they had photos of Fred to take to medical centers and hospitals. At one point he said, "We need to know where he is and what happened. Don't worry about that! We need to know!"

"Is there any word from his hotel?" I asked Ben.

"I finally got through to the front desk at the hotel, and he hasn't checked out yet. I told them to hold the room for another night at least."

Later he called them again and reported, "They have a computer system at the hotel that tells them every time a card is used to open each hotel room door. They checked their system, and nobody went into Fred's room after he left except the maid service at about 11:30 their time. He hasn't made it back to his hotel room yet."

Thelma was back on the phone, fending off well-wishers, news junkies, and members of the media. Cindy was handling the front door. And Ben was in the dining room, which I thought of as "mission control". But the children and I had nothing to do but sit and watch the television and wait and fret.

At one point mid-afternoon, Timothy said, "I can't take this anymore, just sitting here and doing nothing. Would it be ok if I go for a walk?"

"Sure," and I patted his hand. "Liz would you like to go too?"

Ben immediately stopped them. "If you go out the front door, you'll be swarmed by members of the media and maybe neighbors. Whatever you do, don't talk to them. Just say, 'We don't know.' And if they continue to pester you, turn and yell, 'We don't know! Leave us alone!' And keep repeating that."

Liz suggested, "What if we, like, go out the back and cross through the Plagge's backyard over to Nicholas Street?"

"That should work," Ben thought out loud. But then he added harshly, "Remember, though, we don't know anything. Don't speculate. This is your family and your privacy. Don't give it away."

As the children snuck off through our backyard and alongside the Plagge's house, I said to the others, "Thank you all so much. I really don't want to deal with the media right now. But also while the children are gone, we need to speculate and plan."

I felt cold-hearted. But I didn't want to speculate in front of the children. Not yet, anyway.

"I know Fred," I added. "He always gets to his appointments early."

I had inadvertently used the present tense again. That both comforted me and upset me. I smiled just a bit, remembering all our arguments about whether it was okay to arrive at places early.

"I'm sure he was there when the plane hit. I don't want to admit it out loud, but between the four of us adults, I have to say I am really scared."

I realize now, thinking back, that I didn't want to say that I thought he was probably dead. I didn't want to voice that thought, and I didn't want the others to think it, even though I was sure they did. I certainly didn't want to say it, in case I was wrong and he was still alive. All I could say was, "I am really scared."

"Don't you understand plain English?" Ben yelled as he answered the front door. He stepped out, and there was considerable yelling outside. Then Ben opened the front door and stood there.

"I'm opening this door so that Ms. Young can hear us," he said in a commanding tone of voice. "Ms. Young and her family cherish their privacy. You must leave them alone in this very difficult period of uncertainty. They and we have absolutely no news about Fred Young. None. When we know more, we will let you know. Until then I must insist on two things: One, you have to assume we have no information until we notify you; trust us on this. Two, you must move off the lawn, off the driveway, and out to the street. This is private property and you are trespassing."

"Who are you? A family spokesman?" asked a voice I didn't recognize. There were other voices, too. Apparently it was a minor media scrum. Ben had positioned himself on the steps looking down at the reporters.

"I am a long-time family friend and a partner with Fred Young at Klein-Staily."

"Can we have your name?"

I peeked and saw Ben take his card case from his jacket pocket and pass out business cards. It was subtle, but it was his way of trying to stay out of the limelight by not saying any more to the reporters.

I smiled at Ben when he came back in and closed the door. "Thanks. I know we'll have to talk to them at some point, but I'm not up to it right now. Maybe tomorrow; maybe when we know more."

While the children were gone, I opened the laptop and checked my email, hoping that maybe Fred had found a way to send a message. There was no message from him, but there were twenty-five new email messages. Three were from news lists I was on; three more were ads, spam, and junk; and the rest were from people asking about Fred. I created a new email folder and just transferred all those messages to that folder, thinking I might look at them later. And then I put up an auto-response that said, "Hi. Thanks for your message. In case you're asking, we don't know anything about Fred. We need to be alone right now. We'll let people know when we do know something. I'm sure you understand. Thank you."

An hour later, Timothy and Liz returned through the backyard.

"We had no problems with reporters or anyone," Timothy said.

"Good. Where did you walk to avoid them?" I asked.

"We just went up to Charles Street and sat under the small trees there, looking out at Candlewood Reservoir. Dad used to take us there all the time when we were little."

"Remember the time we got inflatable boats and, like, went out on the water?" Liz asked. And then she added with an air of maturity, "I hope he's safe, Mom, but we know the situation."

Liz was always a realist, but even she couldn't force herself to say, "He's probably dead."

I began to think about dinner and the evening and overnight. I nearly panicked. I didn't want us to be alone, and I wasn't sure what to say or do.

"Thelma, we'll have plenty of chicken lasagna for supper. Why don't you and your family to join us for dinner tonight? We can make a huge salad, and maybe even have a glass or two of wine."

Her family included her husband Dale and their two children, Seth (16) and Aaron (13). Their children were great friends and classmates of Timothy and Liz. They had grown up together, gone to school together, and played together much of the time.

Thelma called them first and then said, "Sure, they'd like to come and do whatever they can to help," Thelma said. "They'll be here about five if that's okay."

I turned to Cindy and Ben. "I hope you two can stay, too!"

"Sure, we can," said Cindy without even looking at Ben. It just seemed right for them all to be there with us.

Around 4:30 that afternoon, the food began to arrive. It was a tradition in the neighborhood, especially among the full-time homemakers: we made food and sent it to anyone who even *might* be in need.

Timothy and Liz hadn't caught on to the tradition because they were usually at school or somewhere when I was cooking or baking for someone in the neighborhood. They were amused and dumbfounded by all the food people sent. Casseroles, chicken dishes, meatloaf, scalloped potatoes, pies, fresh tomatoes from someone's garden, and of course Mrs. Redding's home-baked rye loaves that she sent to people all the time.

"Timothy, can you please take over the list that Thelma started and write down everyone who has brought something and what they brought? We want to make sure we get the right dishes back to the right people, and we'll need to thank them eventually when we have a chance."

The more sensitive of the neighbors just handed Ben or Cindy the food and said things like "We're thinking about them." "Let them know they're in our prayers." And, "Here's hoping for the best." Other, more inquisitive neighbors tried to peer in through the front door, hesitated a bit, and then asked, "Are they okay?" "Is there anything I can do?" "Would they like a hand with anything?"

Ben and Cindy thanked each of them and volunteered, "There's no news yet. Thanks for your kind thoughtfulness."

Liz had been upstairs in her bedroom overlooking the front lawn. After one of the neighbors left, she came downstairs half laughing and half fuming. "Those reporters are, like, stopping everyone on the way here and then again after they leave. I wish I could read lips, but I think some of the reporters may have, like, offered money for information; I saw one of them pull out his wallet and open it anyway. And I think I saw Mrs. Nelson use, like, the "F" word to one of them."

We all laughed. Maggie Nelson was famous for her colorful language. It had bothered me when we first met her, and I had to explain to the children that they were not to use those words. After a few years, we all got used to Maggie's language, and she became such a neighborhood fixture and good friend that we actually cherished her colorful language.

Liz's telling us about these goings on out front lightened our spirits a bit. When Dale, Seth, and Aaron Hazelwood arrived, Dale was visibly upset by having had to run the gauntlet of reporters, but Seth and Aaron were smiling.

"There are only five reporters out there," said Seth, but we felt like rock stars with cameras and lights and microphones all being shoved at us."

"One of them offered me twenty dollars if I'd give her an exclusive story after our visit," Aaron added. "That's when Dad blew up!"

Dale was still angry but he began to crack a hint of a smile, too.

"When I heard one of them offering Aaron money, I used some choice phrases. And then I said, 'You folks pool your money and give me $500 when we come back out. I'll donate it to the Youngs or to their favorite charity in their name, and then I'll tell you what I know.' I didn't tell them we're staying for dinner and probably awhile after that!"

The four children went to the basement to play some games. A few years earlier, we had finished our basement into a games room and had used some of Fred's bonus money to buy tabletop shuffleboard, foosball, and an air hockey game. The children and their friends had spent hours down there over the past three years. The games room had become a safe neighborhood hangout where all the children could talk and play together.

"Let's see…. There'll be nine of us for dinner," I said. "Ben, I think we'll need to use the dining room for dinner. I hope that's okay."

"Not a problem at all," Ben said as he picked up his laptop and briefcase. "I'll just move into the living room."

Thelma, Cindy, and I made salads and set the table, while Dale took over duties on the front door. He also had to take over Timothy's list of who brought what food. We had turned the ringer back on for our home phone, and Thelma took a call or two before dinner.

There was a feast available with all the different foods people brought. We put Mrs. Redding's rye bread on the table, and we put out Mrs. Nelson's meatloaf along with the lasagna we had made. We put the rest of the food in the fridge for later and even put some in the freezer.

When supper was ready, Dale said, "Why don't I take the seat nearest the door so I can keep answering if other reporters or busybodies show up." I took my usual place at the head of the table, where it had become customary for me to sit because it was closest to the kitchen.

The minute the stories about Fred hit the air during the dinnertime newscasts, the phone started ringing again. Thelma took the first call, and after the caller told her about the news story and asked about our family, Thelma got off the line quickly.

"I turned off the ringer again," she said. "Apparently all the local TV news stories are mentioning Fred, so let's just not bother with the phone for now.

I saw many of the news stories later when they were re-aired on the ten o'clock newscasts, including clips of Ben announcing that there was no news. At some point he must have composed a statement from Klein-Staily saying how valuable Fred is to the firm. "Is", not "was". He said it that way on purpose. "We're all hoping and praying for the best," he added.

Chapter 4 --- **Evening Uncertainty**

After we finished supper, everyone pitched in to help clear the table and load the dishwasher. We put Ben and Dale on scrubbing duty with the pots and pans, and we three women smiled at each other as Thelma told them we wanted to make sure they felt included. Then the five of us adults went back into the family room to watch TV to see if there was any more news. I tried Fred's cellphone a few more times, but I had pretty much given up hope.

"Timothy, would you mind checking all the phone messages? Just write down who called and a brief note about what they wanted, okay?"

"Sure thing, Mom."

A few minutes later, he yelled out, "Holy Cow! There are 154 messages here! How long is this going to take?"

"It won't take long," I answered. "Maybe Liz, Seth, and Aaron can help."

The others tried to sneak back down to the games room, but Timothy stopped them. "Hey, come on guys! Let's get this done. I'll listen to a message, announce who it's from and what they want, and you can take turns writing it down."

"Should I delete each message after we've taken down the info?"

"I think so," I answered. "But if there's anything too confusing or complex to put in a brief note, save that message and write a note and put a star next to it so I'll know to listen to that message myself, later."

It didn't take them long. After about five minutes, they had worked out a pattern and could deal with each message in only ten or fifteen seconds.

When they were nearly done, they began giggling and laughing together. I was glad they were having some brief moments of fun together, but I wondered what on earth they found so funny in any of the messages.

I went back into the kitchen, where they were sitting around the table. I smiled. "What's so funny about the messages?"

They all looked a little embarrassed.

Finally Aaron piped up, "There are so many people calling to ask if there's any news about Mr. Young, that we were trying to think of a good answering message to put on the phone, like 'We don't know if he's....'" and Aaron trailed off into silence when he saw my face.

I was hurt inside and yet I understood: they wanted some comic relief. So I controlled myself, quite admirably I thought.

"Some things can be funny even now when we're so distraught," I said. "I understand. I know you children were having fun and I don't want to spoil it. But it does bother me, too. I can tell from the looks on your faces that you understand how I might feel, and I really am not upset that you were having fun with this. In fact, there are many callers who probably need to get a good, blunt message. But maybe it would be better if you went back down to the games room when you discuss things like that."

"Okay, Mom," said Liz. "We have, like, only about five calls to go."

I smiled again. "Thank you." And I gave each of them a hug. As I did that, I looked at the message pad and saw what else was causing the giggles. It turned out we had, according them, received messages from Batman, Homer Simpson, and Alicia Keyes, all wanting to bring pizza and asking which kinds we would like and if two dozen would be enough.

I tapped the list and smiled again. "I see you're having other fun, too. Phone them back and tell them I want broccoli and artichokes on my pizza. And I think we have room for three dozen pizzas in the freezer in the basement, so make sure you ask for plenty!"

- - -

While Timothy and Liz finished taking down all the phone message information, Seth asked, "Is there any more news on TV Ms. Young?"

"Not really, Seth. The politicians are all getting into it now, though. 'We are strong!' 'We will rebuild and be stronger.' 'We will not tolerate… blah, blah, blah.' I don't know how they do it."

He groaned and the others grimaced. They all knew how much I disliked politician's blathered empty phrases. Back when I was working for Arkero Foods before the children were born, I had done enough public relations work to recognize the strategies, and those strategies were out in full force that day: maintain a tough veneer; seem compassionate whether you are or not; be determined; don't commit to anything. I could almost say the speeches along with them, word-for-word; I sighed silently.

By eight o'clock, it was clear that the others would have to leave soon. Seth and Aaron would have schoolwork, and so the Hazeltons would have to leave, and Ben and Cindy couldn't stay forever either.

- - -

Finally, I had to accept the situation even though I didn't like it. I didn't want to be alone that night, and I didn't want the children to be stuck with just me in the state I was in. But part of the growing up process for our children ... yes, I thought "our", not "my" children ... was dealing with and coping with the tragedies and uncertainties of life.

"Damn," I said out loud. I rarely swore at all, but even though all that loss of life was a catastrophe, I was upset to be thinking this was a tragedy for us, when we didn't know for sure. There was a good chance it was a tragedy for us, but I didn't know, and I didn't like having those thoughts.

Everyone looked at me sharply when I uttered "Damn". I covered for my inner thoughts and announced, "Well, you can't all stay here forever. Thelma and Dale, your boys must have schoolwork to do. Thank you for coming over today, Thelma. And thank you for everything you did here today. I don't know how we'd have made it through the day without you four."

And then before they could say anything, the doorbell rang.

It was Jeremy Hall again. Dale was both indignant and impish at the same time. "I hope you have the $500," he yelled so the other reporters could hear.

"Sir, we just have a few questions ..."

Dale interrupted him, yelling, "You are trespassing and we're calling the police. Get off this porch and get off the lawn!"

"Well! That felt good." Dale was smiling as he came back to the family room, and we all smiled with him.

I turned to Ben and Cindy. "You two have also been a tremendous help today. Thank you so much for giving up your day and evening to be here and to help us in so many ways."

Thelma said, "Susan, would you like me to come back tomorrow?"

My inside voice screamed "YES!" but my outside voice was more cautious. I really appreciated Thelma's help and comfort, but I didn't want to take advantage of her generosity. I replied, "Why don't you call after your boys are off to school? I'll have a better idea then."

"Good plan," Thelma replied. "But call me **any**time if you need **any**thing."

We had been good friends for a long time. It was more comforting than she knew to hear her say those things. I knew she wasn't just saying empty words; I knew I could count on her if I needed her.

We called the children up from the games room, and everyone said goodbye, with hugs all around. Even the four children hugged everyone, including each other. There were no giggles and no hesitations. The children felt it, sincerely. There was a closeness between us all, and the hugs told me that they cared.

The children and I stood in the foyer with the front door open as the Hazeltons and the Gruvels left. "Let's just watch to see what happens," I said.

The reporters shouted questions at Ben as he was getting into the car, but he was very formal in his response. "You have my statement for now, and you have the statement from Klein-Staily. I have nothing to add to those statements. Now would you please make room at the end of the driveway for me to back out?"

They moved over to the side of the driveway but as soon as Ben was gone, they crowded around the Hazeltons with shouts and questions. They even tried to isolate Seth and Aaron, the way wolves try to isolate the young from a herd of deer. Thelma and Dale took the boys by their hands and almost circled them to protect them from the onslaught from the reporters.

Dale held up a hand. After a minute or so, they realized they had to be quiet if Dale was going to give them any information at all.

When they had been quiet for a few seconds, Dale began. "Ladies and Gentlemen. Have you collected the $500?"

The children and I couldn't contain our smirks and chuckles. But the reporters were not amused. They started shouting questions again.

Once again, Dale held up his hand until they were quiet.

"Until you come up with the $500 for the Youngs' favorite charity, I have nothing to add to Mr. Gruvel's statements." Then he and Thelma put their arms around each boy and walked home.

As we were getting ready to close the front door, a police car came by. The officer told the reporters that there had been several complaints about people blocking the street and harassing a neighbor. He made it clear that they were to leave right then and not bother us.

I could see that having media crews, trucks, and other vehicles lining the street would be unpleasant for the neighbors. I felt guilty: it wasn't right that everyone else had to put up with so much in a situation involving our family, even though I knew there was no reason for my guilt.

While the reporters shuffled around a bit preparing to leave, the officer came to the door. He was young, maybe in his mid-twenties. He spoke slowly and quietly to us.

"Ma'am, I hope this helps. We've had six or seven calls about those reporters, so I thought I'd stop by to shoo them away, for now at least."

"Thank you so much, officer! I'm Susan Young, and these are our children, Timothy and Liz."

"Our". I was determined not to say "my" yet.

"Nice to meet you Ma'am,' and he nodded to each of us separately. "I'm officer Dunwall," and he gave me his card. "If there are any problems at all during the rest of the night, call the number I've written on the card. It will go right through to one of us assigned to the Candlewood area, and we can be here in just a few minutes."

- - -

We watched him speak harshly to the lagging reporters and then wait until they were all gone before he drove away.

Slowly we closed the front door.

I pulled the children to me once more and held them tight. I didn't want to smother them, but I needed comforting from them, and I wanted to comfort them, too, if they still needed it.

I almost lost it, but I held myself together. I simply couldn't lose control completely in front of the children. Instead, I started acting like a politician and couldn't believe what I was saying:

"We have to try to remain strong. We still have no idea where your father is or what happened to him. I'm holding out hope that he is in some medical center or hospital. If he is in one, then the people that Uncle Ben has working there in New York will find him. But we also have to be ready to deal with the uncertainty of not knowing. If your father didn't make it through that attack, ..." and I broke off, choking back a sob. I hadn't wanted to say that out loud, but there it was.

I chickened out. "Well, let's not talk about that right now. We'll deal with it, if and when we have to."

And then I quickly went on, trying to distract the children a bit. "Timothy, I know you brought your books home. Even if you don't have any specific homework, I want you to read ahead or work ahead in some of your courses. One hour is all, and then we can all take a break. Liz, unless you have some homework, would you mind going back to the phone and collecting any new messages?"

I smiled and added, "and please don't change the outgoing message!"

I busied myself cleaning up and putting things away in the kitchen.

"Mom," Liz called out. "There are, like, another ten messages here! When do you think we'll be able to use the phone again? I was hoping to call some friends from school."

"It will probably be okay to call your friends, but promise me you won't say anything about your father or about us other than that we don't know anything and we're concerned. Use those words. If a friend asks you more, say, 'We've all agreed not to say any more about it for now. I hope you understand.' They'll understand. Oh, and if you do call your friends, find out what schoolwork you need to do for tomorrow."

Liz knew I was right about what to say and what not to say, and she agreed.

She also knew I was right about the schoolwork, but I think she wished I hadn't thought about it. I kissed her on top of her head as she went back to work on the phone messages.

While the children were occupied, I sat on the sofa in the family room and let my mind wander. I missed Fred whenever he was gone. I hated the thought of not having him home tonight or ... I couldn't let myself go there yet.

Chapter 5 – Reflecting

I met Fred at a Christmas "social" when we were juniors at Kansas State University in Manhattan, Kansas. Twice a year, the Home Economics students and the Agricultural Business students got together for a social event. The practice started in the late 1940s as a way to help students find life partners, and who was I to sneer at it? It had worked for us!

Fred was a tall, lanky, naïve farm boy from western Kansas; he had a square jaw that he set just a bit off center whenever he was thinking. He looked great in a button-down shirt and jeans, but he was so shy, I had to strike up a conversation with him at the cookie-and-punch table.

"Hi, I'm Susan Loeffer." … Pause. … Pause. … Pause. "Well? What's your name?"

"Oh." He blushed a bit. "Fred Young."

"Where are you from, Fred?"

"I was raised on a farm out in western Kansas."

I waited some more. But he didn't continue the conversation.

"I'm from Salina, Kansas," I offered. "Have you ever been there?"

"Yeah. We go through there now and then. Had some good chicken dinners near there a few times."

"I know the place!" I almost gushed. "The Brookville Hotel in Abilene!"

More pauses. He didn't try to get away, and he looked at me often, so I continued.

"What do you farm?"

"Mostly wheat. We used to have a small herd of cattle, but we sold 'em off when we figured out that the land was worth more when we planted it in wheat instead of using it for cattle."

"Really?" I actually was sort of interested but mostly I wanted to keep him talking.

"Yeah. It's something I learned in my first year here at K-State. Look at alternatives and evaluate them. We did that my first summer back home, and that's when we made the decision."

Well, he sure felt comfortable talking about farming. I wondered what else he might be interested in. He didn't return any questions to me about my life in Salina.

So I continued, "My family runs a hardware store in Salina."

He nodded an acknowledgement. He still wasn't looking around for anyone else. It just seemed that he had no idea what to say.

"I've worked in the store ever since I was ten. But when I was in high school and during the summers, I help wait tables at the Brookville Hotel on Sundays. Maybe I've waited on you." I smiled.

He smiled back. "That'd be nice."

His hair was shorter than a lot of guys kept their hair. He had no beard and no moustache and the most unusual grey-green eyes.

"What are you planning to do after graduation, Fred?"

"I'm not sure anymore. I was planning to go back to the farm, and I know my family wants me to, but I don't think I will. We talked about it over Thanksgiving."

I was tentative. "How did they take it?"

"Dad and I had a long talk. They're okay with it, I guess, but, yeah, they're disappointed. After that talk, Mom said, 'We just want you to be happy, son.' And I think that's really how they feel."

"You're so lucky to have understanding parents..." I trailed off.

Fred got a funny look on his face, as if he was concerned. "Aren't your parents understanding...," he looked at my nametag, "...Susan?"

He was interacting!

"Oh, they are, for sure. But I've met so many kids whose parents are really pushing them one way or another. Oh, no, my parents want me to prosper and be successful, at least that's what they say."

"Sounds good."

Fred had been a man of few words back then. Slowly over the years, though, he became quite a social being. He was still shy deep down, but he could command the floor when he was comfortable, and he held his own even in some uncertain social settings.

"So, then, what are you going to do after graduation?" he asked me.

"Well, what do you know?" I thought to myself. "He actually asked me about myself again. Let's see where this goes."

"I'm not sure either. I have some good skills and a varied background. I'm thinking maybe I'd like to work in the food industry somehow."

We smiled at each other, both knowing we were checking each other out for more than just dating. That made me nervous because I didn't know much about him at all. Was this going the wrong way too fast? I added, "But that's a year and a half away yet. There's lots of time to think about it."

Fred said, "Yeah, but it's good to be thinking ahead."

"I suppose. So, what are you thinking ahead about?" I smiled, trying to put on my friendliest non-flirty smile as I asked.

"Well, I'm thinking I might end up in one of those big agricultural business firms. Maybe John Deere or maybe Pioneer or maybe Armor or Swift meats."

"Do you ever think of striking out on your own? You might be a good consultant if you've already used your knowledge for your family farm."

"Not sure I want to take a chance on that, but that's not a bad idea in some ways. I think I would like some measure of success."

"Me, too." I worked to keep from gushing. I loved the way he set his jaw.

I changed the subject. "When are you leaving to go home for Christmas? I finish on the 17th."

"I got stuck with a late exam. Not 'til the 23rd. All my other exams are done on the 17th, though. If you stay here in Manhattan that night, maybe we could go out somewhere."

"I'd like that." It had worked! I had a date with him!

"What do you have in mind?" I asked.

"Oh, I don't know." He wasn't being suggestive or coy. He quite clearly had no idea what to suggest. But he stumbled on, "How about something at the Student Union? Maybe bowling or pool? Maybe a movie?"

"Sure! I'm a horrible bowler, though. How about just a movie?"

We exchanged phone numbers, and sure enough he called me the next day with the movie schedule and the times. We went to a movie the 17th and had a good time, but we didn't say much at first. And then we had some snacks at the café there in the union.

Fred didn't know much about politics or about philosophy, but he seemed interested as I held forth on those and other topics. He was either a good actor, which seemed unlikely, or he truly was interested in what I had to say. He even asked some sensible, thought-provoking questions. What impressed me was that he didn't try to score debate points or to one-up me with his questions. He truly seemed interested.

He walked me home, and as we said our good nights to each other, he didn't kiss me; he just stood there. And then out of the blue he asked, "Where's your hardware store? Maybe I'll drop by on my way home."

I told him, and gave him both our home and store phone numbers. "If you get there around 1pm, maybe can go have a quick lunch together."

I knew it was premature, but I was beginning to have all sorts of fantasies about Fred, and I knew it was way too early to introduce him to the family.

I had no choice, though; he did stop by the store, and we did go to lunch.

I was falling for him. Heck, I'd fallen for him the minute I saw him. I don't know why. I'm usually more rational than that. As we said good-bye after lunch, we wished each other a Merry Christmas, but that was that. No hugs, no mistletoe, no polite cheek kisses, nothing.

My parents wanted to know all about him, but I didn't have much to tell them other than that we'd just met a few weeks earlier, that he lived farther out west on a wheat farm, and that I quite liked him.

We saw each other off and on through that winter. One night in February, after we'd been to a movie, he quick-kissed me goodnight. But that was it. By March, his kisses became a bit more passionate, but he seemed so inexperienced and so eager at the same time.

Finally, one time when we were in the lounge together, I looked at him with what I hoped was a slightly suggestive look. "Sex was a natural dinner-table topic in our house. What about yours?"

He blushed a bit. "Well, my aunt and uncle on the neighboring farm raised white-faced Herefords, and so did we. We talked about animal sex a bit, but mostly in practical, farming contexts. Which cows to breed when and with which steer. We never talked about sex between people."

The truth was, he said, he was a virgin and knew next to nothing about having sex other than that masturbation seemed evil but felt good.

I told him I was a virgin, too, but that I'd had a boyfriend in high school and we had done some heavy petting. In truth, what we had done might as well have been having sex, but I didn't tell him that part.

That night Fred and I went to a motel and made love. It wasn't great, but it was fantastic to be with him and to watch him and feel him come alive. We spent the night and made love again in the morning, more slowly. He was clearly inexperienced; well, so was I but I think I had read a lot more about it than he had. I knew then that we would enjoy exploring our sexual beings together.

Over Easter, Fred stopped to stay with my family for a day, and then he drove me to his family's farm for two days. The families approved of our choices, and we got engaged at the end of the summer before our senior years.

Our plan was to find jobs we could start in the same city after we graduated and then get married before starting our new jobs. The plans worked out wonderfully.

Chapter 6 – Omaha

Fred was a hot item among the recruiters who came to campus during our senior year: his farming background combined with his agribusiness training was attractive. I did pretty well, too. I had some business skills from working in the hardware store, and I had a good, broad training in food sciences and food management.

By April, we had both been offered and accepted jobs in Omaha: Fred with Klein-Staily, an agricultural finance company doing mortgage appraisals; me with Arkero Foods in their marketing division as an administrative assistant. In May we went up to Omaha to meet with our employers, sign the requisite papers and forms, and find an apartment. During our drive there, we joked that we were well on our way to living the Great Mid-American Dream. We both felt more special than just two people trying to live a standard dream, though, and we agreed we didn't want to fall into that trap.

As I sat in the family room that evening, I realized that until that day, we had been living exactly the Great-Mid-American Dream. Little did we know back then just how standardized we would become over the next twenty years.

Our wedding was a typical huge Salina wedding, with over 200 guests. It was a perfect afternoon June wedding, followed by cake and ice cream in the church basement. After we changed from our wedding clothes, we went out to dinner with just our parents before leaving for our honeymoon. They had gotten together and decided jointly to give us $400 in cash to help with the honeymoon and buying things for our apartment. It was a welcome contribution, for sure, since we had no idea when we would get our first paychecks. It was a small fortune to us.

We honeymooned in Colorado Springs, which was nice, even beautiful, but we felt like one of thousands of honeymooning couples there. Again we vowed not to become trite copies of everyone else who was aspiring to the Great Mid-American Dream.

After the honeymoon, we rented a small trailer and stuffed it with our personal things along with a few of the wedding gifts we thought might be useful, leaving dozens of boxes with our parents and suggesting they might want to use some of the other wedding gifts themselves. We laughed, "How many serving platters and casserole dishes will a young couple really need?"

Our apartment in downtown Omaha was a small, sparsely furnished one-bedroom unit with the kitchen and eating area at one end of the living room. It felt like a luxury penthouse after four years of living in student housing. What's more, it was ours!

Klein-Staily was only two blocks from the apartment, and so Fred walked to work. Arkero Foods was up on the northwest edge of town, and so I used our car (actually Fred's) to drive to work each day.

Our relationship grew during the four years that we lived in that apartment. We talked about the meaning of life, about our goals and how those goals had changed somewhat but at the same time hadn't changed at all. We also talked about what we meant to each other, and about having children and buying a house. I often felt as if I was forcing Fred to talk about these things, but he seemed content, maybe even pleased, to do it, too. He never acted as if he had to know everything, and although he encouraged me to do more of the talking, he participated enough to let me know he cared about me and about us.

We lived frugally, which wasn't difficult after our near-penniless student days. We saved all of my income and much of Fred's, putting some of the savings into tax-free retirement plans but saving most of it for a house.

I progressed rapidly at Arkero, and after four years I was the executive assistant to the vice-president of marketing, Vern Jackson. I loved my job: handling press releases and product promotions but mostly controlling Vern Jackson, who had lots of creative ideas, but who also let his imagination go wild now and then and needed reining in.

After four years, Fred and I had saved up enough money to buy a second car and, more significantly, to make a very large down payment on our house on Izard Street in the Candlewood subdivision of Omaha. It was big and beautiful. We took possession two weeks before we moved in and spent every evening there painting and dreaming together. As we put up drapes, I think we made love in every room of that house before we moved in!

I became pregnant about then with Timothy. We were both overcome with joy, and so were our parents. I worked another six months, and after those six months, we just about had the house paid off. Of course, our expenses went up and our total family income went down, but we were prepared for all that. We continued to live frugally and money issues never came between us. Not overtly, anyway.

Arkero Foods was disappointed when I resigned instead of taking a maternity leave. I knew the money from my job would make our lives more comfortable, but I wanted to be a stay-at-home mother, a complete homemaker.

Just before Timothy was born, I sat Fred down at the kitchen table, reached across and took his hand, and said in a very determined tone, "I am choosing to be a homemaker and a mother. I have even studied for this career. I will devote myself to it. You do your work, I'll do mine, and we will be true, sharing partners. When the children are older, I might consider re-entering the workforce, but not until then."

Sometimes I wondered if maybe I was a bit too determined, too pushy.

After the children were both in school full-time, I did take on some freelance part-time work with Arkero, but not much. I saw my job and my career as being a mother and homemaker. As a result, we didn't have all the things that the neighbors had, but we had a rich, wholesome, caring family life.

Chapter 7 – **Preparing**

My reminiscences were interrupted as Timothy came downstairs.

"Mom, I've done what I can to work ahead in some courses, but I think I'll need to talk to Ms. Rashevsky about the math and get her to explain some of it to me. I'll read it again and try to work some of the problems, but I'm not sure I get it yet."

"He came and sat next to me on the sofa, and we watched the news. Shortly after he sat down, the phone rang again. Just once, and then it stopped. Liz had probably answered it.

A minute later, Liz came into the family room fuming.

"I was on the phone with friends," she said, "but the minute I hung up, the phone started ringing again. It was someone from the local CBS station asking about Dad. I told her that we're not talking until we know something, but she wouldn't give up. Finally, I just hung up and turned off the ringer."

Liz sat down on the other side of me. I reached out and touched her arm.

"That's perfect, Liz. Thanks."

Unlike Timothy with his round face, Liz had an oval face, more like mine. In general, Timothy looked quite a bit like Fred, and Liz looked more like me. Timothy had the same calm, quiet serenity that Fred had when I met him. But Liz had an almost fiery temperament. She had learned to control it most of the time, but it was always there, under the surface.

We sat in silence for a while, watching the news recaps. Finally, I admitted to myself that we would have to face the future, both tomorrow and long-term.

"I probably don't need to say this, but we all understand the situation, don't we?"

Timothy and Liz nodded.

"I don't want to be explicit because I know we're all hoping Dad is safe and well somewhere. But we're going to have to deal with the uncertainties. Let's start with tomorrow. You don't have to decide right now, but think about whether you want to go to school tomorrow."

"I don't want to leave you here alone, Mom," said Liz.

"That's alright," I quickly replied. "Thelma has offered to come back tomorrow, and remember, every day when Dad's at work and you two are in school, I'm here alone."

I used the present tense on purpose.

"Oh yeah…." said Liz. And then she added, "Well, if Ms. Hazelton is coming over tomorrow, and if you don't really need us here, I think I'd like to go to school tomorrow. What about you, Timothy?"

"I think I would, too, but how about we wait to decide until tomorrow morning. We might have some news in the meantime. But, yeah, I'd like to get back to school. I can only sit here watching television for so long. I need to get out and get back to school."

I half-expected they would feel that way, especially Liz. She was a social being, and she needed to be with her friends and classmates. Timothy would want to go to school because he was a routine-type person; he needed standard routines and didn't adapt so quickly when those were thrown off schedule.

"Good plan," I added. "I agree. Let's wait to see how things are in the morning. Okay, go brush your teeth and get ready for bed. I think I'll come up, too."

Our home was a standard four-bedroom, two-and-a-half-bathroom suburban home. The children had grown up sharing their bathroom, and over the years they had worked out an acceptable sharing arrangement.

"Liz, where's the message pad from today? I think I'll take it with me and maybe make notes or return calls to a few people before I turn out the light."

Liz picked up the message pad from the kitchen as I turned off the television and the lights, and the three of us made our way up to our bedrooms. I left the telephone ringers turned off for both the kitchen and bedroom telephones; if anyone important needed me, they had my cellphone number.

I plugged my cellphone in to recharge it and sat on the bed, propping myself up with extra pillows. The message pad ran to over ten pages of names, phone numbers, and brief messages. As I began looking through the messages, I saw a number of duplicates from friends and neighbors, mostly just checking to see what we knew or if they could do anything.

"Yes!" I said out loud. "Find Fred and bring him home alive."

Oops, I said that too loud. The children heard me and came rushing into the bedroom. I tried to reassure them, "I was just responding out loud to all the phone messages. There are so many people who are calling to ask if they can do anything. I know they mean well, but it's too much to deal with, so I just blurted out loud, 'Yes! Find Fred and bring him home alive.'"

I tried to smile to the children, but I began to tear up again. So did they, and they got onto the bed, one on each side of me. I let the message pad slide onto my lap and put my arms around each of them.

We hugged again, and then I shooed them off to bed. I was surprised by the feeling, but suddenly I needed some alone time for myself. I hoped they understood without my having to say anything.

After the children went to their own bedrooms, I just sat in the bed for a long time, thinking and reflecting. I missed Fred terribly. I wanted him to be safe and to come through the door. But I was pretty sure that wasn't going to happen.

Chapter 8 – **Drifting Apart**

Fred and I had been *so* in love when we first moved into that house. It was so much more than we had ever imagined possible for us, and then we had two lovely children. Things had been going wonderfully, almost magically, for us. We didn't have all the latest gadgets and other trappings of an over-mortgaged suburban life, but we were comfortable and for the most part debt-free.

Fred progressed slowly and steadily at Klein-Staily in their farm mortgage department. His mentor, Ben Gruvel, had moved on from doing mortgage assessments and was well up in the firm. After six years Fred was handling the mortgage assessments by himself.

Meanwhile, I was a typical homemaker. The house wasn't always as clean as I'd hoped, but of course it wasn't: we had two small children, and I was making meals and looking after most of the details of running the household. It was a full-time job and then some, and I was determined to do my best at it.

We were careful with our money, a pattern we had both been raised with. We began retirement savings plans for ourselves, and we began saving for the children's college educations. We bought serviceable appliances, and we did all the yard work, cleaning, and homemaking ourselves. We bought cars rarely but when we did, we bought demos or used cars. We didn't eat in restaurants very often, and when we did it was mostly in chain restaurants instead of fancy expensive places.

We loved planning vacations, but we were careful with our spending in that area, too, staying four-to-a-room in inexpensive motels and packing lunches or cooking alongside the road in rest areas when possible.

Without realizing it, we were living our version of the Great Mid-American Dream. Over the years, though, things gradually changed. Among other things, Fred wanted nicer cars, and I had to admit some of the features on the higher-end models were nice. And when it came time to replace the major appliances, I wanted more and better features.

I don't know if these changes would have occurred so much if we hadn't lived in such a nice, affluent neighborhood. We had all we needed, and we had more than we had ever dreamed of having. Yet as we saw our friends and neighbors getting nicer things, some wistfulness slowly ate away at us. We didn't stand out as being noticeably less well off than the others, but we knew that most of our neighbors had more than we did.

In the early 1990s, Fred was offered a chance to move to the financial side of the Klein-Staily mortgage operations. He was doing very well in his mortgage appraisal and assessment job, and people throughout Klein-Staily recognized him as a sincere, bright, hard-working and honest man. Ben Gruvel led the committee that approached Fred about the possibility of a diagonal promotion.

Fred was excited about the possibility. "It'll mean a **lot** more money," he told me. We'll be able to afford nicer things and nicer trips."

I was pleased for him that he had been sought out by the partners at the firm, and I knew that having some nicer things, more in line with others in the neighborhood, would be nice, too. At the same time, though, I was hesitant.

"What will it involve?" I asked.

I was thinking he'd be working longer hours, but he'd be home in Omaha more instead of on the road doing farm appraisals, so that overall we'd be together at least as much as we had been all along.

His answer threw me for a bit of a loop.

"I'll have to go to night school and do some intensive weekend courses in finance," he said. "It's been a long time since I've been a student. I'm a little concerned."

He hadn't caught on that I was concerned about **us**, about the family. But my reaction must have clued him in that I had some reservations.

"Yeah, I know," he said. "I'll be away two nights a week for classes, and I'll be studying a lot, the rest of the time. That's why I wanted to talk with you about it before doing anything."

"It does sound like an excellent opportunity ...," I offered hesitantly.

He could sense I wasn't entirely enthusiastic about it. One of the things I had cherished about my life and about our marriage was that we were together. I didn't like the idea of his being gone so much.

"I think I can finish the program in less than two years. That'll include some intensive courses on weekends and in the summers, but we'll be so much better off when I'm done."

He hurried on, "I think Ben and the rest of the partners really want me to do this. They offered me a twenty percent raise starting next week to induce me to do this."

"Twenty percent! Wow!"

I knew Fred was good at his job. But even though we had been comfortable, we had also had to cut corners in various ways.

"The extra money would be really nice." I speculated, "We could take the children to Disney World; we could donate more to charity; we could…"

And I stopped. Fred was smiling.

"Yeah," he said. "I did the same thing. I spent it all in my mind, and yet we haven't even decided whether I should do it."

I laughed. And then I became quite concerned, getting what Fred called my "serious look".

"I know the money would be nice, Fred, but what will it do to us? To our family? I love our life as it is, really."

But Fred wanted a nicer car. I think he felt more of a need to keep up with the neighbors than I thought I did; and yet deep down I know I wanted more things, too: I wanted a cleaning service, I wanted to join a fitness club, and I wanted a finished basement and a main floor family room. I just wasn't as open about the things I wanted.

And so Fred accepted the promotion to the finance department and enrolled in an executive MBA program that involved night courses plus an intensive weekend of courses once a month. It was a struggle for me emotionally to have him lost in his studies and his work so much, but we tried to make sure we still set aside some time for family activities. Before Fred took the new job, he had been noticeably more active in the children's lives than the other dads in the neighborhood. He had even done some volunteer community work. Those activities slowly fell by the wayside as he threw himself into his studies.

When we were dating at K-State, Fred studied seriously, but I don't think he ever was "into" his subjects the way he was into his finance courses. They actually excited him. He tried to explain his excitement about the courses, and I think he was disappointed that I couldn't and didn't share his excitement. And I think that was the first time I had a sense that we might be drifting apart slightly.

Once the coursework was completed, I hoped Fred would be with us more... and he was, a bit, but it wasn't the way it had been. Fred loved his mortgage finance work, and so he worked longer hours and even brought work home with him at times.

We tried to recapture some of what we'd had before his promotion, but it was different. He had his work, and I had a different social life. The children welcomed seeing more of him, and we all enjoyed our first really comfortable vacation together, flying to Orlando and visiting Disney World and all the other sights in style for two weeks.

Around then, we also had the basement properly finished into a really nice games/family room. We really did enjoy it all, but at the same time I think Fred enjoyed *providing* it at least as much as he enjoyed using the actual things we spent the extra money on. He never said anything, but I think that until then he had felt outdone by the other men in the neighborhood whose families had more and nicer things. I had to admit to myself that I began to feel more on a par with the neighbors, too, and I was almost embarrassed to admit it. I had always commented around the house that we didn't really need all those things that the others had and that we had a more wholesome life, but when I think about it, that was just my way of being competitive. It was more subtle than Fred's, but it was still competitive.

- - -

I have moved on with my life, but I miss Fred. I wish he were here now so we could talk about these things. I wish we had talked about them more back then.

- - -

After a few years in the mortgage finance department, Fred was sitting at the kitchen table with the children one winter evening laughing with them as they tried to float what I called "hi-test" cream on their cocoa. If they couldn't do it, they had to make the sound of an animal. None of them could do it, and that was part of the fun.

Liz made the sound of a donkey. Timothy purred like a cat. But there was no sound from Fred.

"I'm a snail," he said, and he just sat there smirking with his lips sealed, and then he tucked his head into his armpit, trying to curl up like a snail. The children groaned and complained, and we all laughed.

The noise and laughter were a real treat for all of us. It felt as if we were reconnecting as a family. I felt a strong sense of love and contentment.

But just then, Fred stopped laughing with the children. He stared at the cocoa in the latte mugs one at a time.

"Layers!" he said. "That's it! Layers!"

"What are you talking about, Fred?" I asked. "Hens laying eggs? They cackle. You have to cackle!" The children and I all started cackling at him.

But he just sat there transfixed.

"Oh," he said finally. "I'm sorry. Looking at the layers of cocoa and cream gave me an idea for how to solve a problem at work."

He tried to participate with us some more that evening, but it was clear (to me anyway) that his mind was on his work problem. For the next few days, Fred couldn't stop smiling. He knew he was onto something, and he immersed himself totally in working out the details. I was excited for him. He was more enthused about what he was thinking about than I had ever seen before, but I wished he could leave work at work, as he had been starting to do until his "Layers" revelation.

Fred's "Layer" thing, as I understood it, involved creating layers of mortgage-backed bonds and pools of bonds. I know that's not quite right, but I never did understand it fully.

What I did understand was that Fred was alive in ways I had never seen before as he threw himself into his work. I missed him, and I think the children did, too. There were compensations, for sure. Fred's ideas went over really well at Klein-Staily, and he received several big promotions and massive bonuses. We never dreamed people made that much money in a lifetime, much less a year. Four years before 9-11, Fred grossed over two million dollars, and even more the next year.

We had the family room added onto the back of the house at the same time we had the kitchen completely redone. We had nicer, newer vehicles. We had ample funds set aside for the children's college and for our retirement, and we had become major donors to local charities.

Oddly about that time, Fred began to seem more pensive, more distant. I tried to draw him out, but he'd just reply, "Oh, it's nothing. Just a wrinkle in the program at work." But he seemed unsettled. I never understood it.

I mentioned this minor change once to Thelma, and her immediate reaction was, "Is he seeing someone else? Are you seeing anyone else?"

I was shocked. It never occurred to me to have an affair. I didn't want to have one, and I couldn't imagine Fred was having an affair. To be sure, I did some minor checking of Fred's cellphone and credit card statements. I didn't see anything, and so I put that possibility out of my mind.

In the end I had no idea what the change was in Fred or why it was happening. I just knew that despite his successes, he seemed lost.

Chapter 9 – Financial Setback

We were riding high financially and socially. The children and I spent a month in Europe one summer while Fred continued to thrive in his work. we missed Fred on the trips he couldn't take with us, and I think he missed us, too. Yet he was proud as a peacock, moving to the top of the neighborhood pecking order, becoming a managing partner at Klein-Staily, and securing a large corner office at work. I hadn't realized how competitive Fred was, nor how much status mattered to him; also, I was more than a little embarrassed as I realized how much I enjoyed the higher social status we had as a result of his successes.

We didn't want the children to think everything would be easy for them; we still made them do chores around the house. Timothy had to do the lawn mowing while Liz and I did the gardening; and they both had to help with the laundry and with the dishes. The children groaned and complained about the chores, but I was determined they would learn to contribute to the family.

One thing I was clear about: the children were **never** to know how much Fred had been earning nor how much we had saved. I'm sure they had an inkling about it, but I didn't want them thinking we had so much money we could afford to buy them everything they wanted.

I was glad I had insisted on that.

About a year before 9-11, something went wrong with Fred's work. I wasn't sure what it was, but it had something to do with falling crop prices.

After a few months, Fred called a family meeting. That was really strange -- we'd never had a family meeting. Never. None of us knew what to expect. One Sunday after church, Fred announced we'd pick up KFC on the way home and have a family meeting. The children were pleased about the KFC, but we were all concerned. The children were on their best behavior, afraid they had done something wrong. I was fit to be tied; he hadn't said anything to me about any issues that needed discussing.

The children had barely seen their father in the previous few months. I'd seen him some, but not much. During that time, I tried to provide as much emotional support as I could for him and the children, but I didn't know what to do or how to do it.

When we had pretty much finished the chicken, Fred told us that things were going very badly for him at work. His programs, through no fault of his own, were falling apart. We should prepare that he would not receive any bonuses this year, and he might have to look for another job.

The children and I were shocked. Stunned.

"What happened, Dad?" Timothy asked.

"It's fairly complicated, Timothy, but remember that layered program I thought of when we were trying to float cream on our hot chocolate…"

And we all smiled, remembering how **un**animated he had been, frozen in his chair at the table, staring at the clear glass mugs of cocoa.

"… That program was great as long as mortgage appraisers were doing their jobs properly. But many of them became super careless and the program went into a tailspin. It was that program that was the cornerstone of Klein-Staily's recent successes, and it is in considerable difficulty as a result of those poor mortgage appraisals."

"Like, what does that mean for us?" asked Liz, ever the practical one.

"I'll give you the best-case and worst-case scenarios," Fred said.

"Best case, I'll lose my partnership but be kept on at Klein-Staily at a drastically reduced salary. Worst case, I'll lose my job and not be able to find anything paying much better than minimum wage."

That petrified the children. I was upset that Fred had put it that way.

"Fred!" I scolded. "Tell them the truth about what that means for them.

He was puzzled.

And so I added, "While your father was doing so well, we saved enough for your college educations, and we have saved enough that we can probably continue to live here in this house for at least the next twenty years even if he is fired tomorrow and never earns another cent. We will undoubtedly have to cut back, and our cutbacks may seem drastic to you two… probably even to your father and me. But we can survive this comfortably enough. And remember that's the worst-case scenario."

They breathed sighs of relief, knowing we could stay in our home. But Fred was bothered. He didn't want to look like a failure in their eyes and he hated being contradicted and criticized in front of them.

I was upset with the way Fred told us what was happening, and I was upset that he hadn't talked about it with me earlier. I had no idea why he did it that way, but it seemed wrong to spring it on the children and me the way he did.

That night, after the children went to bed, I confronted him. "All right, Fred, what was that about?"

"I'm in trouble at the firm. Johnson and his cronies can't wait to get my scalp. That's what it's about."

"Why did you have to tell the children? And why tell them like that?"

"I want them to know so they won't expect things to go on as they have been, and I didn't know how to tell them except straight out like that."

"Couldn't you have softened it somehow? As I told the children, we have enough set aside to live comfortably the rest of our lives."

He looked at me somewhat quizzically. "Do we really? How much do we have? I haven't really paid attention."

I knew he hadn't. He had left the saving and investing decisions up to me; all he had said was "Put the money in low-fee index funds. Stock-picker analysts aren't worth their weight in recycled scotch bottles."

I pulled out the latest financial statements for our accounts. We had nearly three million dollars put away. Most of it was in tax-free education and retirement accounts.

It was more than enough for us to live comfortably the rest of our lives.

"We won't have to cut back much," I said. "And if we do, I am about ready to go back to work full time if it matters all that much."

I continued, "But it shouldn't matter. We have enough. Even if neither of us works again, we have our house and cars paid for and we have more than enough for college for the children and for us to live on. The major cutbacks will have to be in our savings, donations, vacations, and social frills like that massive steak barbecue with the high-end scotch and champagne that we put on for the neighbors last summer."

"I don't want the neighbors or people at church to know," Fred replied. "I especially don't want you and the children to suffer socially because of the way things are falling apart for me at Klein-Staily."

I knew he was a proud man, and I wasn't sure whether he was worried more about his own image or about what would happen with me and with the children socially. Quite honestly, I didn't care about the social image.

Who am I kidding? Of course I did. But I also knew it would be good to winnow the wheat from the chaff among our friends.

Fred did his best to try to hold on at the firm and for the family. That was why he made that trip to New York City on September tenth. But things were drifting away from him at the firm, and despite our best efforts, things were drifting apart for us.

And I was drifting asleep.

Chapter 10 – Wednesday Morning

The alarm went off at 6:30 and roused me from such a deep sleep that I was disoriented. I rolled over and reached out my arm, but Fred wasn't there.

Then it hit me: I had no idea where he was or whether he was even alive. All the tension of the day before flooded up from inside me. I struggled to sit up in bed. I didn't want to face the truth.

I picked up my cellphone to see if I had missed a call from Fred. ... Nothing.

I sank emotionally and probably physically too. If Fred was okay, he'd have gotten a message to us somehow. My only hope was that he was injured and in some clinic without access to a telephone.

Telephone! I lifted the receiver to check for messages. Nothing from Fred and nothing about him. There were five or six messages from friends wanting to know if we knew anything, but nothing else.

I have no idea how I managed to get a solid sleep that night, but I think the tension and the uncertainty had worn me out. I forced myself to get up and look after the children. I was drenched with sweat, and so I knew I couldn't avoid having a quick shower.

While I was dressing, I had a weird thought: "Should I dress in black?"

It felt creepy to wonder about that, but Fred would have laughed with me at the thought. We both agreed that dressing in black to show respect for the dead was an overworked tradition. With those thoughts in mind, I put on some dark brown slacks and a cream-colored blouse. Tasteful, and not too colorful. Respectful, but not morbid.

I woke the children, giving them each a big hug. As I woke each of them, I sat on the bed for a few minutes, touching their shoulders and caressing them. "No word from Dad overnight," I told them. "And no word from anyone else about him. So it's time to get up and come on down for breakfast."

As I finished talking with each of them, I pulled them up and gave them another hug. I was wary of smothering them, but I needed comforting, too; hugging them was giving me what I needed from them right then.

I started the coffee and set out the breakfast cereal and juice as usual. The routine felt reassuring, and yet it felt odd and empty too.

When the children were settled at the table and eating, I asked them what they wanted to do. Did they want to go to school or did they want to stay home? I would understand either way.

"Mom," said Liz, "if Ms. Hazelton is going to, like, be with you and, like, keep you company, I'd just as soon go to school. But if you, like, want us here with you, I'll stay home."

Timothy said, "Me, too, Mom. If you need us here, I'll stay home. But I think I'd rather not miss any more school than necessary."

I loved their replies, and I loved them, too. "Yes, I think Thelma will be here, so you two go ahead and get ready for school. I'll get in touch with you right away if we learn anything new."

And then I added, "I know Uncle Ben has been busy ever since it happened, trying to locate any information he can about your father."

"So … what's on after school today?" I asked, trying to return to some sense of normalcy.

"I have soccer again," said Timothy. "And I may have to go see Ms. Rashevsky about this math we're just starting. I guess that'll depend on whether I understand it in class today."

"What about you, Liz?"

"I don't think I have anything on after school today. Like, what day is today? Wednesday? No, nothing. But Mom I'd like to spend some time with Becky Sanderson if that's okay. We talked for a while last night, and she said, like, she went through stuff like this when her dad was overseas and they didn't hear from him. I know it's not really the same, but she seems to understand."

"Sure," I said. But I didn't let up much. "What time should I expect you home?"

"How's five o'clock?"

"That'll be fine, Liz, but no later than that, please. And you, Timothy?"

"I should be able to make it by five, too."

I continued the routine as well as I could. "Everyone have their homework? Textbooks? Library books? Do you want some snacks?"

I gave the children an extra hug before they left and reminded them, "I'll be sure to let you know the minute I hear anything. If you want to come home, have the school call me, and I'll come get you immediately."

Then I added, "Remember: if anyone asks, we haven't heard from your father and we're not sure how he is. Nothing more. Right?"

After they left, I wandered aimlessly through the main floor of the house, but after about ten minutes I realized I had to get on with life. I picked up the dishes and put away the things from breakfast, but when that was done, I had to face my aloneness. I knew in my mind the odds were low that Fred would be coming home, but in my heart I was holding onto some slim hope.

I collapsed onto the stool at the kitchen counter and screamed as loud as I could. It felt good, but it didn't help either. I put my head in my hands and hoped none of the neighbors heard it.

I was jarred from my misery when the telephone rang. It was Thelma.

"I saw your kids walk by. Are they going to school?"

"Yes. We talked about it a bit last night and then some more this morning. I told them I'll let them know the minute I learn anything. And, no, we haven't heard a thing, Thelma. I'm beginning to fear the worst."

"I'll be right over."

"Fear the worst." I resented the euphemisms people used for dying and death, but during those few days I understood why people used them, especially since we weren't sure what had happened to Fred.

After we sat at the kitchen table with our coffee, we looked at each other. Neither of us knew what to say or what to do. "Seth and Aaron are pretty concerned," Thelma offered. "Well let's face it, so are Dale and I."

"What are your plans for today?" she asked. "Will you stay here and wait for some news? Or is there anything we can do, you and me together?"

"I don't know. I don't want to leave the house in case we get some news. But I guess I'd better start thinking about plans."

"What sort of plans do you want to work on, Susan? Can I help?"

I appreciated her concern, her offer, and the questioning tone --- she was genuinely asking if I wanted her help. If it had been someone else, it would have been different, but I knew Thelma wasn't trying to butt into my life.

"I don't even know what to consider," I said. "I don't want to plan for the possibility that Fred didn't make it..."

Argh. Another euphemism. But I still couldn't bring myself to say out loud what I was thinking and fearing: he might be dead.

I went on, "But I don't know what else to plan for. I feel pretty lost right now."

"How about supper?" suggested Thelma. "Let's think about supper. If there's no news by suppertime, why don't you and the children come over to our place for supper tonight?"

"Oh, Thelma, that sounds wonderful."

I didn't want to leave home, though, until we knew what had happened to Fred. And so I added, "But the neighbors have brought over plenty of food for the next few days, and I really don't want to leave home until I have a better idea what's happening..."

"What's happening..." another way of saying "Until I know whether Fred is dead, alive, or injured somewhere." I smiled to myself, laughing with Fred inside my head and my heart, thinking about all the fun we had had using euphemisms sarcastically.

I looked up and saw that Thelma was smiling a concerned smile back at me. "Oh, Thelma, I was just smiling, remembering how Fred and I would make fun of all the euphemisms people use for 'death', 'dead', 'dying', and what-not, and here I am using them myself."

She nodded slightly, and I went on. "I know the odds are pretty high that Fred didn't make it... "

I smiled again and said bluntly. "Didn't make it. Hmph. What I mean is, 'Is dead.' I just don't want to do anything about it in case he is still alive somewhere. I just can't go there, at least not yet."

"I get that, for sure."

"If we don't hear anything by tomorrow, I'll start planning for a future without Fred – ugh, another euphemism! but for now let's plan other things."

"Okay." Thelma reached across the table and squeezed my hand. As she did, the doorbell rang.

"Let me get it," said Thelma, "in case it's the press."

I guessed it was because I heard Thelma say quite firmly as she opened the door, "Oh! You've returned with the five hundred dollars!"

I couldn't make out the response, but it must have been somewhat indignant because then Thelma let loose. "You have the statements," she said. "And you are now harassing the Young family. We have the local constables on speed-dial. If you aren't gone in five seconds, we're calling them. And we will definitely want you charged with trespassing. Do we need to get a restraining order against you?"

She didn't slam the door. Instead she stood there, glaring out the door until the reporter mumbled some answer, and then she kept the door open as she watched him walk back down the driveway.

"That was almost fun," she said. "Almost, but not really."

"We'll probably have to deal with reporters all day." I agreed. "Let's draft another statement and hand it to those who show up, okay?"

We giggled a bit as we began with a choice phrase or two, but in the end we drafted a very proper-sounding statement:

> To the best of our knowledge no one has heard from Fredrick Young since his email to his wife on Tuesday morning. We have no further information about him. When we do, we will issue another statement. Until then, please honor our request for privacy.

We decided that statement was what we would read over the phone to anyone who called.

But for the written statement we added,

> If you leave a business card with your email address, we will get in touch with you when we have any news.
>
> If you return uninvited, you will be considered trespassers and we will call the police, who have already had to remove some people.
>
> Thank you, The Young Family

We printed off a dozen of these statements.

"I wonder whether we should print another dozen or so of these statements with a different conclusion for the children and me to carry with us when we're out of the house."

Thelma thought it was a good idea, and so we printed up a dozen statements saying,

> We have no news about Fredrick Young. When we do, we will make a public statement. Until then, please honor our wish for privacy.
> If you keep trying to question us, we will consider it harassment, and the local police have already agreed to support us in this.
>
> Thank you for your understanding,
> The Young Family

"You know, Thelma, I've worked with the media off and on for many years. I doubt if these statements will deter many reporters for long if they think they can get a story. We can have these things ready just in case, but I'm not sure they'll do much good."

"Yeah," she replied. "So let's move on to something else. I'd say 'Let's go someplace nice for lunch to distract us' but I know you don't really want to leave the house right now. So how about we plan dinner? We all ate here last night, so as I started to say earlier, why don't you and the children come to our place for dinner...." And she stopped. "Oh yeah. That won't work if you don't want to leave the house yet."

I looked down at my hands and shook my head. "I can't. Not today."

And then I looked up at Thelma and forced a weak smile. "We have loads of food here. You saw everything that came in last night, and there will probably be a few more things today. This afternoon let's plan another good meal for all of us. Maybe Ben and Cindy will be here, too."

That seemed to make sense to Thelma. But we were both feeling unsettled. It was hard to just sit there.

We turned on the television, but there was no news. The four hijacked planes were clearly the work of terrorists; governments and politicians were issuing statements of outrage; George Bush was safe; and New York City was still in a state of chaos.

That last bit of news, that New York City was still in a state of chaos, gave me a sliver of hope. I called Ben to see what his people had found out in New York, but I knew the answer before I called – if he had found out anything at all, he'd have called me or come over.

"Ben, it's Susan. We haven't heard anything about Fred, yet. Have you?"

"Not a word, Susan. We still have people making the rounds of the clinics, emergency rooms, … and temporary … sites."

"More euphemisms," I thought to myself. I knew that he meant 'temporary morgues' but couldn't bring himself to say that.

Ben added, "We've sent people to the sites of the collapsed buildings. They tell us it's still too hot there to do any rescue or recovery work, but they are pitching in at the sites to do whatever they can."

"Thanks, Ben."

"If there isn't any news about Fred by this afternoon, we'll issue another statement from Klein-Staily. And Susan…?"

"Yes?"

"Don't worry. We'll make sure you're looked after both now and in the future."

"Thanks, Ben. Let's stay in touch even if there's no news."

After we said our goodbyes, I suggested to Thelma that maybe we could go through the phone message list to return calls just to let people know that we didn't know anything.

"That's a good way to spend our time. Maybe it'll head off some repeat inquiries, too."

And then she paused and contemplated something for a moment.

"You know, girl, you probably should hold a press conference about this. That might actually be easier than dealing with reporters one at a time. You could get it all over with at once. ..."

I groaned. And I dug in my heels.

"I'm not doing that – not today anyway. And I'm certainly not doing that if we don't know anything new. Why sit in front of a bunch of reporters who will keep trying to find new angles for a story by peppering us with questions when we really don't know what's going on. No, I'm not doing that. Not today. I'm just not up to it."

Cindy Gruvel called. "Have you seen the paper yet? Look at page two."

"Thanks, Cindy. Let me take a look and then I'll call you back."

I got the paper and spread it out on the kitchen table. There on page two was a photo of Fred with the headline, "Local Executive Feared Lost in Attacks".

I was livid. I was hurt. I was in agony. I was overwhelmed with emotions. It felt like a major intrusion into our lives, as if everyone in Omaha had some right to share in our personal and family feelings, and I resented everyone for that. This was our problem, our situation, our potential grief, our cause for concern, ... but I controlled myself.

"I guess they got this photo from their files. It's the portrait Klein-Staily had done when Fred was made a managing partner a few years ago."

Saying that helped calm me down. After all, the headline was exactly right. Fred was an executive... I noted that I had that thought in the past tense... 'Fred *was*', ... and I was determined not to speak about Fred in the past tense again, not yet, anyway.

And Fred was indeed "feared lost", whatever that meant. Another euphemism for "feared dead"? Or maybe he escaped and was suffering from amnesia, wandering aimlessly. I knew I was clutching at straws.

The article didn't have a by-line, but it had quite obviously been written by someone who had connections at Klein-Staily, probably with Ben or someone in Ben's office. It laid out the background fully and carefully, but how did they know it all?

Ben had issued a statement on behalf of Klein-Staily:

> We at Klein-Staily, along with the rest of the world, are shocked and horrified by the devastating terrorist attacks. We join everyone in mourning the losses of so many lives.
>
> For those who have been asking, neither we nor his family have had any news from or about Fred Young since those attacks occurred.
>
> Fred is a valued, talented managing partner of Klein-Staily. He went to New York to meet with representatives of Cantor-Fitzgerald about a new agriculture-bond structuring program he was developing.
>
> We are all hoping for the best, and we are sending our hopes and prayers to Fred and to the entire Young family.

The article concluded with a very pointed reference to Ben's and then Dale's interactions with the press the previous evening.

> Ben Gruvel, Senior Managing Partner at Klein-Staily told reporters that he and the Young family would let people know as soon as they learn anything more about Mr. Young. Gruvel and a neighbor who refused to be interviewed both pointedly said the Young family did not wish to be bothered at this point but that they would issue an update on the situation this afternoon.

"Are you okay with all this?" asked Thelma.

I thought for a second or two.

"Yes and no. Yes, I'm glad that Ben and Dale are helping out right now, but there are some important 'No's' as well. I don't like the fact that reporters are probing, even though I know that's inevitable. And I don't like relying on Ben and Dale so much... or on you for that matter. I have always felt strong. Even though I seemed dependent on Fred, I had a sense of inner strength, but I lost that yesterday, and I don't like that."

"So what are you saying, Susan? Do you want me to leave?"

"Oh my god, no! I love having you here. I need you here right now, Thelma, and I hope you can stay today, too. Please!"

I hadn't meant to insult Thelma. I hoped she wasn't upset.

"That's okay, Susan. I know what you meant. I can't imagine what you're going through right now. So, shall we get started on these messages?"

"Let me call Cindy first. Maybe while I'm doing that, you can go through the list and put stars next to the ones you think I should call first?"

"Good idea." And so Thelma started through the list while I called Cindy.

"What do you think?" Cindy asked.

"I thought it was pretty good, and I was glad Ben issued a statement from Klein-Staily. It was a nice one. I wish the reporters would take 'no' for an answer, but I understand why they don't. What did you think?"

"I liked it. That's a great photo of Fred, and they said nice things. I think Ben wishes it had been more forceful, but I also think overall he was pleased with it."

"What was with the 'will issue a statement this afternoon' quote? What statement and who is going to make it?"

"Golly, Susan, I have no idea. I wonder if someone was guessing or trying to put pressure on you or the firm to say something."

"Well, I didn't say it, so I'm off the hook," I said with a slight chuckle, knowing full well that I wasn't off the hook at all, but I knew that Ben and the firm would issue another statement and that's what the quote was about.

"Cindy," I added, "why don't you and Ben join us again for dinner tonight? As you saw yesterday, we have 'meals for millions'. If we get much more today, I'm not sure we'll have anywhere to keep it."

'Meals for Millions'! That was a term Fred coined, referring to the Memorial

Day potluck picnics back in western Kansas, where everyone brought so much food that they couldn't possibly eat it all. The phrase just slipped out.

"Sure! We'd love to," said Cindy. "But Ben may have to show up late or leave early, depending on how things are at the office."

She didn't have to say it, but I knew Ben would be putting us at the top of his various lists of things to do, which meant he would have a lot of other paperwork to catch up on, too. I hoped he could join us, but I'd understand if he couldn't.

"We'll certainly understand. We appreciate everything Ben and the firm are doing to help out."

"Okay. I'll wait 'til this afternoon to see what Ben is up to, but I'll try to get there about 5 myself, ok?"

"Perfect! And thanks, Cindy."

I took a breather to make a fresh pot of coffee. My brain had been spinning at full tilt for over an hour, and I needed some time to refresh my mind and my emotions. It was odd how doing some little chore like brewing a pot of coffee helped settle my mind and thoughts.

As I was brewing the coffee, I took a piece of paper towel to clean a small spill on the counter and for some reason thought of our first apartment in Omaha, where we used paper towels instead of Melitta filters to make our coffee. I stopped what I was doing and just stood there for a few moments, thinking to myself and wanting to share that memory with someone. I started to turn toward Thelma to tell her about that memory, but then I decided not to share too many memories or thoughts with anyone else, not even close friends. I'm not sure why I decided that, but it felt as if this memory was for Fred and me, and not for others.

That decision at that moment was important. It helped shape the rest of my life. I had always been a private person when it came to my thoughts and feelings, but it felt important to me that I use some care in what I said and shared after that moment. I had a sense that I would have to look after myself, that I wouldn't have Fred with me to share looking after each other.

Chapter 11 – **No News**

Thelma hadn't made much progress with the phone message list, and so we sat together to go through it, discussing each of the messages briefly. Like me, Thelma was amused by some of the children's additions.

"Well, who do you want to call first?" Thelma asked.

I didn't really want to call anyone, but I knew it would be a good idea.

"Let's start with Dr. Franks," I said.

Dr. William Franks was the senior minister of our church, Third United of Omaha. The last thing I wanted was to spend any time at all with a minister or with church elders, and I hoped to head them off by calling him.

"Maybe if I call him, I can explain that I don't need anything, and I really don't want any visitors right now."

When I called the church, of course I had to explain to the receptionist, "No, we don't know anything about Fred, and of course we're very concerned. Could I please speak with Dr. Franks?"

"Sure. I'll get him on the line right away."

I expected she would listen in, and so I chose my words carefully.

Dr. Franks came on the line, "Hello, Susan. I'm so glad you called. Is there anything at all that we can do for you?"

"Dr. Franks, I wanted to thank you for your call yesterday. It means a lot to me and the children to know that you and the members of the church are thinking about Fred and about us."

"Susan, we're all here for you. Let us know what we can do. Would you like one of us to stop by sometime to be with you, to talk, and to pray together."

I had been dreading that, but I had known I would have to face it.

"Thank you so much, Dr. Franks, but I think we need our time to ourselves right now. The Hazeltons from up the street and the Gruvels from Klein-Staily have been a great help so far, and I think that's all we really need."

"We understand that Susan. We will do our best not to intrude on your lives during your time of uncertainty, and we will respect your need for privacy, but please do not hesitate to call me or anyone else here at the church as soon as you know anything or if you need anything at all."

He was saying that I should be sure to call him right away to set up the funeral, at least that's what it sounded like to me. I didn't really mind; in fact, I was grateful that he had very politely and subtly sidestepped the issue for the moment.

"Thanks, again, Dr. Franks. I'll be in touch soon," and I hung up.

I looked at Thelma and saw she had an eyebrow half-cocked, as if she was asking what that was about.

"Thelma, I really don't want anyone to come over to counsel me or to pray with me. I know the children and I may need some counseling of some sort later, but now isn't the time. I called Dr. Franks first and said what I did to him to try to head off any further intrusions from the church. I know they mean well, but I will be happier if we wait to meet with those people until after we hear from or about Fred."

And then, out of the blue, it occurred to me, "I wonder how the children are doing... I hope they're ok... I'm concerned about them... I hope they're coping all right."

"You've nurtured a strong family in every way, Susan. Don't worry about them. They'll come through this fine. It'll be rough, but they'll be okay."

I replied, "Well, if there's no word by tomorrow morning, we'll have to assume he didn't make it," I said. "I'll hold out hope, but things don't look good, do they?"

Thelma was brilliantly non-committal. "Okay."

We spent the rest of the morning with me making calls and Thelma answering the door. I used our landline to make the calls, wanting to be sure my cellphone was available in case Fred or Ben called. My hopes were fading, but I didn't want that line to be busy just in case.

The calls were hard. People wanted to chat, to be involved somehow, but I wasn't ready for all that involvement yet. I did my best not to put people off, and I tried to keep the conversations short.

For example, the Brownings had children the ages of Timothy and Liz, and we'd gotten to know them through school and scouting activities. They seemed like nice people.

"Hello, Nancy, this is Susan Young."

"Oh! Susan! Is there any news about Fred?"

"No, nothing. We haven't heard from him. Even though Klein Staily has people working all over New York City, trying to find out anything they can, there's no news at all. I just wanted to let you know."

"Oh, Susan, I'm so sorry and so worried for you and your children. Is there anything you need? Anything we can do?"

"Thanks for asking, Nancy. I really appreciate it. But for now we're okay. I'll be sure to let you know, though, if we need anything."

"Okay."

"Nancy, I'm trying to call everyone now who has called or stopped by. One thing is that we probably won't be able to call everyone individually again when we do have some news. I hope that's okay and that everyone understands."

"Of course. Listen, can we stop by with some food for tonight? Or maybe for the weekend?"

I laughed.

"Thanks, Nancy, but the neighbors here and the families in our church have already brought more food than we can eat, and we're running out of room in the fridge and freezer. But I'll save some, and we'll try to have your family over to share it sometime after a week or two, okay?"

"That sounds great. But in the meantime, be sure to let me know if there's anything we can do."

"Thanks, Nancy. I will."

I went through about twenty calls, all of them like that. And after those twenty calls, I checked all the messages that had accumulated while the phone line had been busy with me making all those outgoing calls, adding a couple of more names and numbers at the end of the list for people who hadn't called the day before.

Meanwhile Thelma had her work cut out for her at the door, mostly greeting friends and neighbors and explaining to them that we didn't know anything about Fred.

Only one reporter came by, thank goodness. It was a journalism trainee from the local college program. Thelma was brusque with her at first, but when she realized it was a student, she carefully explained that we had no news and that we would let everyone know when we had any.

"Well, do you think I could have just a word with Mrs. Young?" asked the student, who was already developing the persistence that had annoyed me so much in most reporters.

"No." Thelma reverted to brusqueness. "We'll let you know when there's any news."

Just as I was finishing my twentieth call, Thelma came into the kitchen holding a gift card in her hand. "This is from someone named Betty. She wouldn't give me her full name but said you'd know who it was. She said, 'I know lots of people are bringing food by now, but in a week or so they might want some pizza.'"

It was a $25 gift card for a nearby pizzeria.

"What a thoughtful gift!" I said as I attached the gift card to the fridge with a one of the spare fridge magnets. "Betty. ... Hmmm. It must have been Betty LeDuc! Was she slim, bordering on skinny with a pixie cut?"
"That's her! And yes, this is a great idea. I'll have to keep pizza gift cards in mind for the future."

I added Betty's name to the bottom of Thelma's list.

We took a break from messages and struggled with organizing the food people had sent.

"Let's have 'clear-out-the-fridge' lunches and dinners," suggested Thelma. She seemed enthusiastic about the idea.

"Good idea!" I replied. "We'll start with food that's taking up a lot of space or food that won't be very good if we don't eat it right away."

"Let's get rid of the melons, especially this half cantaloupe. We can have it for lunch, can't we?"

"Absolutely! Let's do," I agreed. "We'll have that and some of this leftover chicken lasagna so I can put it back in a smaller container."

And so we got to work, organizing my fridge like it hadn't been organized for years. It was a little embarrassing to have Thelma pull stuff out from the back of the fridge and alternately laugh and groan.

"Eww, what's this?" We laughed and chucked some moldy mess, container and all, into the garbage. "I sure hope it wasn't one of the kids' science projects," Thelma said, and we laughed some more.

"Maybe we can get together and do this at my place," she added. "I expect I have some real monsters lurking in the back of my fridge," as we laughed some more and grimaced together at the thought.

At noon, Ben called. I grabbed at the phone, hoping for news.

"Ben!" I put it on speaker so Thelma could hear, too.

"Hello Susan."

"Oh, oh," I thought. He was using measured tones. It scared me. I reached out across the kitchen table and took Thelma's hand.

"We haven't learned a thing, Susan," said Ben.

I slumped an inch or so in the chair as I relaxed my grip on Thelma's hand.

Ben went on, "We've had people check every hospital, every medical center, every emergency center, and every other possible temporary site, Susan, and there is no sign of him. We've rechecked with his hotel. They haven't seen him, and he hasn't returned to his room. Judging from what the police and others are saying, there must be over two thousand people still missing. Man, that's a lot of people to be missing. No sign of them anywhere."

"Well, thanks for everything you're doing, Ben. It means so much to us.

"We'll continue looking, Susan. I've faxed a photo of Fred to several different people for distribution, and of course I'll let you know if we find anything."

"Thanks, Ben."

And then I continued, "I don't know if Cindy told you, but you're invited here for dinner again tonight. We have more food than we can eat or store right now. The neighbors have been so thoughtful and generous."

"Yes, she called me right away to tell me. I expect I can be there by 5:30. I hope that's okay."

"Of course it is! Thanks, again, Ben. See you then."

Chapter 12 – Facing Reality, Slowly and Reluctantly

That afternoon, I replied to more phone messages. Everyone seemed glad to hear from me, and making the calls became easier as I continued making them.

Maybe what I *should* say is that it became less difficult to make the calls; it was always hard to talk about Fred that day since we had no idea what had happened with him.

Worse, with every minute that we didn't hear from him and didn't hear anything about him, it became more and more likely that he had been killed in the attacks. It was so difficult to face that fact head on, but it was seeping into my consciousness.

Mid-afternoon, Thelma asked, "What are you going to do about that thing in the paper that said there would be a statement this afternoon? Pretty soon you're going to have to deal with more reporters…"

I let my head sink slightly. I wasn't looking forward to fending off the inevitable onslaught of reporters.

"Why don't you call Ben and get him to deal with it?" Thelma suggested.

"I'm sure he'd be happy to do it," I replied, "But it's us. It's our situation. I think I'd better start handling some of these things myself."

Saying "start" seemed significant as I said it, but it wasn't as if I had never handled tough situations before. I had dealt with the press in my job with Arkero, and I had led most of the discussions with the children's teachers on meet-the-teacher nights. I knew I could learn to handle anything new that might happen. But to say "start" seemed to mean something more significant now that Fred might be gone. However, instead of letting that realization get me down, I said, "So I guess I'd better get to it. Would you like to help me draft a statement?"

"Sure. Why don't we start by recycling the statement we wrote this morning?" and we picked it up to read it again.

> To the best of our knowledge no one has heard from Fredrick Young since his email to his wife on Tuesday morning. We have no further information about him. When we do, we will issue another statement. Until then, please honor our request for privacy.

"Well, that won't do!" and we both actually laughed at how inappropriate it was for a press release. "I was feeling a bit frustrated with the media when I wrote that. I should have known better."

And so I modified it:

> To the best of our knowledge no one has heard from Fredrick Young since he and I exchanged emails on Tuesday morning. We know he had an appointment yesterday morning at 9am with Cantor-Fitzgerald in the North Tower of the World Trade Center, and we know that no one who was in the Cantor-Fitzgerald offices has been heard from since the terrorist attacks. That is all we know, and we don't want to speculate about anything else at this point.
>
> We are very grateful for all the kind and caring messages we have received from everyone. We want to thank our friends and neighbors for everything they have done and for all their offers of assistance; and we especially want to thank all the people at Klein-Staily for their help, trying to locate Fred in New York City and trying to help us determine what happened. Knowing we have so many supportive friends has been a tremendous help and inspiration during this time of uncertainty for the children and me.
>
> When we know more, we will let you know.

"What do you think?" I asked Thelma.

"Damn, girl, you're good. That is wonderful."

"Well, remember I had some experience with this sort of thing at Arkero Foods. Can you think of anything else I should change or add?"

"Nothing. It looks fine to me. How will you distribute it? At the door?"

"Printing it as a hand out might be good," I replied, "but I think I'll do a mass email to all the media outlets. I'd rather they all get it at the same time and not stampede to our door to get the handouts."

I let my eyes bug out just a bit, and we both groaned at the thought of a reporter invasion.

I got to work collecting email addresses from the internet and creating a mailing list.

"That's genius," said Thelma. "What can I do to help?"

I stopped in the middle of compiling the email list.

"Listen to me, Thelma. You have been a great help. All day you've been helping with the phone, you've answered the door, and you've provided more time and emotional help than I would have dared to ask for. Once I get this email sent to the press, we'll be bombarded with calls again, and so if you can stick around a bit longer to help with those calls, I'd really appreciate it even though that's more than I should expect."

"Okay," she said. There was a hint of something in her voice. I didn't know what it was – Disappointment? Exhaustion? Wanting to get away? Wanting to help more? I had to check to see. I was afraid I had imposed on her too much already.

"Oh, Thelma, I'm sorry. You've done so much already. If you need time to go home and look after things there, I'm sure I can deal with the press now. It's time for me to do this. Go ahead."

I smiled at her, a smile that said "I'm okay and thanks." I sat up a bit, as if I was about to push my chair back to stand up, but I didn't move toward the door. I didn't want it to seem I was trying to get rid of her, but I wanted her to feel free to leave.

Thelma started to get up, and I knew from that movement that she had other things she wanted to do besides look after me. I was embarrassed by how much I had relied on her, but I was also relieved that I had picked up on the subtle signal when she said, "Okay."

"Well, I do have some things to look after at home. Why don't I go do some of those things and come back in a couple of hours to help with dinner?"

I smiled at her again and walked her to the door. We hugged and then she left.

As I closed the door, I felt as if it was the first time I was truly all alone, with the children at school and no one else in the house. I'd been home alone almost every school day since the children had begun going to school, and I'd even been home alone that morning after they left for school, but this felt so different.

I sensed it would be the beginning of a long period of aloneness. I just stood in the front hall and let that sink in.

And then I went upstairs and threw myself onto the bed and cried and screamed. I hadn't realized just how much I had been holding in. I picked up a table lamp and was about to throw it against the wall, but instead I managed to hold onto it and yelled, "Damned terrorists!"

That helped relieve the tension, but it didn't get the emails written and sent, and it didn't help locate Fred, and so I washed my face, lightly re-applied some makeup, put on some fresh clothes, and went downstairs to finish the press release.

I sent the message to a large list of media people whose email addresses I could find. Then, to be inclusive, I created another email list for friends and neighbors. That list included the children's schools, Dr. Franks at the church, Ben and others at Klein-Staily, and all the neighbors for whom I had email addresses.

I was right. The phone started ringing right after the message was sent.

The first call was from the local CBS affiliate, not two minutes after I sent the mass email press release.

"Hello, Mrs. Young?"

"Yes."

"This is Janice McKay calling from CBS-Omaha. Thank you for your message explaining what's going on with Mr. Young. I know you must be going through a lot right now, but would it be okay if we send a reporter to your home to interview you about your husband and how you're dealing with it?"

I wanted to blurt out something rude to her like, "No! And leave us alone!"

Instead I said, "Actually, we have no information, and we do not wish to grant any requests for interviews at this point. I hope you understand."

"Of course, Mrs. Young. How are the children coping with this?"

She was a typical reporter who wouldn't take "No" for an answer. I controlled myself. I knew I would have to learn to.

I very politely responded, "As I have told others, we do not wish to have our privacy invaded at this point and do not wish to respond to *any* questions. We'll let you know when we have anything else to say. Thanks for calling, though."

I hung up even though she was still trying to ask another question.

That scenario played itself out maybe ten more times over the next hour. And in between phone calls, there were four or five different reporters who came to the door, some with cameras and others with full camera crews. If I recognized them from previous visits, I gave them the more blunt handout that Thelma and I had worked up in the morning. If I didn't, I gave them the printed the copy of the press release, half-smiled, and closed the door.

Chapter 13 – **Planning for Contingencies**

Just before five o'clock everyone seemed to arrive at once. Timothy and Liz came home from school past the Hazelton's house just as they were leaving to come to our house, and as they were all walking up the front walk, Cindy Gruvel pulled into the driveway.

The first thing everyone wanted to know was whether there was any news about Fred. I asked the others to make themselves at home in the family room while the children and I went upstairs for a few minutes.

"Oh, sure," said Thelma. "Cindy and I can start getting things ready for dinner, and we'll get Seth, Aaron, and Dale to help."

"Put your schoolwork in your bedrooms," I said to Timothy and Liz, "and then come into our bedroom."

"Our" bedroom. I still couldn't say "My" bedroom.

When they came in, I was sitting in the middle of the bed, propped up against the headboard, and they sat on each side of me.

"How were things at school?" I asked. It felt forced and artificial, but it was the only way I knew to get started.

Liz answered first. "Everyone seemed, like, in shock. They seemed like they wanted to say something about Dad, but, like, didn't really know what to say or do. The teachers all looked at me with, like, you know, like, sort of a different look?"

Timothy added, "Yeah. No one wanted to raise the subject, but they all seemed like they wanted to know."

"Becky was okay talking about it," said Liz. "At lunch she, like, broke the ice with the others sitting with us and said something like, 'Anything new about your dad, Liz?' Then the others, like, felt free to talk about it, too. I told them, 'The main problem is we just don't know,' and that's, like, all I could say to them. I started to cry a bit, but they were all so nice. Like, each one of them came over and gave me a hug. I was, like, bawling by the end of it all, partly for Dad and partly cuz of all the love they were giving."

"How was it for you, Timothy?" I asked.

"Coach Potter took me aside before soccer practice and asked me about Dad. He said, 'Young, you be sure and let us know at the school if we can help you out in any way. Not knowing is horrible, I'm sure.' The guys at lunch didn't look at me or talk to me. I think they wanted to, but didn't know how. So near the end of lunch I just blurted out, 'There hasn't been any news about my dad, yet. We're all pretty worried.' And they all sort of nodded and said some nice things."

"Good," I said. "How did the math go, Timothy? You seemed worried about that last night."

He beamed. "Oh, it was fine. It turned out that I had a pretty good grasp of the geometry axioms and had done enough of the problem sets on my own that Ms. Rashevsky was pretty impressed. But, man do I have a lot of homework to make up from missing just that one day of school! Reading in history, a poem to analyze for English, more math problems, reading in biology, and a conversation to study in Spanish. Whew!"

"What about you, Liz?" I asked.

"Same here," she said. "I never realized how missing a day of school, especially that last hour study hall, can lead to so much homework!"

"Well, after dinner we'll shoo everyone out and you two can get to work instead of playing games all evening with Seth and Aaron in the basement."

They both complained in the most good-natured way possible, faking groans while laughing.

I wanted to talk with them some more about the possibility that Fred was dead, but I decided to wait until the others had left and the children had done most of their homework. I felt that at that stage we should talk about it just between us and not with the others present. I knew I would talk about it with the other parents when the children weren't present, but I wanted my talks with the children to be just between us at first.

"Okay, let's go down and see what everyone has decided we should have for dinner."

- - -

The table was set for all nine of us again.

"The guys set the table," said Cindy, "while Thelma and I rummaged through the fridge to collect the food for supper."

Thelma continued, "We decided on the scalloped potatoes, meatloaf, and bean with bacon casserole. I hope that's okay. They're all lined up here on the counter to start warming them in the microwave when Ben gets here."

Cindy said, "Let's not wait for Ben before we start heating up the food. He said he'll try to be here around five-thirty, and it'll take us until after that to get the food ready."

About twenty minutes later, while we were heating up the meatloaf, Ben arrived. As we gathered somewhat informally in the kitchen, Ben told us, "There's no word yet about Fred. We had two of our associates working all last night and all day today, looking for any news of him. I called the hotel again. They still haven't seen any indication that Fred has been there. I told them to keep the room again tonight but if Fred isn't back there by noon tomorrow, we'll have someone pack up his things to have them sent back here. I hope that's okay with you, Susan."

I slumped a tiny bit, knowing that Ben was merely acting on what we all expected was true: Fred didn't make it.

As we went into the dining room, I asked everyone to remain standing and to hold hands around the table. The children were on either side of me, and I squeezed their hands as I said, "Let's all say a private prayer for Fred."

We bowed our heads, and stood like that for awhile, holding hands. Finally I said, "Amen."

Then Cindy announced, "the meatloaf is ready. Why don't I slice it in the kitchen and bring it in on a platter?" As she did that, the talk turned to food chatter, like "Please pass the potatoes," and "Is there any of that special rye bread left?"

When we were nearing the end of the meal, Dale said, "No one else wants any of that cherry pie, right?"

The four children immediately made it **very** clear that they wanted some, and Thelma and I both said we'd like small pieces. "Ben? Cindy?" Dale asked.

"I can't speak for Ben," answered Cindy, "but I think I'd better pass on dessert today. I've already eaten wayyy too much these past two days."

"Me, too," said Ben. "You folks go ahead though."

I smiled outwardly but snorted inwardly. Ben had said that as if he was giving us permission, as if we needed his approval. I knew he didn't totally mean it that way; I knew he was just saying he didn't want any pie and that he hoped we wouldn't make a big deal about it, but it still rankled a bit. He was acting like the big shot he was, and not only did he not need to do that, it seemed inappropriate in our home.

"So, seven of us want pie, but two of us want small pieces," said Dale. "How about I cut it into sixths and cut one slice in half for Thelma and Susan?"

Everyone approved, with Seth smiling devilishly as he said, "Okay, but can I have the biggest sixth?"

"Fun-neeee," added Aaron, who then looked at the rest of us and said, "That's one of Dad's favorite lines. Seth just stole it."

After dinner I announced, "Seth and Aaron, I'm sure you both have lots of schoolwork to catch up on, especially after staying here all last evening to play games, and I know Liz and Timothy do. So how about we have a study hall in basement? No games, though," I admonished them. Just school work."

"We'll have to go home to get our homework," said Seth eagerly. "Okay? We'll be back in five minutes."

Once the children were settled in the basement, I asked the others to join me in the family room. I looked at them all and began, "We know the chances are slim that Fred is still alive. We all need to be open and honest about that. I'm not giving up hope, but I want to be realistic and talk with all of you about what to do over the next few days."

"What do you have in mind?" asked Ben.

"First of all, Fred and I have enough put away that the children and I will be fine financially, so don't any of you worry about that."

"And there must be some life insurance, too?" said Dale with a questioning tone.

"There is," replied Ben. "Klein-Staily provides insurance for all its employees. I'll go over the details with Susan later."

Bless Ben. I didn't want the financial details of my life known to everyone, not even my close friends.

"I've sent a statement to everyone in the media," I said, and even though they had received it, I read a copy of the email message I had sent out.

"That's good," said Ben, "And just before I left the office, I sent out another formal statement on behalf of Klein-Staily."

"Thanks, Ben. I'm gradually trying to call everyone who has telephoned or come by, thanking them and assuring them we'll let them know as soon as we find out anything."

"Where do you go from here?" asked Dale. "What's next?"

"I just don't know. That's why I wanted to talk with you four."

Cindy seemed a bit quiet, as if something was on her mind, and so I asked her directly, "What do you think Cindy?"

"It's probably too early to even say this, but I wonder whether you might consider thinking about having some sort of memorial service for Fred." Even though she had hedged the suggestion, she blushed a bit and seemed embarrassed.

"Cindy," I said, trying to reassure her, "I want to be realistic, and I think you're right. It hasn't even been thirty-six hours since the attacks, but if we haven't heard anything by tomorrow afternoon, I'll start making some arrangements. I know it seems early, but if Fred is dead or isn't found soon, I don't want to wallow in the sadness and uncertainty, and I don't want the children to be dragged down by it all."

Saying it all that way seemed so harsh, so definite. I had always had a hard head for making decisions, but this one overwhelmed me. Cindy got up and came over to where I was sitting and put her hand on my shoulder.

"There's nothing to be ashamed of about being realistic," Ben said.

I took a deep breath and looked up at Cindy. "Thanks for saying what you did, Cindy. I hadn't let myself think like that, but it's time to move in that direction. If it turns out that Fred *is* alive somewhere, I know he would understand."

We talked some more about plans. Who should speak; where should it be held; when should we do it? But I didn't want to do anything definite until the next day.

Chapter 14 – Getting through another night

A little before eight-thirty we heard giggling and laughing from the basement. I told the others, "Well, they've been quiet down there for nearly two hours. It sounds as if they're deciding to take a break." I excused myself and went down to talk with the children.

"How is everything going down here?" I asked.

"Pretty good, Mom," said Timothy. I'm pretty much caught up on my math and my reading. I just have to write out my analysis of this poem." And then he added sarcastically, "The others have been giving me some **very** helpful suggestions."

"I don't want to hear them!" I fake-scowled and then laughed.

"Would it be okay if we play until nine, Mom?" asked Liz.

"Sure." The scramble was on as the four of them closed their books and went to the air hockey table.

When I got back upstairs, Dale and Thelma were making their way to the front door. "I think we'd better go home now," said Thelma. "We've overstayed our welcome."

"Nonsense!" I smiled at the two of them, "You're always welcome here."

"We may take you up on that," said Dale. "Let me know when you get more cherry pie."

Thelma jabbed him gently and went to the basement stairs to call Aaron and Seth. "Time to go home now, boys. Let's go."

"Aww," whined Aaron. "We just started a game."

The four children slowly made their way back upstairs to the family room and we all said our goodbyes, with hugs all around again.

Cindy said, "Susan, I know Ben has some things he wants to go over with you, so I'll go back down with the children and get them to show me some of the games."
"Okay, but I hope we won't be too long. I expect the children haven't really finished their schoolwork yet."

When they had made their way to the basement, Ben and I sat at the kitchen table, and I poured us each a glass of wine.

"Susan, how are you doing? Really?"

"I think I'm still in shock, Ben. I'm coasting on nerves and adrenalin."

Ben smiled. "Okay, how about financially? I want you to know that the firm will look after you, if necessary, until things are settled."

"That's nice, Ben, but I think we're okay for now. We have a good amount set aside in education and retirement accounts, and Fred always insisted that we keep a portion of our savings set aside in what he called 'liquid' assets."

"I want to let you know a bit more about his life insurance situation. At Fred's age and given his position at Klein-Staily, the firm had a little over five million dollars' worth of life insurance on him."

He paused. I gulped.

"Wow! That's more than we'll ever need! Why so much?"

"It's a declining balance, term life policy," Ben explained. When Fred was made partner, the benefits for his life insurance were bumped up that high. It happens for everyone in the firm, but the benefits decline over time. After a partner reaches age 70, the life insurance policy pays only fifty thousand dollars. We all agreed when we set it up that younger partners would need more insurance than the older partners."

"But that's so **much**! We have our own insurance for twenty thousand dollars. We thought that if anything happened to Fred, that would be enough to tide us over until I could sell the house, if necessary, and go back to work. But five million dollars! It's hard to fathom…"

"It's a little more than five million," said Ben. "But here's another shocker for you: it's double indemnity. That means the payout to you will be doubled because … "
He hesitated just a half a beat, "Or should I say 'if'… he was killed while traveling on work for the firm. The payout should be about 10.3 million dollars."

I didn't know what to say. I leaned back in the chair; and then I put my head on my arms on the table. Finally I looked up and said, "That is **so** much money, Ben! What will I do with it... if it happens?"

"Well, just think about it for now. Of course, we'll be happy to manage it for you when the time comes. And one more thing, Susan. I've seen too many people who receive life insurance payouts much smaller than this get victimized or approached by all sorts of people and agencies, asking for money or proposing major investment schemes. Be careful."

"Gosh, I hadn't even thought about that. What do you recommend, Ben?"

"Don't tell ANYONE how much the insurance is. Not even the children. If people ask, just tell them "We're lucky. It's enough we can keep the house, and the children will have their education expenses looked after.""

"Good. I like that. It's nobody else's business how much money we have or don't have."

"Another thing to consider is to lock it in, somehow, to make it difficult to withdraw large chunks of it at any time."

"I'll think about that, but I wouldn't ever want to give up my control."

I think the shock of the situation and about the amount of money involved brought out something in me that I hadn't experienced often: I wasn't going to give up much control over things in my life.

"That makes sense for someone like you. In other cases I'd worry. But prepare yourself. Over the next few years you will hear thousands of sob stories, schemes for investment, arguments for why you should buy things, you name it. Feel free to call me at any time. Just be careful. I've known of too many cases where even trusted friends weren't very trustworthy at all."

"Okay."

"Another thing, Susan. Life insurance companies usually insist on receiving a death certificate before they'll pay. It looks as if there are still well over two thousand people who haven't been heard from since the attacks, and preliminary reports are that those who were in the areas initially hit by the planes will never be found, never identified."

I studied my hands for a few moments, trying to accept the situation, and I started to cry again, softly, for the loss of the man who had come to mean so much to me and to our children. I gulped and asked, "What does that mean? Does the insurance company not pay then?"

"Well, if they become real jerks about it, we can have him declared legally dead after seven years and they'll have no choice but to pay. If that has to happen, though, don't worry – Klein Staily will help you out financially if you need help."

"As I said, Ben, I think we have enough to see us through even if they don't pay off, ever."

"Oh, we'll make sure they pay off, and with interest! Believe me!" said Ben. "I've been on the phone to the insurance company. I know it may seem premature for me to have done this, but I wanted to get things rolling. It looks as if we'll have an airtight case for getting them to pay within the next month or two."

"Really?"

"Remember there are thousands of other households in the same situation," said Ben. "They'll have to come up with some way of dealing with all these claims, and I'm sure they will. If they don't, we'll sue them."

"Thanks for everything you're doing, Ben. I hope you know how much I appreciate it all."

"Our families have been friends for twenty years, Susan. Good friends. And Fred was always my favorite colleague. I probably shouldn't say that, but he was. He was solid, smart, hard-working, creative, and genuine. He seemed a bit down a few times these past few years, especially when his mortgage-bond scheme ran into trouble, but that all happened because of other incompetent people, not because of him. I think he took it all too seriously and too personally."

I quietly noted the prevalence of the past tense in what Ben had said.

"Thanks for the reassurance, Ben. I know the bond thing bothered him, but he seemed bothered or unsettled for other reasons, too. Was there anything else going on that might have affected him that way?"

"I can't think of a thing."

"Ben, don't lie to me. Was he seeing someone else?"

"Not a chance! Some of the others in the firm, like Johnson, referred to him as 'Straight Arrow' because he didn't laugh along with their tales of their own exploits. He was faithful to you Susan. One time last year, though, Fred asked me if I ever wondered what I was doing and why. We talked about it some, but that was the only thing I ever heard from him about his being bothered in any way."

I started to cry again. I don't know why, but I did. I slammed my fists on the table and said too loudly, "I didn't even say good-bye!" and I started crying loudly.

Cindy and the children rushed up from the basement to see what was going on.

I quickly regained control of myself and explained, "While Uncle Ben and I were talking, I realized that your father left for the airport straight from the office. I didn't drive him there. I didn't hug him and kiss him good-bye. I didn't say 'Good-bye.'" And I started crying again.

"Mom," Liz said, "Like, I heard you on the phone when Dad called from New York. At the end you said 'Good night. Remember I love you,' like you always do."

I smiled at Liz. "You're right. I did. Somehow it doesn't feel like enough."

And then I made a quick change in the conversation. "Timothy and Liz, fix yourselves some yogurt drinks if you like. Cindy, would like to join Ben and me and have a glass of wine?"

"I sure would! Your kids are terrors down there. Look at my knuckles! I'll never get the hang of air hockey. If I go down there again, next time it will be to play table-top shuffleboard, not air hockey!"

After everyone was settled at the table, I looked mostly at the children. "I'm sure you two know that Uncle Ben and I were looking ahead, talking about the future."

Their nods were barely perceptible.

"I cannot give up hope that your father will be found somewhere," I said, "I won't! But it would be foolish for us not to think about what to do if he isn't.

For one thing, we have some savings and we have a life insurance policy on your father. Those two things alone will give us enough money to make sure we can stay in this house and that you two can get a good education. Also, at some point, probably sooner than later, now, I'll to go back to work full time."

I looked back and forth at each of them. My speech was met with blank stares and barely perceptible nods.

"I'm telling you these things so you won't worry if Dad isn't found or if he's found dead. Also, Uncle Ben assures me that Klein-Staily will help us out and that there is some life insurance with them, too. I just don't want you two to worry about any of these things, okay?"

Timothy said, "You and Dad made these things pretty clear to us already over the past couple of years. I remember Dad's saying, 'No, we're not flying first-class no matter how much money I earn. We're putting away money for your educations, you two, and we're saving so you will be okay financially if anything ever happens to either your mom or me.'"

Ben added, "If people ask whether you have enough to get by, say something like, 'Yeah, Mom and Dad put some away for our college and Mom will go back to work if she has to.' Don't say anything else. Okay?"

They both nodded.

While I finished cleaning up the kitchen, I thought about everything Ben had said to me. I wanted them to find Fred so badly it hurt. I didn't care if he was injured; I just wanted him. Alive. And back home with us.
I turned on the television to see if there was any more news that might be helpful. Nothing. Absolutely nothing.

I didn't want to give up hope, but the thought that he was dead and wouldn't be found really upset me. I wanted to know. I wanted another chance to say "Good-bye", if only to his ashes. I tried to reconcile myself to never having Fred back with us and to not having any sense of closure, but it wasn't easy. I couldn't do it right then.

Finally, I let myself think about the amount of insurance money involved. I knew that with our savings and our own insurance, the children and I would be comfortable the rest of our lives.

I knew that I would want to go back to work. The work itself would be important just for my own sense of self-worth, even though I wouldn't need the income for extras for the children and me. But ten million dollars!

I knew Ben was right about keeping it all secret. I had read about how vultures went to work on lottery winners, and usually friends and acquaintances were the worst. I hoped that others in the firm who might know about the amounts involved would exercise discretion and that I could hold off having to deal with the vultures for a few weeks, if not forever. That money would mean the children could go to any college they wanted to, and it would mean we could weather any storm.

Mostly, though, I wanted everything kept quiet because I didn't want to think about it. I knew that dealing with the uncertainties about Fred and trying to maintain an emotionally stable home for the children would be time-consuming enough, and I didn't want to have to fend off the vultures at the same time.

Fred had been away on business before, but only rarely had he been gone for more than a night or two. Wednesday night was my third night at home without him. It felt like an eternity.

Chapter 15 -- **Thursday**

Thursday started pretty much like any other day. I got the children up, made coffee, set out breakfast, and sent the children off to school well-questioned and on time.

At breakfast the children and I seemed to want some sense of normalcy. We didn't talk about their father; we didn't talk about the future. We talked about school, about how Cindy Gruvel needed to learn how to hold the air hockey striker, about how neither of them had anything on after school and they should be home by four o'clock.

But we didn't talk about Fred.

Shortly after the children left for school, Thelma called. "How are you doing this morning?"

"I think we're all in a state of numb denial. We didn't talk about Fred once this morning. I guess we're just coasting for now."

"But how about *you*? How are *you* doing?"

"I'm okay, I guess. I think I'll finish up returning the phone calls on the message list, and after that I'll start thinking about a memorial service. I know it's wayyyy too early to say anything publicly, but I think I'd better prepare for something. What do you think?"

"That sounds good. Do you want to go to aerobics this morning?"

I hesitated.

"I know I should, and I know I need to get out and face people again, Thelma, but I'd like to wait until next week. Maybe I can meet and talk with people again then, after we've had a memorial service, but I don't want to explain the same things over and over again to everyone."

"Yeah, I can see that. I'm going to aerobics, though, so I'll make it clear to everyone there that you're ok, you're hanging in, there's no news, and the children seem ok for now. Alright?"

"Sure. And thanks, Thelma. Is there a chance you might be able to stop by for a while this afternoon? Maybe we can start talking about the memorial service then."

I didn't want to impose on her, but I didn't want **not** to see her that day.

"Of course. How about I come over right after lunch?"

I poured myself another cup of coffee and started reading the paper.

The story about Fred on page four had nothing new. Ben had written another release from Klein-Staily saying how valuable Fred had been to the firm and how much he would be missed.

> 'Fred Young was a key player among the managing partners at Klein-Staily,' said Ben Gruvel, a senior managing partner with the firm. 'He was a trusted, brilliant colleague whose work ethic put many people to shame. He will be greatly missed.'

The wording made it clear that Ben and everyone else there thought Fred was dead, and I was ready to accept that. It had been forty-eight hours since the terrorist attacks, and there was no sign of Fred.

The wording also made it clear that Ben was unhappy with the slackers in the firm and that he thought some people there weren't carrying their share of the workload. "... whose work ethic put many people to shame." sounded nice as it applied to Fred, but I didn't see any reason for him to chastise others in the firm indirectly while talking about Fred.

During the morning I made more phone calls, avoided more calls from reporters, turned away two more reporters at the door, and accepted kind wishes from neighbors who stopped by to see how I was doing.

One visit was from Gail Schultz, who lived down at the end of our street, backing onto the Candlewood Reservoir. When I opened the front door, she thrust a bouquet of cut flowers at me.

"Hi Gail," I could only barely contain my surprise. We had gotten to know each other at neighborhood parties, and I don't know whether I was more surprised by seeing her at the door or by her bringing flowers. I thought to myself, "Flowers are for funerals, aren't they? We don't even know yet if Fred is dead."

"These are for you, Susan," Gail said. "I don't know if it's appropriate to bring flowers at a time like this, but I thought having some flowers might cheer you up a bit."

"Gail, this is so thoughtful! No one else would dare do something like this, but I'm so glad you did. These are so beautiful!"

I stuck to my resolve not to say too much, but the white calla lilies she brought were very special for me. I just didn't tell her why.

During the very first trip that Fred and I had made to Omaha when we were making the final arrangements to accept our jobs and to find an apartment, we were walking along and on an impulse I rarely saw, Fred said, "Wait! Let's get some flowers to celebrate the day!" and he dragged me into a florist's shop where he bought the biggest collection of tall white calla lilies I had ever seen. They were gorgeous and spectacular. We loved them so much that we had them shipped in specially for our wedding that summer, and he ordered them for me on our wedding anniversary every year after that. They had become "our flower".

"These are perfect!" I said. "Why don't you come in for a cup of coffee?"

"Oh, thanks, but I really don't want to be in the way here. I just wanted to let you know we're thinking about you."

Tall white calla lilies with big stems. It was as if Gail was bringing me a message from Fred. I didn't believe that for a minute, but I pretended anyway, and the pretense was a great temporary help. As I put them in a tall vase, I said directly to the flowers, "I love you, Fred. Thank you for everything you've done to make my life so full. I'll take this as a sign that you're dead now or that if you aren't, you will be okay."

It was silly, I know, but those flowers seemed symbolic to me -- an indication that it was okay to go on with the preparations for the memorial service.

I had lunch alone on Thursday. I wanted it that way, and yet I felt alone. Before Tuesday, I had cherished my opportunities to be alone, but this was different; it felt like the beginning of a long period of aloneness. I knew I would adapt, but I had no idea *how* I would adapt, and I knew the children would need me to be a stable force in their lives. As I sat at the table finishing up some leftover salad and drinking my third cup of coffee, I closed my mind to the present, trying to dream about the future instead.

But the dreams always seemed to include Fred. I would think about travel, but I wasn't traveling alone; I was traveling with Fred. I imagined myself moving up in the world career-wise, but again I was sharing my life with Fred. I wasn't sure I could ever make the adjustment fully.

Ben called over the noon hour just to let me know there was no news about Fred.

"The only important news," he said," is that the insurance companies are meeting to agree on the standards they will use to determine eligibility for receiving benefits, and we've started the process of filing a claim for Fred. We won't file it without your say-so, but we'll be ready."

"Thanks, Ben." And then I thought to ask, "Do you think the insurance benefits can be kept quiet from people there at Klein-Staily? Even if we don't talk about it, will there be leaks from Klein-Staily?"

"Good question! I'll make sure everyone here who might know about them is sworn to confidentiality. We'll set up a blind numbered account with several layers of paperwork between it and you. It won't be perfect, but we should be able to keep it under wraps pretty well."

"Good. I don't want to deal with any of that right now."

"How are you and the children doing, Susan?"

"We're coping about as well as can be expected. The children are in school again today, and I'm managing pretty well on my own."

"On your own!?" He sounded shocked or upset or maybe both. "Do you want Cindy to come over? Or can we take you all to dinner tonight?"

"I'll be fine, Ben. Thelma is coming over this afternoon, and I think I'll take the children to dinner over in Council Bluffs tonight. I need to get out, but I don't really want to run into anyone I know; not yet, anyway."

"Okay, ... well be sure to stay in touch and let us know if there's anything more that anyone here at the firm can do."

Thelma arrived shortly after Ben and I hung up, and we went right to work, planning the memorial service for Fred. For some reason, the arrival of the calla lilies that Gail brought made it easier for me to go ahead with making the plans, and for some reason I decided not to tell Thelma that they did or why they did. She noticed them, though, and said, "Good grief, who brought flowers at a time like this?"

I shook my head a tiny bit. "It was Gail Schultz. I was surprised, too, and I'm sure my mouth dropped when I opened the door and she held them out to me. She was a bit apologetic, but she said she thought maybe having some flowers would be nice even if it seemed inappropriate to bring them. And you know what? She was right. They're nice, and they do help."

"Oh! I'm sorry I said that," said Thelma. "And I'm glad they're okay and you're okay with them."

"There's no need to apologize, Thelma! I'm sure Gail meant well."

I rushed on. "So, when and where should we have the memorial service?" I asked, quickly changing the subject.

"I guess your church would be the best place?" Thelma suggested.

"Of course you're right. What about having it Sunday afternoon?"

"That would be good, if the church is available then. All the NFL fans would have to give up the Sunday afternoon game, but at least all the die-hard Cornhusker fans could show up."

Thelma had a way of acknowledging things in a straight-forward manner. That was something she and Gail Schultz had in common, and I liked it in both of them.

"I think I read that a lot of football games are being postponed from this weekend," I said, "out of respect for the victims of the attacks."

"I guess having the ceremony at the church means Dr. Franks would have to officiate, doesn't it." I added. "Not that I wouldn't want him to, but I wouldn't want him to go on forever and I wouldn't want him to say anything he didn't know. When my uncle died, there was a new minister in their church in Salina who didn't know him at all. He tried to collect gossip and stories about Uncle Pete, and he spun a few other stories on his own. Most people appreciated his effort, but it felt fake to me. I don't want that for Fred."

"What about you?" Thelma asked. "Will you speak?"

"I know it's not always done, but I will want to. It's a memorial service, and the children and I have many wonderful memories that we would like to share. Well, that I would like to share anyway. I shouldn't speak for them."

"What about someone from the firm?"

"I hope Ben will speak!" I said. I should have asked him. We were on the phone just a few minutes before you called… "

Thelma sat up with a concerned look on her face.

"Oh! I'm so sorry. No, there's no news. I should have told you that. I'm sorry, Thelma. I hope you know I'd tell you if they learn anything."

Thelma seemed relieved but maybe a smidgeon hurt that I hadn't told her. I hated that. I would have to be more careful.

"Oh, that's no problem," said Thelma. "I know you'd let me know right away."

And then she added, "Say, why don't you and the kids come to our place for dinner tonight?"

"That would be nice! I do need to get out, but I don't really want to face people other than you and the Gruvels yet. I was thinking of driving the children over to Council Bluffs for some of that greasy authentic Mexican food we like so much, but I can do that next week sometime."

"I know that place! We like it, but we can't handle the grease and spices."

"How about we just come for dinner tonight and leave after we eat?" I asked. "The children really will need to get ahead on their school work, and I'm sure they won't get much done on Sunday."

"Okay. Now, back to the memorial service," Thelma said. "Who else should speak?"

"I don't know. I really don't want it to drag on and on and on. But should we ask if any others have anything they'd like to say?"

"That might be nice. There might be nice things that others would like to share that you don't know about."

"Okay…." I hesitated.

"Why not?" she asked.

"I just don't want anyone to go on too long. At Ben's birthday party a couple of years ago people were invited to make speeches, and some guy went on for nearly an hour with his rambling reminiscences, only a few of which directly involved Ben. I wouldn't want that to happen."

Changing the subject again, I asked, "What can we bring for dinner tonight? You know what we have and how much we have, too!"

"Don't you bring a thing!" ... pause... "Well, maybe a bottle of wine, if you have some. But don't rush out to the liquor store if you don't!"

"C'mon, Thelma. You know we have several cases of standard table wine in the basement. I'll be happy to bring some 'bloody plonk'. That's what Maggie Nelson called our wine at the last neighborhood party."

Fred and I had tried to educate our palates about wine, but it never really worked. We were happy with what Maggie had referred to as 'bloody plonk', and we even adopted the term for all the wines we seemed to like. After Thelma left, I called Ben. "Ben, I'm sorry to bother you, but are you sure we should go ahead with planning the memorial service?"

"I'm sure it will be okay. Some people might think it a bit premature, but with everything we know about what happened and the lack news of any survivors for the past fifty-odd hours, I'm sure it will be okay."

"Thanks. I'll probably ask Dr. Franks to hold it at the church and to lead it. Will you be willing to speak at the service?"

"Of course. When will it be?"

"I'm hoping for Sunday afternoon. But I haven't checked to see if the church is available then. Why don't I call the church now to set it up?"

After we hung up, I called Dr. Franks to explain what we wanted to do.

"That's an excellent idea, Susan, and if anyone asks, you can tell them it was my idea to hold a memorial service this early."

"No, Dr. Franks. This is my idea. I appreciate your offer, but I want to assume the responsibility for the decision. Does that make sense to you?"

"It certainly does, Susan. May I make one minor suggestion, though? How about we call it a 'tribute' or a 'tribute-slash-memorial'?"

"I like that, Dr. Franks. And will you be willing to officiate?"

"Certainly. Let me check to make sure the church is available then," and he put me on hold. They actually played hymns as their "hold" music.

When he came back on the line, Dr. Franks said, "I'm so sorry, Susan. I forgot we have a wedding booked into the church that day."

"Oh, no. I don't want to put this off too long. What can you suggest?"

"I agree that you shouldn't put it off any longer than necessary. We need a ceremony of some sort to help with the emotional impact of the situation and to help signify Christian experiential and existential love. Remember what Christ told his disciples: 'Leave the dead to bury the dead and follow me.'"

"That might make sense when you know someone *is* dead, Dr. Franks, but we don't know about Fred. That's one of the things that is bothering me about all this."

I went on to explain to him everything that Ben and all the people at Klein-Staily had done to find out anything they could, all to no avail, and that as a result of all they had done I felt comfortable going ahead with a tribute-memorial for Fred.

"Well, of course you're right. Well, Susan, I don't think it would be too early to have the service on Saturday afternoon. Both the church and I are available then. What do you think?"

"I think that will be okay. Can I have a half hour to think about it before we commit to doing it then?"

"Sure."

I thought to myself, "Saturday afternoon? I'll be saying good-bye that soon? Well, if Fred's body had turned up on Tuesday or Wednesday, we'd be having a funeral this weekend, probably, and it seems all but certain that Fred is in fact dead, so why not?"

I called Ben first.

"Saturday? Four days after the attacks. Sure. If he's alive somewhere, we'll know for sure by then. But to be blunt, if his body turns up, you may want to cancel it and have a straight out funeral for him."

"Hmm. I don't know," I said. I sort of like the idea of having a testimonial-tribute-memorial now, and then just a private graveside service if and when his body is found. And Ben,…"

I hesitated, but I knew I had to say it. I wanted to make sure it was our family's ceremony.

"Let me be the person to issue the announcement about the ceremony, okay? Don't say anything about it. It should come from me, don't you think? And I'll send out an announcement via email to the media and to all our friends tomorrow afternoon. Announcing it now definitely would *seem* premature even if we think it isn't."

Next I called Thelma to ask what she thought.

"I think Saturday should be okay," she said. "What are the odds you'll know anything more after tomorrow?"

"Thanks, Thelma. I'll set it for Saturday, then, but let's not tell anyone until I have a chance to announce our plans in emails tomorrow afternoon…. Just in case."

I called Dr. Franks and thanked him for his help. "I think Saturday afternoon at 2pm should work fine," I said. "But I would rather not announce it until tomorrow afternoon, just in case…. Will that be okay for you and the church?"

He hesitated. "Well, that will be fine for me, but I think I'll have to let the church ladies know tomorrow morning that it might happen so they can prepare sandwiches and coffee. I'm sure we can work this out, though. I'll explain the situation to them, and I'm sure they will understand."

"Sandwiches and coffee. I hadn't even thought about those things! They'll need time to prepare, of course." I said. "I have so many things to think about. Thanks for everything, Dr. Franks."

"That's what we're here for, Susan."

"Oh, it just hit me. On the very slim off chance that we decide not to hold the tribute, I will still be more than happy to make a large enough contribution to more than cover the costs."

"Don't worry about that now, Susan, but thank you for thinking about it. Assuming it goes ahead, will you want to speak?"

"Yes. I haven't prepared anything yet, but I expect I'll have something that will run five or ten minutes or maybe a bit longer. I think each of the children will probably want to say something, too, but I haven't asked them. And I've asked Ben Gruvel from Klein-Staily to say something too. I hope all these speakers are okay."

"Of course. This will be a tribute-memorial for you and your family. It should be what *you* want. Would you like me to say a few words, too?"

I appreciated that he asked and didn't assume. His reputation with me went up a few notches because of that.

"Certainly, Dr. Franks. One other thing: should we ask if anyone who's there wants to speak or share a memory? I'm a little leery of doing that in case someone rambles on for far too long".

"Trust me, Susan, I can take care of that. I've officiated for many memorial services in the past and have had the situation arise only twice. In both cases, I interrupted, thanked them, and began praying. If you want someone cut off just touch your ear or something."

I couldn't help laughing. "I'd feel like Madame DeFarge knitting at the French Revolution."

Dr. Franks laughed, too. "Well, let's hope it isn't necessary."

"I'll make a public announcement late tomorrow afternoon," I said. "Is there a chance we can talk again tomorrow afternoon to go over everything again before I make the announcement?"

"That'll be good, Susan. In the meantime, you might want to give some consideration to which hymns you want for the service."

"Oh! Of course! That's another thing I hadn't thought about. Is there anything else we should consider?"

"Well, sometimes people have the funeral parlor drive them to the service in a limousine so they don't have to worry about parking. You may not want to arrive too early…. Or, really, I don't know, maybe you will want to. But if you want to arrive at the last minute and leave early, you might want to arrange for a ride."

"Let me think about that one, Dr. Franks. … Hmmm … No, Fred always liked to get to church early, and he had his favorite parking spot there. I think I'd like to honor him by doing the same thing."

"I know the parking spot. I'll ask the staff here to put pylons in it Saturday morning to reserve it for you."

"That would be very nice. Thanks."

Chapter 16 – **Thursday Evening**

When the children came home for school, I had them sit at the kitchen table. "There are a couple of things," I said. At the last minute, I got nervous about telling them I had been planning the tribute-memorial, and so I began, "We're having dinner with the Hazeltons tonight…"

"Yea!" They chimed together. Both were pleased, and I was so glad the four children seemed to get along so well.

"We're to be there about six," I said, "but tonight we're leaving their place right after dinner so all four of you children can get to work on your homework before the weekend."

"Before the weekend?" asked Timothy. "What's up?"

Good. This would be an easy way to break it to them.

"I've been talking with Uncle Ben, Thelma, and Dr. Franks at the church, and we all agree it would be a good idea to have a sort of tribute ceremony this weekend for your father."

Liz stiffened perceptibly.

"I probably should have told you both more about what Uncle Ben has discovered… or maybe I should say not discovered. The last anyone heard from or about your father was the email exchange he and I had before he left for his appointment Tuesday morning, and his appointment was right where the first plane hit. There has been no trace of him anywhere since then, and Uncle Ben has had an army of people looking everywhere for any sign of him. It's hard to say this, but the odds are really high that your father was killed in the initial impact when that first plane hit the North Tower. It's time for us to acknowledge this. I hope it's okay with you two."

"But what if, like, he turns up later, Mom?" asked Liz. "Won't we, like, feel as if we gave up on him too early then? It'll look pretty silly."

"You're right, Liz, and I'm hoping with all my heart that he does turn up. I miss him so much, and I know I'll miss him even more as time goes by, but it's so unlikely he survived that I see no reason to drag this on any longer."

"Mom, if they find some remains that might be Dad, will we have to go through it all over again and have a funeral?" Timothy asked.

"If that happens, we can have a private graveside ceremony. Uncle Ben says the officials in New York City are saying that over two thousand people are missing and there are probably over a thousand people that no one will ever learn anything about or find any remains of."

"Wow!" Exclaimed Timothy. "Over a thousand families with nothing?" And then he shook his head slowly, "Grieving, worrying, wondering, like us! No body, no information, no remains. Well at least we aren't alone."

"Dr. Franks suggested we call it a 'tribute-slash-memorial'. I like that, but what do you two think?"

"I get it," said Liz. "A tribute because we're not, like, absolutely certain Dad was killed. I sorta like that, Mom. I mean, like, I wouldn't want to say he's definitely dead, but I understand. I like it."

"Me, too," said Timothy. "A tribute–memorial covers things pretty well."

"Now the next thing," I said. "Dr. Franks and Uncle Ben are going to speak, and so will I. It might be nice if each of you could say something, too, but it's up to you. What do you think?"

"Speak?" said Liz. "About Dad? Like, in front of all those people? I'm not sure I can do it."

"I will," said Timothy. "I won't say much, but it's a tribute to Dad. I think we need to be a part of it, Liz. We can tell stories about things we did with him, and we can write it all out ahead of time and just read it."

"I suppose," said Liz. And then it hit her. "So that's why you want us to come home early tonight! You want us to, like, have some time to work on our speeches!"

"That's right, Liz," I smiled as I replied, "and so I'll have time to work on mine, too. I thought maybe I'd go last. Is that okay with you two?"

They nodded and mumbled their assents.

"So, who wants to go after Uncle Ben? He'll probably talk about what a brilliant man your father was. ... He really was brilliant, you know. And I'm sure he'll talk about your father's work ethic and dedication to everything he did. It would probably be best if you each concentrated on a few things about your father that were special to you."

Timothy thought for a moment and then said, "Well I don't care either way. I'll go first if you like, Liz."

"Oh, please do!" replied Liz. "I'll feel so much better if you go before me."

After the children went upstairs to do their homework, I went to the basement for a bottle "bloody plonk". While I was there, I looked around the storage room. We had so many memories: camping gear, sports equipment, boxes of memorabilia for Fred and me, and other boxes for each of the children. I stood there for a minute or two to reminisce, but was on the verge of tears again, so I took the bottle of wine upstairs and sat at the kitchen table to begin working on my talk.

Having to put my thoughts on paper made the likelihood of Fred's death seem even more real. I was trying to write things about Fred, and I didn't want to do it. I didn't want to accept what I had just been saying to the children, that it was unimaginable Fred was still alive.

I pushed the pad away and went to the family room, where I stretched out on the loveseat and closed my eyes, losing myself in my thoughts and hoping for some sort of inspiration.

I have no idea why, but I remembered Dr. Franks' asking me to think about hymns for the ceremony. Seven years earlier, when we were driving to Arizona on a family vacation, we decided to leave the car radio turned off but sing and talk instead. The children sang songs they had learned in school, Fred and I sang songs from the 80s and 90s, and we all sang church hymns together whenever we could remember the words. We had a wonderful time singing at the tops of our lungs. I think the singing and story-telling of that vacation was one of the all-time highlights of our family togetherness, and I cherished the memories.

I tried to remember which hymns we all enjoyed the most. Fred's favorite, as he announced it every single time, was "Number one in your hymnals, 'Holy, Holy, Holy'." Liz's favorite then was "The Wise Man Built His House Upon a Rock", and Timothy's was the rock-gospel, "Put Your Hand in the Hand of the Man". I understood the appeal of the beat, even though it wasn't really a hymn. And what about me? I think I liked "Fairest Lord Jesus". It had a mellowness that appealed to me.

I doubted whether the children's favorites from that trip would be in the church hymnals. I would have to ask them if they had any preferences about hymns to sing. And then I thought, "It doesn't have to be a hymn, does it? Wouldn't it be something if we could play 'We Are the Champions'? Fred and I always enjoyed that song, and the children loved the foot-stomping and hand-clapping that went with it." I would try to include that song in the ceremony somehow.

I started going through our CD collection to find the Queen album, and I played "We Are the Champions". The line, "… and we'll keep on fighting 'til the end …" really moved me. It seemed appropriate for our family right then, even if the rest of the words didn't. I immediately decided that the first half, "We Will Rock You," certainly wouldn't do. I would want to think about it some more.

"Mom, like, why are you listening to that?"

It was Liz.

"Your father and I always liked that song. And it's very inspirational… you know… 'We'll keep on fighting 'til end.' I'm thinking of incorporating it into the tribute ceremony. What do you think?"

"Like, that'd be *so* great! Do you think they'll let us use it in the church?"

"I'll have to ask Dr. Franks about it, but I think so. I listened to the first part, 'We Will Rock You', and I don't think that would be appropriate even though you and Timothy used to love the stomping and clapping."

"Maybe we could start the stomp-stomp-clap just with the people there without playing that song and then lead into 'We Are the Champions'? Would that work?"

I laughed. "Foot-stomping and hand-clapping in our church! I wonder how that will go over with some of the church elders," and we laughed together. "I'll see what Dr. Franks thinks, but I expect he'll be pleased that we want to do something special for our family."

Dinner with the Hazeltons was pleasant, but it felt like a re-do of the previous two nights. There was no news, and not much more to talk about. It wasn't that we were bored with each other's company; it was just that we were tired, and we needed to move on.

We did talk a bit about the propriety of holding the tribute/memorial on

Saturday, and they agreed that it would be a good idea to hold it then to get some sense of closure. And when I broached the idea of using "We Are the Champions" as one of the 'hymns' for the ceremony, Seth and Aaron were very enthusiastic about it. Thelma and Dale liked the idea, too, so that pretty much settled it.

"Susan, would you like one of us to drive you to the church?" asked Dale.

I didn't want to turn them down, and I thought it might be a good idea since I wasn't sure what shape I'd be in for driving. At the same time, I wanted to honor Fred by getting there early and parking in our regular spot, and I wanted to feel free to stay late or maybe leave early, depending how we felt, and so I came up with a compromise.

"I'd like that, Dale. How about one of you drive us in our car and that way you won't have to hang around until the bitter end if you want to come home together. I won't want to leave right away after the ceremony; Dr. Franks says they'll have coffee, sandwiches, and cookies or something afterward, and I'll want to talk with others after the ceremony before leaving."

They liked the plan, and I said I'd call them the next day to confirm that the ceremony was going ahead and to let them know what time I thought we should leave.

As we were leaving, Liz started hugging everyone good-bye, the way we had the previous two nights. It seemed natural as we all hugged each other, but I looked at Liz and smiled inside, wondering, "Is it Seth or Aaron she has a crush on?" The signals were loud and clear. Like me, Liz was an initiator, but at the same time she was subtle enough not to be too obvious.

When we got home, the three of us sat in the living room and shared memories. They were mostly happy memories, but we loved sharing even the unhappy memories.

After half an hour, I said, "Well, it's time for you two to get back to your school work, and if you've finished all your homework, try just jotting down some ideas about what you would like to say for the tribute. While you're doing that, I'll get started on my own talk."

I sat on the loveseat with my legs pulled up and started writing.

"I didn't have a chance to say good-bye."

And then I put the pencil down. I had to think more about what to say and how to say it. I wanted to honor Fred and not have the talk be about me or how I was feeling. I would keep that opening sentence, but I would have to shift gears to talking about Fred quickly.

I knew Ben would talk about Fred's work ethic. I wanted to share things about Fred that were endearing and that captured his personality outside of work. It would be easy and it would be hard. It was easy to think of what a wonderful man Fred had been, and yet it was hard to say it so that it would honor him and pay tribute to him the way he deserved.

I couldn't face it. I just turned on the television instead and flipped through the channels. One of them was showing "On Golden Pond," a movie Fred and I had always liked. It made me sad to think that Fred and I would not be able to have similar experiences and adventures in our golden years. It wasn't fair. We were at the pinnacle of our lives and were just getting things right for us and for the children. I felt cheated, and I hated the terrorists who plotted and carried out the attacks.

At ten o'clock, I went upstairs and looked in on each of the children. Liz was already in bed with a pad and pen in her hand. "Oh Mom, Becky loves the idea of 'We Are the Champions'! Would it be okay if we teens who will be there start the stomp-stomp-clap and sing just the lines, 'We will, we will rock you...' and then have someone start the CD right at that long guitar chord to lead into 'We Are the Champions'?"

"That sounds very moving and very special, Liz. I'm sure it will be okay." And I kissed her good night.

When I stopped in to say good night to Timothy, he had just put his pajamas on.

"What have you thought about for your talk on Saturday?" I asked him.

"Mom, this is so hard. We don't know for sure that Dad is dead but we're talking about him as if he is."

"I know. It *is* hard."

"I mean, I know the odds are that Dad is dead, but it still feels wrong."

"That's okay, Timothy," I said as I gave him a gentle one-armed hug. "I wrote one sentence and couldn't go on from there. One thing that might help is to imagine that it really is a tribute and not a memorial. What if you think it's a big party in your Father's honor and he's right there, looking at us, and we're just telling stories to everyone else who is there to celebrate? Would that help?"

"I don't know, Mom. Is that what you're doing?"

I half-laughed. "No. I just thought of that now, but I think it will help me."

How would I organize my thoughts for Saturday? There were so many memories and feelings colliding in my mind.

Chapter 17 – **Friday**

It was Friday, September 14, 2001. Three days had passed and there was still no word from or about Fred. Three days may not sound like much but we had been on edge the entire time, and we were exhausted emotionally and physically. I'm not sure how the children were holding up, but I knew I would need a rest after the weekend was over.

After the children left for school, I called Ben to see if he had learned anything more about Fred.

"Nothing new, Susan. The people going through the rubble say it will be months before they can clear everything, but they are quite certain that there won't even be remains for the victims who were anywhere near the point of impact."

"Oh my. This is so awful for everyone!"

"I've been in touch with the insurance company several times already, Susan, and there won't be a problem from them. The insurance companies all recognize the difficulty of the situation, and they are bending over backward to avoid any chance of bad PR from delaying their payouts. I'm sure we'll have your money in less than a month. Are you sure you'll be okay until then?"

"I'll be fine financially, but otherwise? This is hell."

"Ben?" I added, "You're still okay with speaking tomorrow?"

"Of course, Susan!"

"I think I'll ask Dr. Franks to say a very few words first and then turn it over to you. Does that sound okay?"

"Sure."

"And then I'll have the children speak in turn, and I'll wrap it up. We'll probably have a hymn or two, too." I couldn't bring myself to tell him about 'We Are the Champions'.

"Would you like Cindy and me to drive you to the church tomorrow?"
"Thanks, Ben, but one of the Hazeltons will drive us there in our car."

And then it hit me that the reporters would all show up at the ceremony and reception. I'd have to deal with that situation somehow.

"I wonder whether after the reception I should meet with the reporters to answer questions. That way the Hazeltons can come home when they're ready and I can drive home later. Maybe I'll ask if the Hazeltons can bring the children home then, too, so the press will leave them alone."

Next I called Thelma and discussed the arrangements with her.

"I'll be happy to drive you there in your car," she said, "and Dale can drive the minivan so we'll have room for your kids when we come home. I like the plan."

"Are you really going to face the reporters right after the ceremony?" she asked. "Will you be able to do that?"

"I think so," I replied. "It won't be right after the ceremony, though; I couldn't do that. We'll have had the reception, and I'll have had a chance to talk with all our friends. I haven't asked Dr. Franks about this yet, but I'll speak with him before I plan it. It shouldn't be too bad. Just some standard questions like 'What do we know?' or 'What's been done to find him?' or 'How are the children doing?' What else can they ask?"

"You're brave. I'm sure they'll come up with something more to ask."

"I'll be ok. I had to handle lots of tough questions when I was working for Arkero, and I know this situation better than I knew any of those"

"As I said, 'You're brave.'"

At noon I ate some more leftovers from the fridge and decided that for supper we should probably have the tuna casserole the Swansons had sent over on Tuesday night. It was three days old, ...

Three days ... ... I had to stop being so melodramatic.

And we could have some fruit salad from the next melon that was taking up so much room in the fridge, and I could add fruit from the basket that the Geddles had sent.

After my lunch I started cutting up the fruit for the fruit salad. It was a good job for me right then. I kept thinking of the things Fred and I had done together and how much I would miss him. But I didn't want to start writing any more of my speech yet. I just couldn't do it.

About two o'clock, Dr. Franks called.

"Susan, I've cleared everything with the reception committee and they're prepared to get together tomorrow morning to make sandwiches and prepare punch and cookies for after the ceremony."

"That's wonderful, Dr. Franks. Thank you. And just so you know, it looks as if we have no reason not to go ahead with the ceremony."

"Alright. What about speakers? What have you decided?"

"I was hoping you would welcome people and explain that even though we have no news about what happened to Fred, it is implausible that he survived the crash and that's why we're having this ceremony now."

"That's good. I'll be happy to do that. Who else will be speaking?"

"We'd like to start with Ben Gruvel from Klein-Staily. He was Fred's mentor and best friend. He'll probably talk mostly about Fred and business. After that Timothy will speak, and then Liz. I'll go last. Then I think just so everyone there feels as if they have a chance to participate, it would probably be a good idea to invite short comments from others."

"What about hymns? Usually there would be two hymns during this type of ceremony."

"Well, Fred's favorite was always 'Number 1 in your hymnals, "Holy, Holy, Holy"'. And maybe we could also sing 'Fairest Lord Jesus'? I know it's not particularly relevant, but I like the mellowness of it."

"I think it's quite relevant, Susan. Those are good choices."

"And Dr. Franks, the children and I have somewhat unusual request…"

"Yes?"

"After everyone has spoken, I'd like to have the children and their friends do something they've been working on. They want to lead the congregation in the foot-stomping, hand-clapping of 'We Will, We Will Rock You', just the stomping and clapping and that phrase, and then have that lead into the companion song played from a CD, 'We Are the Champions'. Will it be okay to do that in the church?"

"Of course it will, Susan! This is for you and your family. We had one family lead the congregation in the song 'Daisy, Daisy', the song about the bicycle built for two, and several have played a recording of Frank Sinatra singing 'I Did It My Way.'"

"Good! The children and their friends will be so pleased. And when that's finished, could you say the benediction and direct people to the basement for refreshments?"

"I think I know 'We Are the Champions' a bit… It should be a fitting piece. It's very inspirational. It's an excellent idea."

"Two more things, Dr. Franks."

"Of course."

"Thelma Hazelton will be driving us there in our car. I'll try to make sure we arrive early so that Liz can go over the sound cues with Mike. He's the one who does the sound for the sanctuary, isn't he?"

"He is, indeed, and I'll make sure he's on hand to look after things. And the other thing?"

"You may have noticed that I'm doing my best to avoid the press for now. I haven't wanted to say anything publicly – it just seemed so premature for us to say anything other than our usual line of 'We have no idea what happened to Fred, and we're doing our best to cope with the uncertainties.' Well, I think I'd like to have a formal press conference after the ceremony, but not until after the reception. I know I won't be up to meeting with them right after the ceremony, but after I meet and chat with friends at the reception, I'll have collected myself and be able to deal with the press then. Would it be okay if we hold the press conference there at the church?"

He paused. "We've never had one here before, but that sounds like a good idea. Probably not in the sanctuary, though, and not in the reception hall. We could set it up in the large Sunday School classroom. That way the press can get set up in advance, maybe during the reception, and not distract others from the purpose of the ceremony."

"Thank you, Dr. Franks. I appreciate your doing all you can to help us out.

And by the way, the children really took to the idea of calling this a tribute, not just a memorial service. That was a wonderful suggestion."

After we hung up, I turned my attention to writing an announcement about the tribute-ceremony and came up with this (after many edits):

> The Young family will be holding a tribute-memorial ceremony for Fredrick Robert Young tomorrow at 2pm at the Third Congregational Church [United Church of Christ], Dr. William Franks presiding.
>
> The last anyone heard from Mr. Young was an email exchange he had with his wife, Ms. Susan Loeffer Young, on Tuesday morning before leaving for his nine o'clock appointment with Cantor-Fitzgerald in the World Trade Center. The first terrorist plane hit the tower where Cantor-Fitzgerald has its offices just before nine o'clock. Nothing has been heard from or about Mr. Young since then. He has not been found in any medical centers, hospitals, temporary clinics, or other sites. Authorities say that over two thousand people were killed in the crashes and collapses of those buildings, and they speculate that there will be no recovery possible of the remains of many of those victims. Fred Young is missing and presumed dead.
>
> Friends are invited to attend the ceremony and our tribute to the life of Fred Young, and to join the Young family at a reception in the church hall following the ceremony.

I emailed that message to all our friends. And then I added this for the media email list:

> Ms. Young and the Young family have appreciated the respect shown by the members of the media for the Young family's privacy.
>
> To thank you and acknowledge your respect, Ms. Young would like to invite you to ask all the questions you have at an interview session **after** the reception. The large Sunday School classroom at the church has been reserved for this question-and-answer session.
>
> Ms. Young asks that you not ask her questions during the reception because that time is for her and her friends. She will be happy to answer any and all questions after the reception. Dr. Franks and the church staff will be happy to show you the large Sunday School classroom where you can set up.

> Finally, Ms. Young asks that you not intrude on her children's lives. She will do everything she can to answer your questions tomorrow.

When the children got home from school that afternoon, they were visibly upset. It seemed a reporter had caught up with Timothy and walked with him to where he usually met Liz.

"He didn't tell me he was a reporter, Mom. He just started asking me how I was doing. I didn't know who he was. I thought maybe he was a friend of the family or something. I told him I didn't know anything, but he just kept walking along with me, asking me questions. I told him that we're a strong, tight family, but I don't know how I'll get over Dad's death and that I'll miss all the things we did together. Oh Mom, I'm so sorry. I know I should have told him to leave me alone, but he was so persistent, I didn't know what to do."

"It sounds as if you did alright, though."

"I don't know. At one point I broke down when I started to tell him about how much I loved Christmas time with Dad."

"What did he say then?"

"He just patted me on the shoulder and said something like, 'I'm sure you'll be fine. You're a strong, bright young man and you have a good support network. I'm sure you'll be fine,' and then he patted my shoulder again and hurried away somewhere."

"Well, that's a good lesson for all of us, Timothy. I think you handled it very well. But we know the reporters are going to be relentless. To head this off, I've arranged a press conference to answer all their questions tomorrow after the reception. Dr. Franks will set it up in the large Sunday School classroom. I don't want you there to be subjected to any questions, so the Hazeltons will bring you home in their minivan before that begins. Okay?"

"I'm sorry, Mom, I just didn't know what was going on, and then it was too late."

"Don't worry about it. It sounds as if you did an excellent job under those circumstances."

"Here's some fun news, though," I added. "Dr. Franks likes the idea of you children and your friends leading the congregation in stomp-stomp-clap with the chorus, 'We will, we will rock you,' and then 'We Are the Champions'! He's making arrangements for Mike, their sound technician to meet with you, Liz, before the tribute, to cue up 'We Are the Champions' right where you want it. I think I'll introduce you and your friends right after everyone finishes speaking."

"Yea!" They were both excited about the prospect.

"How many of your friends will be there and want to help with it, Liz? I know you two should be the overall leaders, but I was thinking we'd ask them to join you at the front of the church to do this."

"Mom, this is, like, so cool!" Liz said. "Becky will be there for sure, and I know a couple of others were interested when I told them about it."

"And Seth and Aaron!" added Timothy. "I didn't mention doing the song to anyone else, but I'll call some of the guys from the soccer team who said they'd be there and ask if they'll help. This will be great."

I knew it would be great. But I also knew I'd be crying like mad, having the children singing to the world. Still, it seemed like a good idea.

"I'm thinking we'll all join in singing along with the CD," I said, "and then when we're done, Dr. Franks will say a benediction and invite everyone to the reception. I won't speak with the media until you've left with the Hazeltons after the reception."

"That's a good plan, Mom," said Liz, "but I think I'd better control my excitement, like, about the song and get working on my speech now! What about you Timothy?"

He led the way upstairs, and I got back on the computer.

There was a flood of messages from friends about the ceremony, and there were a few questions from members of the media. I ignored them all and wrote another message to the media list, copying Ben and Thelma:

> I have just learned that a member of the media approached my son after school without identifying himself as a media member and without my being present. He then also refused to take 'no' for answer from my son when my son tried to avoid answering any questions. This is highly unprofessional and intolerable behavior. The editor and

publisher must see to it that there are consequences for this.

I sat on that message for a while. I wanted to cool off. If I had sent it then, I might have been able to head off the publication of the story, and I probably should have, but based on what Timothy said, it sounded as if he handled himself well. I did, however, want to cause some difficulties for whoever did it. When I recall this moment, I'm both embarrassed and pleased. I'm embarrassed that I felt so vindictive, but I'm pleased that I followed through.

After supper, the children took turns using the phone to call their friends and get them lined up for the song the next day.

"Don't stay on the phone with Becky too long," teased Timothy. "We both have lots of calls to make!"

"Ok, and don't you spend an hour the phone with Sandra, either," Liz shot back.

"Sandra?" I thought, trying all the while not to react. "Who is Sandra and what's this about?"

I looked through the messages from our friends. They were mostly messages of condolence, offers of assistance, and a few subtle and not-so-subtle questions about "What if he isn't dead yet?" I ignored the last type of messages but sent out thank you notes to the others.

The messages from members of the media were to ask if they could bring cameras and recording equipment to the press conference. I responded that I didn't know for sure, but I didn't see any reason why they shouldn't.

Later that evening I decided to email my critical message to the members of the media. Half an hour after that I received a call from Jeremy Hall.

"Ms. Young, this is Jeremy Hall calling from the World-Herald to apologize."

"I suspected it was you. But I had thought you're too experienced and too professional to have stooped so low as to ambush my son on his way home from school. I'm very upset about that."

"You're right, Ms. Young. And I have no excuse. I won't even try to manufacture one. It was a thoughtless and unprofessional move on my part. At the very least, I should have identified myself when I started speaking with him."

"Yes, and you should have taken 'no' for an answer! How can we teach young men that 'no means no' when older men like you don't seem to understand that?"

"You're absolutely right, Ms. Young. I never thought about it that way. Please accept my apologies."

"What are you going to do about it? Is it too late to kill that story?"

"Unfortunately, yes, it is too late. It has already been sent off to the printer.

"Mr. Hall, I emailed that message half an hour ago. You should have killed the story then."

"You're right, but it wasn't my choice. I submitted the story a couple of hours ago, and it went through the editor and re-write an hour ago. When I received your email, I went to the editor and asked what we should do. I admitted to him that I hadn't identified myself properly. He looked at the story and didn't see anything harmful and decided to go with it anyway."

"Mr. Hall, it's not just that there wasn't anything harmful in the story. It's the fact that you invaded our privacy at a very difficult time, you didn't identify yourself, you took advantage of a minor without parental consent, and you didn't take no for an answer! Both you and your editor should know better than this and both of you should face repercussions. I hope the publisher deals harshly with both of you."

I wanted to slam the phone down, but I didn't. For some reason, I just held onto it, leaving him hanging, and didn't say anything.

Finally he said, "I'm very sorry, Ms. Young. I'll try to make it up to you any way I can. For starters, I'll make sure to collect the five hundred dollars for your charity that your neighbor kept insisting on, and please let me know if there's anything else I can do."

And then it hit me, and I got off the phone quickly.

"Thank you, Mr. Hall. Good-bye."

I was sure, given his obsequious tone, that Jeremy Hall had been called on the carpet by his editor and publisher. I wondered whether they had threatened to fire him for his unprofessional conduct and whether he was trying to do anything he could to ward off any further complaints I might make. I filed that idea in my mind. I'd have a better idea after the press conference the next day.

After I checked with the children to see how they were coming with their speeches, I realized I had to get started on mine.

I stayed awake for maybe another hour or two, trying to write out what I would say at the ceremony. After a struggle, I decided I would just jot down points I wanted to mention, but I wasn't sure what order to put them in. After twenty minutes, I went back downstairs to get the laptop so I could write out ideas using it and then rearrange them. It would be much easier that way.

I had often been upset when Fred brought his work laptop to bed, and it felt dishonest for me to be using mine in bed, but it was convenient and so I did it. The thoughts poured out in no particular order.

- Didn't say goodbye.
- How we met; what attracted me to him.
- His determination to avoid debt.
- Community involvement.
- Time with children (relate to what they say)
- Holding hands as we watched television.
- Generosity.
- Anniversaries/flowers

I knew there would be more. I would have to get back to it and write more in the morning.

Chapter 18 – **Saturday Morning**

Saturday mornings were traditionally sleep-in mornings. We always had breakfast together at about nine o'clock, earlier if we had a family outing planned, and we tried to maintain a somewhat relaxed atmosphere.

That morning, Saturday, September 15th, I wanted to let the children relax, sleep in, and loll about, but inexplicably we were all up and dressed by seven-thirty, so I suggested we sit around the kitchen table to come up with ideas for our talks and then I'd fix a big breakfast for us about nine-thirty or so.

I confessed to them that I hadn't been able to write much and read off the points I had made.

"Those seem fine, Mom," said Timothy.

"But what will you say about each of them?" asked Liz.

"That's what has me hung up," I said. "There's so much to say, I don't know where to start. I want to include pithy, memorable stories but not too many either."

We worked solidly for the next hour. The children took breaks to pour themselves orange juice, and I drank at least two cups of coffee.

"I want to talk about how much your father loved singing 'Holy, Holy, Holy' and all the traditional Christmas carols," I said.

"I want to talk about the overnights with the scouts," said Timothy.

"And I'll, like, talk about that excursion on the reservoir with the inflatable boat," added Liz.

We continued in that vein for the next hour, swapping stories. We knew we wouldn't use them all, but it felt so good to be remembering all the fun and pleasant things about Fred.

Just before I was ready to start fixing breakfast, Thelma called. This time when I answered the phone, I made sure I let her know we had no more news.

"I'm sorry, Susan."

"That's okay." And then I went on, "The children and I have been having a very good morning, sitting around the kitchen table, swapping stories about Fred that we want to include in our talks."

"Good. I just called to see how you're doing. Do you need anything?"

I have no idea why, but I answered, "Yes, we need two dozen casseroles and a dozen cherry pies," and we both laughed.

"Okay, well how about I come over around one-thirty and we can leave after that?

"Perfect."

I turned to the children and asked, "Have you given any thought to what you'll wear this afternoon?"

"I thought I'd wear my 'Queen' t-shirt," said Timothy with a perfect fake straight face.

I pretended to try to swat him with the spatula I was using to make the eggs, but a bit of egg flew at him. He artfully caught it and flung it back at me, and we all had another good laugh.

But we couldn't put the situation out of our minds. I broke off laughing and looked solemnly down at the frying pan, remember the wonderful weekend breakfasts we usually ate together as a family. We'd sit around the table and chat about the week and about the weekend plans. This was our first weekend breakfast without Fred. It wasn't easy.

After a moment, I looked up and smiled. "I know you were teasing me. Seriously, it would be nice if you wore your coat and tie. What about you Liz?"

"Well, since the 'Queen' t-shirt idea is out, how about ripped jeans and a tank top... ... Just kidding, Mom! Don't throw the eggs at me!"

She continued, "I have a dark skirt that I can wear with a white blouse. What will you wear, Mom?"

"I think you both know I usually feel more comfortable in slacks, but today I should probably wear the only suit I have that still fits me. It's not dark, but it's not too light either. I'll wear it with a cream crepe top. And I think I'll put on one of your father's darker neckties ... maybe tie it loosely ... we'll see. I'm not sure. What do you think?"

"I like the idea of wearing something of Dad's," said Timothy. "Would it be okay if I wear one of his ties, too? Do you suppose he has any older dress shirts left from when he weighed less that might fit me too?"

"Oh, Timothy, that's, like, the greatest idea!" said Liz. "Maybe I could wear one of his shirts too?"

I loved the ways they wanted to pay tribute to Fred, but I didn't think any of his clothes other than his neckties would fit either of them. Fred weighed well over 200 pounds naked, and Timothy and Liz were both slim and light, the way Fred had been when I first met him. I wasn't complaining about Fred's weight, though, because I had put on about thirty pounds myself since we'd been married, all despite my best efforts at the gym and trying to cut calories.

When we had cleaned up the breakfast dishes, we went upstairs to explore the depths of the closet, looking for things the children could wear to the ceremony. Timothy came up with a blue oxford dress shirt that Fred hadn't been able to part with, and it was only slightly too big for him. Liz found a slightly larger and frayed white shirt that we all thought might work. And we all selected neckties.

Before they left the bedroom to try on their finds, Timothy asked, "Mom, do you think it would be okay if I wore a pair of Dad's socks, too?"

I opened Fred's sock drawer and said, "Take your pick." There were about fifty pairs of dark blue, dark brown, and black socks.

After about ten minutes we reconvened in our bedroom. Liz's use of the white shirt and burgundy necktie with her navy skirt was stunning. It all worked very well together. And Timothy looked dashing in the clothing he had decided to wear.

My choices weren't so good. My suit was a herringbone grey tweed, and it didn't go with my cream-colored blouse, and so I tried it with just a white one, which was better. Liz helped me arrange a dark blue striped necktie so that it wouldn't look so forced and artificial.

"I like this look for you, Mom," she said. "Very professional!"

"Thanks, Liz. You two both look spectacular! Now let's get out of these clothes and make sure we know what we want to say. After the ceremony, there will be a reception in the church basement, and then you two are coming home with the Hazeltons in their minivan while I stay and deal with the press."

Liz said, "Mom, you are going to be great at a press conference! You look great and you're always so, like, calm and reasoned, like, all the time. Is it okay if we hang around to watch?"

I hesitated. I didn't want any questions addressed to them. Finally I said, "Well, maybe okay, but only if you stay at the back of the room with Dr. Franks and *don't answer any questions from the reporters!* I've had words with Jeremy Hall on the telephone, and I don't think he'll bother you anymore, but there's no telling. And don't speak to them at the reception, either, okay?"

"Got it, Mom," said Timothy, somewhat chagrined about having answered questions the day before on the way home from school.

"Timothy, you did nothing wrong yesterday. Mr. Hall knows full well that he is obliged by journalism ethics to identify himself to you as a reporter and that he is not to interview any minors without permission from their parents."

And then it occurred to me… "There may be a lot of people at the ceremony you don't know; there might even be some I don't know. They will likely want to console you, express their admiration of your father, and express their sympathies. Be prepared for that. But if they start asking questions, keep in mind what happened yesterday. Reporters have all been told *not* to ask any questions during the reception, but, as I said, be prepared."

"What should we say, Mom?" asked Timothy.

"Try to come up with some stock answers that are real. You know, something like, 'I loved my dad and I'll really miss him. Thanks.' If someone persists, it's perfectly fine to ask them if they're from the media. And if there's even a hint of a hesitation on their part, just say, 'well I really don't have any more to say right now,' and walk away."

I went on, "I think that as long as I keep planning and preparing, I'll get through this okay myself. But the ceremony is going to be difficult. Let's all make sure we have plenty of Kleenex with us. And it would probably be a good idea for me to have some touch-up makeup with me. Maybe you, too, Liz?"

The children went back to their rooms, and we all changed back into what we called our weekend grubbies. I knew I needed to think more about what I would say, and I was sure the children would as well. I think Liz was on the phone with Becky quite a bit, too, planning "We Are the Champions."

My own notes needed fleshing out for sure. It took me another two hours to come up with this list, which I've saved on the computer ever since that day, along with all the messages and replies.

- I didn't have a chance to say good-bye.
- How we met; what attracted me to him. His shyness then. Our first date. His stopping by for lunch on his way home at Christmas.
- Wholesome farming background
- ~~His determination to avoid debt.~~ That was more me, I think. And maybe not good to mention as if we were superior to others.
- Our love as we bought our home and started our family.
- Community involvement. Assistant scoutmaster. School class trips. Neighborhood fund-raising even when busy.
- Generosity. "We have more than we ever imagined. We have to share."
- Board of Junior Farmers.
- Time with children (relate to what they say)
- Holding hands as we watched television.
- Anniversaries/flowers. Take the ones from Gail.

I printed the list in sixteen-point font so I'd be able to see it when I put it on the lectern, and then I had the children do the same thing with their notes.

About twelve thirty, I suggested each of the children have a snack and then take turns showering and getting dressed.

"Mom," said Liz, "You won't believe what Becky and I have worked out for 'We Are the Champions'. It makes me feel as if we can handle this now. I'm so glad we're doing it."

She hugged me and then ran upstairs. I could see she was beginning to cry again, just a bit.

Timothy asked, "Mom, why is Ms. Hazelton driving us to the church?"

"I wasn't sure I'd be up to it, Timothy. And when they offered, I thought it would be a good idea to have someone else do the driving."

"But you'll be okay afterward?"

Timothy had a penetrating mind sometimes.

"I think I will. I'll likely have calmed down before facing the media; and if they don't rile me too much, I'll be fine. Otherwise I'll make sure someone else drives us home. If I know Uncle Ben, he will want to be present at the press conference; he could give us a ride if we need one."

"Okay. Good. Mom, I love you." And he came over and hugged me.

I couldn't stop the tears.

"I love you, too, Timothy." I hugged him back, and then he turned and went upstairs.

This was not going to be easy.

Chapter 19 – **The Ceremony**

Thelma came over a little before 1:30. She noticed right away that we were all wearing neckties, even though Liz and I had ours done up very loosely, more like scarves or ribbons than neckties.

"Were those all neckties that Fred used to wear?" she asked.

"Yes," I answered, "and the children are each wearing one of his shirts."

"Well you all look great, and the idea of wearing some of Fred's things for the ceremony is wonderful."

She prompted considerable laughter and discussion when she announced, "Seth and Aaron wanted to wear their 'Queen' t-shirts or hoodies, but I wouldn't let them."

"See, Mom? We wouldn't have been the only ones!" chided Timothy.

"Yes, you would have," I shot back, "because Ms. Hazelton wouldn't have let them wear theirs!"

Oh, oh. … I glared at them. "Li-izzz? Ti-mo-thy? I hope none of your friends shows up in rock-style or rock-star clothing."

"We have no control over them, Mom," smirked Timothy, and then he went on in a serious vein, "but I don't think they will. They know this is supposed to be a ceremony paying tribute to Dad, not a teen dance." He was developing a sense of when things are fun, when they are appropriate, and when the two converge.

Inside the church, I went to the sanctuary and put the calla lilies in front of the altar. I wasn't sure that was the right place for them, but since we didn't have a casket or an urn or anything, I wanted something there, and I wanted to be able to refer to the flowers in my talk.

While I was doing that, Liz and Timothy found Mike to go over their plans with him. I overheard some of their conversation…

> "Do you think we should ask people to stand in the aisles for this?"
> "Don't play this too loud. Just loud enough that it will be significant, okay?"
> "Can you cue it up to start right at 3:50 on the disk? We just want

the last two choruses."

They had obviously thought very carefully about what they wanted.

- - -

I met Dr. Franks in the corridor, and we went to his office to go over the order of the service. It was all pretty straight forward. I jotted down the items on the back of the notes I had prepared.

- Dr. Franks, invocation, opening remarks
- Holy, Holy, Holy
- Ben
- Timothy
- Liz
- Fairest Lord Jesus
- Me
- Invitation for others to speak
- Me introduce children
- Benediction
- Reception
- Press conference

"Dr. Franks," I asked, "Would it be okay if you don't say anything about how 'it's a bit unusual...' or anything like that? Just say we're here to pay tribute to Fred?"

"Sure. I like that," he said.

"And as you saw from my emails, I asked the reporters not to ask us any questions after the ceremony or during the reception. I'll answer all their questions afterward."

"That'll be fine. As soon as the ceremony is over and during the reception, Mike will go to the classroom to make sure there are enough chairs and enough outlets and power cords if they need any."

And then he continued, "I expect people will be arriving any minute now. Would you like to greet them, or should I round up your children and have them wait here with you?"

"Let's wait here and go in with you when the service is about to begin. I don't really want to speak with others until after we've all had a chance to celebrate Fred's life."

"Excellent." And he went to get the children.

As he went to get them, I wondered how they were holding up. Getting them involved with the song had not only distracted them but had also energized them, but I didn't know if that was a good thing or a bad thing.

- - -

At about five minutes after two, Dr. Franks walked down the center aisle with us following him. The front row was reserved for us, with the Hazeltons and Gruvels in the row behind us. As I expected, the sanctuary was packed. Even the balcony was full. I let myself slip into a grain of cynicism as I wondered how many would be there if the Cornhusker's game against Rice hadn't been postponed.

Dr. Franks, true to his word, opened "We are here to pay tribute to Frederick Robert Young, a loving father and husband, a brilliant executive. A genuine, caring man who has done so much for all of us…"

I noted the word choice, "has done" not "did". Bless Dr. Franks.

After the hymn, Ben spoke. He began by explaining, but not in so many words, why we were having the tribute-ceremony. He went on to describe Fred's eagerness to learn and his drive to be successful when he joined Klein-Staily twenty years earlier. He praised Fred's dedication and creativity; and he subtly patted himself on the back for having found Fred on the recruiting circuit back then, for having trained him in mortgage appraisals, and for having the insight to encourage Fred to study finance and move into the realm of farm mortgage financing. He didn't mention the problems that had arisen in the past few years with the farm mortgage bonds.

Timothy spoke next. He told people about how much he had enjoyed the camping outings when his father was an assistant scoutmaster. He spoke of the pride he felt when his father went with them on a school trip. And he told a story I'd never heard.

> One summer, when I was nine and Liz was seven, we were both bugging Dad to increase our allowances, but he wouldn't do it. He said, "If you want some extra money, you'll have to earn it." But we had no idea how to earn any money, so Dad took us over to Miracle Hill golf

course, across the highway from Candlewood. "I don't think this is illegal," he said, "but if you walk onto the course over here, away from the clubhouse, you can go through the trees and tall grass, looking for golf balls. You can collect them and sell them to golfers and maybe even to the neighbors."

As we were walking onto the course, Dad said, "Remember two things: always keep your attention on where the golfers are so you don't get hit by any crooked drives. And never, never pick up a ball if there are any golfers in sight or who might have just hit it."

When we came home two hours later with our pockets bulging with golf balls, Dad suggested we take backpacks the next time. And then he said, "I've spoken with the golf pro to make sure this is okay with him. He says you're not to go there on weekends or after about four-thirty in the afternoon because there will be too many golfers on the course then. He even said he'll buy the balls from you for a quarter apiece and then resell them in bags."

Liz and I earned several dollars a week each summer doing that for several years until the new golf pro caught up with us one day and told us not to do it anymore unless we wanted to buy a club membership. That was disappointing, too, because we had found an old butterfly net and were scooping dozens of balls from the water traps and ponds.

I knew the children had done this, but I hadn't known that Fred had suggested it or that they had been shooed off the course. It was amusing but also a bit embarrassing. Still, it was a good story to share about Fred, and I was glad Timothy told it.

Timothy tried to give a little insight into the anguish we felt on Tuesday and were continuing to feel because of the uncertainty.

"We know," he said, "and yet don't want to admit that we know. Thank you all for coming today. This tribute to our father…"

He looked at Liz and smiled and then at me, and then all three of us couldn't control our tears. …

He began again. "This tribute to our father is your way of helping us accept and admit to ourselves what we know: Our father was a wonderful man and we miss him very much."

Through my tears, I noted the past tense, the acceptance of Fred's death. And then Timothy came to the front pew and hugged each of us.

I think it was impromptu after that because it wasn't on the schedule, but Dr. Franks gave us a bit of a break by offering up another prayer.

At the end of the prayer, he said something about the Fredrick Young Memorial Fund. Huh? What was that about? I hadn't caught it all, but I would have to ask him later when we were alone.

Liz went next. I was so proud of her – thirteen years old and facing several hundred people, telling them about her father. The tears flowed again. Liz was about to start her talk, but then stopped and looked at me. And smiled.

She didn't hesitate after that.

> I miss my Dad. He was strict but he was also kind and loving. He wanted the best for us, but he wanted us to grow up being kind, generous, and hard-working ... like him. Even when he was working his heart out on some project, he was always with us, and he was always there for us.

I was pleased that Liz had seen this side of her father. He had been working so much the past few years, I was afraid he had been ignoring the children.

> I want to share two stories with you about my father. The first one is work-related. One day when we were little, we were sitting at the kitchen table having hot chocolate when Dad said, "You know, cocoa tastes even better when it has a bit of cream added to it." And then he went to the fridge to get some "high-test" cream; at least that's what Mom calls it.
>
> Before he would let us pour any into our cups, he said, "I think cream will float on cocoa if we put it on a spoon and lower it gently into the mug. Shall we try it?"
>
> And just to add to the fun of it all, we decided that anyone who couldn't float the cream had to make the noise of an animal. Well, wouldn't you know, Dad couldn't do it, so we told him he had to make the noise of an animal. He just sat there and smiled, and then he tucked his head into his armpit and said, "I'm making the noise of snail.

> They don't make any noise."
>
> We groaned and complained. Then suddenly Dad stopped, as if something was wrong. He just sat there staring at the glass mugs we were using that we hoped would show off the cream on top of the cocoa. Finally, he said, "Layers". Just that one word. Mom said, "Layers? You're a hen? Then you have to cackle," and we all cackled at Dad! I never understood what happened to Dad then, but I guess he had discovered something really important for work.

Later, Ben told me how much he appreciated that story because he had always wondered what had inspired Fred's layering financial innovation.

> The other story is about the Saturday we went boating. Yup. Dad got us out of bed early and took us to Wal-Mart, where he bought an inflatable raft. We took it over to the reservoir and spent the day there paddling around and having a wonderful time. The thing was though, we were having so much fun boating that we forgot to put on sunscreen and were seriously sunburned. Mom threw us all into cold showers the minute we walked into the house, and that helped a bit.
>
> Dad and Mom always tucked us in when we were little, taking turns reading with us and singing bedtime songs with us. I don't know how it became a bedtime song, but both Timothy and I always loved it when Dad sang "The old woman who swallowed a fly" to us and tickled us on the line, "... that wiggled and jiggled and tickled insider her."
>
> I will cherish those memories and many more the rest of my life.

And then Liz walked down and we had another three-way group hug.

Next we sang "Fairest Lord Jesus." It was a nice break before my talk.

I began, "I didn't have a chance to say goodbye." And already I had troubles stopping the tears. But I went on. I was not going to leave out anything in this tribute to Fred.

In addition to the points I had outlined in my notes, I emphasized what a loving, caring man Fred had been, referring to each of the stories the children had told. But I also told about our close relationship and how we had grown together.

I cried off and on during my talk, but every time I cried, I would take a break and then talk some more. At the last minute, I decided not to tell the story about the calla lilies and how they had become "our" flowers; it was our story, and I wanted to keep it just ours.

I think I spoke for fifteen minutes or so. When I finished, I decided to take charge and instead of turning the ceremony back over to Dr. Franks, I asked if anyone else had memories they wanted to share. There were several and, bless them all, they weren't endless.

Dale Hazelton talked about meeting on the street when they were looking after children on weekends, about barbecuing together, and about the closeness that had developed between the families.

Mrs. Plagge, our backyard neighbor, told about how Fred and later Timothy would mow her backyard now and then and how we always made sure she was included in so many things we did.

Joshua Klein, one of the two founders of Klein-Staily, then made his way to the front of the church.

> For those of you who don't know me, I'm Joshua Klein of Klein-Staily. What a wonderful tribute this has been to Fredrick Young. He was a brilliant man who, through his creativity and use of layers, as this beautiful young lady has mentioned, helped recreate the entire world of mortgage finance. Klein-Staily owes Fred and his family a great deal. Thank you all for coming today ….

I couldn't believe it! Joshua Klein was thanking them as if he had invited them and as if it was his show. I thought to myself, "What a controlling s.o.b." I was livid inside, but I didn't show it. Instead, I stood and interrupted him,

"Thank you for your kind words and thank you so much for joining us here today Mr. Klein for our tribute to Fred."

He nodded. He knew what he had done, and he knew what I had done. He came over to me and shook my hand and shook hands with the children, and then made his way back to his seat.

Before he could get there, I announced, "The children and their friends would like us to join them in a celebration of looking forward with strength."

I almost continued to talk, to explain what they were about to do, but instantly I remembered how upset I'd been with Joshua for trying to take over something that was ours; I didn't want to do the same thing to the children.

Timothy and Liz stood up. They gestured to Seth and Aaron to join them and they went to the front of the church.

Timothy said, "A number of our classmates and friends are here to help us pay tribute to our father. I hope you will all come up and join us. "

After the commotion ended with about twenty young people joining the others in the front, Liz announced, "We are not really going to sing, but we are going to sing along with the song 'We Are the Champions', just the last two choruses, and we'd love it if all of you would join with us.

Timothy took over in perfect tag-team fashion, "We're going to start with the rhythm from 'We Will Rock You...' and then when we've all sung that a few times, Liz will signal us to stop that and we'll sing "We Are the Champions."

Liz again: "So if you'd all please stand? And it might be nice if we could mostly form a huge circle around the pews all around the sanctuary. We'll start the rhythm while you all make your way out to join us."

Dr. Franks was beaming. He was clearly of the "Let's make church more relevant" school. I was beaming, too. The children had such poise.

The four children started.

Stomp-stomp-clap. Stomp-stomp-clap.

People were smiling and crying at the same time. The strength and the mix of emotions were overwhelming as people smiled in recognition and went out to join the circle.

Stomp-stomp-clap. Stomp-stomp-clap.

More joined the circle until it was crowded. Others who couldn't get out very easily sat in the pews and joined from there.

Stomp-stomp-clap. Stomp-stomp-clap.

Liz started the chant. "We will, we will rock you." Stomp-stomp-clap. Stomp-stomp-clap.

They continued and were almost dancing as everyone made their way to the outer aisles.

"We will, we will rock you." Stomp-stomp-clap. Stomp-stomp-clap.
"We will, we will rock you." Stomp-stomp-clap. Stomp-stomp-clap.
"We will, we will rock you." Stomp-stomp-clap. Stomp-stomp-clap.

And then Liz held her hand up and Mike started the music. Everyone stopped stomping and clapping and stood there as the guitar wailed. It was perfect.

We are the champions, my friends,
and we'll keep on fighting 'til the end.
We are the champions;
We are the champions!
No time for losers,
'Cuz we are the champions of the world.

By the time we finished singing the chorus the first time, everyone was in tears, and everyone was holding hands and swaying to the music.

We are the champions, my friends,
And we'll keep on fighting 'til the end!
We are the champions;
We are the champions!
No time for losers,
'Cuz we are the champions …

And everyone, especially the children, all at the tops of their lungs, added "… of the world."

Dr. Franks made his way from the congregation to the center aisle in the middle of the sanctuary. He didn't look around at anyone, and he didn't smile. He was clearly very moved as he said a brief benediction.

After he said "Amen," he paused for a moment and then added, "The Young family would like to invite all of you to join them as we continue this celebration of Fred Young's life. There are refreshments available for everyone downstairs in the Community Hall. May I suggest that you now let the Young family have some private time here in the sanctuary? They will join us downstairs in a few minutes."

Dr. Franks nodded to the back of the sanctuary, where several church members opened the sanctuary doors. And then he walked back to the front of the sanctuary and stood with us while everyone else left. It was a good strategic move on his part; otherwise some of the people would have wanted to speak with us right then and there, despite his suggestion that we would like some private time. The Gruvels and Hazeltons, by exiting from the front, also helped move people toward the back.

I felt as if I didn't really need any quiet time, ... but of course I did. The Champions song had nearly everyone in the church in tears, especially with "... and we'll keep on fighting 'til the end." It was so moving and so draining; and it felt so appropriate after the 9-11 attacks on Tuesday.

After everyone had left, Dr. Franks came and talked with us. "There are always some people who don't want to stick around for the reception and so they try to speak with the family here in the sanctuary or in the foyer while the family is making its way to the basement. How would you like to handle it? We can either go out into the foyer on our way down to the community room, or I can take you there the back way so that you can avoid the congestion out there."

I thought about it for a few seconds. I had avoided people long enough. It was time for me to interact again. I knew there would be people in the foyer who would essentially be trying to jump the queue to talk with us, and I did want to get down to the reception, but I also wanted to speak with everyone I could.

"I think I'll go down through the foyer," I said. "There will be some people I'd like to thank for coming but who might not be able to take the stairs to go down to the reception. What about you children?"

Liz immediately said, "I think my friends will be the first ones to the food table. Will it be okay if we go down the back way with Dr. Franks?"

Timothy agreed, and the three of them left.

- - -

I hadn't planned it, but I loved being alone in the sanctuary. I went back to the altar, picked up the calla lilies, and just stood there, saying my own little prayers to and for Fred. It was surprisingly calming as I stood there.

I must have stood there for at least five minutes. Finally, I knew I had to face the mobs of people, and I realized I couldn't leave my children on their own in the reception hall for long, and so I slowly walked back up the aisle, out of the sanctuary, and into the foyer.

As bizarre as it may seem, that walk back up the aisle felt life-altering.

Part Two: New Beginnings

Chapter 20 – Reception Realization

When someone goes through what looks like a distinctive change in their life, it always seems there should be some specific event that led to the change, but for me there were several significant moments.

Certainly the terrorist attacks on September 11th, 2001, were significant for me. Without those attacks, Fred would still be with us. But there were other little moments, too, like when I looked at the coffee filter and decided not to say so much about our past together. Or when I looked at the calla lilies and decided not to talk about them. Or when I decided to take charge of the tribute and ask others to speak before Dr. Franks could ask them. Or when I shut Joshua Klein down.

For me, though, the truly defining moment felt as if it occurred when I walked back up the aisle by myself in the empty sanctuary. It was as if I was acknowledging to myself and to the world that I was alone and that I was responsible for my future. It wasn't so much an event as a realization that created such a significant moment for me.

I'm sure that if Fred hadn't been killed in the terrorist attacks, we would eventually have gotten to where I did in some vaguely similar ways, but that solo walk back up the aisle gave me the feeling that I was making an important symbolic statement to the world, even though no one else in the world saw it. I had said goodbye to Fred; I was on my own; and I was going out to face friends, family, and the rest of the world as me, Susan Loeffer Young, and not as Fred's wife.

Even though that moment was significant for me, I know it wasn't really anything special: I had always had some confidence in dealing with people socially. My parents had raised me to be an independent, self-reliant person; I was given plenty of responsibility at the family's hardware store; and I felt and developed even more confidence waiting tables on Sundays at the Brookville Hotel. I had been successful at Arkero Foods, and I had always played an important role in the children's three S's: school, scouts, and sports. I was well-prepared for my new role in life, whatever it might become. And yet that particular walk felt and still feels significant for me.

Also, I think we had been edging toward important changes within the family. Fred was slowly retreating from his role in the go-go finance world, the children were getting older, and I was ready to take on more, beyond my role as full-time homemaker. Given who I am now, I know that I would likely have done more with myself and my career outside the home during the next few years after 9-11 anyway. It's just that I would have done something different, with fewer financial resources, and certainly with a less public side to it all. But I was headed in that general direction, and Fred was ready for a break, or so it seemed.

Walking up that aisle, carrying the calla lilies, I resolved to use the time and the money to think about what I wanted in life for the children and me. I resolved then that I would not let anyone take control of our lives, for example as Joshua Klein had subtly tried. I knew that what he had done was terribly unimportant, and yet I knew it was important to me, too, that I not let things like that happen. I was pleased with how I had handled that situation. I hadn't embarrassed him in public and yet I had re-taken control, and he knew it.

With this understanding, which clearly didn't all come to me in those thirty seconds or whatever it took to walk very slowly up the aisle, I resolved to make sure I maintained control of our lives but without embarrassing or hurting others. I hoped I could maintain that resolve.

The crowds had thinned in the foyer; it wasn't a mob at all. It was just a group of friends and kind people wishing me well. Several of them commented on the calla lilies and others tried to hug me gently so as not to ruin the flowers. Some also commented on how moving the last song had been, led by the children.

I greeted each of them, thanking them for coming and making sure I let each of them say something about Fred if they wanted to. They all had nice, general things to say and yet it was immediately clear that most of them really had no idea what to say. We didn't know for sure that Fred was dead, and they didn't want to say anything implying they thought he was dead, and so it was awkward for them and for me, too. I developed a set of stock phrases that I hoped would ease the discomfort for them and for me, too.

> "We're still holding out hope, but we've had no word."

> "It has been a very difficult time for the children and me, but we have to accept the reality of the situation."

> "No, not a word from Fred or about him. Nothing."

"Thank you so much. Yes, he was a brilliant and caring man."

And, "Thank you for coming. Won't you please come down to the community hall and join us for the reception?"

On the way down the stairs to the community hall, I met Jeremy Hall coming up the stairs. I glared at him accusingly, hoping he had not pestered the children.

"Oh, here you are Ms. Young," he said. "I wanted to let you know that not only have I *not* interviewed anyone about your husband, but I have also made sure none of the other reporters here has either. We have nine reporters here, and we'll wait upstairs for you until you're ready."

"Thank you, Mr. Hall. I appreciate your concern. Have you all gotten some food?"

"Not yet. We'll wait until the press conference is over and have some then if there's anything left."

"I'll make sure there is."

"Oh, and by the way," he said. "I've given the five hundred dollars to Dr. Franks for the Frederick Young Memorial Fund."

"Thank you," I replied. I would have to ask Dr. Franks about that fund. I knew that memorial funds were frequently created when people wanted to do something after a friend or relative died, but we didn't know for sure that Fred was dead.

There must have been over three hundred people in the Community Hall when I got there. Greeting them all and speaking with them would take quite a while, but I tried not to rush any of them; I had avoided everyone for four days, and I wanted to make sure no one was left out or felt slighted in any way.

There was no formal reception line, but one soon formed informally as people lined up to speak with me. Many of them had already spoken with the children, with the Hazeltons and Gruvels, or with Dr. Franks, but they still wanted to speak with me.

They wanted to express sympathy for what we were going through, but it was difficult for them to do that without expressing condolences "for our loss". I resolved to just let it go; they wanted to commiserate somehow, but they didn't know how to choose the right words. I thanked them and let them know how much the children and I appreciated their thoughts.

During a break, I spoke briefly with Thelma Hazelton, thanking her for everything they had done.

"Oh, don't, Susan. We're so happy we could help out." And she continued, "That song was a great choice, especially capturing the spirit of the nation after the attacks on Tuesday, but more specially showing the determination of your family. It was perfect."

"Whew. I'm glad you think so. I wasn't sure how it would be received."

Cindy joined us and added, "I think some people were puzzled by the song, but by the time we finished, there wasn't a person in the church who didn't understand and feel the strength it was offering your family."

Dale came over and chimed in, off topic, "Lucky thing we got down here when we did. The children were wolfing down the food pretty fast. I guess there aren't usually twenty or thirty hungry teenagers at events like this. Ben and I cautioned them to make sure they left plenty of food for the other guests, and Dr. Franks spoke with the church ladies. I guess they made another run to the store for supplies and are making more sandwiches now. This has been quite an event, Susan."

Just then a cheer went up from the children as more sandwiches and cookies arrived on the food tables.

Cheryl Hill who worked with Fred at Klein-Staily waited until most of the others had spoken with me, and then she came over to talk. Like the others, she hugged me. And then she said, "Susan, Fred was a very special man at the office. He always made sure everyone was looked after. He was ready to take full responsibility for his mortgage-backed bond program, but Ben and Joshua knew the full story and wouldn't let him. Even though he was a bit withdrawn during the past couple of years, he was a man everyone at the firm deeply respected and trusted."

I started crying again and hugged her. It meant a lot, coming from her.

Later, when I had a chance to speak with Dr. Franks, he mentioned that there had been some large donations to the memorial fund, and he wanted to know how I might want to use the funds. "I had no idea about this, Dr. Franks. It actually caught me off guard when you mentioned it during the tribute. I'm really pleased that so many people want to do something to honor Fred. Why don't we meet sometime next week to discuss it? I'll phone your office on Monday to set up a time, okay?"

Again, I was taking control. I was determined to keep doing it, too.

Eventually people began to leave and say their goodbyes to us, saying things like, "It was a lovely tribute," "Let us know if you need anything," "Fred was a terrific person," and so on.

After most of the people had left, I went into the kitchen to thank the ladies who had gone above and beyond the call of duty to make sure there was plenty of food for everyone. "You all helped make this special day even more special. I hope you all got something to eat yourselves."

They all nodded and smiled, and then Dorothy Kunig laughed, "Oh don't worry about that! We always get something to eat before we put out the food for everyone else."

The others there laughed and hooted, but I knew it was only partly true. They always made sure there was plenty of food for everyone.

"Is there some way I can put together a tray or box of sandwiches and cookies for the reporters who are up in the classroom waiting to talk with me?" I asked.

"Done," smiled Dorothy, and she indicated two platters they had already prepared.

Back in the reception hall, I spoke with the children and the Hazeltons about the press conference and about arranging transportation for the children if they didn't want to stay.

"Mom, I've never seen a press conference," said Liz. "I'd like to stay."

"What about you, Timothy?" I asked.

"Well, I'd sort of like to stay, too, but I don't want to have to answer any more questions."

"That's part of the agreement with the reporters," I said. "I've told them I'll answer all their questions, but they must not address any questions to you children."

"Okay, Mom," said Timothy, "I'd like to stay, too, then."

"Good. I'll need to freshen up a bit before we go up to the press conference. We can go up in a few minutes now."

Chapter 21 -- **Press Conference**

After we said our goodbyes to the Hazeltons, the children carried the platters of sandwiches and cookies upstairs to the classroom. As Jeremy Hall had said, there were nine reporters seated in the room. None of them wanted to appear too greedy by making a rush for the sandwiches, and so the children set the platters on a side table and drifted to the back of the room, where they stood between Ben Gruvel and Dr. Franks.

I had dealt with the press before, but never like this, and my nervousness grew as the reality of the situation began to sink in. There were two light standards with bright lights pointed at a lectern in the front of the room, there was a full-sized video camera and operator, there were several photo-journalists with cameras snapping away, and there was what looked like a forest of microphones attached to the lectern, all with their logos facing the video camera, vying for attention.

I hadn't prepared anything specific to say, but I wanted to start off with an introduction before opening the floor for questions.

> First, I want to thank all of you for being here now and honoring my request not to approach us during the tribute ceremony or during the reception. Your doing this has made things so much better for us, allowing us to focus on the tribute to my husband.
>
> Next, I'd like to reiterate what we know and what we don't know:
> - My last communication from Fred was an email I received from him Tuesday morning before he left for his appointment with Jordan Singer at Cantor-Fitzgerald on the 101st floor of the North Tower of the World Trade Center.
> - When a friend called to tell me about the first plane hitting the North Tower, I immediately tried to call Fred's cellphone, but the call wouldn't go through. We tried constantly over the rest of the day and most of the next day, but we never reached him.
> - Ben Gruvel and his colleagues at Klein-Staily also tried repeatedly to reach Fred that day without success.
> - The hotel where he was staying has a computer system showing when a room has been entered and with which keycard. Fred's room at the hotel was entered only by the maid to clean it. Fred never returned to the hotel.
> - For four days, Klein-Staily has had several people constantly scouring medical centers, hospitals, temporary morgues, and

- every other place they could think of, looking for Fred. They also hired several people from Wilson Detectives in New York City to look for him or for any sign of him.
- Apparently nearly three thousand people were killed in the attacks on the Twin Towers --- you probably have the up-to-date estimates.
- Of those, authorities have informed Klein-Staily that there will be nothing recovered of any of those who were near where the planes hit. There may be more than a thousand families, just like ours, with no idea what happened to their loved ones and no evidence that they were killed in the attacks.

I went on, "Mr. Hall, you have graciously apologized to me for intruding on our privacy, and we appreciate it. We also appreciate your assistance with this get together. Would you like to start with the first question?"

Jeremy Hall seemed only slightly embarrassed. Apparently he had developed a thick skin over the years. At the same time, I didn't really want to embarrass him so much as make a point to the other reporters that if they respected us, we would respect them.

"Yes, Ms. Young, we would like to honor your request that we not ask your children questions, so could you please describe how they are dealing with the disappearance of their father?"

I'm afraid I hemmed and hawed a bit. I felt as if I should have anticipated the question and had a better answer prepared. I think what came out was something like this:

> "It hit us all very hard. The shock of unexpectedly losing someone close to you is difficult to imagine. As soon as I knew what had happened, I rushed to their schools and had them come home with me. We cried, we held each other, we surfed the major news telecasts, and we hunkered down. We had no idea what was happening, and we had no idea what had happened to Fred. We were determined, with the assistance of some very kind and helpful friends and neighbors, not to make any public statements until we had some information for you. We hoped we would know something more to tell you today, but we don't. I'm sorry.
>
> "As for the children, Timothy and Liz, along with two of their friends, helped with meals, with answering the telephone, and with answering

the door. But after Tuesday, there was no reason for the children stay out of school. They went to school the rest of the week."

I smiled at the children.

"From what they've told me, their teachers, their schools, and their classmates were all very kind and understanding."

Jeremy Hall started to ask another, follow-up question, but I shook him off and took a question from CBS reporter, Janice McKay.

"Ms. Young, how will you get by? What if the insurance company denies your claim for the life insurance until you have proof of his death?"

I thought it was crass yet at the same time realistic for her to have asked those questions that way.

"I have thought about this problem a bit, Ms. McKay. It's a good question."

I could see the wheels turning in all the reporters' heads.

"Fred and I were always careful about saving our money. We have enough readily available to see us through for a while, and I'm ready to go back into the workforce soon. Even if the insurance company doesn't pay, we'll be able to stay in our home and in our community.

"Beyond that, we have been assured that if the insurance company declines to pay, we can have Fred officially declared dead in seven years, and they will have to pay then. Representatives from Klein-Staily have been in touch with the insurance company, and they are confident that even if nothing more is discovered about what happened to Fred, we should receive the insurance benefits within a month or so.

"Next?"

"Nathan Crowley, ABC news," said a polished-looking young man I'd seen at our place often on Tuesday and Wednesday. "How much will you be collecting from the insurance company if and when they pay off?"

Now that **was** a crass and rude question. I tried to fend it off a bit.

"I don't know the exact amount," I said, but I knew that wouldn't suffice, and so I continued, "I've been assured that it will be enough to provide for my children's educations and for my retirement. Whatever it is, I will likely have Fred's colleagues from Klein-Staily manage it for us."

Crowley wasn't happy with the reply but he sensed that he would get nothing more from me on that score.

Back to Jeremy Hall.

"Ms. Young, Dr. Franks mentioned the Frederick Robert Young Memorial Fund. Can you tell us something about that?"

"I would love to, but I had no idea that such a fund would exist or would be created. Just before I came up here, Dr. Franks told me there is over three thousand dollars in the fund already and that there will be many more contributions over the next few weeks. I am completely nonplussed by the outpouring of generosity from everyone. Dr. Franks and I have agreed to meet soon to discuss the situation.

"Next?"

"Jennifer Amin, NBC Financial News. Ms. Young, what was the nature of Mr. Young's business with Cantor-Fitzgerald in New York City?"

"Ms. Amin, I'll tell you what little I know. Fred was always on the lookout for new investment strategies, and apparently he had found one. He and his Klein-Staily colleagues decided to develop and promote the strategy with and through Cantor-Fitzgerald, and Fred was there to seal the deal, but that's all I know about it."

Jennifer Amin again.

"Ms. Young, it's no secret in the finance world that the mortgage-backed bonds developed by your husband had fallen in value seriously over the past two years. Did this fact play a role in Klein-Staily's decision to take Cantor-Fitzgerald on as a partner this time?"

"Ms. Amin, I know very little about the details of the mortgage-backed bonds that Fred developed. If Mr. Klein, who spoke at the tribute, were here, I'd refer your question to him. But since he isn't here, I'll tell you what little I know. Everyone at Klein-Staily says the mortgage-backed bond arrangements that Fred worked out were on solid ground, but only if the farm mortgage appraisers did their jobs carefully. Apparently not all appraisers did their jobs carefully. And so even though Fred's work was not the source of the problem with those bonds, everyone in the firm agreed that it would be prudent to take on a partner, and Cantor was the logical choice."

I hoped I hadn't said too much. But I really wanted to defend Fred.

"Next?"

They were already wracking their minds for questions. This was the part of press conferences I didn't like. They didn't know what to ask, but they felt as if they should keep asking questions.

"What about you, yourself, Ms. Young? What are your plans?"

Good grief. This was the type of stuff I had expected, and I didn't want to shut them down but I also didn't want to go on endlessly with meaningless speculation.

"As I said, Fred and I had expected that I would go back to the work full time at some point in the near future. I've done some consulting with Arkero Foods on a part-time basis for the past seven years, and that is likely an option I will explore – that or some other full-time opportunity. At the same time, I want to make sure my children are well looked after, and so anything I decide will have to take them into consideration for sure."

I actually thought that with the insurance money, there would be no reason for me to work, and so I carefully added, "I would also like to do things for our community and for our city. The outpouring of good wishes today and over the past week meant a great deal to us, and we as a family want to thank everyone for what they have done. I am sure that I will also want to spend more time working with various projects in a way that will reflect our gratitude."

Geez, that felt almost like a political speech. Little did I know...

"Next?"

"Ms. Young can tell us more about how your friends and neighbors reacted and helped out?"

"Sure, some of you experienced their help during the week as they helped preserve our privacy," and I smiled knowingly, trying not to smirk but to add some lightness to the occasion. Some smiled back; some shuffled their feet.

I hurried on, "But seriously, we had literally hundreds of phone calls, email messages, and visits from people offering to help. Some people brought food; others offered to do some driving or to pick things up for us so we wouldn't have to go out. The Candlewood neighborhood is pretty close-knit. We have frequent neighborhood get-togethers and we always pitch in whenever we sense that there even **might** be a need."

"More politician-like talk," I thought to myself.

I wasn't sure whether I should single people out, but I really wanted the Hazeltons and Gruvels to know how much I appreciated their help.

"In addition to everything that everyone did, I really must make special mention of everything the Hazeltons and the Gruvels did for us. Thelma Hazelton was with me much of the time for the first few days, helping with just about everything. And her family spent the first three evenings with us, too. We have always been close friends, but they showed us the true meaning of friendship this past week. And Ben Gruvel from Klein-Staily and his wife, Cindy, were more help than you can imagine. Ben mobilized every possible resource to try to find Fred or to find out any information they could, and then he got onto the insurance company right away. Meanwhile Cindy was there with us, too, helping out in every way possible. Without the help of those two families, I don't know how we would have survived the past four days."

I hesitated briefly, "If there are no other questions, you can see that Liz and Timothy have brought up some cookies and sandwiches for you. I have one continuing request, and that is that you not invade my children's privacy. But from now on, I will be happy to answer any of your questions. So now, won't you please help yourselves to the food."

I asked the children to come up to the lectern with me while the reporters milled around the food platters. As we stood there, each of the reporters came by and shook our hands, expressed their condolences about our situation, and thanked us for the food and the interviews. Others snapped what sounded like thousands of photos.

After all of the others left, Jeremy Hall tentatively approached us.

"Timothy, I've apologized to your mother, and now I want to apologize to you, too, for interviewing you the way I did on Friday. It was inappropriate, and it won't happen again."

Timothy was a bit taken aback. He wasn't sure how to respond.

"Thank you, Mr. Hall. I appreciate your letting me know."

Good Lord, Timothy had wonderful social graces.

On the way back down the stairs to the reception hall, Liz stopped right in the middle of a flight of stairs and confronted me about my parenting.

"Mother," she scolded, "you can't protect us all our lives. You've got to let us make mistakes. It's, like, the best way to learn. It is almost insulting that you don't, like, trust us with reporters. What Timothy said to Mr. Hall was fabulous. Sure Mr. Hall shouldn't have done that, but Timothy handled it really well. And I would, too."

I stopped mid-step on the stairs and leaned against the handrail. She was right. It completely caught me off guard, though. With Fred gone, it was clear that I had intended to become overly protective, and I could see that not only would it be a big mistake, but it wouldn't work with Liz, who had a mind of her own.

I looked at Liz very seriously and said, "You're right, Liz. Timothy, you did handle that unwarranted interview very well, and Liz I know you would too. I was just so eager to keep the press out of our lives that I went too far in that direction. Thank you, Liz."

And I hugged them both again. It was an apologetic-asking-for-forgiveness type of hug and very different from all the desperate, clinging, consoling hugs we'd had the previous four days. It felt strange, but it also felt like important progress in so many ways. We were no longer focusing on Fred's disappearance; we were talking about the future, and the children were standing up for themselves.

Liz went on, "But aside from that, Mom, you sounded like a pro in there, like the way you handled the questions, answering what you wanted to and side-stepping other things."

"The odd thing for me," I replied, "is that I felt like a politician or something. I've done public relations work all my life, but not like that."

I added, "I really don't think it should be anyone's business how much money we are likely to have, but I felt like a politician trying to cover up a scandal or something."

The ladies were just finishing up when we got back to the kitchen. They had wrapped up the extra cookies and sandwiches for us, but I said, "Oh gosh, no! Why don't you folks take them home for your families?"

I learned later that about half the people holding receptions told the kitchen helpers to take the leftovers home and about half took the leftovers themselves.

"I know this must have cost your group quite a bit," I said. "How should I pay for it?"

"Oh, we usually leave that up to Dr. Franks," said Marva Smith.

"Okay, I'll discuss that with him when we meet to talk about the memorial fund next week. And again, thank you all for everything."

Chapter 22 – **Emptiness**

The drive home from church was a huge letdown emotionally. We had been coasting on adrenalin for four days; the intensity of wondering whether Fred was alive, and the sparks of energy from the uncertainty had died with the tribute ceremony. We expected few press inquiries after that day, and we knew our friends and neighbors would soon stop calling and visiting. It was time for us to move on with our lives.

"How much did you two eat at the reception?" I asked Timothy and Liz.

"I stood near the food table with some of my friends from the soccer team," answered Timothy. I don't know for sure, but it was a *lot*."

"My friends and I stood over by the wall, like, watching the soccer players," giggled Liz, and then she added, "We all probably ate more than we should have just so we could, like, walk past the soccer players."

Timothy groaned an embarrassed groan.

"Well, I was so busy with the reception line that I didn't eat a thing," I said. "I should have realized a reception line would form unofficially even though we hadn't planned for one. It doesn't matter, though, I'm glad we had a chance to speak with everyone. Anyway, I didn't eat, so I'll have a snack when we get home, and then maybe we can make sandwiches for a late Sunday supper. How does that sound?"

The children mumbled their "Okays," which I interpreted as a sign they had both eaten quite a few sandwiches and desserts during the reception and didn't really want to think about eating right then.

With that discussion ended, the emptiness hit again. What would I do? What would the children do? What should I do to help the children?

I wanted to escape. I wanted to escape *with* them, and I wanted to escape *without* them. I wanted to be alone, and yet I didn't want to be alone at all. I really needed to think.

When we got home, I ate some leftover salad. I wasn't hungry but I knew I should eat something healthy instead of snacking on junk.

Meanwhile, the children fought over and then negotiated the use of the telephone. I knew it wouldn't be long before I put in a second phone line.

Fred and I had talked about it, and I knew it was time.

There were so many things to think about, so many things to do. I tried to prepare myself for the things I'd have to start doing on Monday. ... But I couldn't. I knew we had the rest of the weekend still ahead of us, and I felt so lost. I would try to muddle through and provide whatever I could for the children, but I didn't know what they needed, and I wasn't sure I could provide it even if I managed to figure it out.

"Mom?" It was Liz. "Is it okay if we have Becky over this evening to play some games? Maybe I can invite Seth and Aaron, too?"

"Sure," I said, and I thought, "I really don't want us to impose on the Hazeltons too much. They have their own lives to lead, too." But then I thought, "Well of course! The children have been good friends for years and have often gotten together to play games here on the weekend. This should be no different." And so I added, "Of course."

I wondered again if there was any romantic interest between Liz and either Seth or Aaron. If there was, I was both pleased and concerned. I hoped I could deal with the changing teen lifestyles.

Timothy emerged next. "Mom, some of us are going to go bowling later this evening. I hope that's okay."

"Of course," I answered. "Who all is going?"

"It's sort of a group thing. Some of the guys from the soccer team and a few girls from school."

"Will Sandra be there?" taunted Liz.

"Yes, she will," and Timothy was clearly embarrassed.

He recovered quickly, though. "And so will Marcia and Beth and Sarah and Kit. Any other questions?"

He was being overly defensive and it was cute. I smiled to myself and realized they would both be gone in just a few years, and I would be on my own, completely. I loved them, and I loved that they were growing and developing and maturing, but it frightened me, too.

"How are you getting there, and when are you leaving?" I asked.

"Bob Kapov is coming by about seven o'clock to drive some of us."

Ah. He was double-dating but not calling it that. I think Liz realized it, too, but she decided not to taunt her brother anymore because it looked as if she and Becky were essentially hoping to double date with the Hazelton boys, and she didn't want to be taunted or teased about that.

Anyway, the children had their distractions planned for the evening. I was pleased for them. ... And so lonely.

At least there would be children in the basement during the evening.

I went into the family room and sat on what had become my side of the loveseat. I just sat there. I didn't turn on the television, and I didn't pick up a book or turn on any music. I just sat there.

I had no idea what I wanted for the rest of my life. I had been so content, living the "Great Mid-American Dream" with Fred that I hadn't really examined my life. I knew that in the coming years I would want more than just sitting around the house, even if Fred were still with us. I had been feeling a little restless over the past few years, and so I knew there had been germs within me of looking for more. But I wasn't ready – not yet anyway. I thought that perhaps within the next month or so, I might see about returning to Arkero Foods full-time even though we probably wouldn't need the money. I had loved working with them, and I knew they had liked the work I had done for them during the past seven years on a free-lance basis.

I looked around and wondered how long I would stay in our house. I had always loved going "home" to the same house in Salina, Kansas, when my parents were still alive. And the thought of having Timothy and Liz visit with spouses and children was a wonderfully warming thought. I decided not to sell the house until they finished their educations at the very earliest. I'd have to see after that.

The social chaos began at about six-thirty, when Becky arrived. Although she and Liz were very close friends, I thought I sensed her checking Timothy out a few times before he left. I wondered if she was disappointed that he was leaving.

Liz got on the phone right away to invite Seth and Aaron over, and they were happy to accept the invitation. They loved playing games and just being social in our basement games room; we had built the room with exactly this sort of thing in mind, and I was delighted to see it put to this use, especially this weekend.

Right after the Hazelton boys arrived and went to the basement with Becky and Liz, Bob Kapov drove up the driveway to pick up Timothy.

I knew they wouldn't be bowling for five hours, but on Saturday nights Timothy had a curfew of midnight. As he started out the door I asked, "Where do you think you might go after bowling?"

"Sandra says her parents want to meet us and are preparing a late-night barbecue. That sounds like a lot of fun. Don't worry, I'll make sure Bob gets me home by midnight," he smiled.

And then he added, "I like Sandra, Mom. And I think she likes me, too. I've never really had a girlfriend before, and I think she might become my girlfriend. See you later…" and he was out the door.

I didn't know what it meant to have a boyfriend-girlfriend relationship anymore. I had read that it would mean more time together and more sex than young people had when I was young. I dreaded having to have "The Talk" with the children, but it was clearly time.

"Maybe tomorrow after church," I thought.

From time-to-time the game-playing noises stopped in the basement, sometimes for ten or fifteen minutes at a time. I wondered whether they were playing kissing games or maybe talking quietly about things they didn't really want a parent to overhear.

Yes, it was time to have "The Talk".

I didn't want to embarrass the four of them, and so when I heard noise from the air hockey game, I went downstairs to see if they wanted anything. When I got to the games room, they'd had plenty of warning and were all active. It looked as if maybe they were trying to play team versions of the air hockey with Liz and Seth versus Becky and Aaron. But they all seemed a little flushed and a little too earnest.

Yes, it was time to have "The Talk".

"I'm not sure whether any of those dozens of pizzas that celebrities were offering this week actually arrived..." I smiled, and the children giggled. "But we have some frozen pizzas down here in the freezer. Would you like me to put one in the oven?"

They all loved the idea.

"That would be great, Ms. Young," said Seth. "I know we all ate wayyyy too much at the reception, but neither Aaron nor I had any supper, so I don't know about the others, but I would really like some pizza!"

"Me, too," chimed in both Aaron and Becky.

"Okay," I said. "… How does broccoli, artichoke, and feta pizza sound?"

They all made appropriate gagging noises except Aaron.

"I've never had that," he said, "But if that's all you have, I'll try it."

I laughed. "All we have is all meat or deluxe pizza. I'll make one of each."

When they were baked, I put the pizzas out on the kitchen, called the children, and retreated to the family room again, so as not to intrude. But they called me in.

"What will you do now, Ms. Young?" asked Becky.

Chapter 23 – "What Will You Do Now?"

"I'm not sure, Becky," I replied. I sighed as I shook my head slightly. "Everything is so up-in-the-air."

"Mom, you mentioned going back to work. Were you serious?" asked Liz.

"That's a good possibility, Liz. I've already been doing a lot of community work along with some part-time consulting. I'll probably continue doing those things while I think about what else I'd like to do."

And then it occurred to me to ask the children what their thoughts for the future were. "What about you children? What do you think you would like to be doing, say, ten or fifteen years from now?"

Nobody spoke up, and so I turned to Becky and addressed her directly. "What about you Becky?"

"That's so far off, Ms. Young. I want to go to college somewhere, maybe at Creighton here in Omaha or maybe to UN-Lincoln. And, I'd like to travel some, so I'm hoping I can get a job that involves a lot of travel."

"I'd like to travel, too," said Aaron. "But I know my parents have high hopes for Seth and me to go away to some top school somewhere."

He smiled, "Maybe I'll pick a college far away so I can travel some."

I turned to Seth, "What about you, Seth?"

He hesitated a bit. "I know our parents want us to go to a top college and do well, but you know what? I'm not sure what I want to do. I'm thinking maybe I should work or travel a bit after high school before I go to college. You know, take time to figure out what I want before I spend all that time and money spinning my wheels."

"That's a great idea," said Liz, almost but not quite gushing. The wheels were spinning, all right --- in Liz's mind! --- I could see she wanted to think about going to college about the same time he did. Then she looked at me. "Mom, I don't know what Dad did, exactly, but I hope I find something like that, something I really like and can really get into."

After the children finished the pizza, I offered to drive Becky home. The girls walked to Hazelton boys to the foot of the driveway and said their goodnights, and I took my time getting the car out of the garage.

On the way home from Becky's, Liz was quieter than usual.

"What's up, Liz?" I asked her.

"Mom, am I too young to have a boyfriend?"

"I don't think so," I offered. I decided not to tell her about the crushes I'd had on boys when I was her age or younger. "Why do you ask? Are you wanting one of the Hazeltons to be your boyfriend?"

She smiled an embarrassed smile, "Yes…. Seth. He's nice, he's smart, and he's cute. But he's older than me. Is that okay?"

"I think so," I said. "What does he think?"

"He said he likes me, too, and he asked me to go with him."

"What does that mean?" I asked with some trepidation.

She sensed my concern and laughed, "Oh, Mom! … It just means we'd be boyfriend and girlfriend."

- - -

"What will you do now?" The question stayed with me all weekend: when I went to bed that night, the next day at church, and as we sat at home on Sunday afternoon. Well, honestly, the question stayed with me for a number of years, but it was foremost in my mind for those next few days.

I knew I would have many details to take care of, including meeting again with Dr. Franks, meeting with a lawyer, and setting up some sort of investment plan with Ben. I would be busy doing all those things. And the children were quickly growing up; just keeping ahead of them (or, for that matter, trying to keep up with them) would keep me busy, too.

But what would I do? As I pondered the question, I remembered the interest and aptitude tests we had taken in high school. The counselors told me the tests indicated an aptitude and interest for organization and service, which was pretty much what I had decided on for my life as a full-time homemaker. But now, with Fred gone and with the children maturing rapidly, I realized I would want more. But how much more and what type of "more"?

I was determined not to rush into anything. Ben had warned me that people would be after my money, and I guessed that would mean they would be after my time as well. I had learned from the PTA and scouts that those activities, while important when our children were young and involved, were not what I wanted to do for the rest of my life. I wanted to do more, to help make some kind of difference somewhere, somehow.

I smiled at myself. I knew that helping with school and scouts and other activities was making a difference, but I wanted to make a different kind of difference; I wanted something bigger, but I had no idea what.

On Sunday after church and before lunch, I had the children sit at the kitchen table with me.

"Oh, oh," said Timothy, "is this another family meeting like the one Dad called to let us know things weren't going so well at work?"

Liz's head jerked up. "Mom? What's wrong?"

I smiled at them as I chastised myself slightly for having done it this way. "No, there's nothing wrong ... that I know of ... and yes, I guess this is like a family meeting."

They relaxed a bit but were curious to the point of being on edge.

"I think it's time we talk some more about boy-girl relationships," I said.

I couldn't tell whether they relaxed or tensed up or maybe both.

"I know you both have boyfriend-girlfriend relationships," I said, and I'm happy for you. I just need to lecture you about a few things..."

"Don't worry, Mom," Liz laughed at me. "We've had all the stuff at school about safe sex." And she actually smirked a bit.

I didn't laugh. Instead I said, "I hope so. You, too, Timothy?"

He just nodded and seemed a bit embarrassed.

"Well, no matter what they teach you about safe sex, I need to talk to you about relationships, but I don't know where to start. How about I let you know that before I went to college, I'd had several boyfriends ... no, not at the same time ... and I believed I was in love with each of them. Your father, though ... I'm not sure how many girlfriends he'd had before we met. Not many, I think.

"Falling in love with someone is wonderful. The excitement, the happiness, the desperation of wanting to be together, it's all wonderful. You tell each other at the beginning how wonderful it is and how you can't imagine ever being with anyone else, and then you find yourselves drifting apart for a whole host of different possible reasons. And sometimes it's very painful when it ends.

"My lecture is that I hope you enjoy it, love it, and live it fully. At the same time, don't sacrifice yourselves for it. Don't let your schoolwork suffer, don't give up options you want to pursue just for the sake of the other person.

"And one more thing: when things don't feel right between you, talk about them! You won't know what to say, and you won't want to hurt the other person, but if you don't talk about them, problems fester and the relationship gets worse instead of being saved. And if things still don't feel right, don't stay in the relationship. Okay?"

The children had blank looks on their faces. I couldn't tell if they were bored or embarrassed or maybe a bit of both.

Timothy broke the silence. "Mom? Sandra and I aren't there yet. But we might be in the future, and I have no idea what to do about sex. We've kissed and hugged, and that's really good, but I have no idea what to do or how."

I surprised by his forthrightness. Liz giggled, but only bit. She was eager to hear what I had to say.

"Well, I'm not going to be explicit about anything," I answered. "I will say this, though. Take your time and talk with each other about what feels good and what you might like to do. Also, let's make sure we get a couple of the best books for you to read."

"Is that how things went for you and Dad?" Liz asked.

"Sort of, I guess. He was quite shy, and I had to talk with him a lot about sex. But over the years we became very good lovers for each other. It didn't just come naturally, though; I really don't think it does for any couple. We tried lots of different things and did our best to make sure we were both happy with what we were doing."

The children seemed contented with that discussion, and so I suggested, "Well, shall we start working our way through all this food we have?" and we had lunch.

The Huskers hadn't played the day before because of the terrorist attacks. And the NFL didn't play any games that weekend but decided to extend their season by a week. I don't know what other people did that Sunday afternoon, but I took a walk over to the reservoir and continued to contemplate the question, "What will you do?"

Chapter 24 – Dealing and Coping

"Susan, is there a chance you can come in to the office this afternoon?"

It was Ben Gruvel; he had called me about nine o'clock Monday morning.

"Sure, Ben. What's going on?" I asked.

"There are several things that we need to talk about to help with getting things settled. There's nothing to worry about; it looks as if the insurance company is ready to make the full payment on Fred's life insurance, and it looks as if the government is offering some substantial payments to families in order to avoid massive class-action lawsuits.

"Okay," I answered. Is there anything I need to bring or that I should prepare for?"

"I can't think of anything, but I'd like to invite Charles Leamer to meet with us. He's probably the top wills and estates attorney in Omaha, and I recommend that you get started with him as soon as possible."

We met early Monday afternoon. Charles Leamer seemed about forty-five years old and was neither too slimy nor overly solicitous, and, to his credit, he didn't seem rushed either. In other words, he seemed very professional. Also, I'm sure he expected to earn a fat fee for handling Fred's estate.

"Susan," Ben began, "The federal government, the airports, and the airport security services are being sued in a class action suit by the survivors of everyone killed in the attacks. Rather than let the suit go forward, Washington is imposing a settlement. The settlement for each family will be based on each victim's past and expected future incomes."

Charles joined in, "Fred was at the top of the scale that the federal negotiators are using. It looks as if the U.S. government will be sending you a check for six million dollars sometime in the next two months."

I nearly fell off my chair. We had saved plenty of money, and I was going to receive so much from our insurance, too. We didn't need the extra money from the government on top of all that.

"We don't need it," I said, almost plaintively.

Charles said, "You may feel that way now, but don't reject it. If, after you've thought about it, you still don't want the money, perhaps you can donate it to a charitable organization or even maybe create your own foundation."

"I like those ideas," I replied, "You're right. I'll wait and think about it."

Ben added, "We can try to keep the insurance payout quiet and out of the press, but we cannot keep the settlement from the government a secret. Within a day or two, the information will be released and the press will have it. Everyone in Omaha will know about it."

I groaned. "I don't need this."

"That's what we thought," said Ben. "As we have seen before, when there is news of a huge windfall for an individual, friends and relatives turn into vultures. We want to help you prepare for that onslaught."

"Okay, but how?"

"First, if anyone asks, handle it the way you did at the press conference yesterday. Tell them you don't know your financial situation right now but that you are arranging for Charles and me to handle things for you. You will probably be able to hold off most people with something like that. There will be others, though, who will persist. Someone will need some money right now, or someone else will have an investment opportunity that will go away if they or you don't act quickly. They will be very persuasive, and you will have to be firm. Don't necessarily deny them anything; just tell them you can't make any decisions without consulting us."

I think I must have let a skeptical look come over my face.

Charles jumped in to reassure me. "We're just recommending that you *say* that. Ben tells me that you will want to retain complete control of everything. We're just recommending that you act as if we have some sort of veto power over your financial decisions, just as a response to urgent pleas for funds."

I relaxed, but only a bit. "I know we will need legal documents to let Ben and Klein-Staily handle the funds as they come in. After I sort myself out emotionally, though, I may want to take a more active role. It's just that I have no idea what to do right now."

I went on, "Is there anything I need to do to give Ben and Klein-Staily the authority to receive and manage the funds as they are paid to me?"

Ben smiled. "Susan, you had already said you wanted us to manage the funds for you, and so I prepared these documents for you to sign," and he pull out several sheets of paper that he had already signed.

Before I signed them, I looked at Charles. "Who are you working for, Charles? Are you working for Ben? Klein-Staily? or me?"

I'm sure neither he nor Ben had anticipated that question. There was a moment of silence before Charles answered, "I have worked for Klein-Staily in the past, and I have helped Ben set up trusts for his children and grandchildren. But I don't think there's a conflict of interest here."

I hesitated, and then I turned to Ben, looking him squarely in the eyes. "Ben, I'm sure there would be no problem with my retaining Charles, but just in case and just to be on the safe side, I think we should look for someone else who has no connection with you or with Klein-Staily. I'm sure you both understand."

Charles started to babble, trying to reassure me, but Ben saw where I was going. "You were right to ask that, Susan. Charles, Klein-Staily will pay your billed time for today. Susan and I should discuss finding someone who has no connection with me or with the firm."

It had been awkward; I hated having to ask that question, and I was a little bothered that neither Ben nor Charles had considered it.

Charles promised to email some recommendations to Ben, said his polite good-byes, and left. As the door closed, I turned to Ben and said, "Ben, I know you were trying to help, but I hope you won't do that to me again."

And then I went on, "Ben, I don't want to delay any more than necessary about having you named as the manager of the funds. That was not what my concern was at all."

I smiled tentatively, again, hoping he would understand.

"It's just that if something happens to you or to me, I want to make sure the legal situation is clear and clean. I need a good, experienced lawyer, and while it has to be one that you can trust and work with, it has to be one that I can trust as well. Does that make sense?"

"It does, Susan, and I'm a bit embarrassed that I didn't discuss selecting a lawyer with you sooner. I won't make that mistake again."

The people at Klein-Staily were beginning to get the picture. I wasn't going to go along with things just to avoid any confrontations. At the same time, I hoped I was polite. Striking a balance was something I wanted to be careful about.

"Thanks, Ben. I knew you would understand. Now, let's look at the forms you need signed. I do want you to manage our funds, and I know we will have to have agreements in place now, before the funds arrive."

Ben just sat there and looked at me for a few seconds.

"Susan," he said. It seemed he used my name a lot when talking with me. "You seem like a tiger mom guarding her cubs today. What's going on?"

"Ben," I responded, using his name in return, "One of the things I was raised with, and in fact one of the things that you have emphasized and that I learned watching and living with Fred, was to try to prepare for the unexpected. If something were to go wrong, and I have no idea what it might be, I want to prepare as well as I can and be able to keep looking after myself and the children. That's all.

"As of now, Fred and I have saved nearly three million dollars on our own. We were frugal, and we invested as Fred recommended, in low-fee index funds. But I managed the day-to-day finances for the family. We were a good team, then, and I want to carry on in that same spirit."

Ben looked down at the table briefly. Then he looked at me directly. "Did Fred tell you not to invest with us, not to have us manage your savings?"

"No. Why do you ask?"

"It always puzzled me that even though he was a genius in developing our mortgage-backed bonds, he never invested in them or in any of the funds that used them. Do you know why that was?"

"Not really ... but maybe... He said we should diversify our assets. He said that on one hand his salary and bonuses were the return we earned on his talent but that on the other hand he wanted our savings invested in something else, something that didn't depend on and wasn't related to him. It made sense to me, especially when things started going wrong with the mortgage-backed bonds."

I changed the subject. "But let's look at these forms you want me to sign, okay?"

The forms set out what Klein-Staily would do and what they were constrained to do. I added some conditions: no actively- managed funds – just index funds. And no less than eighty percent in stocks. Ben readily agreed to those add-ons.

Ben had set the management fee for my portfolio at 0.41%. I knew that was higher than the management fees for index funds I wanted in the portfolio, but Ben explained that managing the portfolio would involve more than just buying a few mutual funds. I didn't begrudge him the money, and I knew Ben would look after us as well as he could.

"Ben, I hope you understand that I trust you. I wouldn't want anyone else to manage our portfolio. I raised the red flag about Charles only to make sure I get independent legal advice, especially since there are some people here that I don't trust the same way I trust you."

Ben smiled. "Thank you, Susan. You have no idea how much I appreciate your saying that."

Chapter 25 – **So Much Money**

That evening I thought some more about our financial situation. It looked as if we would be far richer than Fred or I ever imagined; the house was paid for, and so were both cars. I figured that if we had a hundred thousand dollars a year, that would be about double what we would really need. Fred always said to count on no more than two percent return and to reinvest whatever was left over to provide for inflation. That meant I'd need only five million dollars invested at two percent to get the income I thought would be more than enough for us.

What would I do about the rest of the money? I wanted to create trusts for the children for when they were older, and I wanted to set money aside for their educations. But what else? I had no idea what to do with so much money. I didn't want a bigger house, I didn't want more cars, I didn't want a summer home, I didn't want a boat, and I didn't really want to travel a lot more, not without Fred.

It looked as if charities would be major beneficiaries of Fred's death. It felt crass to put it that way, but that's the way it was.

I determined then, not to talk with anyone about the insurance payout. Even the children were not to know how much money was involved. I wanted them to be comfortable, but I also wanted them to behave responsibly. We had a better-than-comfortable life as it was, and we didn't need to go around flaunting our wealth.

How could I head off all the problems that we might face?

On Tuesday morning I met with Dr. Franks at the church. In the three days since we had held the tribute, the Fred Young Memorial Fund had grown to over five thousand dollars, and Dr. Franks was confident it would grow more over the next week or two.

"This is a fairly substantial amount for a memorial fund, Susan. Have you given any more thought to what you would like done with it?"

"Well, Dr. Franks, I've been thinking about it but I haven't come to any decision yet. I'm content for now to leave it in your hands as a trust. If our financial situation ends up being better than we expect, we will likely want to consider a number of options. But let's just wait and see.

"Meanwhile, what would be an appropriate donation for the church group that looked after the reception? They did such a marvelous job, even rushing back out for more supplies at one point!"

"We've never had a reception that big before. But I think they spent over three hundred dollars on the supplies..." and he looked at me somewhat hesitantly. "If you can't afford that much, I'm sure we can use some of the Memorial Fund receipts ..."

"I'm okay for now, Dr. Franks, and I would just as soon not touch the Memorial Fund, but I'm sure the circle could use some extra funds, so how about I donate five hundred dollars to them?"

"That's very generous of you, Susan. Are you sure you can afford it?"

"I'm sure we can, but thank you for asking. Ben Gruvel, says we're likely to receive a substantial settlement from the federal government, and if that happens, we'll have nothing to worry about financially."

Dr. Franks seemed somewhat surprised, but he recovered quickly, "All right, but just in case, Susan, why don't I just hold onto this check for a few days before depositing it."

Another paternalistic figure trying to look after me!

Again I smiled. Why did I feel I had to smile when I was rejecting offers from men who wanted to advise and control me? "No, Dr. Franks, trust me. I know what I'm doing. We can afford this, and we will likely want to do more in the near future."

I held out the promise of more mostly because I expected I would, indeed, donate more to the church in Fred's name; but I also did it to let him know I intended to be in charge of my own life and that I was willing to live with the consequences if I made any mistakes. That was, after all, a major belief of mine: Everyone should live by the motto, "Think hard, make your own decisions, and accept the consequences."

Ben called me a week later to warn me that the news would be out soon about the government payout to the survivors of the victims and to confirm that because of Fred's income and age, we would, indeed, be receiving a check for six million dollars during the first week of October.

"Have you given any more thought to what you would like to do with and about the money?"

"Yes, I have. I liked Charles' suggestion of setting up a foundation, but I don't think I want to do much more than think about it right now. I need to see a lawyer soon to set up all these things. I guess managing money isn't cheap, is it."

"Great idea, Susan. But you know the press will be onto you first thing tomorrow. What will you say to them?"

"Hmmm. I guess I'll say pretty much what I've said all along, that we have enough to live on for now, that with our savings and with Fred's life insurance, we expect to be okay financially. ... No, that won't be good, will it."

"No, it won't, especially not for the families that received only a few hundred thousand dollars in comparison with the settlement you'll get."

"Explain to me again why I'm getting so much, and why others might not get much at all."

"The whole plan is to head off lawsuits. If Fred were negligently killed in an accident, the courts would look at his past income, his age, and his expected future income in awarding damages. They'd likely come up with a number even larger than six million dollars. But if someone the same age earning only ten dollars an hour were killed in a similar accident, the payout to the family would be much smaller because the loss in income to them would be much less. At least that's the basis of the settlement."

"That makes sense but I can also understand why poorer families would be resentful about the wealthier families receiving larger payments."

"I can understand it, too, but keep in mind that their loss of expected future income is also much smaller."

"I'll have to think some more about questions I might get. I want to be prepared. You know, like, 'Don't you feel bad about getting so much money when others are getting less?' Ugh."

The news of the settlement payouts hit the wire services overnight. There wasn't an itemized list of who would receive how much, but it didn't take much digging for anyone to figure out that Fred had been a high earner and that he would likely have earned a lot of money over the next twenty-to-thirty years.

At 7:30, the phone rang. It was Jeremy Hall, which didn't surprise me.

"Ms. Young, this is Jeremy Hall. Have you heard the news about a payment that is being made by the federal government to the families of the victims of the terrorist attacks?"

I remembered from my days at Arkero: turn a question back on the reporter to get more information before answering.

"Yes, Mr. Hall, I've heard a bit. I don't know the details though. Perhaps you can fill me in?"

"It looks as if people who were younger and who had high expected lifetime incomes will receive the most. By my rough calculations, you stand to receive about six million dollars. What's your reaction to that?"

"Wow!"

"Just, 'Wow!'?"

"That's a lot of money!"

"Yes, it is. What do you think you'll do with it?"

"I have no idea! I can't even guess at this point. I'm sure we'll use some for the children's educations, of course, and some for our continued living expenses. I'll probably want to put some into a retirement savings plan for myself, too. But it's really hard to know. I'll probably just leave the funds with Ben Gruvel of Klein-Staily to manage for us until we have a better idea. He is already looking after things like this for us."

"Of course. One more thing, Ms. Young."

I knew what it would be --- the 'fairness' question. "Yes?"

"According to the news releases we received overnight, families like yours will receive large sums but other families will receive much less."

Bless him for not having tried to play the "fairness card" ... yet.

Instead he simply asked, "What's your reaction to the news that different families will receive different amounts?"

I thought to myself, "Redirect the question to get more information."

"Have the news releases said anything about the basis for the payments? I wonder if that would explain the differences."

"Yes, they said, and I'll read this to you, 'There have been numerous class-action suits filed on behalf of the victims suing the federal government, its agencies, and its contractors for damages resulting from the terrorist attacks on September 11th of this year. To deal with these claims expeditiously, the government is using tables based on life expectancy, work practices, past court settlements, and past incomes to determine the lost income for each victim's survivors.'"

"So, court awards and settlements are based not so much on what people need or what they have, but on what they have lost, in some sense?"

"I think that's right."

"If that's the case, I think the government is doing nothing the courts wouldn't do but without nearly so much legal hassle and expense? That will probably save the taxpayers millions of dollars."

I added, "And, off the record, I can imagine some law firms are not entirely pleased…"

I shouldn't have said that, but I thought it would be interesting to see whether Jeremy Hall's newfound integrity in dealing with our family would hold up.

He laughed and said, "Ms. Young, I'm sure you're right, and you needn't worry; I won't report anything you say to me if you say it's off the record. You have been very helpful. Thank you very much. And let me add that … well, I think I enjoy interviewing you."

Huh? What was that about? Whatever it was, I'd have to file it for future reference.

I fielded a few more calls from reporters that morning and told them all the same thing. Then, at about eleven o'clock, I called Thelma Hazelton.

"Thelma, I need to get out, away from reporters. How about we go to lunch, my treat? There's a new French place that opened last spring called 'Le Voltaire'. Would you like to give it a try?"

"Oh, I've heard great things about it! I was supposed to get a pedicure at noon today, but I'll cancel it for sure. Let's do this!"

Over lunch, I explained to Thelma some details about the government money we were expecting. "I'm sure the papers will be reporting this by tonight or maybe tomorrow morning, but the federal government is imposing a settlement on all the possible class action claims and we're going to receive maybe five or six million dollars."

I let that sink in.

Thelma's eyes got bigger and she said, "Well, ..." and then she said, "Wow! ..." followed by "That doesn't begin to make up for losing Fred, does it. ... And it'll sure change your lives."

"It certainly will, Thelma, and I'm not sure how to deal with it. With our savings and with Fred's life insurance, plus with my going back to work, we'd have been fine money-wise. We really don't need this, but I still have to deal with it somehow."

I didn't tell her how much we had saved up, nor how much we would receive as life insurance. I didn't want **anyone** to know. And to make the point stronger, I emphasized that I was planning to go back to work soon.

"To think that earlier this week I was worried about what to do about a few thousand dollars in the Memorial Fund at the church, and now this. It's almost overwhelming. Almost."

Thelma smiled, "When you say 'Almost', that means it isn't overwhelming. What do you have in mind, Susan? Huh?"

"I think I might like to start a foundation in Fred's name."

"What a great idea! What would the foundation do?"

"I'm not sure, but I'm thinking maybe something to do with financial aid for rural youngsters who want to go to college? But I just don't know."

I looked at her seriously and asked, "What do you think?"

"That sounds good, but would you have to spend time reading and assessing all the applications for financial aid each year? Or would you just turn that job over to the colleges?"

"I hadn't even thought that far. I'll have to think about it a lot more."

"Let me know if I can help," said Thelma.

Those words were music to my ears. I so much wanted her to be a part of my life, and yet I knew my life was going to change in ways I couldn't anticipate.

"I sure will, Thelma. Thanks!"

Chapter 26 – Teen Relationships

We ordered a very French lunch and had a wonderful time chatting about nearly everything. At one point I smiled, perhaps a bit shyly, and asked, "You know about Seth and Liz, don't you?"

Thelma was quite obviously surprised. She almost shrieked, "What?"

"Liz seems to be attracted to Seth, and she says the feeling is mutual."

Thelma got a very serious look on her face.

"Well!!!! That's the last time he's going over to your house to play games in the basement until you install a video camera down there!"

And then she burst into laughter.

"I had no idea, girl. I was glad the children were getting along so well, and I think it's cute. … Seth, huh? … when Aaron is her age. Interesting. Well, I guess it's time to have 'The Talk' with the boys."

"Good. I had 'The Talk' with Liz and Timothy last Sunday, and it went pretty well. It'll be good if Seth and Aaron hear it from your end, too."

And then I got a bit of a scared look on my face.

"Thelma, I have no idea what goes on with teen romances these days, and it does concern me. I love you and your family, and like you I think it's 'cute', but it worries me."

"It worries me just a bit, too. Teen romances don't often end well. I hope they're both mature enough to keep the family friendships intact no matter what else happens."

"I'm not sure," I said, "but I think Liz's friend Becky and your Aaron might also be involved somewhat. It seemed like a double date the last time the four of them were together in our basement."

"Aha! Aaron did say something about Becky. She lives over on the other side of the reservoir, and she's in his and Liz's class at school. I don't think I've met her, though."
Suddenly Thelma got an evil-pushy-mom look. "What's her dad do? What's her mom like? Is she a tramp?" and we both laughed.

"Wait a minute!" I stopped laughing and glared at Thelma. Putting my hand over my heart, I asked, "Are you implying that *my Liz* is a tramp? And what kind of playboys are you raising, huh?"

After we stopped laughing, I got serious. "Thelma, just so you know, during my version of 'The Talk' Timothy did ask me about sex. I promised I would get them some good books on sex and teen-age relationships. And I think you should know that Liz seemed **very** interested. I'm not sure they're ready for this; I know I'm not ready for them to be ready for it, but I do want them to have a decent idea about the importance of caring and relationships. I hope that's okay with you."

"It sure is. But I'm not about to pass down our copy of **The Joy of Sex** to the boys, so after lunch let's hit Barnes and Noble to get some books."

At the bookstore, we found maybe a dozen books that looked promising. We were both a bit embarrassed, and we even tittered a little as we took them to the reading area to sort through. I don't know why we were embarrassed, though; I'm sure lots of parents have bought books about sex for their children.

"Should we get about two each and then share them?" Thelma asked.

"I don't know. ... If we do that, will it be like we're suggesting they experiment? I'm not ready for them to do that, and I don't think they are either, to be honest."

"I get that. Let's downplay it then, but we do want them to be prepared and knowledgeable, don't we?"

"Absolutely!"

And then I wondered out loud, "Oh! I wonder at what age I should get Liz started on the pill."

I tried for a penetrating look, then, as I asked, "As the potential grandmother of my daughter's child, what do *you* think?"

Thelma laughed, "My parents started me on the pill when I was in 11th grade. What about you?"

"My parents didn't know. I had to go to student health at K-State to get on the pill. I don't want our children to have to sneak around like that, though. So.... what do you think?

"Two months after I started on the pill, I started having sex. I think Dale and I both accepted that we'd been 'active' before we met each other, but we didn't talk about it too much. What about you and Fred?"

"Hah! I spent two years on the pill for nothing. Fred and I were both virgins when we met. I'd had several sexual 'encounters' in high school, but no intercourse because I was afraid of getting pregnant."

"Yeah, it's important that the kids not have children until they're reasonably well set. Everything I read tells me that having children too early is a major reason young people aren't very happy later in life."

I pondered. "I wonder how many parents of boyfriends and girlfriends have talks like this. Imagine if I called up Sandra's parents – she's the girl that Timothy seems attached to – and suggested a parental get-together about teen sex!"

"Never gonna happen," I added. "Are you going to call Becky's parents?" and we laughed some more.

We both selected three books on teen relationships and sex and agreed we would suggest sharing them. I was still uncertain about whether that was a good idea, but it seemed preferable to having the children sneak around sharing the books they were most interested in.

That night at dinner, I told Timothy and Liz that I'd bought the books and showed them the books. They were a bit embarrassed but they were also pleased and eager to get started on them.

"Oh, I think Becky has this one," said Liz. "I read parts of it at her house. It's pretty good but a little bossy. 'Do this'. 'Don't do that'. But it seems ok, I guess."

So … she had been reading about sex on her own and not just in romance novels. I was actually pleased, even relieved.

"Just so you know, the topic came up at lunch today with Thelma."

"Oh Mom!" said Liz. She was clearly embarrassed. "How could you?"

"Well, it turns out that Thelma didn't know you and Seth are 'going together', and we're both fine with it. We just want you all to be careful and to have good, healthy relationships."

"Oh Mom!"

"We went to the bookstore together to buy some books; she bought some different ones for Aaron and Seth, but we'd be happy if you four share any of the books you find particularly good. You'll notice that we focused on books that deal with the importance of relationships. Even if these relationships don't work out, it is really crucial that you continue to be pleasant and kind with the other person."

I looked at Timothy, who seemed to be trying to avoid eye contact.

"What do you think, Timothy?"

"I think I need to read some of these books. I don't know, but I think Sandra probably has read some already."

After a pause, he asked, "Mom, is it okay if I don't know stuff but she does?"

"It sure is. As I told you, that's how it was between your father and me."

"Well, we've had some information in our health science class and again in biology class, but the teachers never really seemed to feel comfortable with it. I'm looking forward to getting into these books. Which one do you recommend?"

"I don't know. They all looked reasonably good while we were looking through them at the bookstore. Liz didn't think so much of this one I guess, so why not try one of the others."

"Okay," and he picked it up and started upstairs.

"Timothy, maybe you should do your homework before you start reading about sex. You, too, Liz."

They both laughed and chimed together, "Sure thing, Mom."

I hoped I wasn't implicitly giving them the idea of having orgies. And I knew I didn't want our basement to become known as a sex pit. I prayed I was doing the right thing.

I wished Fred was with me. I really wanted to talk with him about it.

And so while I cleaned up the kitchen after supper, I imagined I was talking with him and tried to imagine what he might say. It was hard.

> Me: Fred, the children are involved in teen relationships now, and I'm just a little concerned.
>
> Fred: What's there to be concerned about?
>
> Me: Don't be so quick to just write it off! Teen-age love can be good but it can be devastating when it falls apart.
>
> Fred: We'll be there for them when that happens. The kids are strong, and you're good. It'll be fine.
>
> Me: But what if someone gets pregnant?
>
> Fred: They're not having sex are they!!?
>
> Me: Not yet. At least not that I know of. But it's going to happen. Teen-age sex is much more common now than it was twenty-five years ago, when you and I were teens.
>
> Fred: Good grief. Don't even let them date then!
>
> Me: That's how I feel, too, but they're already involved with others. Liz is 'going with' Seth Hazleton. I know he's older than she is, but they're a good match. I can't help thinking about them and hoping they'll be careful with each other.
>
> Fred: Seth? Not Aaron? Hmmm.
>
> Me: Why 'Hmmm'?
>
> Fred: They're both good boys, but a three-year age difference at their ages seems pretty substantial to me. He'd better not "take advantage" of her. Will Liz be okay, seeing someone that much older than she is?
>
> Me: Oh, Fred, sure she will. She's a tough little lady, and she has gumption. She won't be pushed around or talked into anything she

doesn't want to do, that's for sure.

Fred: What about Timothy?

Me: I think he's shyer, more the way you were. He's seeing a girl named Sandra. Do you remember his ever mentioning her?

Fred: No, I don't. What's she like?

Me: I have no idea. Well, yes, I do. So far, their dates have been group activities like bowling; and her parents had a bunch of the young people over to their place for a barbecue one evening. I haven't even asked what her parents do or where they live.

I laughed to myself.

Me: I'd better get on that. Oh, and Timothy thinks she's more experienced about dating than he is.

Fred: That is like me, all right. It wouldn't take much to be more experienced than me when I was his age.

Me: Well, what should I do?

Fred: I don't know. Maybe hope they meet people like you who will help them and guide them?

Me: Oh, thanks. But seriously, I'm at a bit of a loss. I went out with Thelma, and we each bought books about teen relationships for them. I'm hoping those will help.

Fred: It seems to me they also need to be lectured about safe sex and birth control.

Me: Yes! They say they've had the talks about those things in school, but I'm still worried.

Fred: Don't be. They're good kids, and they're smart. They'll look after themselves.

Me: I don't know. I hope you're right.

Fred: As long as they're alive, they'll be okay.

Well, that didn't work very well. I was hoping to get more detailed advice from my pretend conversation; I should have known better.

But my imagining what Fred would say became more helpful as I thought about it. My imaginary conversation made me feel close to him, and it reassured me in some vague way. Also, it helped me understand that yes, indeed, no matter what happened, they would be okay.

> Me: Oh Fred, I miss you so much! I wish you were here. I wish you hadn't gone to New York that day. Oh Fred …

And I began to cry. I went into the half-bath and washed my face with cold water. I knew the children would be okay. That helped.

But I would still try to make sure the children looked after their futures while they were exploring their teen relationships.

The next morning just as the children were walking past the Hazeltons' house, Thelma called. She could barely contain herself.

"Susan, we've got to get together this morning!" She was laughing, almost hysterically. "I hope you have nothing on this morning and can come up for coffee."

Thelma greeted me at the door, smiling and stifling her laughter.

As I sat at their kitchen table, she poured the coffee and blurted it out. "You should have heard the boys this morning! I had 'The Talk' with them last night. Actually, Dale and I did it together, and it went well, but as they were leaving the house this morning, Aaron whined to Seth, 'I guess you'll be walking to school with Liz now. Does that mean I'm stuck in a relationship with Timothy?" He actually said it that way!"

All I could think was that I wasn't ready yet for gay relationships in my family. I'd welcome them if they happened; I just needed to prepare myself. But I laughed along with Thelma.

"Poor Aaron," I said. "But maybe he and Liz can meet up with Becky after they drop Seth and Timothy at high school."

"I think Becky is sort of Aaron's default girlfriend. I think he'd like to be with Liz. I hope they sort it all out amicably."

"So, You and Dale had 'The Talk' with the boys last night. How did it go?"

Thelma laughed again. "Well I don't think Dale was ready for it; to tell the truth, I don't think he'd ever have been ready for it."

"I don't think Fred would have been ready, either," I added.

"Neither of us had picked up that Seth was interested in Liz. After supper, I filled Dale in and then we called the boys to come to the living room to talk with us. I opened it up with 'So Seth, Ms. Young tells me you and Liz are going together.'"

"You should have seen his face! It turned bright red. Anyway, I think the talk went pretty well. At least our children will know we care about them and that we want them to care about each other, too."

*Chapter 27 – * **The Memorial Fund**

"Susan, I told Dale about your financial situation. He knew you and Fred had always been … 'careful with money' was the phrase he used. But the big payout from the government surprised him. I hope it's okay that I told him."

"Of course. I really don't think husbands and wives should have secrets, but I know we all do … did… do… did… Oh, Thelma …"

Thelma came around the table and hugged me. I really needed that. I'd missed having a loving, comforting hug when I needed one.

After I settled down, I asked, "Did Dale have any suggestions about what we should do financially?"

"Mostly he was envious, I think," replied Thelma, "but he tried not to show it because he really doesn't want to be like that. But other than that, he likes the idea of your creating a Foundation."

"I think I'll keep a small amount of the government money, as a backstop in case things go wrong somehow," I said, "but I'll also add in whatever is in the Memorial Fund that is being held by Dr. Franks at the church."

"Dale wondered the same thing I did, though. How would you decide who gets the money and how much?"

"I'll really have to think carefully about that," I said. "I want the money to go to students who wouldn't be able to go to college otherwise or who might have to work more than they should to stay there, but I have no idea how to get them to apply for the money, and I have no idea how to decide. I guess I'll need a board of directors and all that nonsense. Ugh."

"Have you seen a lawyer about it?"

"Not yet. Ben recommended one, Charles Leamer, but he has other legal dealings with Ben and others at Klein-Staily, and I want one who would be independent. So both he and Ben recommended Allison Cameron at the Costello firm. Do you know anything about her or them?"

"Not a thing. I've never even heard of them, but that just means that they don't advertise where I might see their ads; maybe that's a good thing?"

I saw Allison Cameron the next week. When we met, she said, "We're a large firm of specialists, Ms. Young. I'll be happy to help you with your estate planning and management, but then I'll turn you over to Harold Yoder. He's our foundations specialist."

First, we drew up a will, leaving my estate to the children, divided equally, and with their children (if and when they had any) to get their shares if my children died before I did.

"You have a potentially very large estate, Ms. Young. This will do for now, but you may want to adjust things after a few years. Most people do change their wills as circumstances change, and it's fairly easy to do."

"Okay," I said. "I also know I should specify someone to look after the children if I die before they come of age, whatever that means. Right?"

"Yes, and we'll need to deal with several issues here. First, who would you like to have appointed as guardians?"

"Fred and I had already named Dale and Thelma Hazelton in our earlier wills," I said. "I'd like to continue with that."

"Fine. And do you want them to manage your financial estate in trust for your children, too? It could be a large amount of money, judging from everything you have told me."

"Actually, I'd like Ben Gruvel of Klein-Staily to manage all the trusts and potential trusts. Will that be okay?" I love and trust both the Gruvels and the Hazeltons. But my concern is that if for some reason the children decide they want a lot of money, it would be easier and better for Ben to assess the situation than if the Hazeltons were involved. My children are smart and can be persuasive; I'd like to take that pressure away from the Hazeltons."

"I see. I don't have many clients who think that way, but it makes sense. So now let's set up the trusts you want for the children."

Allison explained all the legal ins and outs about creating trusts for the children. She suggested that I create some education plans for the children and create separate trusts for them as well. The tax issues were overwhelming, and I just deferred to her on all of those complications.
"All we're doing today is creating the trusts and accounts," she said. "As the money arrives, you can have Ben Gruvel put it into the various trusts.

I was happy with all of her suggestions, and so we turned our attention to naming Ben as trustee for the trusts. I wasn't happy with having to name a backup trustee in case Ben died before the trusts were given to the children, but I asked her to have Ben designate a chain of backup trustees. I knew he would choose people who were honest and who had no axe to grind about Fred's mortgage-backed bonds.

- - -

Next she called in Harold Yoder to discuss foundations with me.

Harold carefully and clearly went through what would be required to create a tax-free foundation, but he did so by asking me questions about my goals. It was instructive and it helped me understand what I wanted.

I wanted to help rural and small-town students go to college or university, but I didn't want to have to entice them to apply for scholarships, and I didn't necessarily want them to have to go through the college or university admissions offices to apply. What's more, I wasn't eager to have to decide that only certain colleges would benefit from being able to offer the scholarships. Also, I didn't want the funds to go to students who wouldn't need them.

"I'd like the scholarships to be available for any student from a rural area or small town in Kansas or Nebraska who wants to attend any accredited college," I said. "But I would somehow like the scholarships to have an impact on students who wouldn't be able to afford to go to college otherwise. They wouldn't have to be the top students; they can just be students with reasonable potential and from less-well-off backgrounds. Can that be done?"

Harold assured me it could be done but the details would require work.

"I expect to be able to start with a little over five million dollars for these scholarships, but I want the funds to be ongoing; I mean I want funds to be available until long after we're all dead."

"Then a foundation with an endowment is what you want," Harold said.

"So once I endow the foundation ... let's call it the Frederick Robert Young Foundation, okay? ... Once I endow it, then it will be up to the foundation's directors to determine how the funds are used?"

"You can provide a statement of goals, but you can't get too detailed about what people can do with the funds a hundred years from now. To create a foundation that will do what you want, we'll have to incorporate it, and you'll need a board of directors. We can structure it so that you will have control for as long as you want it. The important thing at this stage is to make sure the board of directors is always composed of people you like and trust."

"Okay." I immediately thought of Thelma and Ben, but then I worried, "I guess I can't have Ben Gruvel as a director, can I, since I want him to manage the endowment funds."

"That's right. But we can still structure it so that he sits in on board meetings if you wish."

"Good. The one thing I must insist on," I said, "is that the Foundation never commit to spending more than two percent of the funds in the endowment in any given year," and then I explained to Harold that the funds should be invested mostly in stocks with some in bonds and even less in liquid assets.

He looked at me somewhat questioningly. "Do you want this in the charter of the foundation?" he asked.

"Yes, at least some guidelines and ranges would be good. I don't want to be too conservative or too aggressive with the endowment."

In the end, we decided to create the foundation with me as the chair and with control, but with Thelma and Dr. Franks as unpaid directors. It took several weeks of meetings with Harold and Ben and Thelma to work out some of the details. It was a great experience for both Thelma and me as we learned more about what she called 'sweating the details' and what Harold called 'preparing for contingencies'. Both concepts suited me well.

- - -

Once the details were clarified, I met again with Dr. Franks to discuss both the memorial fund and the foundation.

"Susan, the memorial fund is now over six thousand dollars," he said with some pleasure. "What would you like to do with that money?"

I explained to him that I wanted to use the memorial fund as part of the foundation endowment.

He looked a bit disappointed, and I knew he had hoped the money would be used in the church, and so I headed off his concerns as quickly as I could.

"Dr. Franks, I know that names are important, and I know that money can get switched all around pretty easily. Here's my full plan, and it includes the church."

I handed him a check for one hundred thousand dollars.

"I am making this donation to the church in Fred's name. My preference would be that it be used to create or add to the endowment fund for the church to provide for ongoing operational expenses. I know it won't generate a lot of income each year, but it could provide a base for building a larger endowment fund."

He was stunned. "Susan, this is so generous. I don't know what to say. We do have an endowment fund, but it isn't very large. This will be a great addition to it. But again, 'Can you afford this?'"

"I've spoken with both Ben Gruvel of Klein-Staily and Harold Yoder from Costello, and they both assure me I can afford it. Fred and I had plenty of savings, plus he had a good life insurance plan. We don't really need all the money we're going to get from the government settlement, and so I've created some trusts for the children and set some aside for my own living expenses and retirement, but I've decided to use the bulk of that government payout to create The Frederick Robert Young Foundation. The reason I want to add the memorial funds to the foundation endowment is that I think it would be a great way to show others what is happening with their money. What do you think?"

He was completely taken off-guard, but he recovered quickly. "I think I see what you're saying. You could leave the six thousand dollars here and donate another ninety-four thousand dollars to the church, or you can donate a hundred thousand dollars and then use the memorial funds for a part of the foundation endowment. It works out the same way, I guess, at least in terms of the dollars and cents."

"Yes, but if we say we're adding the memorial fund proceeds to the foundation endowment, I'm hoping that will attract even more donations to the foundation from outside the church ..."

Dr. Franks readily agreed to serve as a director of the foundation.

So did Thelma Hazelton. But I could see my life was changing, and so one day I said to her, "Thelma, I wonder if you would consider being the managing director of the foundation... I'd still want to maintain some minor control, but would you like to be salaried and look after the day-to-day details?"

She was flabbergasted. I hoped I hadn't insulted her. I knew that, like me, she hadn't really done much work outside the home over the past fifteen years. I had no idea what her qualifications were, but I knew she was careful, intelligent, and considerate.

"Susan, you don't know what you're asking! You don't know if I'm qualified or if I can do the job. This is just so ... weird."

"Thelma, I know you pretty well after fifteen years of close friendship. I know you're smart and you're careful, and I know you have basically the same values that Fred and I have ... had ... have ..."

The correction probably wasn't necessary, but at least I wasn't choking up and crying when I made it.

"You could do almost all the work from your home," I added, "and the foundation would cover all your office expenses. Give it some thought."

She hesitated about six seconds, staring at me the entire six seconds. "Okay, I've given it some thought. I'll do it!"

- - -

After a few meetings with Ben, Harold, and Dr. Franks, Thelma and I called a press conference to be held again in the large Sunday School classroom at the church. We made it clear in the announcement of the press conference that I would be discussing what I would do with the funds we would be receiving from the government.

We quickly realized that to fit everything into everyone else's schedules, we would have to hold the press conference at 8am on Thursday; both Ben and Harold would have to leave early, but we wanted them there initially to emphasize the importance of the Foundation.

This time, there were no lights, just one person with a hand-held video camera, and only four reporters. Dr. Franks made sure there was coffee available, and we brought in some muffins from a gourmet bakery.

After thanking them for coming, I opened with a semi-prepared speech:

> Today we are announcing the creation of the Frederick Robert Young Foundation, to honor the memory of my husband, our children's father, who died during the terrorist attacks on September 11th. We are grateful to everyone who has contributed to the Frederick Young Memorial Fund. Those contributions, along with a sizable portion of the insurance proceeds, and with pledges from Fred's friends and colleagues at Klein-Staily, will provide an endowment that will fund the Foundation's activities for the foreseeable future.
>
> The primary goal of the Foundation is to provide academic assistance for young people from rural and agricultural backgrounds. Both Fred and I grew up in rural areas, and we were deeply indebted to those who helped us along the way. It is the hope of our children and me that others will be similarly helped with the financial assistance provided by this foundation.

As expected, Jeremy Hall had several questions. His first one was, "Ms. Young, can you give us some idea how large the foundation endowment will be?

"We are in the early stages of establishing the legal framework for the Foundation but we wanted to make this announcement now to reassure everyone who has contributed to Fred's Memorial Fund that every penny of their contributions and much, much more will be put to good use and that a lasting memorial will be created in Fred's name.

"We will be using all of the contributions to the Fred Young Memorial Fund for the foundation. Thanks to the efforts of Dr. Frank, Ben Gruvel, and Harold Yoder, as well as you Mr. Hall, we have now raised over ten thousand dollars in donations and pledges for that fund, and we hope others will continue to contribute to the fund.

"But also..." and I hesitated for emphasis and dramatic effect, "we will be using nearly all of the six million dollars we have received from the federal government settlement to endow the foundation."

That revelation caused quite a stir... And several more questions.

Jennifer Amin from NBC asked, "That's a lot of money. How will it be managed, and how will it be dispersed?"

"Well, of course Ben Gruvel of Klein-Staily will be managing the endowment for us. As part of his and Klein-Staily's contribution to the foundation, and in addition to their already sizable cash donations, they have agreed to charge a minimal rate for the management fees, well below their costs, for which we are very grateful.

"The dispersal method is yet to be determined by the Board of Directors of the Frederick Robert Young Foundation, but we plan to fund scholarships to any accredited college or university for students from small towns and rural areas in Kansas and Nebraska. The children and I talked it over together and with others, and we all agreed that this foundation would be an excellent way to honor Fred's memory."

Jeremy Hall: "Have you created a Board of Directors? Who is on it?"

"Mr. Yoder from the Costello law firm," and I gestured to him, "has drawn up the incorporation papers for the Foundation. As much as I would like to have him and Ben Gruvel on a five-member board of directors for the corporation, we wish to avoid any potential for conflicts of interest, and so we are limiting the board of directors to include just me, Dr. Franks from the Third United Church," and I indicated him, "and Thelma Hazleton, who will also serve as day-to-day manager of the Foundation. The five of us will meet together to establish the by-laws of the foundation and to clarify the dispersal process."

Back to Jennifer Amin: "Ms. Young, you are giving away almost all of the money you will receive from the government. What will you live on?"

Was she really that nosy? That dense? Oh well...

"Fred and I saved quite a bit while he was alive; also, we have some life insurance proceeds, and I am considering returning to the labor force. And I'm holding back a small portion of the government settlement funds to prepare for any contingencies."

Before she could pursue the details, I added, "With the help of Ben Gruvel and the help of Harold Yoder's partner, Allison Cameron, I have also created some trusts for the children to provide for their education. I'm not being frivolous in creating the Frederick Robert Young Foundation," I smiled, almost as a put-down, "Our family will be comfortable without most of that government settlement money."

I continued, "Fred was an important man in the lives of his family and many other people, and we'd like to honor Fred by doing something to help others. The children understand this and are in complete agreement with the plan. As they come of age, it is our expectation that they will be added to the Board of Directors."

Chapter 28 – **Constant Changes**

Several weeks later, Dr. Franks called me. "Susan, an opening on the Church Council has come up because the Oliver family is moving to California. I wonder if you would be willing to serve on the Council."

"Gee, Dr. Franks, I'm flattered that you asked, but I have no idea. What does it involve?"

"Church Council meets monthly to oversee the operations of the church, something like a Board of Directors. All the other Council Members agreed that you would be a good choice to serve on the Council. It seems all the more appropriate now, after your large donation."

"Well… Can you give me a rough idea how much time is involved in addition to the monthly meetings? I'm not sure I'm ready to make any major time commitments right now; I want to make sure I can still provide time and support for my children."

"That's why we would like you to be on the Church Council, Susan. You're level-headed and careful."

"Thanks, Dr. Franks. So… how much time, roughly?"

"I think the others on the Council spend about four or five hours each month on church business. It's far from onerous. And they've all agreed that newer members of Council will have less responsibility as they join and accustom themselves to the organization and the month-to-month operations. Oh, and Susan, please call me Will."

"Okay… Will, may have a day or two to think about this? I promise I won't need forty days of wandering in the wilderness."

Will actually laughed. "Of course!"

The very next week, the Citizens' Review Board for the police department invited me to join them as well. And so did the Board of Directors of The United Way. I accepted all those invitations, but I turned down most further requests to join various boards of directors.

I could see where my life seemed to be headed, at least temporarily. I didn't need to work to earn money, and organizations would ask me to join them. It was part of what Ben had warned me about. They wanted my time, and there was an expectation that members of the boards would make sizeable contributions to the organizations.

I was both honored and insulted by the requests. I was honored that they thought I could do the job, but I was disappointed that they didn't recognize that I had some abilities along these lines until *after* I received so much money; clearly the organizations were after large donations.

The Church Council invitation I understood: Fred and I had always been generous donors to the church. The invitation to join them wasn't necessarily to get me to donate more than I already had. Similarly, we had always donated to The United Way; but it was pretty clear that the managers of The United Way hoped and expected I would increase my donation to them if I was on the board of directors.

The Citizen's Review Board for the police department puzzled me. They didn't want any money from me, and I had no background that would be useful to them, so why invite me to join their board?

I soon learned that one of the other members of the review board was with the Costello Law firm and had heard about me from Allison Cameron and Harold Yoder. The board members watched videos of both of my press conferences and liked the way I dealt with questions, and felt they could use a spokesperson like me on the board.

I turned down all other invitations to join boards and donate to charities with one exception. Several contacts through the Citizens Review Board put me in touch an organization called LOST; it provided counseling to teenagers who had lost one or both parents in accidents. I donated to LOST, and I was pleased to actually meet with them to help talk with the teens, to help them work through their issues. I hoped what I would learn through LOST would also help me to help Timothy and Liz.

Timothy and Liz seemed to be coping well with the changes. I was determined to be a nurturing and supportive mother, but the demands on my time continued to grow during those first few months. Not only were various groups inviting me to join them, but I also had frequent meetings about the foundation, and I had to run the household, too. I tried to schedule most meetings during school hours so that I could be home for the children as much as possible, but because so many board members of the different organizations had full-time jobs, we had to schedule a lot of the board meetings for the evenings. I didn't like it, and that was a major reason I declined any further invitations. I wanted to be with my children or at least be there for them. For those few months in the autumn of 2001, I was home for them most of the time, but I was out at board meetings on average once a week.

One evening in November I asked the children about their thoughts and feelings about losing their father. I told them I had joined LOST, and I wanted their input.

"It hasn't been too bad, Mom" said Timothy. "Don't get me wrong: I miss Dad – A LOT!! – but everything else seems to be pretty much the same as before and going ok."

"I agree," said Liz, "but I miss, like, the sense of family we used to have. Like, the Sunday breakfasts as a family, and just, like, sitting around as a family. It's just not the same without Dad here."

"Now that you mention it, I miss that, too," added Timothy. "You're here, and you're amazing, Mom, but it's not the same without Dad here."

The more they talked, the sadder I felt – I wasn't enough for them. Well, of course I wasn't, but hearing them say it so explicitly wasn't easy.

I tried not to show my sadness. "What advice would you give other children who have lost a parent?"

"Think about the good times," said Timothy right away. "It's almost like praying, but at least once a day I think about different things about Dad. Sure, some not-so-good times pop into my head now and then, but mostly they're good, and I love the feeling."

Liz nodded. "I think preparing our talks for the tribute/memorial was, like, a big help like that, Mom. Doing that helped me get through these past few months; like, I keep thinking of more things I could have said."

"Thanks," I said. "And now a tougher question, maybe, and I want you to be honest with me. What could I have done, and what can I do, to help with the transition to not having your father?"

The children seemed confused. Maybe they were just reluctant?

"Come on," I said. "Be honest."

"Mom," offered Timothy, "sometimes during that first week it felt a bit like a party atmosphere. I know it wasn't, and I know I enjoyed spending so much time with the Hazeltons and Gruvels, but somehow it didn't feel right."

Liz disagreed. "I thought it was good. Like, I was happy to have the distractions, and I was happy to feel, like, the love and support from everyone."

Liz continued, "Like I told you then, Mom, I thought you were being overprotective. Sorta like you'd lost your husband and weren't going to let anything go wrong with your children."

"These are both helpful and right," I said. "I know it felt like a party atmosphere at times, but I was so distraught and I really needed comfort and support. And, yes, without your father here I felt as if I had to protect you from every possible evil. Anything else?"

They shook their heads.

I went on then. "Speaking of protecting you…"

I smiled tentatively and they looked apprehensive.

"Don't get pregnant, Liz! And don't get any girl pregnant, Timothy! And don't get any STDs!"

They gasped and then giggle-smirked.

"Mom!" said Liz. "We aren't 'doing it'! I won't, at least not until I'm older. Seth knows this, and I think he's ok with waiting. If not, he can just take a cold shower."

Timothy looked embarrassed. "Sandra wants to have sex with me," he said. "But I'm too scared. I just don't know enough and I don't want her to get pregnant or anything."

Wow! This was not going in directions I felt comfortable with.

"Well, I'm certainly not going to encourage you to have sex before you're ready. And I'm not ready for you to be ready. I'm pleased that you're both being careful. So I guess I have a few thoughts:

"First, don't do anything you're not comfortable with. Don't be forced or threatened. I had a boyfriend in high school who threatened to dump me if I didn't have sex with him. He didn't get the chance: I dumped him instead.

"Second, I know I'm gone sometimes, leaving you children here alone. It will be tempting to have make-out parties here when I'm not here, and I don't want that to happen. We don't need for our house to become known as a place where teens can go to make out or even have sex. I will be very upset with everyone if that happens."

"Sandra says her parents are okay if we use her bedroom, and we've made out there a few times when I've gone over to her place to study," said Timothy, "but it's embarrassing."

Liz stared at him. "Really? I don't think I could do that."

And then she looked at me with what I took as a reassuring smile. "But I'm not there yet, Mom, so, like, you don't have to worry."

She continued, "Mom, tell us about the first time you had sex with Dad."

For some reason it felt okay to tell them.

"We were both twenty. We'd been dating for four or five months and I finally had to raise the topic." I smiled as I reminisced. "Your dad was so shy about it. Neither of us had actually had intercourse before, but I'd done some heavy petting … is that still a term? … back in high school."

"What was it like?" asked Timothy.

"I don't think it was great for either of us. We had very little idea what we were doing. We were both terribly eager, though, and we were both relieved to have finally had our first experience. The best part was that we'd had that experience together."

"Where were you, Mom?" asked Liz.

"We went to a budget motel. After we finished, we lay in bed and talked together. Your father actually asked me what he should do better the next time, and we laughed and hugged and slept together. It was much better for both of us the next morning." I smiled again, remembering.

And then I looked at Timothy. "Is Sandra on the pill? Can you trust her?"

Again he was embarrassed. "She says her mom put her on the pill as soon as she and I started going together. She showed them to me, and then she said, 'I've only been on the pill for a month, so we have to wait at least another month just to make sure they're going to work."

I was relieved. "I'm glad she's being conscientious about it."

"I think you both need to know that your first love is not likely to be your only love in life. Also, having sex with someone doesn't mean you have to stay with them. My high school friend Peggy didn't get that, and she was always devastated when a relationship ended. 'But I gave myself to him,' she'd say, 'he has to stay with me.' It doesn't work that way. Okay?"

They both nodded.

"One more thing," I added. "Don't let your obsessions with romance get in the way of your schoolwork. One of the best ways to ensure you'll be happier later in life is to do well in school now. So, go on. Go upstairs and get your schoolwork done. And stay off the phones for at least two hours."

Yes, phones. Plural. We'd had a second line put in, and I was wondering whether I might need a third line for myself; instead, I began relying on my cell phone more.

Chapter 29 – **The Holiday Season**

During the previous summer at one of our neighborhood parties, Fred announced that we would host the upcoming neighborhood Christmas party. Now, with the insurance money, I knew we could afford to do it up big, the way Fred would have wanted, but I wasn't sure I was ready for everything involved with hosting a big, fancy party.

In late November, Kathy Bergman, our next-door neighbor, stopped by for coffee. During our chat, she said, "I'm not sure how you feel about hosting the neighborhood Christmas party this year. I know you and Fred had been planning to have it, but would you like Ray and me to have it instead this year?"

I was so relieved I could barely contain myself. "That would be wonderful, Kathy! Thank you! We'll be happy to do it next year, but this year it would be too much, I think."

"Good. Ray and I had been wondering. We realized you have a lot to deal with, but we weren't sure if we should suggest it. We didn't know whether you would welcome the distraction of hosting the party or whether you'd like to defer it until you're better-settled."

"Thanks for understanding, Kathy. And yes, you're right, the distraction would be good in many ways; but I've had so many things to deal with lately. We'll do it here at our place next year for sure."

"Well, that answers another question we had," said Kathy. "I'm glad you're planning on staying here in the neighborhood. We weren't sure how you'd feel about staying here…"

That remark puzzled me. Maybe some people really do want to start fresh when they lose a spouse, but I was cherishing the memories of living in our family's home, and I certainly didn't want to take the children away from what had been their home all their lives.

"Kathy, I don't want to leave here, not even after the children go away to college. This was the first house that Fred and I bought, and it is chock full of memories for me and the children."

The Christmas season was both happy and difficult for us. The difficult part was that we missed Fred, and that was to be expected. The happy part was that everyone we knew tried to make sure we were included in the

Christmas get-togethers.

The children had school and church and sports and choir parties to attend. There was some awkwardness a few times when Timothy, Seth, and Sandra attended high school events while Liz, Aaron, and Becky attended middle school events. I could tell Liz was feeling left out those times, but she was excited about going to the high school's Christmas dance with Seth, and that made up for it.

The get-togethers for the children mostly involved dancing, games, food, and punch. A couple of them involved blind gift exchanges: bring a gift for someone of your sex. And there was great anguish in the household about whether the children would exchange gifts with their "going-withs", and, if so, what would be appropriate.

I had some simple advice for them: "If you'd like to give Seth or Sandra something for Christmas, let them know so that they can get something for you, too; discuss it with them, and don't try to make it a surprise. If you surprise them with a gift, they'll feel bad if they don't have one for you. And if they're not comfortable exchanging gifts, discuss it with them, but don't push it."

I cautioned the children not to go overboard. "Think of them as really close cousins that you would like to share something with, maybe." I remembered from high school when Tommy Jensen gave his girlfriend about two hundred dollars' worth of clothing. She didn't like most of it, returned it, and dumped him, keeping the money.

And then I added, "And do your gift exchanges with them when you're alone together; don't put your gifts to each other under the family Christmas trees. It should be for you two to share."

"Mahh -ahhm...." Liz said in an almost scolding voice. "We can figure some of these things out ourselves!"

I was about to apologize, but Timothy said, "Maybe you can, Liz, but I think I'd like a lot of help. Like, what should I buy Sandra? Do either of you have any suggestions?"

"Listen carefully," I said. "She'll indicate what she likes but if not, then maybe Liz and I can offer suggestions. But make it personal."

"What does that mean?" Liz challenged me.

"Well, first off, don't give gift cards! Show that you've put some thought into your gifts."

Liz was in a debating mood, "But Seth knows what he wants better than I do. Wouldn't a gift card be the best way for him to get what he wants?"

"You're probably right, Liz, but maybe he'd like something that *you* choose for him; that would be important, too."

I thought for a moment, and then I added, "You've both seen that little ceramic cat that I keep on my dresser? That was the first gift your father gave me for Christmas. We barely knew each other, really. We'd had one date, but when he stopped to visit me on his way home from college, he gave me that cat. He was pretty embarrassed, but I think he was trying to say he wanted us to "go together"; he just didn't know how."

"Had you given him any hints about what to get you, Mom?" asked Timothy.

"Not really. In fact, I don't remember ever mentioning cats, and I definitely wasn't into ceramic junk from the variety store, which is what it was, honestly. But I cherished it anyway because it came from him."

"Why did he choose *that*?" asked Timothy.

"I wasn't sure. I asked him a few years later 'What made you choose that cat as a Christmas gift?' He just said, 'I saw it in the store, and I don't know why, but I wanted to get it for you. I had no idea what you might or might not like, but I wanted to let you know I liked you a lot.'

"So I guess 'It's the thought that counts,' is true, at least sometimes."

It had become a tradition in the neighborhood to have our massive get together two Saturdays before Christmas. The Bergmans hadn't held it before, and Thelma and I were wondering what it would be like.

"They're Jewish, aren't they?" asked Thelma.

"I never asked," I said, "But yes I think they are. It'll be interesting to see what happens. I seem to recall their saying 'Merry Christmas' at times, but I wonder if we should say 'Happy Holidays' when we greet them."

And so I did just what I had been advising my children to do: ask.

I called Kathy and said, "Kathy, I'm wondering if you folks are Jewish."

She laughed and said, "Don't be shy about asking! I'm glad you did. Yes, we are, but we're quite reformed and quite modern."

"Well, are you okay to hold the 'neighborhood *Christmas* party' then?"

"Of course. Christmas is mostly a secular and seasonal holiday these days, so it doesn't matter to us. We're happy to wish people 'Merry Christmas' and to serve all sorts of wines and meats – even pork! As I said, we're quite reformed and quite modern."

I breathed a double sigh of relief that I hadn't committed a *faux pas* by asking and because they seemed happy to be hosting the party.

"Well, I think maybe just to be inclusive, perhaps we should call it a 'Holiday Party' from now on, especially this year when you're hosting it."

"Okay," said Kathy, "I like that. And just so you know, we will have some slightly ethnic appetizers in addition to the standard ones."

I could hear the smile and pride in her voice.

"That sounds fabulous! I can't wait to try some."

It was, indeed, fabulous. The Bergmans decorated their house and had special motion-activated ~~Christmas~~ *Holiday* lights and bells at their front door to welcome us all. They even had a Christmas tree! When I asked Ray Bergman about the tree, he developed a very fake serious, indignant voice and exclaimed, "It's not a Christmas tree, it's a Hanukah bush," and then he laughed. "That's what the orthodox Jews call them when they give in to the demands from their children to get a tree. We just call it a Christmas tree and go with the flow."

Speaking of flow, they had all sorts of standard red and white wines available, but they also put out some Manischewitz and Mogen David for us to sample. I tried both, but they were awfully sweet. I could see having them maybe as an aperitif or something, maybe, but I didn't really care for them.

"These are mostly ceremonial wines," Kathy said, "We don't drink them very often otherwise. *But* they were the wine of choice when we were teenagers. We used to sneak a bit from our parents' stash every time they were away. We thought we were such big stuff..."

Aside from the usual appetizers of cocktail wieners, meatballs, veggie trays, meat and cheese trays of all sorts, and plates of cookies everywhere, Kathy put out some deep-fried matzo balls with a spicy sauce, some mini-bagels with creamed cheese and lox, and some deep-fried potato latkes. We all really enjoyed the additions, and the children made me promise to get the recipes from Kathy.

- - -

Long before we moved to Omaha, the Third United Church had decided to forego holding Christmas Eve and Christmas Day services. Instead they held a combined Christmas service and pageant on the last Sunday before Christmas each year. It had become so popular they started holding two services, the first one at three in the afternoon and another at seven in the evening. Fred and I always loved the tradition of going to the evening service, even when the children were really too young to be staying up that late. I knew the children liked it, too, and so we all just expected we would go to the evening service that year as well.

About a week before the service, Timothy asked, "Do you think it would be okay for Sandra to join us for the church Christmas service? I've told her about it, and she says she'd like to come with us."

"I'm sure she can," I said. "This would a great way for us to get to know her better and for her to get to know our family better, too. Should we plan on picking her up at her house?"

"I'll call her and find out."

Ten minutes later, Timothy was back downstairs.

"Mom, her parents would like to meet you, too. They've invited us over for some appetizers and snacks before we go to the service. ... And just to warn her, I told Sandra we'll have to leave her place before six o'clock at the latest to make sure we can get a parking place and a decent seat."

"That sounds wonderful," I said. "But let's check with Liz and make sure she's ok with it, too."

Liz wasn't all that pleased. "Like, how come we get to go to his girlfriend's house instead of, like, doing something with my boyfriend's family?..." and her voice trailed off.

"That was stupid of me. We spend lots of time with the Hazeltons. I'm sorry, Timothy. Let's do it."

She paused, smiled impishly, and then said, "I wonder if the Hazeltons have, like, a church service that night I could go to with them…"

It turned out they didn't. In fact, the Hazeltons didn't really have a church or go to church. Liz had just said that to stir things up a bit.

I thought of suggesting that Liz invite Seth to join us, but that would make for awkward seating in the car, and I didn't really want to acknowledge her attempts to provoke her brother (and me, too). It turned out that I didn't have to hold back.

"Mom, maybe the Hazeltons would like to go to the service, too."

I could see the wheels turning in her mind again; she was such a cunning little schemer.

"We always invited them to join us in the past and they declined," I said, "But you can try again."

Within twenty minutes, Liz had it all organized. She was going to have dinner with the Hazeltons, who were then going to drive Seth, Aaron, Becky, and Liz to the service. I was going to be chauffeuring Timothy and Sandra. That was okay with me, actually, because I wanted to get to know Sandra and her family better.

"Well, the arrangements certainly have changed now, haven't they! Do me a favor, though, children. Let's make sure the three of us sit next to each other with your friends on the other side of you from me. This year I'd like to maintain some of the family feeling for the three of us. Okay?

"Timothy, are Sandra's parents planning to come to the service? If so, there will be room for us all to go in our car now that Liz is being driven there by the Hazeltons."

"I don't think so, Mom. Should I invite them?"

"Ask Sandra what she thinks. Talk to her about it."

After another fifteen minutes, Timothy was back. "Sandra says her parents would love to come, but they have something else they're doing later that evening."

"Okay, so it will be you, Sandra, and me in our car; and Liz, Seth, Aaron, and Becky in the Hazelton's car. That means whoever gets to the church first needs to save places for all seven of us so we can all be together. And Timothy, you should probably let Sandra's parents know that Liz won't be joining us for supper that night."

On the way to Sandra's house, we picked up potted poinsettia to take with us for her parents. I wasn't completely at ease with meeting them. These were the parents who had told their daughter it was okay for her to have sex with my son in their home. Fifteen-year-olds! But I tried to put that thought out of my mind as we drove there.

Their home was a standard large suburban three-bedroom brick ranch with a two-car garage. They had some nice lights on the two pine trees in their front yard, and we could see the big decorated tree in the corner of the living room as we walked up their front walk.

Sandra's mother, Lanny Overhill, answered the door wearing a very brightly patterned caftan with her grey-streaked hair done up on top in a very artistic bun. She was warm and welcoming as we entered their home and Timothy handed her the pot of poinsettias. She gushed over the plant, then set it on a table, and gave Timothy a big hug. Then she turned to me and hugged me, too. That seemed somewhat prematurely familiar to me, but the way she did it made it feel genuine and welcoming.

While Lanny was hugging me, Sandra went to Timothy and reached up and kissed him. I think he was embarrassed, and I think she was having fun as she put her arms around his neck and laughed.

He laughed with her. "Mom, Sandra warned me she was going to do that. I was sort of prepared, but I wasn't sure."

I laughed too, realizing that she had been teasing him. I'd met Sandra once or twice before at some of the get-togethers in our games room. We said "Hi," and then she came over and hugged me. I guess they were sort of a hugging family. I didn't mind it; in fact, I had missed being hugged after that first week when everyone was hugging everyone.

Rodney Blair, her father, emerged from the kitchen wearing a Christmas apron with bells and reindeer all over it. We smiled, and he wiped his hands on his apron and came over to shake hands with me. I was a bit disappointed that he didn't hug me, too, but he seemed somewhat more formal than Lanny and Sandra.

He said, "I've just put together a few appetizers --- you know, the frozen things from the grocery store. I hope that's enough."

"Of course it will be. Timothy said you were having us over for just a light snack."

The light snack-dinner was pleasant, and there was more than enough food for the five of us. During the meal, they politely asked how I was doing and if there was any hope of any news about Fred.

"We're doing well, all things considered," I told them. "The shock and the uncertainty were difficult for all of us to accept, but the loss of Fred has left a big hole in our lives, for sure."

Lanny asked, "You have a daughter, too?"

"Yes, Liz. She's with her boyfriend and some other friends now, and they will all be joining us later at the church."

I felt awkward sitting there. I hadn't socialized with people I didn't know for quite a few months, and I wasn't sure what to say. Fortunately, I didn't have to say much because Lanny and Rodney seemed more-than-pleased to have an audience. We chatted about the War in Afghanistan, all of us agreeing that we hated the idea of another middle-east war, but we didn't see much option based on what we knew. Rodney argued that the Taliban couldn't be beaten without a large-scale massive invasion, and even then he didn't think they would stay defeated.

"Their devotion to their religion is intense," he said. "And they held out successfully against the Russians for a decade, with our help of course."

Lanny added, "The US should have learned by now that the enemy of our enemy is not necessarily our friend. Middle east alliances can change overnight."

It was then that I asked, "What do you two do for a living?"

That seemed crass, but I couldn't think how else to ask it.

"I teach sociology at Creighton," said Rodney, "and Lanny teaches history at UNO."

I think not knowing they were professors until then was good. If I'd walked into their home knowing they were professors, I'd have felt ill-at-ease and shy.

Lanny turned to me and asked, "What about you?"

That caught me off guard, but I recovered pretty quickly.

"Before the children were born, I was an executive assistant at Arkero Foods, but I quit when the children were born. After the children started school, I began consulting with Arkero on a free-lance basis, doing marketing plans and public relations. I'm not sure now. I may go back to work full-time, but I still feel as if I need to consider other options."

Timothy looked at me very curiously, as if to ask, "What options?" He didn't have to ask, though, because Rodney did.

"What options are you contemplating?" he asked. "I saw the news clips of your press conferences, and I should think almost any major firm in the area would jump at the opportunity to hire you in their marketing and public relations departments."

I actually blushed. "I'm really quite taken aback," I said. "But thank you. And yes, even if I don't end up back at Arkero full time, I'll almost surely be doing that same kind of work somewhere, somehow."

I thought about telling them about all my recent work with the church, the United Way, the Civilian Police Review Board, and LOST, but I didn't want to sound as if I was bragging about how popular and busy I was. It seemed I might be saying, "Look at me. Look how important I am," and I didn't want to do that.

Instead I just told them about LOST and how I wanted to try to help children who had lost a parent but who didn't have the advantages Timothy and Liz had. They were interested and wanted to hear more. I explained a bit about the group, but then we realized it was nearly six o'clock and we had to get going.

There were hugs around before we left as we wished each other a "Merry

Christmas" and made vague commitments about wanting to get together again soon. While we had been at her parents' home, Timothy and Sandra had been pretty much non-physical with each other after that initial kiss. On the way to the church, though, Timothy and Sandra sat in the back seat, snuggled together, Sandra with her head on his shoulder and Timothy with his arm around her.

I lectured myself: "Susan, this is not your romance; this is not necessarily Timothy's life-long love. Don't get all worked up about it."

I had to admit, though, they made a very nice-looking couple -- cute enough that I had to stop myself from shedding a romantic tear.

"How did you two meet?" I asked them, not directing the question to either one specifically.

Sandra said, "I set it up. We knew each other a bit from our classes, and I thought he was good-looking, and so one time when he was walking alone, I caught up with him and walked alongside him. He was so easy to talk with, and we got along really well, and so I started trying to walk with him more often after that. I think the time we walked together down the hall with our arms touching the whole way, the electricity could have lit up all of Omaha."

"I knew who Sandra was," said Timothy, "and I thought she was cute and smart and nice, but I had no idea what to do about it. I was just too shy to call her out of the blue or anything, but our walks and talks really put me at ease ... made me feel comfortable with her.

"And the arm-touching thing Sandra mentioned? It was real. At least it felt real to me, too, and so I finally summoned up my courage and suggested maybe we could go for pizza together at lunch sometime."

"Hey, that's right! And we never did that. You still owe me a slice and a Coke!" and again Sandra laughed, teasingly.

The church service itself was splendid. I had always been less enthusiastic about these Christmas services than Fred was, but this year, being there with our children on each side of me felt extra special. We all thoroughly enjoyed ourselves. We sang the carols loudly and with what can only be thought of as Christmas joy, and we smiled at the cute young children acting out the nativity story. A few times I felt a twinge of sadness, missing Fred, but I didn't let it get to me then while we were having such a good time.

When the service was over, I called Thelma on my cell phone to let her know it was time to come and pick up the children; and then on a whim I suggested that she and Dale and all the children join us at our place for hot chocolate and cookies. She loved the idea, and so did the children.

Hot chocolate... Cream... Layers...

And there were nine of us again, sitting at the dining room table, another coincidence. The sensation swept over me as we were preparing the hot chocolate. I wasn't superstitious, but these things all seemed very symbolic; and to tell the truth I welcomed these emotional little symbols, even though I had no idea what they were symbols of.

Dale asked, "So this is what you were referring to, Liz, when you told the story about Fred acting like a snail?"

We all laughed at the memory. It felt good to laugh about it and not cry, at least not outwardly; I could tell we were progressing. Of course the children all had to try to float cream on their hot chocolate, proclaiming it was a contest for all of us, including the adults, along with the same rule: if you couldn't get the cream to float, you had to make the noise of an animal. Dale was keen to try it; Thelma and I went along less enthusiastically.

"No snails or turtles or whatever doesn't make a sound this time," said Timothy, and again we all laughed at the memory.

The only ones who could float the cream were Aaron and Sandra. The rest of us were quite impressed, and the cacophony of animal sounds as the rest of us failed was hilarious.

Chapter 30 – Christmas Day and into the New Year

Christmas Eve and Christmas Day were sad days for all three of us because Fred wasn't with us. Honestly, I wanted to skip them, but I knew we couldn't. And the children did their best to help us cope.

When Fred was alive, we had hot dogs and coleslaw for Christmas Eve dinner and spent the rest of the evening listening to, and singing along with, Christmas carols while we wrapped presents. "Is there any different paper?" "Who has the tape?" "Who knows how to tie decent bow?" were all familiar questions every year.

We always insisted the children go to bed early on Christmas Eve so Santa Claus could fill the stockings. Then Fred and I would share a glass of wine and a traditional kiss in front of the fireplace before filling the stockings. It was a family tradition to put unusual underwear in the toe of each person's stocking and then fill the stocking with gadgety-gimmicky little gifts, along with Christmas candy, and candy canes.

I did my best to carry on the tradition, and so did the children, but without Fred we had fewer gifts to wrap and less confusion about who was using the scissors or tape. We were finished in no time, and so we hung the empty stockings from the mantel and sat together on the couch to watch some Christmas specials on television.

At nine o'clock, I announced with an attempt at seasonal gaiety, "Okay, children. Time to go to bed or else Santa won't stop here to fill your stockings."

Timothy and Liz had been acting strangely all evening, which I had attributed to Fred's not being there, but when I tried to send them to bed, they just sat there on the couch, smiling at me.

"Not tonight, Mom," said Timothy. "We're doing your stocking!" and the two of them grabbed my stocking from the mantel and scurried upstairs with it to one of their bedrooms.

They had decided to play Santa Claus for my stocking. They secretly planned to change the family traditions to suit our changed family circumstances, and I was thrilled beyond belief.

The secrecy was probably a good idea. It boosted our morale tremendously for the next few days – mine because I was so happy they had done it, and theirs because they carried it off so well.

After about twenty minutes, Liz came back downstairs. "Mom?"

I was reluctant to look because I didn't want to spoil their surprise at all, and so I stared out the back window as I answered, "Yes?"

"We don't want you to see your stocking until morning. Is that okay?"

"Sure. Is it okay to turn around now, though?"

"Okay, and we don't really want to see our stockings until tomorrow either. Would it, like, be okay if we bring your stocking into your bedroom in the morning and the three of us open our stockings there?"

"I love it!" I exclaimed. "I'll take your stockings up to the bedroom and fill them there now. What a great idea!"

When I was buying things to put into their stockings, I told myself that after their recently expressed interests in sex, I'd buy extremely **non**-sexy underwear for both of them. Timothy got boxers with butterflies on them, and Liz got full-sized cotton panties with flowers printed on them.

The children were beside themselves with excitement on Christmas morning. It was like the old excitement, when they were so eager to open their gifts, but this time it was because they wanted me to see what they had done for my stocking. They burst into my bedroom at 6:30, shouting, "Merry Christmas!" and piled onto the bed with my stocking.

I tried to get out of bed to get their stockings for them, but they wouldn't let me. "No, Mom! You have to open your stocking first!" said Timothy.

They were giggling and having a blast.

As I slowly took their gifts out of my stocking, they continued their giggling, and soon I joined in.

"Sugar-free candy?" And then I burst into laughter as I read the label, "'Guaranteed to taste better than cardboard'? You know you both are going to have to try this with me!"

As I feared, they had included a thong for me. "You've got to be kidding!"

And then, "What is this? Broccoli? An artichoke? Feta cheese? What's the story here?"

"We put them in plastic bags, Mom, so they wouldn't mess up anything else," said Timothy, but I just looked them blankly.

"It's for the pizza you threatened to make one time when we, like, have friends over," laughed Liz.

I laughed along with them and hugged them both.

"Thank you! This is a great gift. And I hope you and your friends are willing to try that pizza!"

"Of course, Mom," said Timothy. "Actually, we're hoping you'll serve it for New Year's Eve…" and they both looked at me tentatively.

"What?"

And then it clicked.

"Ohhhh… You want to have a New Year's Eve party here?"

"Would that be okay, Mom?" asked Liz.

"Of course! Just tell whomever you invite, 'No drugs and no alcohol'!"

They nodded their tired nods as if to say, "Yeah, yeah, we know."

I glared at them. "Make it clear to your friends that we want a safe and legal party, please. Otherwise, there won't be a party."

"Okay, okay," they chimed together.

"How big a party do you two have in mind?"

"I don't know what Liz has in mind," answered Timothy, "but the basement really can't hold a lot of people comfortably. Maybe twenty?"

"So maybe we can invite, like, eight or nine friends each?" added Liz.

That sounded good to me, and I was interested in hearing how they would select which friends to invite.

"Maybe stick with about seven friends each initially and then when others hear about it and beg to be invited, you might be able to add them to your guest lists? And be sure to get clear whether they're bringing a date so things don't get out of hand."

Later, as Timothy and Liz were planning the invitation list, I heard Timothy and Liz discussing the Hazeltons… "Well Seth started out as your friend," said Liz. "He should be included on your list."

Timothy groaned, and they both laughed. They knew what they were up against with Seth, Aaron, and Becky, and whose list they should be on.

"Let's split up Aaron and Seth on the guest lists, at least in our minds," offered Timothy. "That way we both get to invite the Hazeltons and you get to invite Becky, and I get to invite Sandra. Then we can invite six more people each."

"Well, okay, maybe," said Liz, "but, like, that means I'll have more of my friends here. Sorta. Are you okay with that?"

"I think so. After all, even though you're going with Seth, he's my friend, too. Besides, right now I can think of only three other couples I'd like to invite. With those six people, plus Sandra, Seth, and me, that's nine already. What about you? It'd be you, Aaron, Becky, and six more. Would that be okay for you?"

I was delighted to hear the give and take between them. They had grown closer after we lost Fred, and the more general sense of friendship with the Hazeltons helped, too.

"Tell your friends they'll have to find their own transportation here and home," I said. "I might be able to drive a few of them home, but I'd rather not if we can avoid it."

Between Christmas and New Year's Eve, they drew up their guest lists and invited their friends. Sandra's parents offered to help chaperone the party, and I was delighted to accept their offer since I wasn't sure I wanted to be the only parent there. And then the Hazeltons called and suggested they help, too. And so we ended up with eighteen teenagers in the basement and five adults in the family room.

All week, we planned the menu and made sure we had plenty of soda pop, chips, dip, and appetizers on hand. We also bought some frozen pizzas of all varieties, including two cheese pizzas to which we planned to add feta cheese, broccoli, and artichokes.

Both Dale Hazelton and Sandra's father, Rodney, decided not to drink more than the small glass of champagne we all had at midnight so they could safely drive some of the teen guests home. When all the guests had left, Liz and Timothy came and sat in the family room with me.

"We'll clean up in the morning," I smiled.

Liz and Timothy looked at each other with strange looks, and I added "I hope it's not a huge mess down there…"

Liz shrugged and said, "It's not bad. It won't take long."

"How was the party?" I asked

"It was great, Mom," said Timothy. "It was just what a New Year's Eve party should be… games, music, dancing, food. Thanks!"

I looked at Liz, who seemed a bit less enthusiastic.

"Liz?"

"Oh, it was great, Mom. It's just that, like, I don't think Aaron and Becky are getting along all that well. And I like them both so much that I don't like to see that."

Timothy offered, "Sandra wondered if Aaron is jealous that Seth is going with you."

"Oh no!" said Liz. "I hope not. I like Aaron a lot, but I'm going with Seth."
Then she glowered at Timothy, "You shouldn't have told me that, Timothy. Now I'll feel awkward around them. Mom, like, what should I do? How should I deal with this?"

"Just be as nice as you can the whole time. Don't be dishonest with them, but at this point it might be a good idea not to discuss it with either of them. It's awkward, but let's make sure we all maintain a good friendship between the families."

"But what about Becky? She's, like, my closest friend!"

"I don't want to seem too cavalier about this," I contributed, "because I like your concerns, Liz. You don't want anyone to get hurt, I know, but boy-girl relationships rarely last and can really mess up boy-boy and girl-girl friendships. Keep in mind that if the four of you try to be friendly and civil, things will work out."

"I hope so, Mom. I'd hate to lose any of them as friends."

I let the children sleep in until ten o'clock on New Year's Day. When I got them up for breakfast, I told them we'd been invited down to the Schultzes for hot dogs and burgers to watch Nebraska play Miami in the Rose Bowl, which was also the NCAA championship game that year.

"But before we do anything else, we have to clean up the basement," I pronounced.

Liz got big-eyed and groaned and whined, and Timothy looked at her very seriously saying, "C'mon, Liz, you knew we'd have to face this."

As I was going down the stairs, they started laughing behind me. When I got to the basement, I saw why. The basement was spotless. The children and their friends had collected all the drink containers in clear bags to be returned or recycled, and they had all the garbage collected in big garbage bags.

"Part of having a party includes cleaning up!" said Liz, "and so we got all the kids to help and it was done in, like, under ten minutes."

"You children are amazing. Thank you so much! If you get the garbage and containers out to the garage now, and bring the vacuum down with you when you come back, I'll take care of cleaning up the rest."

I wasn't sure the children would want to go to the Schultzes that evening. They seemed increasingly attached to their boy- and girlfriends, but the issue never arose. It was as if they still wanted to do family and neighborhood things, too. Of course, it helped for Liz that the Hazeltons were there, but there were several other teens there, too, and they all just seemed to hang out together.

The only downside to the entire get together was that Nebraska lost the Rose Bowl amid much controversy about whether they should even have been invited to play in the national championship game.

When we left to go home after the game, the Bergmans joined us, and as we all got to their driveway, Kathy said, "The holidays are so much fun, getting together with everyone," and she began hugging everyone.

"Hugs all around," said Dale, bless him. I had missed all the hugging we had done after Fred disappeared, and it felt good to be hugging all our neighbors.

And just as happened back then, all the children hugged each other. Timothy prompted it by hugging Seth and Aaron, and then Liz joined in with all of the hugging. I watched her and Aaron's hug. She kept it a tad more formal than it had been back in September, and it looked as if Aaron wasn't going to press the issue. They seemed to be resolving things implicitly... for then, anyway.

Suddenly Ray Bergman said, "Let's just stand here in the middle of the street, hold hands in a big circle, and sing 'Auld Lang Syne' together.

We loved the idea, and as we started singing, other neighbors came out and joined us, so we sang it again. And again, and again. After four choruses, we had a circle of about twenty people singing "Auld Lang Syne", a tradition that has been carried on ever since that night: a half hour after the Rose Bowl game, everyone in the neighborhood meets in front of the Bergman driveway and sings "Auld Lang Syne" together.

Chapter 31 – Marking Time, Trying to Adjust

Over the next few months, I gradually but very cautiously eased into my roles with the charitable organizations, and the children carried on with their school and their romances pretty much the way most teenagers do. There was a huge emptiness in our lives because Fred wasn't there, but we were slowly building new yet somewhat different lives.

The changes were more dramatic for me than for the children. I had always been a homemaker at heart, albeit one who was involved with clubs or groups that involved our children, but over those few months my growing involvement with charities and community organizations began to take up much more of my time. I tried to do the preparation work while the children were at school, but I couldn't avoid having to attend some meetings in the evenings, which meant leaving the children home alone after dinner.

I'd read stories about children who had major parties when their parents weren't home, and the children's delight in the movie **Risky Business** didn't ease my mind much; but both Liz and Timothy were very good in that regard. I tried to make sure I was there every day when they got home from school, and I tried to make sure we had healthy meals every evening. The children pitched in by cleaning up and doing the dishes each night, whether I was home or off at some meeting.

In early February, Ben asked me to meet with him to go over all our financial matters involving the insurance proceeds that he was managing for us. He wanted to make sure that I was okay with the investment plan he had laid out for us, and he wanted me to see a tax consultant. "When we created the trusts for your children, and when you endowed the foundation, we minimized your tax exposure," Ben said, "but we should probably meet every once in awhile to go over your accounts and to answer any questions you might have."

"I hadn't even thought about needing someone to look after my taxes, but of course you're right. My tax situation will never be easy anymore, will it?" and I groaned.

Those early months of 2002 when we setting up the Foundation and getting it operational were particularly time-consuming. Thelma was the perfect choice to be the managing director of the foundation; she met with financial aid officers of at least ten different colleges and then set out her proposal that the endowed scholarships be advertised in all the high schools of

Nebraska and Kansas. The scholarships soon became known as FRY grants, named for **F**rederick **R**obert **Y**oung. It was an easy way to refer to the scholarships, and Thelma blitzed the high schools with information about the funds and how to apply for them.

I continued to insist that the funds should go to students who would otherwise have to borrow too much and take on too much part-time work to attend college successfully, and I wanted the funds to be available for promising but not necessarily star students – the star students would generally have access to other financial aid plans.

"Do you know there are some students who try to hold down full-time jobs at the same time they are taking a full course load?" Thelma said. "Are these the students you want to target, Susan?"

"Exactly," I said. "If they're struggling that much financially, let's see what we can do."

Ben explained to the board members that even though the investments would ordinarily yield much more than two percent each year, it would be prudent to take out only two percent from the endowment each year and then reinvest any extra income so the fund could grow and maybe try to keep pace with inflation. "Education isn't cheap," said Ben. "It is becoming more expensive every year. If the foundation is going to help students in the future, we have to make sure the base of the endowment grows over time so that the annual income from the endowment can keep up with rising costs."

Ben didn't need to say that. I had insisted that it be written into the charter of the Foundation. After I pointed out that it was in the charter, we agreed that the annual amount taken would have to cover Thelma's salary and expenses as well as the scholarships. We set our initial annual budget at a hundred thousand dollars and worked from there.

"If we grant a scholarship to a freshman," Dr. Franks asked, "what will he or she have to do to keep the scholarship?"

I answered, "I should think that as long as the student is in good standing and making normal progress as defined by their college, that should be good, shouldn't it?"

"Will the foundation fund them for four years?" asked Thelma.

"Hmmm," I said. "I see the problem. Every scholarship we create puts the foundation on the hook for four years of funding. We'd better start small this year or we won't have any funds to use during the next few years. I'm guessing that roughly we should give out a quarter of the expected annual income this year with the rest reinvested?"

We all agreed on that plan. It turned out, though, that Thelma was short-changing herself on travel, office, and salary expenses. When I learned that she was planning to take only ten thousand dollars a year to cover everything, I confronted her at one of our morning coffees.

"Thelma, I love what you're doing, but you can't do it that way. You have to get at least ten thousand dollars upfront, in salary, for yourself; and then you must also bill the foundation for your office and travel expenses."

"I know," she said, "but I just want to do what I can to contribute and make sure it all gets off the ground."

"It's a well-endowed foundation," I said. "We don't pay rent to hold our meetings, and we have amazingly low expenses, thanks to you and Dale. Administrative overhead of twenty thousand dollars for an endowment of this size is nothing. That leaves eighty thousand dollars for scholarships, or enough for twenty thousand dollars each year in new scholarships at today's tuition fees."

"Okay, but let's revisit this next year, when we see how much or how little time is involved. Twenty thousand dollars a year for scholarships out of an endowment of five million dollars just doesn't sound right."

"It is, though, because that's just for one year's worth of scholarships. When we're fully up and running, we'll be giving roughly eighty thousand dollars each year in scholarships," I said. "Now, how should we divide it up?"

"Let's suppose a student without the scholarship would work part-time enough to net, say, a hundred dollars a week. That works out to roughly three thousand dollars during the school year. How about we use that as our starting point?"

"Good!" I said. "So this year we can grant six scholarships of three thousand dollars each. We've had some set up expenses and legal fees now, and we might have other legal and accounting fees in the future, so let's try to set our target as granting six new scholarships each year. Then as tuitions go up and as the earnings on the endowed funds go up, we can reassess how many scholarships to grant each year, along with how big they should be."

"You know," said Thelma, "once the scholarship program is up and running, at any one time there will be twenty-four FRY students in these two states, and maybe more! That's a pretty sizable impact."

I smiled. "I'd like that, and I'm sure Fred would have approved."

- - -

The Police-Civilian Review Board took much more time than I had expected, and I had to work hard to get a handle on what we were doing. I had thought the board would discuss overall policies of the Omaha Police Department, but that was only a small part of what we did. We spent more time on residents' requests for a greater police presence and on citizen complaints about the police department in general.

Prior to our first meeting, it became clear that I had been recruited for the Review Board to help with public relations both within the police department and with the public at large. I think that was one reason I accepted the invitation: they weren't after any kind of monetary donation; they wanted me for my experience and skills (at least as they perceived my skills). They wanted me for who I was and what I could contribute as a person, not as a financial donor. That was a refreshing change from so many of the other requests I received.

Reviewing the issues was time-consuming. I often found myself sitting up at night while the children were doing their schoolwork and even later, after they went to bed, reading through all the documents and thinking about them.

One case that illustrated what we did and what I had to do involved the shooting of a teenager named Michael DeVere by a police officer named Lucian Smith. The facts of the case were pretty clear-cut: the teen had been joking around with his friends and had removed the orange piece from the front of a toy gun – the orange piece that is on toy guns to clearly identify them as toys. He then carried that toy gun into a variety store, brandishing it now and then for his friends to see. The clerk immediately called the police, who arrived in less than a minute, saw the boy pointing the gun at his friend, not at the clerk, and ordered him to drop it. Instead of dropping the gun, the teen turned toward the police with the toy gun still in his hand. The police officer, believing the gun was real, shot the teen in the shoulder.

The parents of the teen were upset, as were some members of the community who deplored increased violence in general, but especially from police officers. Our response was measured:

> We have reviewed the file about the shooting carefully. Our conclusion is that we do not wish to blame the victim, and we have made a great effort not to blame him for the shooting.
>
> Likewise, we must also understand the difficulties faced by law enforcement officers when having to make split-second decisions involving people brandishing weapons that are not clearly identified as toys.
>
> Balancing these concerns, we do not see any compelling reason to reprimand the officer involved. The evidence is clear that Officer Smith warned the teen to drop the gun; and he purposely tried to avoid shooting the boy in his torso.
>
> We understand the teen was trying to have fun with his friends and was not trying to rob the store. By all reports, he never threatened the clerk, nor did he say anything to indicate he was planning to rob the store. We also understand that while the clerk had not been threatened explicitly, she wanted the police to come, just as a precaution, not knowing what the teen would do next.
>
> We understand, too, that when a police officer shouts "drop the gun" to someone who is inexperienced, they may become confused and not drop the gun but instead turn to where the voice comes from. We believe the victim's assertion that he thought the voice was from the storeowner and he was just turning to show the owner that the gun was a toy.
>
> Nevertheless, we cannot find that the officer did anything wrong in this case.
>
> We have three recommendations to make, based on the case.
>
> 1. The orange pieces on the nozzles of toy guns are put there for a purpose. The dangers of removing them must be made clear. We want this case to help spread the message.
> 2. We find the officer followed all procedures to the letter.
> 3. If the teen and his parents are unsatisfied with our findings,

we urge them to seek legal counsel.

The other members of the board were not altogether pleased with my insistence on adding the third recommendation, but I knew a finding like ours had only internal authority, within the police department. We had no legal authority to head off a lawsuit, and I believed that we should be clear that our decision would not foreclose that option.

Also, the board members were not altogether pleased with my decision to visit the teen and his parents to explain the decision, but it worked out well. Initially, the parents were angry: angry with their son for having done what he did, angry with the police officer for shooting their son, and angry with the police board for its decision. But as I sat with them and talked with them, it was clear to them I wasn't there as a police department spokesperson; I wasn't there so much to defend the police or our decision, but to explain it and to let them know we felt concern for their son and about his injuries.

Learning not to be defensive and combative was something I picked up when I was working in the family hardware store back in Salina, Kansas. Being defensive and combative only made things worse. Those same lessons served me well at Arkero Foods as I took on more public relations work with them, and those lessons helped with my work on the Citizen-Police Review Board as well.

Our decision in that case, along with the fact that the Citizen-Police Review Board had gone out of their way to help the teen with transportation to and from his physical therapy sessions while his parents worked, was faxed to various members of the media as a standard press release. And the reporter Jeremy Hall was on the phone to me right away about it.

"Ms. Young? This is Jeremy Hall calling from the World-Herald."

"Hello, Mr. Hall," I said with some reservation. I was about to let him know that I had guessed what he was calling about, but I remembered to ask, not guess.

"What can I help you with today?" I asked.

"I just read the press release from the Citizen-Police Review Board in the case of the teen shooting by Officer Smith, and I can see your hand in that. I wonder if we could get together to talk about it."

"Get together?" I thought. "What's this about?"

"I can probably answer any of your questions on the phone, Mr. Hall. Do we need to meet?"

"I think it would be helpful," he replied. "I'd like to talk at length with you about the case, and we'd like to do a photo for the story."

I wasn't keen on it, but I knew it was part of the job.

"Okay. I have some time available this afternoon. Where should we do this? Would it be easier for the paper if I go there?"

"Our photographers are always on the go and actually are only rarely here in the press room. Why don't we meet for coffee somewhere?"

We agreed to meet that afternoon at the Garden Café for coffee. It was only about two miles from home, and it had great pastries. As I pulled into the parking lot, I reminded myself, "Yes, the pastries are great here, but be careful. Do you really want a photo in the paper of you chomping down on some pastry? With crumbs on your face? And powdered sugar on your sweater?"

Jeremy Hall had everything arranged with the management, and we went to a private room for our interview and photo session.

"Let's begin just sitting here and chatting," he said, "while Lee snaps some photos. Then he can get on to his next assignment..."

"Great idea, Mr. Hall!" I smiled. "And then he won't be around to photograph me as I spill my coffee or something."

"First, would you mind calling me 'Jeremy'? And may I call you 'Susan'?"

I wondered what he was up to, but that seemed fine with me. "Sure."

"To begin with, Susan, I'll be using a voice recorder so that anything I report is accurate. And any time you want to go off the record, let me know, and I'll turn it off."

"Thank you, Jeremy."

"How did you end up getting involved with the Civilian-Police Review

Board? Do you or did your family have any history of working with law enforcement or any of these sorts of things?"

"Quite honestly I was surprised by the request that I join the review board. Do you know why they asked me?"

"I can guess," Jeremy said, "but tell me."

"They said they had seen my press conferences on television and had read your reports about us after Fred disappeared. For some reason they liked the way I handled things."

I then added, "Off the record now."

Jeremy reached out and stopped his tape.

"We both know the Police Department has received some unfavorable press over the past few years, and they need to clean up their image. Several of the review board members told me explicitly that was why they were looking for someone like me to join them."

He turned his tape recorder back on and then asked, "What financial compensation do you receive for being on the Review Board?"

"Reviewing and discussing all the submissions to the Review Board is a daunting task. I don't know about my fellow Review Board members… they're all much more experienced at this than I am, but I find I'm spending roughly at least ten hours each week on Review Board matters. And that latest case took even more time.

"The monthly honorarium for serving on the Review Board is two hundred dollars, but I don't keep the money. Instead it all goes to the Frederick Robert Young Foundation."

"I anticipated as much. What about compensation for your expenses? Commuting? Office expenses? Things like that?"

"I suppose I could bill the city for those expenses, and maybe some of the board members do, but I don't. I'll see, but I don't think I'll need to."

While we were chatting, Lee took quite a few photos, mostly of me, but also some of the two of us talking. I shuddered inwardly to see what they would use, and I secretly hoped there would be a lot of news to fill the paper and so they would decide not to fill the space with a photo.

After Lee left, Jeremy and I discussed the case.

"I didn't realize that personal visits to people who make submissions were part of your job there," said Jeremy.

"They aren't," I said, somewhat emphatically. "In several instances, though, I have visited people to discuss their submissions. Usually it's to meet with people who complain that the police don't do something about noise from their neighbors or who want increased foot patrol service in their area. This case was unique, though."

"How so?"

"Well, first, shootings by anyone in Omaha are extremely rare, as you know; I can't remember the last time I heard of a police officer shooting anyone here. And second, this was a sad case that came about because some teens were having fun together but hadn't really thought carefully about the possible consequences. They're all good kids. They just got carried away. I'm so glad the victim is expected to make a full recovery."

"How and why did the Review Board arrange transportation for him to receive physical therapy?"

"That was my idea. I knew the young man had made a mistake, but I wanted to make sure he got some help. His parents both work, and so it would be difficult for him to get to all of his physical therapy sessions. I offered to drive him to the sessions when I could, and we provided taxicab vouchers for him when I couldn't. We discussed it when I met with him and his parents."

"Susan, I can't believe that it is standard procedure for members of the Civilian-Police Review Board to meet with complainants. What on earth led you to do that? And how did it go?"

"Both the teen and his parents were angry about the shooting," I agreed. "They were very hesitant about meeting with me and, to be honest, I went to the meeting with more than a little trepidation. But I looked at his background and his family and thought, 'this young man has so much potential.' I hoped to do something to encourage him to think about his future. I think that visit actually did help him.

"During our talk, his mother mentioned that he was signed up for physical therapy but they weren't sure how often they could get him to his sessions. It was then that I said, 'I'll make sure that's not a problem. I'll drive you if I can, and if I can't then the Review Board will pay for the taxi service.' I made arrangements with one of the taxi firms in town to pick him up either after school or from his home. 'No side trips,' I made clear to him and his parents, 'But we'll make sure you can get to your physical therapy. We want you to recover fully and go on to lead a happy, productive life. We want you to look forward, to decide about and prepare for your future.'"

"Susan, that's not in the budget for the Review Board, is it?"

"Off the record," I said, and Jeremy turned off the tape recorder.

"Of course not. I told the taxi company to send the bills to me. That's off the record, though."

"Okay, but why?"

"Why what?"

"Two whys," Jeremy replied. "Why did you do it? And why do you want your contribution to be off the record?"

"As I said before, I did it because it seemed to me the young man was genuinely a decent person who had a good future ahead of him; I didn't want his anger about having been shot to have too negative an impact on him. And I don't want to publicize my contribution because I'm not a Pharisee. I don't need everyone to know about what I do for other people. If it comes out that I played a role, I'll just say I used my Review Board expense allowance to cover the taxi fares."

Jeremy could see that I wasn't going to claim either my expenses or the taxi fares. But he had to let it drop.

"Would you like something to eat?" he asked. "They have fantastic baked goods here."

"No, thanks. Does this mean we're finished now? That wasn't too bad," I actually laughed, and so did he.

"We're not quite finished, though," he said as he got a very serious look on his face.

"Oh, oh," I thought, "What's coming up? Is this why he wanted to meet with me in person?"

"Susan, this is all off the record now," and he put his tape recorder away.

"Okay. What is it that you want to talk about?"

"Are you aware that a number of influential people in Omaha are suggesting that you would be an excellent candidate to run for the Senate in this coming fall's election?"

"Good grief. No."

"Yes. You have tremendous name recognition and, as I can attest, you have poise and integrity."

"I'm flabbergasted! I can't imagine life as a politician."

"Well, I wanted to let you know so you can think about it."

"Well ... thank you for the advance warning." I hesitated and then continued, "I'll think about it, but probably I'll think mostly about how to decline any suggestion or offer."

Part 3: The World of Politics

Chapter 32 – Politics : Susan Young :: Oil : Water

As I drove home from the meeting with Jeremy Hall, I wondered who he had been talking with and how my name had come up. Had he been encouraged to speak with me to gauge my interest?

I really couldn't imagine me as a Senator, but I could see how it had happened. Fred's disappearance had been in the news, and I had dealt with the media carefully. I did, indeed, have name recognition going for me -- that plus my own way of dealing formally but cordially with the media.

I decided not to say anything about it to anyone else right then. I needed more time to think about it. What might I hope to accomplish as a Senator? What impact might my running and possible election have on the children? Did I really want to endure the micro-inspection of my life and of the children's lives? Did I really want all the tensions and stresses of public, political life?

I really wished Fred had been there to talk with me about it. I tried another imaginary conversation with him, but it didn't help. I decided I'd think about it for a few days, and then discuss it with Thelma before mentioning it to the children.

I wasn't allowed the luxury of waiting that long, though. The next morning, Thelma called me as soon as the children left for school.

"Put the coffee on, girl, we need to have a long session," and she hung up before I could say anything more than, "Hello."

I opened the door for her, and there was a photo of me staring back at me from the front page of the morning paper that Thelma was holding. It must have been a really slow news day if Jeremy Hall's article about me and the Civilian-Police Review Board was on the front page!

I took the paper and started to read Jeremy's article, which seemed pretty fair and accurate until the last few paragraphs. I was reading those as Thelma swaggered to the kitchen table with her coffee.

Yes, she swaggered.

I felt both forewarned and betrayed by Jeremy in those last few paragraphs.

> Ms. Young's handling of the Officer Smith case for the Civilian-Police Review Board comes as no surprise to those who know her. Her compassion for the shooting victim, combined with her insistence that Officer Smith was blameless in the shooting, have won her admirers from all walks of life.
>
> "Susan has always had compassion and skill, a valuable and rare combination," said Vernon Jackson, Vice-President of Marketing and Product Development at Arkero Foods, where Ms. Young has done considerable consulting work over the years. "She has the makings of being a great leader for our country."
>
> Echoing Jackson's observation, Joshua Klein of Klein-Staily where the late Fred Young was a partner, agreed. "Susan has the ability to be perceptive and analytical yet at the same time to let people know she cares about them as individuals. I don't know what her political ambitions might be, but I will support her unreservedly."
>
> And when the parents of the victim in the Officer Smith shooting were asked about Ms. Young, they had nothing but compliments. "We were so angry," said the teen's father. "We didn't want to see anyone connected with the police after that board let the cop off without even a hand-slap. But she really did make us feel like she cared about what had happened and about our son. She even took the time to drive him to and from his physical therapy sessions since my wife and I couldn't do it most of the time."
>
> Ms. Young has not made any public statements indicating her interest in running for political office, but it appears she has considerable support without even trying.

"Nice picture of you," Thelma offered somewhat fake-off-handedly as we sat at the kitchen table. "Now be straight with me, girl. Was that story planted to test the waters for you politically?"

I just sat there with my mouth agape, staring at her.

"Oh my god," I said finally. "Jeremy warned me about the political angle when we talked yesterday, and it left me completely dumbfounded. Now that you ask, though, I have to wonder *very* seriously whether he and others are trying to get me to run for the Senate."

"You'll be a shoo-in if you do," said Thelma. "Everyone in Nebraska knows who you are. Everyone has seen news clips of you and how composed you are. It's only a question of whether you want to do it."

"I don't know," I said quietly. "The children and I are adjusting to so much already. Do we really need to go through the trauma of a political campaign, possibly moving to Washington, D.C., and a completely new type of life? I love it here. I love our friends; I love our neighborhood; and I love the familiarity we have with Omaha. What do you think?"

"I know you have what it takes to do the job, and I know you have what it takes to make the transition. You're smart, you're organized, you care, and you handle yourself well in difficult situations. I know you can do it if you want to. It's just a matter of whether you want to."

"I don't know. And look at these names in the article! Joshua Klein? Vern Jackson? Why them, I wonder. I'll have to find out whether Ben Gruvel has had anything to do with this and whether Jeremy Hall played a role in initiating the idea or is just being used as a go-between."

And then it dawned on me. "Okay, how much did you and Dale have to do with all this speculation?"

She just sat there and smiled at me. I wanted to jump across the table and alternately strangle her and hug her.

"Do you remember that last Foundation meeting we had? You had to leave early, but Ben, Will Franks, Harold Yoder and I stuck around. I don't know who raised the idea, but it was enthusiastic and unanimous that we should form an ad hoc committee to explore your candidacy.

"I'm sorry. Maybe we should have checked with you sooner, before it all came out this way. But quite obviously we've been busy. Ben got Joshua Klein on board, Harold talked to Vern Jackson, I talked to Jeremy Hall, and then he talked with the victim's family. I think his next step is to profile your work with LOST."

"I'm really upset that this was all done without my knowledge or approval, Thelma. You should understand that. I'm not going to decide anything without talking about it at length with Timothy and Liz. I will ***not*** be pushed into anything."

I looked at her angrily, but the anger melted, and I said, "You're just lucky I love you so much."

"Now don't go all mushy on me, girl. You're going to have to be hard-nosed if you want to be a Senator."

Thelma's eyes were twinkling with an inner laughter. She was truly enjoying this conversation, and that infuriated me. I wasn't enjoying it at all.

"Thelma, what's going on? Why are you enjoying this so much? Can't you see how tormented I am by the thought of becoming a politician?"

"I'm sorry, Susan, and I know we should have asked you about running for office sooner ... maybe ... but you know you'd have shut us down from the outset without considering it seriously. And you must know, deep down, how good you would be as a Senator. You must know ..."

"I feel as if I'm being railroaded into something," I complained.

"Then don't do it! I warned the others that you might not want to run for office and that you might even resent our creation of a 'Draft Susan Young' committee. I don't think any of us will be hurt if you decide not to do it. It's just that we know you'd be a superb Senator and that it would be a shame if you didn't give it a shot."

I don't often use sarcasm, but I replied, "Well, thank you *so* much for your permission not to run."

"Oh, Susan." She was crushed. She had never heard me use sarcasm in anger before. "I didn't really think you'd be so upset about this. It's a great opportunity for you, and you know you'd win the nomination by acclamation and the election in a runaway. But, wow, don't do it if you really don't want to do it."

"I'm already busy enough," I replied weakly, "with LOST, the Review Board, the church, the United Way, and the Foundation. And I don't really want to steal any more time from Timothy and Liz."

"Aha!" Thelma pounced. "I knew it! The way you said that – 'I don't' – you're already considering it."

I laughed. "You scheming devil!"

After I sipped some coffee, I continued, "But please stop the work of this ad hoc committee, or whatever it is, until I've had a chance to think about it more and discuss it with the children. I really don't want to be pushed into this."

Thelma said she would let the others know that I wanted some time to think about it but she really doubted whether the movement would be easy to stop. I groaned.

I really was bothered that the others had done all this without telling me, but I knew Thelma was right about everything. I had a good chance of winning the election, and I would do a good job as Senator.

When the children got home from school that afternoon, I was tight-lipped about Thelma's visit. The children didn't mention politics, much to my relief because I needed at least one more day to contemplate it before even raising the possibility with them.

The next morning it was clear I'd have to make a decision soon. The newspaper carried another story by Jeremy on page two, "Will She Or Won't She?" It quoted Ben, Harold Yoder, Omaha's Democratic Mayor Mike Fahey, Nebraska's Republican Governor Johanns, the chair of the Civilian-Police Review Board, all saying strong, positive things about me and about my potential candidacy.

I carefully composed an email to Jeremy, Ben, Will Franks, Harold Yoder, and Thelma:

> I'm sure you all know how surprised I was when Jeremy Hall's article came out yesterday. I had never really thought about running for any political office until then.
>
> I really must consider my other obligations, too, though: the church, The United Way, LOST, the Civilian-Police Review Board, and the Foundation, not to mention my children.
>
> Please stop pushing me with these articles and whatever meetings you've been holding. I need some time to think about this and to work through all the issues with my children.

About mid-morning, Kathy Bergman from next door and Gail Schultz from down the street showed up at the front door. I knew why they were there, and I invited them in for coffee.

"Are you really seriously considering running for Senate?" asked Gail.

"What can we do to help?" asked Kathy.

I tried to act calm and not get all politician-sounding when I answered.

"You know, I'm not really sure. There's so much to consider, and the thought had never crossed my mind until two days ago when that reporter mentioned it to me. I'm plenty busy now; I really don't need to try to enter the world of politics on top of everything else."

Gail said, "We all know you're busy with various organizations, but you can get someone else to take over for you at most of them, for sure. And you'd be so good as a Senator."

Kathy added, "Please think about it. Let's talk about the things that are worrying you, okay?"

"Well, first off, there are Timothy and Liz. I haven't discussed it with them. If I won, they'd have to move to Washington, D.C., and leave their friends and schools behind. They'd be graduating from a different high school. That would be quite a change.

"What's more, I'm comfortable raising the children here in Omaha where I have a good sense of what is going on and what they're doing. In Washington, I'd be working all the time. It would be a new environment that I'm not sure they're ready for yet. Am I being overly protective?"

Kathy countered, "I've seen you with your children, Susan, and I've known you and them for nearly a decade now. They are rock-solid. They have strong moral compasses. They might even grow and flourish in a DC environment, away from the safety of the old Omaha suburbs."

"Really?" I asked. "I'm not sure *I'm* ready for that yet, even if you think *they* are."

Kathy continued, "Your children have good social skills. They'll make friends quickly there, and they'll also quickly figure out which kids are going to be good friends and which ones will be ... what should I say? ... less-good friends?"

"In other words," said Gail, "'Yes', you are being overly protective. What I wouldn't have given for the opportunity to live in DC for six years as a teenager! I'd love to have the chance to immerse our children there for six years! What a wonderful opportunity for you and your children!"

"What about the house? What about moving? What about the pressures from all the lobbying groups? There's just **so** much to consider..."

"If you want to take the challenge, those things will all work out, and you know we'll all do everything we can to make it happen," said Gail, "and to make it work for you."

I glared at them. And I laughed at the same time. "You had already anticipated my objections and questions. Right?"

They laughed, too.

"We sure did," answered Kathy. "After that story in yesterday's paper, we spoke with my husband, Ray, and with Gail's husband, Harry, and the four of us all agreed it would be a big loss to the community, to Nebraska, and although this sounds melodramatic, to the nation as a whole if you **don't** run for the Senate."

I promised to let them know my decision soon, but warned them that I really needed to discuss it at length with my children.

When the children got home from school that day, they were brimming with questions and excitement.

"Mom?" said Timothy, "Seth says you might run for the U.S. Senate?"

"I really don't know, Timothy. The thought had never occurred to me until Jeremy Hall mentioned it when he was interviewing me for that article in yesterday's paper. I think, though, that Thelma and Dale and a few other people have been working on the idea without telling me."

"You'd win, like, for sure, Mom," said Liz. "I can't see why anyone wouldn't vote for you."

"Well, I do think there's a better than even chance I could win," I agreed, "but we need to talk about a lot of different things before I can decide what to do."

"Like what, Mom?" asked Liz.

"We would have to move to Washington, D.C., for one thing," I said. "You would have to say good-bye to your friends, and you'd graduate from a different high school."

"Also, for the next seven or eight months I would be on the go, campaigning, meeting with people, writing speeches, and lord only knows what else. I've always been determined to be here for you children, and I'm not eager to spend so much time away from you two."

"We'll be okay, Mom," said Liz, "We'll even, like, help all we can."

"Before you get too enthusiastic about the idea," I cautioned them, "Think about everything some more. Let's draw up a list of things to consider, okay?"

In the end, we made two lists, a campaign-pre-election list, and a post-election-if-we-win list.

The pre-election list:
- All my current obligations.
    - I could resign from the Board of Elders at the church in no time. I was there only because I had made a major donation to the church. They didn't really need me.
    - I could resign from the United Way. They named me to their board of directors just to get me to donate more money.
    - The Civilian-Police Review Board. I could maybe stay with them for a while, but I would have to resign eventually.
    - LOST. LOST didn't take a lot of time. I could probably continue with it even if I won the election.
    - The Foundation was a different story. I could leave more of the decision-making to Thelma and the Board of Directors, but I wasn't keen to do so.
- Time with and for the children.
    - The children offered to do more cooking and cleaning.
    - I promised we would eat out more, but not just fast food.
    - The children said they really wanted to be involved in the campaign. They offered to do all the menial tasks they could.
- Money. Who would pay for everything? I had no idea, but I would leave that responsibility to whatever group had been so eager to get me to run for the Senate.

- Chaos and communications. If I decided to run, we would each have a cellphone, and we had to promise to answer calls from each other.

The idea of getting a cellphone apiece was a big plus for the children.
The Post-Election list was harder:
- The children's friends.

"I don't really want to move and, like, have to say good-bye to everyone," said Liz. "Not to Becky and Aaron, and certainly not to Seth."

"And I have some friends I will have a hard time leaving, too, mostly Sandra" said Timothy.

I noted they both said "will", not "would", which I took to mean they were in favor of the idea. But I wanted to make sure.

"If you two are still going with the same boyfriend and girlfriend after the election, I know it will be hard to leave them. That shouldn't and won't be the only deciding factor, but it will be important. Think about it carefully. Please."

I added, "To be really blunt, most romances don't last when people live in different cities. When I left Salina to go to K-State, my boyfriend, Albert Mauer, and I promised we would love each other forever. Within three weeks one of my high school friends told me that Albert was going out with someone else in town. And that happened everywhere at college; almost all of my dorm mates lost their hometown boyfriends before Christmas that year. I just want you to be prepared."

"Mom, like, you don't need to be so brutal," said Liz.

"Later in life things might work better. I've known marriages to last forever with the partners commuting to see each other when one works in one town and the other works somewhere else. But in those cases, both are working and can afford to fly all over creation to be together."

"I have to admit I'm concerned," said Timothy. "Sandra is the only girlfriend I've ever had, and she chose me; I didn't really choose her. I like having a girlfriend, and I'm glad it's Sandra, but I have no idea whether I'll ever find anyone else if she and I split up."

I bit my lip to keep from laughing. Timothy was so handsome and tall and so nice, I knew he'd have girlfriends all his life if he wanted them.

"I think Sandra likes having a boyfriend, too," he said. "I think she'd find someone else if we moved away. That makes me sad."

"Here are some things to consider," I tried to explain. "First, if someone is going to start dating around the minute you're gone, maybe that's a good sign, you know, that they liked being in a relationship with you so much that they're looking for something to replace it."

"Second, if you can't hold the relationship together with email, phone calls, and infrequent visits, maybe it wasn't meant to last. That doesn't mean it's wrong to have that relationship now – there are lots of good things about temporary relationships that are positive and caring."

"And third, I know of some married couples who dated for a while, broke up for even a few years, and then got together again before they got married. I know of one couple that started dating each other again twenty years after they had dated in high school."

"The point is, it's not the end of the world."

"Mom, Seth and I have talked about the future some. Does that count?"

I fake-stifled a shocked look, smiled, and then said, "Liz, honey, I'd be surprised if you hadn't talked about the future. You and Sandra, too, Timothy. That's how you find out what the other person is like and whether you want to commit to them. If you don't like what their plans are for the future, and if you don't want to be a part of those plans, that's a good sign the relationship is unlikely to go anywhere."

"So what else belongs on the list?"
- "Moving!" said Liz, and I agreed. Where would we live in Washington? Would we sell our house in Omaha?
- How much would I have to work? Would I be gone all the time?
- Could I handle the pressure of single-parenthood plus a pressure-packed job?

"Also, drugs. I don't know how exposed to the drug culture you are here in Omaha," I said, "but I'm certain it's better developed and more prevalent in Washington, D.C. That worries me. I know that at some point you may want to experiment, but I also want you to be safe."

Timothy then surprised me with this insight: "Mom, if you don't run, you'll always wonder whether you should have."

I hugged him. "That is so perceptive!" I said, "but I don't want to run if I think I might resign before completing the six-year term."

"Six years?" asked Liz. "Really? If you're elected to the Senate, it would be for like six years, not just two?"

I had forgotten that the children didn't take their civics classes in Omaha until they were high school freshmen, and Liz didn't really know much about politics and government yet.

"Yup," answered Timothy for me. "Senators are elected for six-year terms; members of the House of Representatives are elected for only two-year terms."

"So, if we decide to do this ... and notice I said 'we' because I won't do this unless you two want to do it, too ... if we do, you would both graduate from a high school there in DC, not here. Liz you would have plenty of time to adjust and fit in if we go, but Timothy you'd be transferring in the middle of your junior year. Think about that. You have your friends and clubs and sports activities here; you'd have to start all over again there."

"Mom, I don't really have such close friends here that I'd die if could never see them again. Sure, Bob and the guys on the soccer team are good friends, but I can play soccer there, probably, and get friends that way."

He added wistfully, "I would miss being with Sandra, though."

After some thought, he went on, "Six years? Geez, I'd just about be through college by the end of your first term."

"Well, let's all think about it," I repeated. "If your friends ask about it, just say we're considering it. And feel free to discuss it with your friends. Some extra input might really be helpful."

"I know you'll want to discuss this with your friends tonight, so after dinner let's put a moratorium on using the telephone for two hours. Let's get schoolwork done, and I'll start thinking of more pluses and minuses, okay?"

Chapter 33 – Wishy-Washy and Determined

We had a quick salad, and I some heated up leftover hamburger-macaroni-tomato casserole for supper. I told the children to leave the cleaning up for me that night while they did their schoolwork.

"I'm serious about doing your schoolwork," I said. "In two hours come down here and be prepared to tell me what you've been working on. Only after you pass that quiz will you be allowed to use the phone."

The telephone must have rung at least three times in the next twenty minutes: Seth for Liz, Sandra for Timothy, Becky for Liz. I told them all that no one could use the telephone for the next two hours.

Cindy Gruvel was also one of the callers. Immediately I asked my cynical self, "Is she making this call on her own or has Ben put her up to it?"

"Susan, it's Cindy. Do you have a few minutes to talk?"

"Sure." I almost added, "as long as it isn't about politics," but I figured that wouldn't stop whatever people were trying to organize.

"I know you've seen the articles in the paper, Susan, and I'm sure you've figured out that Ben and I played a role in creating this buzz about your running for the Senate. I hope it's okay that we've done this…"

I still couldn't decide whether Cindy was calling on her own or on behalf of the ad hoc committee to "Draft Susan Young".

"Well, really, I don't know what to think," I said. "I was certainly dumbfounded when the idea was first mentioned…"

"And now?"

"The children and I had a long talk about it this afternoon, and we'll talk more tonight and tomorrow. I don't know what to think at this point."

"We'd like to have a steering committee get together soon, Susan, maybe even before you decide whether you want to run, to help you decide, and to answer any questions you might have."

"That seems a bit premature," I said. Things looked as if they could easily get away from me if I didn't urge caution, serious caution.

"What we really want to do is make sure you know there are many, many of your friends who will do whatever we can to help. We'll help you get elected, and we'll help you by taking over things you might want to spin off if you decide to run. We'll help you move, we'll help you organize a staff, we'll help you set up constituency offices here in Nebraska, we'll help you do anything we can help with…"

"Slow down, Cindy! You and the 'many, many friends' you mentioned are way ahead of me. I know you're all trying to be helpful, and you all really want me to run, but you and everyone else involved are going to have to slow down, or the answer will certainly be 'no'!"

"Well we certainly don't want that to happen," replied Cindy, "and so I'll drop it. I just want you to know there is a groundswell of support from a *lot* of people."

And then, to try smooth things a bit, Cindy asked, "How are you three doing these days?"

"I think we're okay, all things considered," I answered. "The kids are adjusting well. Both seem to be involved in *very serious* romances," I added in a very serious sounding voice. "And I think we're all slowly accepting and adjusting to Fred's not being with us. There's a really empty feeling that affects us all, but we're coping pretty well."

"Good. Why don't you and the kids come over for dinner this Friday night?"

"I'd love that, Cindy, but I can't speak for the children anymore. I'll have to see what plans they have for the weekend. … Oh, wait, I know they're planning to go to the high school basketball game and then have friends over afterward."

"Okay…"

I sensed that she wanted to invite me over anyway so I could meet with the "steering committee", and I was glad she let it go.

"Cindy, we'll probably order some pizza for a quick supper Friday night before the children leave for the basketball game. Why don't you and Ben come and join us for pizza about 5:30?"

"That would be wonderful. It's been too long since we've seen your kids, and it will be good to catch up."

"My only request is that you two not push me on the idea of running for the Senate, okay?"

Cindy laughed, "Of course, Susan! No politics on Friday night."

- - -

Pizza night was great fun, but it wasn't exclusively a pizza night. The children had decided to have a Cheetos-only, all-orange party after the basketball game, and they insisted we all had to have some crushed Cheetos on at least one slice of our pizzas as well.

"Why a Cheetos-only party?" asked Cindy.

"We were getting, like, bored with the usual chips and dips or hot dogs or pizza for our get-togethers," answered Liz. "And Cheetos are, like, such fun! You have to sort of, like, forget about everything else and let the orange colored dust cover your face and fingers. We thought it would be fun just to forget about neatness and, like, cut loose with the Cheetos. We'll take plenty of photos!"

"Well, that certainly sounds creative,' said Cindy, tentatively."

"I just hope the rec-room carpet doesn't become permanently stained orange," I said.

"Why not, Mom?" asked Timothy, "An orange carpet down there will look great!" and he laughed as he added, "And the only drinks we're having are orange pop and orange juice."

Liz said, "We're all going to wear sort of, like, orange-colored clothes for the party, but the high school colors are black and gold, so we figure gold-ish orange or orange-ish gold should work well both at the basketball game and later, here at the party."

I looked at Cindy and Ben and reassured them, "Don't worry. We have a limit of eighteen teenagers who can come to the party, including Seth, Aaron, Becky, and Sandra, along with Liz and Timothy. It'll be fine."

After the children left for the game, we chatted a bit about what we believed and didn't believe about how the war in Afghanistan was going. The conversation moved around after that but after an hour or so, Ben said, "Susan, I know Cindy promised you we wouldn't talk about politics tonight, but there's something we need to discuss."

I glared at him. "This had better be good, Ben."

"Have you ever heard of Agbrakan?" he asked.

"I think I've heard the name. Vaguely. Isn't that an ag-biz firm?"

"In a way, yes," replied Ben. "They're an agricultural business public interest group. That's a backward way of saying they're a major farm lobby organization, lobbying on behalf of farmers, mostly in Kansas and Nebraska. Their name combines 'agriculture' plus the two state names. 'Ag' from agriculture – 'bra' from Nebraska – 'kan' from Kansas."

"Oh, yes. I think Fred mentioned them a few times. Why do you ask?"

"They just made a thirty-thousand-dollar donation to the Fred Young Foundation."

"Send it back!" I nearly shouted. And then I took a deep breath.

"I can't have it look as if any lobbying group even *might* be able to buy influence with me by donating to the foundation."

"They are distinct things, though," Ben responded. "The donation is a no-strings-attached donation; in fact, it's a pledge for thirty thousand dollars each of the next six years."

"Six years, huh?" I asked in my most sarcastic voice. "What a coincidence that a senator's term is also six years."

"I can understand your feelings about this, Susan, but you should know that many politicians do set up foundations and do accept what can only be called 'politically-motivated' donations to the foundations. Former President Clinton and his wife are notorious for having done this."

"Well, it's wrong. It's as if votes on key legislation are for sale in a very unsubtle way. Send it back."

"The way you say that with such vehemence…" said Cindy, "it sounds as if you've decided to run."

"Not really," I hesitated, and then I added. "I am just aghast and upset by the skullduggery involved with politics and political financing."

"Well, then, how about we hold onto the check until you decide for sure whether you're running?" asked Ben.

"Hmmm." I paused. But then I went on, thinking out loud, "If I don't run, it would be nice to have the money for the Foundation, but I'm still uneasy about receiving money that is donated just on speculation that it might buy influence and not because people care about Fred and the Foundation. It concerns me. I can imagine others joining in, trying to influence me, just by *trying* to donate to the FRY Foundation, letting me know they tried, and expecting a political favor for having tried."

Ben wasn't very reassuring.

"If you run," he said, "There will be people every day trying to influence you in every imaginable way. Lobbyists and others will all be both a nuisance and an important source of information. By all means, do *not* downplay the demands on your time and on your inner strength."

- - -

The children got a little exuberant during their Cheetos party. They giggled, they laughed, they screamed, and when they came upstairs to leave, they were all laughing as they stopped in the half bath and front hallway to look at themselves in the mirrors. They had orange streaks on their faces, through their hair, and on their clothing. True to her word, Liz had everyone pose for photos – in groups and individually.

"The party was epic, Mom!" said Timothy. "Everybody is going to be talking about it for a long time at school!"

After all the guests had left, I went downstairs to check things out. I screamed and groaned. There was Cheeto dust and globs of Cheeto gunk everywhere in the basement.

I called up to the children. "I'll help with this, but you two have a **lot** of cleaning up to do!"

"Don't worry, Mom," chirped Liz. "We know it's a mess; we're going to look after it."

"We know, Mom," added Timothy as they came downstairs to join me.

Surveying the mess, I couldn't believe it.

"It looks as if Cheeto glop has been ground into the carpet and the furniture!" I said. "If it doesn't come out with the vacuum or just good old-fashioned elbow grease, we'll rent a steamer to clean this up."

Another option, of course, was to hire someone to come in and do the cleaning professionally, but I didn't want to do that. I knew we could afford it, but I couldn't get past my old thrifty habits.

More importantly, I didn't want the children to get even a hint that it would be okay to make a big mess and then let me pay to have someone clean it up. I wanted them to remember that they had responsibilities and shouldn't become cavalier about either money or their own behaviors.

"Let's leave it for now, but tomorrow is a work day," I said. "We'll sleep in as usual, but we'll have to start the cleaning by nine."

"Mom," complained Timothy, "usually we sleep in longer than that on weekends. Can't we wait to start the cleaning until 10?"

I reluctantly gave in.

"Okay," I said, "but this is going to be one heck of a task."

I looked at them both again and couldn't believe it. There were Cheetos in their hair, on their hands, in their clothes, everywhere.

"Shake all the loose food off your clothes and out of your hair down here," I said. "Then go up and shower, both of you, tonight. Don't put it off until morning. And when you get undressed up there in your bedrooms, don't let too many of the Cheeto crumbs get onto your beds or floors."

- - -

The next morning, I heard them moving around upstairs and whispering to each other at 7:30. I wondered what was going on, and so I reluctantly pulled myself out of bed, showered and got dressed. By the time I got downstairs, I could hear the two of them down in the rec room, and so I went down to join them.

"Mom," said Liz, "We are, like, *never* doing this again. What...a...mess! Cheeto crumbs are ground into, like, everything! And we'll have to scrub down all the games to get rid of the Cheeto gunk. There's even orange dust on the ceiling! Ugh."

"We'll collect up all the garbage and pop bottles now," said Timothy, "and then after breakfast we'll start dusting and vacuuming and washing everything down.

At ten o'clock, just as we were about to start cleaning, the doorbell rang. It was Thelma, along with Seth, Aaron, Becky, and Sandra.

"When Timothy and Liz spoke with the boys on the phone this morning and told them what the cleanup was going to involve, the others decided to help, and so we stopped at the Hy-Vee to rent some steamers, too, just in case we need them. One for the carpet, and one for the furniture."

All six of the children were smiling and quite pleased with themselves.

"When did all these phone conversations take place, anyway?" I asked.

"While you were still in *bed*," said Timothy pretending to be judgmental and superior. "Liz and I just woke up on our own, and when we got together, we decided we didn't want to put off the cleaning all day. We called our friends to explain that we probably wouldn't be going out with them until much later, after the cleaning was done."

"Seth wanted me to go to the mall with him today," said Liz. "I told him, like, I couldn't until we got the rec room cleaned up."

"When I thought about the mess from those Cheeto wars we'd had down there, I knew we had to help," said Seth. "I called Aaron to the phone to get him to agree, and then we called Becky and Sandra."

"The boys told us over breakfast what they were planning," said Thelma. "Let me tell you, I wasn't surprised to hear about the mess down there after I saw the boys when they came home last night. I barely recognized them. Cheetos all through their hair and clothes! Orange faces and hands – even their eyebrows and eyelashes! I made them strip at the door and head straight to the shower! Well, kids, get to it!"

Thelma actually screamed when she went down the stairs and saw the mess. "Oh..my..GOD! How could you kids do this? Aagggghhhh."

Seth, Timothy, and Sandra took charge of organizing the cleaning. Sandra started vacuuming, beginning with the ceiling! There was orange dust everywhere! The others began dusting and washing all the items in the room.

"Man," said Aaron, "This foosball table is a mess!"

He and Becky dusted and washed all the players, the playing field, and especially the handles.

"Eww," said Becky, "The handles are coated in orange, sticky crud from everybody's hands. It was fun cutting loose last night, but what a mess!"

"Oh no!" exclaimed Timothy. "Look at the air holes for the air hockey game! They're all clogged with Cheeto dust and gunk."

Liz got out our little hand-held vacuum cleaner and started vacuuming the air hockey table, but then she said, "I don't think vacuuming will, like, get everything out of all those holes. We can turn on the game to blow the stuff out, I guess, but, like, it'll probably blow it all over the room."

"So let's vacuum it to clean it as well as we can now so there'll be less dust later," Seth suggested. "But it looks like we'll be doing every job two or three times, just to get everything cleaned up the way it should be."

Timothy added, "I guess this is going to be what Ms. Rashevsky calls an 'iterative process.'"

Seth groaned, and Sandra put down the vacuum cleaner, "Okay, Smart Guy, come over here and help me 'iterate' this ceiling."

I winked at Thelma and said, "Why don't you and I take some more of this garbage upstairs while the children clean up here."

My plan was for Thelma and me to go upstairs and have coffee together while the children cleaned.

I added to the children, "Why not stop for a while at noon for a lunch break, and we'll have leftover Cheetos and orange pop for lunch, okay?"

Timothy threw a Cheeto at me. "No more Cheetos for awhile, Mom. But you and Ms. Hazelton might want some," and he approached me menacingly with a bowl that still had some Cheeto crumbs in it.

While Thelma and I sat at the kitchen table with our coffee, we could hear the vacuum going, and they had the music turned up loud so they could hear it over the vacuum.

At various times, the children came upstairs for more paper towels and more garbage bags, but they threw themselves into it.

"Susan, we have to talk about a couple of things," said Thelma. "Is now a good time?"

I frowned, wondering what she was up to. "I suppose so. What's up?"

"First, when the boys stripped at the door last night, they had Cheetos in their underwear! What kind of place do you run here, anyway?"

I faked a shocked look. "Oh no! What did they say happened?"

"Well, I've never heard of Cheeto sex, so I wasn't too worried, but I wanted both to tease you about it and to let you know. They swear it was just the boys that got into stuffing Cheetos in each other's pants and shirts…"

"Well, I *want* to believe it was just the boys," I said, "so let's believe them. I would hate to think anything got out of hand between the boys and the girls."

"What else?" I asked.

"Ben and Cindy were here last night. We recognized their car. Did you three talk any more about your running for the Senate?"

"Mostly not," I said, "at my request. But I think they were checking out my possible positions on a number of policy issues. They encouraged me to talk about Afghanistan, Saudi Arabia, energy, the push to use corn for ethanol, and other topics, too. It didn't dawn on me until I went to bed that maybe that was part of what was going on… Thelma!?"

"What…"

"Have you been on the phone with them this morning?"

"Yes, and I think they're even more enthusiastic about supporting your candidacy now after your conversations last night."

"Well, you folks have to stop this. I hate the thought that people are plotting behind my back. Anyway, one thing I wasn't so sure would go over with Ben was my take on farm subsidies. I told him that I think the programs are keeping landowners well-supported but farmers and farm workers aren't benefiting nearly as much."

"How's that?" Thelma asked.

"If government programs increase the demand for wheat, then farmers want to plant more wheat and gradually end up outbidding each other to rent or buy more land. The farmers who own land are better off, but only because the programs basically just drive up the price of farmland."

"Wow! You said that to Ben? How'd he take it?"

"You talked with him this morning. What did he say to you?" Answer a question with a question. I was slowly learning.

"He said he hoped it wouldn't come up during the campaign, but he also said that if anyone could win in a farming state with your views about farm subsidies, it would be you. Susan, I don't understand it all, but I know he's right that you can win."

"Well, maybe. But just so you know," I said, "I would never advocate getting rid of the subsidy programs instantly. Mostly I just want the government to stop creating new ones. And then maybe we can slowly begin to phase out a few others, like especially the ethanol program. That one is just plain ridiculous, making us burn less efficient fuel and driving up the prices of grains, and why?"

"It may be a good idea to have other sources of fuel besides oil," I added, "but right now it looks like another boondoggle for farmers, especially the farmers who own their land. I hope everyone realizes that if oil is going to get super expensive, some people will figure that out all on their own, long before it actually happens. They'll be the ones who will develop the processes and networks for ethanol production and distribution. We don't need the government to get involved in that."

"It'll be interesting to see how that plays out," said Thelma.

"Anyway," she continued, "You can trust Ben and Cindy *and me* not to try to push you around. I'll quit for now, and I'll let you know about other activities that might be going on in anticipation that you will run."

She added, "I don't think you understand, Susan, how many people are behind this attempt to get you to run for the Senate."

Chapter 34 – Making the Decision

Over the next few days, as I reflected on all the life changes I had been through in the six months after losing Fred, I came to accept two things.

First, he was gone, and he wasn't coming back. I thought I had accepted that during the first week after 9-11, but deep down, I knew I hadn't – not really. It continued to throw me for a loop, especially at times when I needed someone to talk things over with. I missed him terribly and I often spoke with him, in my mind anyway.

The second thing was that despite all the pain and grief we had felt, I had weathered it all reasonably well. I had stood up for the children and for myself all along the way; I had taken control of my life, and I hadn't succumbed to very many of the pleas for funds that Ben had warned me to expect. I felt an inner weakness in my loneliness, but I knew, too, that I had a strength that would serve us well.

That realization was a big reason I was willing to consider running for the Senate. Another reason came from Timothy's insightful comment – if I didn't do it, I would always wonder, "What if I had run? Could I have won? Could I have made a bigger difference in the world?" I knew those questions would haunt me if I didn't run.

Probably the most compelling reason for running, though, was all the support that so many friends and neighbors offered and promised would be available from all over the state. I was repeatedly reminded that many people in the state knew who I was because of Fred's death in the terrorist attacks and because of all the news stories about him; and then later there was all the publicity about us and about the Foundation. Apparently, I had handled myself well during the crisis, the funeral, the ensuing stories about our financial situation, the creation of the Frederick Robert Young Foundation, and the issues at the Citizen-Police Review Board.

Thinking only from my own perspective, I had pretty much decided to give serious consideration to running. I didn't want to think only from my own perspective, though; I wanted to consider the children, my local commitments to various organizations, and the very different lifestyles we would be thrust into. Also, I loved my friends, our neighborhood, our house, and Omaha; I wasn't sure I wanted to move away from the wonderful support, community, and memories we had.

I continued to press the children about their thoughts on moving and how much our lives would change if I ran and was elected. The two things that concerned me the most about uprooting the family from Omaha and moving to Washington, D.C., were how much my being a senator would take me away from the children and how much they might miss their friends in Omaha.

I truly wanted it to be a family decision, and so in our talks, I often said, "If **we** decide I should run…"

"If we decide I should run," I told them, "it's a major commitment. We can't start this process and then change our minds after a month or even after a few years. If I'm elected, I can't say to everyone, 'Oh, thanks for everything you've done on my behalf, but I've changed my mind, and I don't want to be a senator after all.' I will have to stick out the race, and the full term if I'm elected. If I run, we'll be committed to running, winning, and serving, so let's talk it through as well as we can."

The children were pretty much in awe of the idea that their mother might become a senator. They were also pretty much in awe of the idea of getting their own cell phones, and I wanted to make sure they weren't going along with my running just so they could get their own phones.

"Mom," Liz asked, "Is there, like, a chance the Hazeltons might move to Washington, D.C., if you win?"

I had been thinking about that myself. It would be wonderful to have Thelma with me in Washington, but I didn't know if Dale could change jobs or whether they would even be interested. But I had certainly been toying with the idea of asking Thelma to be on my staff in Washington.

I didn't say these things to Liz right then, though. Instead I said, "Let's not get ahead of ourselves. First, we need to decide whether I should run. Once we make that decision, then we can ask them."

Liz smiled. It was almost a shy, yet coy, smile, as she ventured, "Well I've, like, already mentioned it to Seth and Aaron, Mom. They both think it'd be, like, cool to live in Washington for at least the next six years."

"It's awfully expensive, compared with Omaha," I said, "and it's such a different culture there…"

"What's different about the culture?" Timothy asked.

"There are so many people there trying to influence politicians and bureaucrats; there's so much going on that you can't trust. And there are serious ghettos in Washington, D.C. I get the impression that our lives in Omaha would seem very mild and tame, compared with life in DC."

I went on: "I don't know. Maybe it would be good for you children to be exposed to more than our serene lives in Omaha, or to experience more, different lifestyles than we see here or on our trips; but changing our lives for the next six or more years… I just don't know."

Thelma called a couple of days later.

"Susan, we need to get your name on the ballot."

"What do you mean?"

"In order to get your name on the ballot for the primary election, we need to have the paperwork filed by next weekend. All we need is a form signed by you and two thousand signatures by registered voters."

"Oh my! How hard will that be?"

"Susan," Thelma said somewhat condescendingly, "we can get the signatures in less than a day. They won't be a problem. What we need from you, though, is the go-ahead to start collecting the signatures and begin campaigning."

"Okay." I hesitated. "I'll let everyone know my decision tomorrow evening. Will that leave enough time?"

"That'll be perfect!"

That night before we went to bed, I asked the children to sit with me so we could talk some more about whether I should run for the Senate.

"I've tried to emphasize," I said, "that if I run, I'll be away from home a great deal. I'll be at meetings, I'll be traveling all over the state to meet with campaigners and voters, and I'll be expected to make hundreds of public appearances. And when I'm not gone, I'll need to be working on speeches, drafting position papers, and who knows what else."

"You've made that all pretty clear to us so far, Mom," said Timothy. "I think we can handle that. Actually, I'd love to do whatever I can to help."

"Me, too," Liz added quickly and enthusiastically.

Timothy went on, "I think it will be so cool to be on the inside, helping and learning more about how politics works. Just think how valuable this experience will be for us, no matter how things turn out!"

I caught that he had said "will", not "would", and smiled.

"Yes, it will be a valuable learning experience for us all," I half-laughed. "But I'll need your help around here, too, especially with meals and other household tasks. Okay?"

They nodded. I wasn't sure whether the nods meant, "Yes, we understand" or "Yes, we're willing to pitch in at home to help."

I continued, "I hadn't thought much about politics at all except as a voter until a month or so ago. We all have *so* much to learn. We need to learn all we can from everyone, but I worry about all the pressure that professional politicians will be putting on me … and on us."

"It'll be, like, interesting, if not fun, Mom," said Liz.

"Maybe so," I said, "but I need some assurances from you two."

Timothy and Liz looked at each other and grimaced.

"What kind of assurances?" asked Timothy. His tone of voice revealed skepticism and concern.

"Well, for starters, you absolutely **must** keep up with your schoolwork. If you won't seriously commit to that, I won't run. Your futures are more important than some foray I might make into the world of politics."

I had no idea how to enforce it, but I knew I wouldn't let them help with my campaign if they were letting their schoolwork slide.

"Also, we'll need to work and co-ordinate carefully about meals, school, social activities, and everything."

"Mom," said Timothy, "I've heard something about using the internet to coordinate schedules. Maybe we can look into something like that?"

"That's a great idea!" I said. "And a third thing: I know this isn't a problem right now, but we all need to be careful about what we say to or in front of others. Anything and everything can be reported in the news, so please watch yourselves. But for now I need to know if you two are willing, even eager, to do all this. I won't run if you have doubts."

"The only doubts I have," said Liz, "are, like, being away from Seth. I really like him, Mom."

"I really like Sandra, too," added Timothy, "but I don't want to let that stand in the way of this opportunity."

Then he looked at Liz and said in a somewhat condescending big-brother way, "Liz, I know you and Seth are close. When it's just the guys laughing and goofing around, it's really clear how much he cares for you. I don't know, maybe it's because I'm there, but he doesn't ogle other girls or go along with the guy-talk stuff with the other guys. With email and all, I think you two will be able to stay in touch if we end up moving."

Liz almost swooned, she was so happy to hear this from Timothy. She leaned over and hugged him.

"He says those things to me when we're alone," said Liz, "but it is, like, so reassuring to hear you tell me this."

I didn't want to rain on her parade, but I interjected, "Keep in mind, you two, that people get lonely when they're apart. Remember what I told you about my first year in college, how all my dormmates either lost a boyfriend to some other girl or left their former boyfriends for someone else. Be realistic, but also be honest with each other."

"Mom," asked Liz, "do you think that if you and Dad had been, like, dating in high school you would have, like, stuck together if you hadn't both ended up at the same college? ... Or even if you had?"

"That's hard to say; I never really thought about it. ... Now that you ask, though, I can imagine that we might not have stayed together. He was so handsome that I'm sure some other girls would have made a play for him. I'm surprised he wasn't already going with someone else when we first met."

"What about you, Mom? Would you have dated other boys in college?"

"To be honest? ... Maybe. I didn't date all that much in college anyway, but I wanted to go out, and I wanted to go out with boys, not just with roommates or dormmates. I just wasn't asked out all that much. If your father had been a solid boyfriend before college, I know I'd still have been lonely ... I might have ... Anyway, I'm glad it didn't happen that way and that I was able to snag him early on, before anyone else could."

I smiled as I said that, but I had a sense that my answer didn't satisfy either of them. I got the feeling that they were a bit disappointed to learn that Fred and I might not have ended up together.

"Would you have actually two-timed Dad and gone out with someone else?" Timothy asked.

"I really can't say. I know that if some boy had shown interest in me or flirted a bit with me, I wouldn't have tried to stop him much if he appealed to me, but I'd like to think I'd have talked more with your father before actually going out with someone else."

I suddenly didn't want to explore the past and "what might have been" any more. I said to the children, "We have two phone lines. I know you have talked with Seth and Sandra about the possibility of my running. Why don't you call them and discuss it with them?"

"I don't need to," said Liz. "Seth and I have talked about it. We both cried at the thought of, like, not being together, but we also vowed to keep in touch with each other as much as we can.

"Sandra is different," said Timothy. "She really likes me, I know. She says she loves me, and we even talk about a future together. But she always adds something in a throwaway line, like, 'If it happens, it'll be wonderful.' I keep trying to accept that, but if I don't accept it, then I know we'll break up now, and I don't want to. I want to keep dating her and seeing her while we're here. I guess I don't really see her as my 'forever girlfriend' even though we'd both love it if it happens."

And so that night, the decision was made. I agreed to run. I called Thelma to tell her and then sent a group email to the others to let them know. After that email was sent, I called Thelma again.

"I have no idea how to run a campaign. I know we'll have to get other politicians and higher-ups in the Republican Party involved. What would you think of my asking Ben to take care of that part of the campaign? He's been active in the background of the Republican Party for a long time; he'll know what to do."

"I was thinking the same thing!" said Thelma. "He knows all the ins and outs. But there are lots of your friends who will want to be involved, too. I hope you and Ben will find a way to let us all help…"

"Of course! Thanks, Thelma. I'll call him now to see what he thinks."

The call with Ben was an eye-opener. If I had made the call before deciding to run, I might have had second thoughts.

Ben was happy to become the overall chair of the campaign, and in that regard to lead the fund-raising drives and to deal with all the long-time party members who would have to be included and made to feel a part of the campaign. But he also cautioned me about things that hadn't occurred to me yet. I would need a careful description of who I was and what I had done, and I would need to make sure to keep every campaign expenditure separate from my private spending, and that would apply to the children and the campaign workers as well.

I had pretty much foreseen those concerns. But then he said, "Susan, we all know you're going to win. You will have to be prepared to find a place to live in DC, and you'll have to start thinking about hiring a full-time staff. You'll need at least thirty people on your staff in DC."

"Thirty?" I groaned. "That seems daunting in and of itself."

"It won't be," Ben assured me. "There will be holdovers from Senator Tansky's staff after he retires. Some of them will have made a life in DC and will want to stay on, and there will be plenty of campaign workers from Nebraska who will want to ride your coattails. Just don't make any commitments to anyone yet, but I probably don't have to tell you that.

"What's most important right now is getting all the paperwork done so you're on the ballot for the primary. Can you stop by the office tomorrow morning? We'll sign the forms then. And, you need a good bio. I know you can write well, but just do a quick draft and add points to it. We'll get someone on the committee to polish it off, campaign-style."

I felt the control of my life slipping away from me. I couldn't micro-manage every little detail; I was going to have to decide what was important for me and let other people look after other things.

I had learned in the fall that I was probably too controlling for my own good. Liz had made that clear when she criticized me for giving too much advice to them during the memorial-tribute we had held for Fred. These were going to be new paths for me to walk.

I dashed out a quick bio, but I wasn't sure what to say about my positions on various policies. I did, however, mention the terrorist attacks and the war in Afghanistan. I said quite bluntly that given the confused state of politics in the Middle East, it wasn't clear that we could accomplish a quick solution to terrorism, but I believed we could not let Al Qaeda and the Taliban continue unchecked. I hated the thought of more war, but I believed continued military action would be necessary.

It was after 10:30 that night when I finished writing the quick bio. When I logged onto the computer to email it to Ben, I had over a dozen messages already congratulating me and offering assistance. A notable message was from Jeremy Hall, who said, "I'm delighted you'll be running for the Senate, and if there is anything at all that I can do to help, please let me know."

That message puzzled me. I knew Jeremy couldn't work on my campaign, not even quietly or behind the scenes, and maintain the ethics of journalistic objectivity, and so when I sent the bio to Ben, I also forwarded Jeremy's message along with it.

"What do you make of this?" I wrote to Ben. "I thought journalists were supposed to be objective and detached."

Ben wrote back almost immediately.

"Jeremy Hall is skilled but very ambitious. He knows you have a high probability of winning, and he would happily forego his journalism career in Omaha to work with you and for you. It might not be a bad move to let him ride along. How do you two get along?"

"Let's talk about it tomorrow," I wrote back. "I'll see you at 8."

When we met, I told Ben that I didn't completely trust Jeremy but it did look as if he would be very helpful.

And then the penny dropped. "Ben, was this all set up by you two?"

"Not exactly, but we did talk about it together."

"I know I have a lot to learn, Ben, but please don't plan my life for me."

He looked at me very seriously and replied, "Susan, no one will ever plan your life for you. I know you well enough to know you won't let that happen. But you are going to have to adjust to having other people do things for you. Figuring out what and how much you can delegate and how much you need to control will be a major part of your transition."

"I did all that at Arkero when I was there, Ben, but it looks as if this will be on a much grander scale."

"Okay," I sighed as I tried to accept it. "So let's get to work."

Chapter 35 – **Launching the Campaign**

"Well, the die is cast." That's what Fred always said after he made a decision, even after he played a card in UNO! He loved that phrase.

In my case, the die was definitely cast. I was running for the United States Senate and there was no turning back.

After I met with Ben, I emailed my brief bio to Jeremy Hall with the note, "Ben suggested I ask you to polish and/or rewrite this for me. Can you do that and still be a journalist at the paper?"

He replied, "Yes, I can. I just have to make sure I don't cover any of the senate race from now on, and I have to be very careful about how I cover any issues that you might address." Twenty-five minutes later he emailed me a smoother, more polished rewrite of the bio I'd sent. He clearly was an effective and efficient writer.

Next I called Thelma. "Let's do lunch. ... I'm trying to sound like a high-powered professional," I laughed. "But seriously, let me take you to lunch. We have so much to talk about."

"Oh, I can't today, Susan."

I was disappointed. I expect my pause led her to continue, "I'm meeting people from the different college campuses to explain more about the Foundation scholarships. The meeting is at ten this morning, and I have no idea how long it will last. I'm on my way out the door now."

"Can you call me when you're done? We need to set up a time to get together soon."

I had decided to leave the signature-gathering to Ben and the people he knew from the party, but I wasn't sure how much else I wanted to leave to them. For one thing I knew I would need a wardrobe makeover, but I didn't want to be "dressed" by some political advisor who didn't know me. Instead, I called Gail Schultz from down the street and asked if she would like to come up for coffee and give me some wardrobe advice.

"I'd love to!" she said. "I can be there in half an hour."

While I was waiting for her to come up from their house down by the reservoir, I started a pot of coffee. Next I wrote Ben and Jeremy again.

> Dear Ben and Jeremy,
> I love the rewrite you did of my bio, Jeremy.
> It occurs to me that we may want to have another press conference soon to announce my candidacy. But before I face the press, I really need to study up on current issues so I can speak intelligently about them. What do you two recommend besides reading the morning paper?

Ben was quick with a reply.

> Absolutely. How about we hold a press conference at the end of next week just as your nomination papers are being filed? That will give you a week to prepare as much as possible. Would it be okay if we begin policy discussions either tonight or tomorrow evening, just you, Jeremy, and me? Too many people at these thinking sessions leads to too much talk and not enough thinking.

Ben's email was quickly followed by another from Jeremy.

> Yes, be sure to read the paper, but I also suggest that you subscribe electronically to the New York Times, The Wall Street Journal, The Christian Science Monitor, The Kansas City Star, and The Telegraph. And yes to a meeting. I'm available both tonight and tomorrow.

I invited them to come over that evening at about eight o'clock.

Gail and I had a wonderful time discussing the appropriate wardrobe for running for office. We agreed that basic navy would probably be best for me, with a full suit, a blazer, and a grey skirt and grey slacks. We also liked the idea of a tweed sportcoat for visits with more rural audiences.

"What about jeans?" Gail asked. "You're going to be invited to all sorts of agricultural events, you know."

"What a great idea!" I grimaced. "I'll have to start going to aerobics class more often if I'm going to fit into my jeans. What sorts of tops do you recommend?"

"I expect you have some nice, simple blouses that would be fine, don't you? Why don't we look?"

Gail definitely was not shy about it. We went up to the bedroom and started going through the closet.

"I haven't given all of Fred's clothes away yet," I said. "I just can't get rid of everything right now, so I saved some of his older, slimmer things for Timothy, in case he wants them."

"That's really nice," said Gail. "And by the way not everyone noticed, but I thought it was wonderful how each of you wore something of Fred's at the Tribute last fall. That was so touching!"

As we went through the closet, Gail selected three blouses and two shirts she thought would work well with basic business suits. "You'll be on the road and traveling a lot, Susan. As I understand it, most politicians have a dozen or more shirts and carry a few with them when they travel, too. Maybe you can expense them?"

"I have to keep all my personal and political expenses separate," I said. "I'll see what the lawyers think. Starting right now I want there to be absolutely no chance that there could be even a whisper of a sense of impropriety or scandal involved with the campaign."

I pondered, "Two dozen shirts? Wow! What have I signed up for?"

"Oh, this grey tweed suit is **really** nice! Very professional. I remember it from the Tribute. It's definitely a keeper for the Senator."

Gail was the first person to refer to me as "The Senator". It made me uncomfortable since I hadn't even won the nomination yet … but I liked it, too.

"Here's an idea," said Gail. "What if you wore one of Fred's neckties whenever possible and even remotely appropriate while you're campaigning? Is that too crass?"

"I don't know," I was tentative. "I like the idea of having Fred with me, in a way, during the campaign, but I won't use his having been killed to win the nomination and election…"
Gail quickly responded, "Absolutely. Besides, it would probably backfire if anyone ever suspected you were doing it to play on people's sympathies. Still I just love the close, romantic notion of the two of you on the campaign trail together this way. Do it and I promise I won't say a word to anyone."

"A woman politician might want a bit of color in her public wardrobe," I said. "More than just grey and navy. What do you think?"

"Of course. You don't have to look exactly the same every day the way men politicians seem to. What else do you think would work?"

"I don't know… Burgundy? Dark green? I don't know. That's why I called you… I like your fashion sense, so what do you think?"

"Well, grey slacks and grey skirts will work well with all those colors if you want to mix and match. What about some pastels to lighten things up?"

I hesitated. "I don't know… I wonder if pastels might stand out too much and look too flashy. I could see going for royal blue, though."

"That would be good," and then her eyes lit up. "You might also want to consider something a shade darker than Cornhusker red to show your loyalty to them and to Nebraska as a whole. Cornhusker red is probably a little too much for campaigning, but something close would be good."

"I like that thought," I said, as I felt myself being drawn more and more into strategizing in the political world.

Just then my cellphone rang. It was Thelma.

"It was a quick meeting. They'd all read all the material I had sent out, surprise, surprise, and are on board with our program."

"That's great, Thelma! Thanks. Gail's here now. We've been discussing the clothing I'll need to run for office, but we're just about finished, so maybe you and I can meet at noon after all?"

I looked at Gail and added, "I'm hoping Gail will go shopping with me sometime in the next couple of days…"
Gail nodded enthusiastically as Thelma said, "Brilliant choice. She has excellent clothes sense."

We said good-bye and then I turned to Gail, "I have to go meet Thelma soon, but how about we go shopping tomorrow? We'll do it up right and have a fancy lunch somewhere, too!"

She beamed and said, "I'd love that! Thank you so much for including me in this part of the campaign. I want *so much* for you to win, and I really want to help somehow."

At lunch I asked Thelma how much she wanted to do on the campaign and later. "I don't know a thing about it, but I know some politicians hire staff members to work on their campaigns. Would you be willing to become a paid campaign staff member for my campaign?"

"Don't be a fool, Susan! Of course I will. I'll even become a full-time *volunteer* so you can use your campaign funds for other expenses."

I smiled at her. "Thank you! You're terrific. Let me ask you a tougher question then …"

And before I could continue, she said an enthusiastic, "Yes!"

"But you don't know the question, Thelma."

"Okay, Smarty, what's the question?"

"Would you and your family be willing to move to DC if I'm elected?"

Her mouth dropped open, but before she could speak, I continued, "I would need a personal assistant and I would want to offer you that job. I just don't know how mobile Dale can be in his work, or whether you would even want to give up your lives here in Omaha."

"Right off the bat, yes, I'd love it. But I don't know about the rest of the family. We'll have to discuss it; it wouldn't be easy."

Then she smiled back at me and said, "Well, we both know that Seth would love it. I don't need to ask him," and we both nodded knowingly.

"They're so young," I said. "It doesn't seem right to think long term about them, but I love you and your family so much, I can't help but think about whether it might work out for them."

"I know, but we really had better not get ahead of ourselves."

When the children got home from school, I was in the middle of making a gigantic pot of chili.

"Who's coming for dinner?" Timothy asked.

"No one that I know of. I just want to make sure we have lots of meals ready for you two to heat up on nights when I can't be here."

Just then, Liz bounded down the stairs and threw her arms around me.
"Oh Mom!" she exclaimed, hugging me tight. "Seth just told me on the phone that you want Ms. Hazelton to be, like, your personal assistant in Washington if you win the election! Oh Mom! I hope, I hope, I hope!"

"She's perfect for the job, but we can't get our hopes up too high. First, I haven't even been nominated. I need to win, and then … maybe … We don't even know if Mr. Hazelton will want or be able to make the move."

"Wow, Mom," said Timothy. "That would be so cool if we could all still be together there."

That evening, Ben, Jeremy, and I sat in the living room discussing strategies while sipping some 'bloody plonk'.

Ben had been very busy all day. First, he called the party leaders for the state to confirm that I would be seeking the nomination.

"They seemed enthusiastic," he said. "I think several of them had senatorial aspirations themselves, but they all realized that you would defeat them soundly in a primary and that you, more than anyone else, would be a shoo-in come November. They all got on board quickly, and they'll have the requisite number of signatures by tomorrow afternoon. I've asked them not to file the papers until next week so we can plan to hold the press conference announcing your candidacy at the same time."

"Thanks, Ben. Let me fill you two in on what I've been doing. First, I've asked Thelma Hazelton to work on the campaign, and she says she'll do it full-time as a volunteer so that we can save the campaign funds for other uses. But I think she should hold off on doing it as a volunteer because she'll need the money; it's expensive to live in DC, and I've asked her to be my personal assistant in Washington if I'm elected."

Ben and Jeremy looked shocked.

"Why on earth did you do that?" asked Ben.

I hadn't expected that reaction, and I became defensive. "She is amazingly competent and well-organized, she knows me well, she knows my likes and dislikes, and I want her there with me if she and her family can work it out. I didn't ask her to be my **legislative** assistant, just my **personal** assistant. I mentioned it to her so that she and Dale could discuss it; DC is so much more expensive than living in Omaha, and I wanted them to have a chance to think about it carefully."

"Have you made any other job offers?" Ben asked, trying to control himself. I had no idea what I'd done wrong, but I had clearly upset him.

"No, why?"

"Because you have to save most of those jobs for the party faithful, that's why. I know Thelma would be an excellent personal assistant, though, so that will actually work out very well."

Ben adjusted to go with a different flow very quickly, a talent that had helped him become a senior vice president at Klein Staily.

"Are you planning to offer any other jobs to your friends before November?" Jeremy asked.

"No, I wasn't planning to, and I certainly won't now, especially in light of your and Ben's reactions."

I barely stopped myself from saying that he'd be welcome to apply for the job of press secretary for me.

"Okay," I added, "no more talk about patronage jobs or any other kinds of jobs. But I wanted to let you know that I had done that."

Jeremy went on, "You said, 'first...' What else have you done today that's campaign related?"

"Oh. I invited Gail Schultz to go through my wardrobe with me and discuss attire for the campaign and onward. She is very fashion-aware and very perceptive about what is called for in various situations. We're going shopping together tomorrow to fill out my wardrobe."

I saw that look again on Ben's face... "Oh no. What's wrong?"

Ben tentatively said, "The party has several experts on staff to help with wardrobe, hair-styling, makeup, you name it. Would you mind if one them joined you on the shopping trip?"

"Yes, I would, Ben. I know I need to learn to delegate, but my appearance tells people who I am. I'm not delegating that to someone I don't know. I trust Gail's judgment on the overall wardrobe and concept. Once we're done, you can send your party dresser over to go through my closet to assess things, but I'm going with our instincts initially."

"That'll be fine, then," Ben smiled and raised his glass as a toast.

I smiled and raised mine, too. We had reached an understanding and were ready to move on.

"The main thing we need to work on tonight is anticipation of the questions reporters might ask at the press conference," said Ben.

They both liked what I had to say about terrorism and the war in Afghanistan:

> "I don't think we should seek revenge, not for the sake of revenge anyway, even though al Qaeda killed my husband; but I think they need to be stopped before they launch any more terror attacks. Between us, I'm very pessimistic about the outcome there. I know we cannot just turn the other cheek or bury our heads in the sand, but that means we have to be prepared for a long, difficult war on terrorism there. In the longer run, though, it's probably at least as important that we rethink U.S. foreign policy so that we don't create more excuses for Islamic and other terrorists to attack us."

"That's beautiful," said Jeremy, "as far as it goes. If you say things like that, though, there are several questions I would ask as a reporter if I wanted to give you a hard time. I'll send them to you tomorrow, okay?"

Ben jumped in, "Like what?"

"Okay. Here are a few:
- How long should we stay in Afghanistan if we can't win?
- What do you think a victory there would involve?
- How will we know if and when we win?
- What kind of foreign policy, if any, can we pursue in the Middle East that won't upset radical Islamists?
- To what extent has our selling weapons to despots there contributed to the anti-American sentiment?"

"Good questions," said Ben. "You'll need to think about them, Susan."

"Next, what about poverty?" asked Ben. "What policies can we pursue to help reduce the amount, the severity, and the effects of poverty?"

"From what little I know, much of poverty results from lack of education or training, and much of it is related either to having children too early or to single parenthood. Maybe instead of funding colleges and universities so much, we need to think more about keeping students in school and also about teaching the trades."

"That's a good start," said Jeremy, "but you'll lose whatever university vote isn't already voting for the Democrats if you say it that way. Maybe emphasize encouraging young people to stay in school and suggesting more support for the trades is good."

"I'm sure you're right. And one reason Fred's Foundation is providing scholarships for colleges is that it bothers me that children from middle- and upper-class families get so much support for college and university while those who don't go to college end up paying taxes to support them. I'll keep that thought to myself, though, because the last thing I think the government should do is spend more money on **anything**."

Ben nodded thoughtfully. "What about out-of-wedlock births and single-parenthood as they relate to poverty?"

I sipped my wine to give myself more time to think. Finally, I replied,

> "We have a welfare mess. Ever since we began the War on Poverty, we've created programs that involve loads of spending but haven't been very successful, if they have had any positive effects at all. I think the welfare reforms begun with the Republicans and Clinton together are a good start. At this point I would encourage more family planning be taught and that young teens be taught the importance of waiting to start families. I know that's minor now, but it's important for the longer run."

I added,

> "As a society, we care about people in poverty, and we want to do what we can to help them, but it has to be with programs that don't treat the poor as victims of much more than poor decisions – it has to be with programs that don't keep people trapped financially or emotionally in poverty. I think the phrase, 'a hand up, not a hand out' is a good one, but there has to be some stable sense that if

people make mistakes, they'll be helped along the way as they try to straighten out their lives."

Ben looked at me hard. "There's pretty good evidence that if people know there's a safety net, they make more mistakes. How do you react to that?"

"We need programs that take that into account. We all know that incentives matter, and so I would favor an extension of the reforms begun in the 1990s."

Jeremy got a serious look and asked, "Okay, what sort of extensions?"

I smiled at him. I loved the grilling, but I hated it, too. I knew I'd have to face even more grilling in the future, but I wanted all the tough questions thrown at me that he could think of.

"Off the top of my head, I think we need to figure out how high the social safety net should be, and we need to make sure people don't face massive disincentives when they try to work their way out of poverty. But I also think I'll need to read, study, think, and discuss that more during the next week."

I looked at Ben and said, "Ben, I know there are 'official' Republican positions on all these topics, and I think I'd be much more comfortable with the Republican positions than the Democrat positions, but how much will I be expected to toe the party line?"

He smiled, "This isn't Canada or England, where elected politicians are expected to vote with their parties all the time. Still, the closer you can come the better on the issues where you're comfortable. ... or even where you're not completely comfortable."

"Here's an example," I said. "I personally feel very uneasy about abortion. I don't like the idea at all. And yet I know that abortion is one way to reduce the seriousness of poverty, especially when it arises from early out-of-wedlock pregnancy. I'm glad the Supreme Court made the decision it did in Roe v. Wade, and I think women should be allowed to make up their own minds about abortion. I hate the thought of abortion, but I don't think it's appropriate for well-to-do politicians to tell a poor, struggling teenager not to have one."

I looked back and forth between Ben and Jeremy. "Will that wishy-washy position fly with the party faithful?"

Ben looked at Jeremy. "Jeremy, you probably have a better sense of this than I do. What do you think?"

"The anti-abortionists will be extremely unhappy with this view, but ninety-nine-point-nine percent of them will still vote for you rather than a democrat. And it's a view that will likely keep the independents and the Democrats-for-Young in the fold."

"Democrats for Young?"

"It's not an official group, but there are lots of Democrats in Nebraska who will support you **because** of a position like that."

When we said goodnight, both of them hugged me and kissed me. Their hugs and kisses felt good, but they caught me off guard too; I knew I didn't want any romantic involvements at this stage, but the physical contact reminded me that I liked it and was missing it.

Jeremy particularly affected me. He was closer to my age; he was good-looking, and he was interesting for sure. However, I had no idea whether he was involved with anyone, and I had no idea whether I wanted any involvement with anyone I would be working with so closely. I decided not to encourage him ... at least for the duration of the campaign.

- - -

Shopping and lunch with Gail were just what I hoped for. We chattered the whole time. She told me how much she and her husband Harry admired Fred and me, and how impressed they were with our children – "polite and active" she said, "Not just listening to others, but asking good questions, too. Our kids are a tad overwhelming, I think."

I had noticed that their children seemed pretty rambunctious at times, but I replied, "Really? They're just bright, energetic children!"

We settled on a red blazer for me, a couple of conservative-looking dresses, two more blouses, and a medium-green three-piece suit. We laughed about what a three-piece suit meant for me: slacks, skirt, and jacket, as opposed to Fred's three-piece suits of pants, vest, and jacket.

Then Gail said, "For farm visits, you'll need some more casual things, too – a couple of plaid shirts, for sure, and be sure to wash them at least five times before you wear them! Also a bomber-length denim jacket."

I agreed and so at the end of our expedition, we stopped at The Paddock, a tack-and-saddle shop, where I got those things, some new jeans, and a leather belt made for jeans. I balked though when Gail suggested cowboy boots.

"I don't think I should get the boots," I said. "They would seem so fake. I think my own walking boots will do for farm visits, don't you?"

"As long as you can square dance in them!" and we laughed again.

"That actually sounds like fun! I hope it happens!"

Over the next few days, Ben, Jeremy, and the children all posed questions for me to consider. Ben seemed concerned that I wasn't a standard Republican, whereas Jeremy and the children were more concerned about getting me elected, urging me to offer giveaways to everyone and to soft-pedal some of my small-government views.

"No! I won't offer giveaways," I said, determinedly. "The government is already spending too much money. But I'll try to figure out ways to slip past some of those issues. One thing I will probably counter with is, 'I think more programs like the ones you're suggesting should be left to the states and municipalities for their consideration.'"

There were meetings and more meetings; phone calls and more phone calls; emails and more emails. That week was super hectic.

After four days I said to the children, "I knew I'd be busy, but I have to figure out how to cut down on the meetings and messages soon. I can't maintain this pace even though I know I have a lot to do right now. I just don't want to feel this way for the next six or seven years."

"That's okay, Mom," said Timothy. "It's pretty exciting for us, and I think Liz and I are coping pretty well so far..."

"So far?! It's been only five days. We have a long row to hoe. After the press conference when we announce my candidacy, let's take a break, go over to Council Bluffs for the day, and do some hiking."

"Okay, Mom," said Liz, "but, like, don't you think it'd be better if we did some hiking in Nebraska?"

I was flustered. I hadn't adjusted yet to the idea of planning my day trips around an election campaign, but then I said to myself, "Remember, you told yourself that if you were going to do this, you were going to do it flat out. You can still spend a day with the children, and that's the important thing for you."

"You're a good political advisor, Liz. I want to spend the day doing something with you two, but we can do it here in Nebraska. Let's get out the maps and guidebooks to find a place to go."

The phone rang twice while we were trying to decide where to go. I said, "We'd better get used to this. Let's just let it go to the answering machine right now."

We decided on the Platte River State Park because we could walk along the bluffs overlooking the railroad and the river. We had never been there even though it was less than an hour away, and we were excited about having a day off from the campaign even though it had only just begun.

The phone messages were just about meetings and campaign details. Nothing crucial. I emailed Ben, Thelma, and Jeremy to let them know that the next Saturday, I would be unavailable because I was going to Platte River State Park with the children. They responded positively, but I sensed that really they all wanted me to campaign 24-7.

The press conference and the announcement went off without a hitch. Barry Jones, President of the Republican Party was there, and so was Senator Tansky, who was retiring. It was clear Ben knew what he was doing, and it was clear the party machinery was geared up for launching my campaign.

After the formal announcement of my candidacy, which came as no surprise to anyone, there were a few softball questions.

"What do you think should be done about Afghanistan?" I gave the answer I'd given to Ben and Jeremy the prior week.

"Why are you running for the Senate?"

I wasn't entirely prepared for that question, but I wasn't entirely **un**prepared either; I had thought about it a lot over the previous few weeks.

"I think I can make a difference," I said. "A difference for my children and the world they will live in, a difference for the people of Nebraska. I have thought about the state of the nation quite carefully over these past seven months, and it is clear we need fresh ideas, the kind I can take to Washington."

Well... I knew that was a bunch of empty political gibberish, but no one called me on it. It made me feel just a touch cynical to be spouting those platitudes, even though I honestly believed them.

After the announcement and the press conference, Ben and Cindy hosted a campaign-launching fancy cocktail party in my honor at Champions Run Golf Club. They made sure everyone was there, including Barry Jones and Senator Tansky, but also including the Hazeltons, the Schultzes, the Bergmans, Sandra's parents, Becky's parents ... and everyone who had sent congratulations. I think over two hundred people were there, all wishing us well.

The six teenagers were there, too: Timothy and Sandra, Liz and Seth, Aaron and Becky. I warned them, "Do not! I repeat 'Do NOT' sample someone's drink! Not even the dregs of a leftover drink!"

Liz glared at me. "Mo-om." She stretched it over two syllables.

I nodded. "Right. Sorry." I still had a ways to go in trusting my children.

They were terrific that evening, accepting well-wishes from everyone, but then asking people about themselves; I was impressed with the way they handled themselves in this social, political setting, and I was even more impressed when I saw them helping out the wait staff, who were overwhelmed by the unexpectedly large size of the crowd.

At the peak of the party, Ben took a microphone and introduced me as "the next Senator from the State of Nebraska."

My instinct was to look around to see who he was introducing. It still hadn't taken over my mind and body that he might be talking about me. I recovered in a split second, though, hoping my naïveté hadn't been too obvious. I had to recover quickly because the next thing I knew, Ben was inviting me to go to the microphone to say a few words.

"Thank you, Ben and Cindy, for this lovely get-together to kick off our campaign. It is really wonderful to be here with all of you, especially under less trying conditions than those when we all got together last fall for the Tribute to my husband."

I was becoming a political animal, and I knew it. My reference to Fred's Tribute was calculated. But I didn't want to play it up too much.

"I hope you all know how much I appreciate your support and how much I am looking forward to working with each one of you."

And then I caught my children by surprise, but I really wanted to make sure they were included.

"I expect you have all noticed the young people here who pitched in to help the staff because the crowd was so much larger than anyone expected. I'd like to introduce each of them." It seemed like a calculated political move on my part, but it also made the children feel special – at least that's what I hoped for and that's what they said later.

Interestingly, Jeremy Hall wasn't there. He decided not to be too public about his support, and so he was off covering the aftermath of a hit-and-run auto accident.

When the party was over, I made a point of hugging Ben and Cindy and thanking them profusely for everything. And later that evening I sent them a message thanking them again.

I added, "How does financing for something like that cocktail party work? Am I allowed to repay you for it? Can it come out of campaign funds? I really don't want there to be any questions about our use of campaign funds, but I also don't want you two going overboard like that."

Cindy wrote back, "Don't worry about it. It's something we wanted to do for you, to help celebrate. It's not a campaign expense; it's a celebration, so just don't worry about it."

Chapter 36 – The Nomination

The next morning the children and I got up early, packed a picnic, and left bright and early for Platte River State Park. I was looking forward to just ambling with Timothy and Liz along the cliffs and playing together in the water at Stone Creek Falls.

For the most part that was what we did. Something I should have expected, though, was that lots of people recognized us; we had been in the news, and there was considerable interest in my campaign. Most people just smiled at us, but a few spoke with us, wishing me well and said we had their vote. Some even offered business cards with their names, addresses, and phone numbers, offering to work for the campaign in their towns or neighborhoods.

I thanked each of them who said something about the campaign, and if they wanted to chat, I was happy to do so for maybe a minute or two, but mostly I wanted to be off, doing something with the children. At least that had been my goal when I proposed the outing. I saw that day as our last day together before the campaigning began in earnest. Yet the children enjoyed the public aspect of it, too: the glamour of being recognized and being talked to was pretty special for them.

On the way back home, we stopped at a small Mexican restaurant in a plaza on the edge of Omaha. It was the kind of place where you could get authentic Mexican food, made from scratch and cooked on site; it was exactly the kind of place that Fred and I loved finding.

While we were eating, Liz noticed that the people at the other tables were looking at us but trying not to stare. "Mom, like, why aren't you going over to talk with those people?"

"It's their dinner time; I don't want to intrude or interrupt them. And I hope they will also honor our privacy for now."

"Well, I think you should at least go and, like, speak with those who are staring at us," Liz said, almost pouting.

"Not tonight," I said. Maybe later in the campaign I'll become more assertive.

"Mo-om..." two exasperated syllables again.

I looked around and nodded to those who were smiling or staring at us.

When one of the couples indicated they'd like me to come speak with them, Liz was beside herself. "Go! Mom, go!"

I went to speak with the couple and as I got there, other customers crowded around. It turned out they all wanted to meet me, to shake my hand, to wish us well.

It was small and unexpected but it was also overwhelming, and when we tried to pay the bill, someone had already paid it for us. I learned from that experience to speak with the cashiers as we went into a restaurant to make sure no one picked up the tab anymore. I didn't want there to be even a sniff of bribery in the campaign; even though most of the people who wanted to do things like that for us had only the best intentions, we had to be cautious, too.

Most of the campaigning to win the nomination involved traveling to various towns and districts to meet with the local Republicans. I had told Ben that I would go to all the meetings and appearances that he set up anywhere in the eastern portion of the state, but I didn't want any meetings out of town on Sundays because I wanted to go to church and be with my family on Sundays, at least to the extent possible.

"Can we co-ordinate a calendar with Thelma?" he asked.

"Sure." I was glad he was including her almost as my personal assistant already. And so Thelma and I set up a shared calendar that we could get access to online. That really helped with the planning and cut down substantially on the phone calls and emails we had been making.

After only a week of campaigning, I was exhausted from all the meetings and speeches. Finally, I said to Thelma, "Would you go with me on some of the trips out to central and western Nebraska? We could maybe spend a night now and then and visit quite a few places all on one trip …"

"I'd love to. What about your kids, though?"

"I think the children are mature enough to handle a night by themselves, but let's think about how to do it."

"Have them stay with us! I'm sure Dale would love it," and she wasn't being sarcastic.

"Let's see what we can work out," I said. "But," and I drew this out with a threatening tone of voice, "if they end up staying with your family ..."

We both laughed. She knew where I was going with it.

"Don't worry. We won't let Seth and Liz sleep together."

I dropped a note to Ben and Jeremy to let them know about the plan, and Jeremy wrote back to Thelma and me, "You won't need to cover all those towns and districts to win the nomination; it's as good as yours. But making those public appearances in Central and Western Nebraska will be good for the campaign overall. If you can, try to arrange to go to church dinners, square dances, farm shows, you know, things where you can meet people in a down-home environment."

Thelma did just that. She planned two trips covering ten or twelve stops for each trip. It was unbelievably hectic, and staying on schedule was difficult.

"I wonder if we can allow more time between stops from now on," I said. "I'd rather not make the people feel that I'm just breezing through quickly. After all, I really do care about what they have to say."

"Absolutely!" replied Thelma. "We'll do that from now on, and for sure we'll do it during the election campaign."

The primary was held in early May, and just as all my friends had predicted, I won the nomination with over seventy-six percent of the vote. We had a big celebration at the Bel Air Banquet Room that evening, much like the one Ben held for us when I announced I would be running, only this one was considerably less opulent. I didn't want the campaign to seem as if it was only for the well-to-do, and I wanted the costs for the celebration to come out of the campaign funds, and so we had simpler hors d'oeuvres and a cash bar. Still, I think there must have been over six hundred people who passed through to offer their congratulations and best wishes.

Two of the other primary candidates came by early to concede the nomination and to offer their congratulations. It was reassuring to have done so well in the primary, but we all knew that winning the election would not be as easy. The major objection to my candidacy within the party was my lack of experience, and we knew it would become an issue during the election campaign, and so I tried to address that issue in my acceptance speech, albeit somewhat obliquely.

> I want to thank everyone here for everything you did to help us win the Republican nomination for Senator from Nebraska. The outpouring of support has been overwhelming, and I look forward to working with all of you for the next six years ... or longer!

At that point, Ben brought out a large framed photo of Fred and set it in front of the lectern. His doing that threw me off a bit. I'm sure I showed my surprise, but I recovered quickly. Referring to the photo, I continued,

> As you all know, my husband, Fred Young, was with us throughout the primary campaign, in our hearts and in our thoughts. And he will most certainly be with us throughout the rest of the campaign and the rest of our lives.
>
> We have worked hard. We have addressed all the issues, and we have made positive, forward-looking proposals for where our country should be headed.
>
> Just as importantly, we have a team of talented, experienced people who are skilled policy analysts. We continue to discuss the issues among ourselves, with you – our supporters – and with the voters. Our openness to **all** the voters, and our determination to deal with the issues without the massive budget overruns we have experienced far too often in the past will be a cornerstone of the campaign as we go forward.
>
> And so now we are ready to take our fresh ideas, along with our concern for people, and run for the Senate! Thank you!

I was tired when we got home, and I could tell the children were tired, too. We dragged ourselves into the kitchen where the three of us looked at each other and did a three-person group hug with our own woo-hoos.

I said, "Now, get to bed! You have school tomorrow! And we're not campaigning again for several days, so you'll both have plenty of time to catch up on everything you've been letting slide. Now, Go!"

Before going to bed myself, I sent a quick note to Ben, Jeremy, and Thelma, thanking them for everything they had done and letting them know that I was going to take the next five days off from campaigning to catch up with the children, get ahead on meal preparations, wind down, and read everything I could about various policy issues.

We all obviously needed the sleep. I woke up at 7:30 the next morning, scurried into the children's bedrooms, and saw they were both still sleeping. I told them, "Come on, get up! You may be late for school, but it'll be close. Brush your teeth and put on some clean clothes. You can drink juice boxes and wolf down some breakfast bars in the car – I'll drive you to school today."

We threw on our clothes, and brushed our teeth, and scampered downstairs, grabbing the juice boxes and breakfast bars on the way.

"This is not the way breakfast will be on school days," I said, "but there will certainly be days when we can't do any better, so let's make sure we have healthy food the rest of the time."

When I returned from dropping them off, I sat down at the laptop. There were literally hundreds of messages of congratulations. It was clear that I would need to have someone help handle all my correspondence. I didn't want to delegate that responsibility, but I knew I wouldn't have the time or energy to keep up with everything until I did, and I had no idea how to delegate what portions of the correspondence. In the end, I decided to look after the messages and emails myself for the next couple of days, alternating between doing that and trying to prepare better meals for the children.

One message took some care in answering. It was from Jeremy: "Would you like to go out to dinner tonight or tomorrow night to celebrate?"

He was asking me on a date. I liked it, and I had come to like him. After his initial blunder with Timothy the previous fall, he had been kind and extremely helpful. I didn't want to turn him down. And yet I didn't feel ready for the dating world; what little time I had away from campaigning had to be for our home and family.

That message required some care because I was actually missing some romantic male companionship in my life, and I would have been happy to explore the possibilities with Jeremy. Yet I wasn't sure it would be wise to get involved with anyone while my children were still at home, at least not in any distracting way. And as I thought that, I realized that, yes, I did want to date; and, yes, I did want to date Jeremy; but, no, I wasn't shopping for a mate – I didn't need one, and I didn't want one.

I responded, "Thank you! That sounds lovely, but I think I'd better decline … for now anyway. I really need to get my feet back on the ground, spend more time with the children, and think more about all the life changes we are facing. Maybe in a few weeks?"

I hoped he would read my suggestion of "Maybe in a few weeks" as a positive sign and not a flat-out rejection.

I wrote a generic thank-you note to everyone who had emailed me, and then I copied and pasted it into my replies, making sure I got their names right. My goal was to make sure I said something personal to each of them but without having to retype everything. After I got going, I could write maybe one letter every thirty seconds, but I didn't. Instead I lingered a bit over each one and averaged maybe two minutes per message. I reminded myself that spending that much time on the messages was a luxury I wouldn't be able to indulge in the future.

- - -

In the afternoon, Thelma dropped by.

"I accept," she announced.

"What?" I had no idea what she was talking about.

"I accept your offer to become your personal assistant in Washington, D.C."

I threw my arms around her and said, "Oh, Thelma, I'm so glad. I figure I can probably cope without you, but having you there will make it so much better."

"Dale checked with his head office, and they'll accommodate some changes for him if we go. He'd have to commute some and travel a bit, but I think he would actually like to try that. Overall, though, I think his company wants to have an indirect in with a Senator," and when she said that, we both scowled and groaned.

I shook my head. "I guess things like that will just keep happening."

"One thing, though …" Thelma said with a touch of hesitation. "We've checked, and it's really expensive to live in D.C. I'll have to ask to be paid starting now. Is that okay with you?"

"Of course it is! I offered to hire you as an assistant months ago!"

"I know. I wouldn't dream of asking, but it's SO expensive. We haven't decided what to do about our house here in Omaha. Have you thought any more about what you'll do?"

"I try not to because I haven't won the election, but I know I'll have to think about it. We can afford to keep this house and hire someone to look after it when we're not here. I'd like to do that, not rent it and not sell it. I'd like to think of this home as our emotional base, if nothing else.

If you want to do that, maybe I can use some of the money we invested from Fred's life insurance to buy two houses in DC and rent one to you for the amount I'd have to pay in taxes or something like that…"

Thelma just sat there stunned.

"You would do that? Do you know how much houses cost in D.C.?"

"I have a vague idea, and the way things are going in the housing markets, I'd probably be able to sell them in six years for a profit… Ugh, I'll have to check with the tax lawyers to see how that would work … but, yes, I'd do that. That's how important it is for me to have you there with us. I'll just ask that you not tell anyone about this offer. It's impulsive, I know, but you and your family are so special for us… "

"If there's a tax problem, maybe you can lend us the money to buy a place or something?"

We agreed I would check with the tax lawyers to work out something.

Thelma changed gears and said, "Susan, you should see the applications for the FRY scholarships. There are dozens from top students, but we're following your goal and sifting through the applications to find students who are very, very good but who most likely wouldn't qualify for other scholarships. We are going to make several families very happy."

I was delighted with those developments.

"One criterion I hadn't expected to emerge," she said, "is that several of the applicants lost a parent in the past few years. I hope it's okay with you if we tend to favor them just a bit."

"It sure is!" I enthused. "Those are the very types of students who would otherwise work too many hours on their jobs and take out loans that would be way too burdensome. That is just excellent!"

"I don't think we should make that an official criterion, though," Thelma suggested, and I agreed.

"But I like the connection with our family. Thanks for doing that."

Chapter 37 – The Summer Campaign

"You don't want to peak too early." It was Barry Jones, head of the Nebraska Republicans. "It's probably a good idea to keep moderately active on the campaign trail now, but save up for a big push in October."

"I don't know," Jeremy countered. "Keeping Susan's name and photos out there now will maintain all the momentum the campaign has built up. We don't want to lose what we have. We need to keep feeding it."

The two of them wrangled for a while, and eventually I settled on a compromise, limiting my summer public campaign appearances to no more than two or three per day and no more than four days a week. Also because of our experience at the small Mexican restaurant, I decided to visit smaller, family-owned restaurants for lunches both in Omaha and on the road. I wanted to run an inclusive campaign, and I wanted to show all segments of society that I was serious.

When school was out for the summer, Timothy and Liz became full-time volunteers for the campaign.

"I know you both could get good summer jobs if you wanted to," I told them, "but I'm glad you want to work on the campaign. To thank you, I'll bump your allowances up for the summer, and I'll put some money aside in special 'mad-money' savings accounts for each of you."

"That isn't necessary, Mom," said Timothy. "We want to help you win!"

"And, like, we already got cell phones! Don't forget those!" added Liz. "This is so exciting!"

The children were great workers. They proofread speeches and campaign materials, they stuffed envelopes, they helped draft automatic responses for email, and they traveled with me when I went out of town. Having them along with me that summer was wonderful. It was just the three of us, often, going to various events all over the state, and we had a lot of time together to help our family bonds become even tighter.

A few weeks after I'd won the nomination, I was working late at the campaign office. Jeremy stopped in to go over some position papers he had drafted on my behalf. I had to tone down the rhetoric in some of them – they just weren't me. And I reminded him, "No giveaways! I'm not even hinting that I'll propose or even support giveaways. The problem with a big government budget is that all the cronies use all their energy trying to get government grants for their businesses and pet projects instead being productive."

He wasn't fully on board with that view, but he was fully on board with supporting me, no matter what. I still didn't understand why he felt that way. I was suspicious, wondering whether he was after my money, after me for sex, or just what was going on.

With those thoughts cautioning me, I still thought it would be fun to go out with him. I looked at him and asked, "If your invitation to go to dinner is still open, how about tonight after we finish up here?"

That caught him by surprise. He abruptly stopped what he was doing and said, "Sure thing! Just let me make some calls…"

"No, no," I said. "Don't change any plans. We can do it later," and I opened my laptop calendar, expecting to set some time and date later.

"No, let's do it tonight. I didn't have anything special or important planned. Let me make the calls…"

And while he made his calls, I phoned the children to let them know they'd have to microwave one of the meals from the freezer.

"Okay, Mom," said Liz. "I'm going out with Seth after we eat, and I think Timothy and Sandra have plans, so, like, there's no big rush tonight."

"I'm glad you two haven't sacrificed your social lives for this campaign," I said. And then I couldn't stop myself as I added, "I know it's not a school night this summer, but please don't stay out too late."

Liz actually laughed as she fake-whined, "Mo-om!"

Jeremy took me to a cozy mid-range restaurant called The Red Ruby where we were able to chat and get to know each other in a setting that wasn't too romantic and wasn't too business-like. It was perfect for us.

As we talked, I learned he was single and not seeing anyone. "Luanne and I lived together for a couple of years but it didn't work out. That ended three years ago, and I've sort of been drifting since then."

"Jeremy," I asked, "why did you interview Timothy last fall the way you did?

I've watched you since then, and you seem quite scrupulous about journalists' ethics. What was different then?"

He looked down at the table and then back up at me. "I got carried away with wanting that story. Your email message that evening really affected me. The editor wouldn't kill the story because he knew it was a good one, but that made me determined to make it up to you and Timothy somehow. I always thought of myself as an honest, ethical reporter, and your email message made me rethink what I had been doing."

"Don't you think you've done enough penance? You don't have to keep working with the campaign, and I can tell that your affiliation with the campaign affects the types of stories you can cover for the paper."

"You're right; it was a type of penance at first. Self-imposed. But that was back when you held the tribute for your husband. When I saw you in action then and in the events and stories after that, throughout the rest of the fall, I became attracted to you in many ways."

Gulp. I wasn't sure I was ready for this, but I went along with it … sort of.

"Oh?"

"Of course. You're quite attractive, you know." He paused and looked at me but I tried to keep a straight face. "Also, you're stronger than titanium, you think about details and impacts, you're smart, and your eyes are beautiful, especially when you smile."

I couldn't take the heat right then, and changed the subject.

"How old are you, Jeremy?"

"Thirty-eight … but I'll be thirty-nine this fall. Why?"

"I was just curious."

I was also trying to head off discussions of romance. But I think we both knew what I was doing and that we would likely end up in some sort of relationship in the not-too-distant future.

I really wasn't ready for anything yet, though, and so once again I changed the topic. "You know, Jeremy, you have been a godsend in many ways. You helped organize the press conferences last fall -- you subtly organized the other members of the media to make our lives less unpleasant then; and you have been a great help with the campaign."

I rushed on before he could reply in any way. "I know that you were one of the people behind the push to get me to run for the Senate. Let me be blunt. What's in it for you?"

"Lots of things. For starters, I get to be part of a winning team. That's important. But also I recognized your political savvy and your electability right from the start. I wanted to do what I could to make it happen. ..."

I started to speak, but he cut me off.

"Also, I've never met a woman like you, someone so straight and so unambitious and yet so qualified. I knew early on that I wanted to get to know you better, but I knew I would have to bide my time because of my faux pas with Timothy; I'd have to work with you when possible, and let you get to know me better."

We were involved in a type of mating dance, trying to get to know each other. I had no idea how to do that – I had only done it once before, and that was with Fred more than twenty years earlier. It was fun doing it again, and it certainly was nice having Jeremy interested in me.

We sat there talking, exchanging stories, until it was clear we had stayed past closing time.

I knew I'd had too much to drink, and I thought he had too.

"Let's get cabs to go home," I suggested. "I don't know about you, but I probably shouldn't drive tonight. I'll take a cab or get a ride back to the office tomorrow to get my car."

"Cab**s**?" he asked, emphasizing the "s".

"Jeremy, this is our first date. I'm not ready for much more at this point. If I were, though," I smiled, "I'd be happy if it were with you. I like you."

He relaxed and smiled. "I like you, too."

When the first cab arrived, we hugged goodnight and he kissed me before opening the cab door. It was more than a business kiss but we didn't get carried away, either.

The children were both up when I got home at about ten-thirty. Liz looked at me, smirked a tiny bit, and said, "So, Mom, like what's going on that you're staying out so late and not letting us know where you are?"

"Jeremy took me out to dinner. It was really nice."

"Just Jeremy? Mom, was that campaign-related or was it, like, a date?"

"I'd have to say it was more of a date. At least I hope he doesn't try to expense that dinner to the campaign. Anyway, it was very nice."

I tried to change the topic. "So, where did you and Seth go tonight?"

"Actually, we didn't go anywhere. We just, like, stayed at the Hazeltons, watched a movie that Seth rented, and then we, like, talked about schools and houses in Washington. Mom, this is so exciting!"

She didn't let me off the hook, though, as she continued, "Mom, after that thing with Timothy last fall, like, Mr. Hall has been so nice. Not like suck-up nice; just nice. Are you going to keep dating him?"

"I don't know ... I like him, but I'm not sure it's a very good idea to get involved with anyone right now, especially someone I'm working with."

"Well, let me know if you ... like ... want to borrow the books on sex and relationships."

The little imp! She laughed, and I pretended to swat at her, and then laughed and hugged her.

"Timothy," I asked, "How would you feel if I dated him now and then?"

"Actually, I like him, too. And you know when he interviewed me last fall, he seemed nice even then."

"Well, I'm not going to rush into anything," I vowed. "I expect that if I win the election, I may want to have him be my press secretary. But I really have no idea what it means to be dating or in a relationship. I know things are a lot different now than they were twenty years ago."

"Here's a crucial question," Timothy added. "Has he asked to borrow any money?"

"Why on earth are you asking that?"

"Mom, we all know that everyone thinks you have acres of money. We also know that lots of people have asked to borrow money from you but you've sent them all to Uncle Ben. It wouldn't surprise me at all to learn that some men will want to date you to get at your money."

"Wow, Timothy, where is that coming from?"

"Bobby Vargas at school said his dad wanted to know if you're dating anyone and if not, he'd divorce his wife to marry you for your money. I was pretty angry, but I think I hid it. And then when I thought about it, I realized there was probably more than a glimmer of truth in it."

"Maybe you're right, Timothy, but so far Jeremy is the only man who has shown any interest in dating me, and, no, he hasn't asked to borrow any money. If he does, I can assure you I won't be going on any more dates with him."

"Maybe he's just subtle," offered Liz. "Who paid for dinner tonight?"

"He did. He asked me out, and so that seemed proper to me."

"As I said, maybe he's just subtle … setting you up for the big sting later."

She was laughing, but she was serious, too. And it gave me pause.

"Oh no." I lamented. "This makes me so sad. I hate to have to be so guarded, but I guess there's no way around it. You're good in the advice-to-daters department, you two!"

As I lay in bed that night, my thoughts were swirling. Would our lives change more because Fred had been killed, or because we had so much money, or because I was running for the Senate? Probably some combination of all three, I guessed, but our lives certainly were changing.

And then there was Jeremy Hall. What was he up to, and what had attracted him to me? I thought about going to bed with him, and I realized I liked the thought. Maybe I would sometime; but if it happened, I wanted to keep it at that level. I wasn't looking for a life partner to take the place of Fred. Having the money meant I was independent – I didn't need someone to look after me now that Fred was gone; I could be with people I liked, and that was very freeing. So apparently having the money cut both ways: it freed me but it also made me more guarded.

At some point mid-summer, Ben mentioned that he thought Jeremy would be a good press secretary or communications director for both the campaign and afterward.

"I like the idea, too," I said. "He and I get along well, and he seems willing to support my small-government agenda. Have you mentioned it to him?"

He answered, "I wanted to see how you felt about it before saying anything to Jeremy or anyone else."

"Thank you, Ben. I know that if and when it comes time to fill out the rest of the staff there, I'll have to let you and Barry Jones handle most of the preliminary work at the very least, and maybe more."

That seemed to keep Ben content. We had implicitly been clashing about control, but we were determined not to let the clashes become overt.

"For Jeremy, though, why don't you tell or ask him right away?" I suggested. "And maybe we should put him on staff and start paying him soon? What do you think?"

"Good idea!" Ben said, and he had it all arranged by the next morning.

The summer campaign went very well. I made numerous appearances, both alone and with the children all over the state. The statewide polls were indicating that we had a very comfortable lead, and we all sensed the strength of that lead when we were out on the campaign trail.

Farmers and educators were not altogether thrilled about my reluctance to endorse more spending for them, but they liked what I had to say about Afghanistan and the federal government debt. The die-hard anti-abortionists didn't like my position on abortion, but they preferred it to the actual promotion of abortion that my opponent was proposing.

Ben did a great job of coordinating visits to different towns and events, and Thelma made sure we had more time for each visit so that I could mingle longer and more meaningfully with the voters. During the summer, it was mostly just the children with me on the stump, but a few times Thelma went with me, and once Ben went along to Lincoln to have some closed-door meetings with the local politicians there while I met with a group of people from the university.

At the same time that all this was going on, Thelma was traveling all over Nebraska and Kansas to speak with FRY scholarship applicants. "We've settled on these six," she said, handing me their dossiers. "The interviews are just to rule them out if they seem like really inappropriate candidates for some reason."

After her last trip, she stopped by to fill me in on how it had gone.

"Susan, the families are all so excited and grateful. Well, all but one. That family clearly has buckets of money – a huge spread, big ranch home, pool, fancy cars, the works. When I asked them why their son had applied for the scholarship, they seemed somewhat embarrassed, and he withdrew his application. I think they were pretty upset with him for having tried such a stunt, but that episode made it clear that we'll have to be careful with applicants all the time."

"Money," I said. "I hate this feeling that I have to be so careful about people like that. What did you do after that?"

"Oh, we have a ranking of all the applicants, so I just went on to the next one, and she's very deserving. I don't know if there will be time, but I know they would each like to meet you."

"Maybe we can work something out for those who are here in Nebraska – maybe combine meeting them with other appearances near them?"

"Perfect! That's what I was thinking, too. It'll be good for the foundation and good for the campaign, too."

Gail had been right about square dances and farm visits; that summer I went to three barn dances, a barn-raising, a christening for a fleet of combines, and the Nebraska State Fair in Lincoln. Some of the volunteers in the office wondered how much time I should spend at the fair because it was becoming less popular every year, but we decided that because of Fred's connections with the farm community, it would be good to strengthen those ties by having me go to the fair.

The children and I made a short vacation of it at the State Fair in Lincoln. Campaign supporters put us up for three nights, and we spent four days and evenings strolling around the fairgrounds passing out flyers, buttons, banners, and especially hats for protection from the sun – hats with "Young for Senate" on them. The really popular hats were big foam hats that people could soak with water to keep cool. They were great advertising because they were so visible and useful at the same time.

Jeremy joined us for the middle two full days that we were at the fair. He must have taken enough pictures to fill ten rolls of film. "These will be great for news clips today and tomorrow, and then we can use some for our late-push material," he said. "And let's make sure we have some with you and your kids."

The children wanted to go on the rides, but not me. During those times I went to some of the flower and baking exhibits, and I'm glad I did. There were quite a few shy people who wanted to shake hands with me or have their photos taken with me, and my going to these exhibits without the children at my side made me more accessible to them.

Most of the conversations with the voters at the Fair were focused on how they admired my courage and strength after 9-11 (most of them couldn't bring themselves to say "after your husband was killed) and how much they admired my generosity in creating the Frederick Robert Young Foundation.

- - -

At the beginning of the summer, I knew I was a bit overweight, and I was determined not to put on any weight during the campaign. "No more cheap carbs for me," I announced to the children.

"But Mom, the places you go always want to serve snacks or basic meat-and-potato dinners. How will you handle that?" Liz asked.

"I have to be strict with myself. I can't even look at snacks most of the time, and if they are forced on me, I'll have to have a small bite and then rave. I'll focus on vegetables and salads whenever I can."

It worked. Controlling my diet and being so active on the campaign trail meant I was actually getting into a bit better shape. Over the summer I lost ten pounds and a dress size. No one really noticed it much, except Gail, who said, "Susan, we need to take you to a seamstress to get those clothes refit."

I refused at first because I wasn't sure I could keep the weight off, and I didn't mind that the clothes fit a bit more comfortably. I promised Gail I would consider it later if I could keep the weight off.

Thelma noticed my weight loss in a different way. "Girl, your face is starting to sag. What's wrong?"

"Well!" I wasn't pleased with either the message or the brutal honesty of it, "I guess I'm just tired. I probably need to build more rest into my schedule. This is all so different and unexpected …"

"No, it's more than that," she said as she stepped back and looked me over. "Oh, I see now. You're losing weight, aren't you … Are you okay?"

I smiled. "I'm not sure if you can see that I'm smiling behind this sad, sagging face. I've lost about ten pounds this summer. But I think the constant running, meeting, and traveling really are taking a toll and causing me to age prematurely."

I hastily added, "and no, I won't be getting a facelift."

"Well at least your hair isn't turning grey yet."

"Only my hairdresser knows for sure," I said, mimicking a very old ad for hair coloring.

"You know, I was feeling uneasy about moving with you to Washington, but the more Dale and I talk about it, the more excited we are. I think we will plan to keep the house here, and Dale will use it as his Midwest base. We'll commute back and forth, but mostly it'll be him doing the commuting."

"You have no idea," she continued, "how much our lives have changed because of all this. Last fall, I was a contented stay-at-home mom. And now I'm in the thick of all sorts of action. It's a life I never imagined for myself. Did you ever think about yourself doing any of this before?"

"Not really. I did enjoy my job at Arkero, and I imagined maybe doing something like that again in a few years. The job and the responsibilities were substantial there, but they were nothing like this."

"I think that's one of the reasons you're so electable. It's not just your name, and it's not just the fact that Fred was killed in the terrorist attacks. It's that you're a reluctant politician, not a slick one. You don't need this, and you didn't seek it; you seem far less power-hungry than any other politician I've heard of, and that's refreshing for the voters."

Then she hesitated. "It's probably none of my business, but maybe it is …"

"Oh, oh," I thought. "What's this about…"

I raised my left eyebrow just a bit, a questioning gesture that encouraged her to continue.

"… is there anything going on between you and Jeremy?"

I almost spit out my coffee as I laughed.

"How did you know? He took me to dinner one evening after we were working late. We've had some lunches together. Nothing more."

"I can tell by the way you two behave. It's like high school all grown up. You glance at each other now and then in ways that indicate 'boyfriend-girlfriend'. It's subtle, but I can see it."

"I hope it isn't terribly obvious to others. We are attracted to each other, for sure, but I just don't want to rush into anything."

"He's been fawning all over you ever since last fall. He's got it bad, girl."

"One concern I have is, what if we date some and it doesn't work out? He's been so good for the campaign, and I would hate to lose him in that respect. I've even agreed with Ben that Jeremy should be part of the staff in Washington …"

Thelma interrupted, "I think so, too. And I can see how Ben feels. He often defers to Jeremy's insight during meetings because Jeremy has some media savvy that we need on the team."

"Do you think it's possible to have him working for us if he and I are dating, too?"

"I can't imagine that sort of thing doesn't happen all the time in politics and business. Date him, have fun, and if it doesn't work out, be good and kind and break up as friends. That's what Dale and I both told Seth about dating Liz. 'We don't want anything to disrupt the close family relationships we have together, so be nice to each other if it doesn't work out.'"

"That's what I told Liz, too!" I said. "You'd think I could remember my own advice! I guess it's easier to say than it is to think about on a personal basis."

Then I smiled a somewhat embarrassed smile. "The children were waiting up for me when I got home from that dinner date. ..."

Thelma gave me a questioning look. She knew there was more than that.

"And?"

"Liz offered to lend me the books on sex and relationships!'

This time it was Thelma who had trouble not spitting out her coffee.

She roared with laughter. "I can't wait to tell Dale! This is **so** funny!!"

"Well, maybe it's a story that shouldn't get around much, though. I don't want to embarrass Liz, and I certainly don't want the whole state discussing my personal life."

"They already are, girlfriend. You're looking good, you have some money, and you're about to become very powerful politically. I'm surprised more men haven't tried to put the moves on you."

"The children said something like that, too, but alas no one else has even hinted they might want to date me ... **not** that I'm really eager to be dating again. I'm certainly not looking for a replacement partner at this point, but some romantic male companionship now and then sounds nice."

"If you want blind dates, I think every woman who knows you is ready to set you up. We all have a bit of Cupid in us. Just say the word…"

I interrupted. "The word is 'No'. I don't want to spend too much time even thinking about dating when we have a campaign and who knows what else ahead of us. If I meet single men who are interested in dating me, I'll probably be somewhat interested, but in a detached way. I'm just not looking for life partner. Not now, anyway."

Chapter 38 – The Autumn Leaves

During a break in campaigning, Thelma and I were having coffee at her place when I asked, "Do you think Seth and Liz are having sex?"

Thelma smiled. "I don't know if they are actually having intercourse, but I'm pretty sure they get into some very heavy action now and then. Why do you ask? Are you concerned?"

"I love them, and they're so cute together. But I don't want Lizzy to get pregnant, not even if it's by the son of my best friend."

"We've had that talk with Seth, too. He swears they're not having sex. Not intercourse anyway."

"I think I should put Liz on the pill. What do you think?"

I hastened to add, "It's not that I want to encourage them to have sex at this age, I just want them to be careful. I know how impulsive teenagers can be, and Liz has a rebellious streak in her. What would you say if I put her on the pill?"

"She's only fourteen," Thelma said. "I wish they'd wait, but I see your point. And I must say, since they're going to lose their virginity eventually if not sooner, I hope it's with each other – they really do seem fond of each other."

That evening I raised the subject with Liz over supper.

"Liz, I don't know where things stand between you and Seth, but I wonder if starting you on the pill might be a good idea."

"Mom!" she said. She was happy, scared, and embarrassed. "Is this, like, something we have to discuss as a family?"

"Yes, I think it is. I don't want to push or encourage either of you to get into sexual relationships before you're ready. But when you think you're ready emotionally, I want you to be ready physically, too."

I turned to Timothy, "I gather you and Sandra are having sex."

He was embarrassed, too. "I'm not sure I want to talk about it, but yes we are. I already told you, Mom, she's on the pill, and her parents are okay with it all. I hope you are."

"I am, Timothy. But it's good for the topic of sex to be in the open, here in the family. It's not dirty, and it's not something to hide. It is something that should be private and special, though, and so I won't be asking much more about it. I'm just glad your first experience is with someone who cares about you."

Liz looked at me with a serious look but a hint of a smile, too. Then she threw her head back. "Oh no," she groaned. "Have you and Ms. Hazelton been discussing this? Like, together?"

"Of course we have," I smiled.

"Don't plan my life for me, Mom!"

"Oh, I don't think you'll have to worry about that! I know you are strong-willed. I mentioned it to Thelma mostly because I didn't want her to think I was pushing you two into a sexual relationship. She understood. I hope you do, too."

Liz relaxed. "Thanks, Mom. And, yes, I do understand."

Things became extremely busy in the fall. The children were going back to school, and the campaign was in full swing.

Timothy was in eleventh grade, and Liz was in ninth grade, and so they and their friends all went to Burke High School. The six of them seemed inseparable, going places together or just hanging out in the basement together. Also, Seth got his driver's license during the summer, and so they were no longer dependent on parents to drive them around.

My one rule that fall was that I didn't want them to have **any** friends over to visit while I was out. They were all reaching ages where "sex, drugs, and rock and roll" was an important mantra, and I didn't want our house to become a meeting place for sex and drugs. I knew, though, that they and their friends loved getting together in the games room, and so I tried to hold as many meetings as possible at home so I could be in meetings upstairs while the children were together with friends in the basement.

The campaign was grueling: meetings, meetings, and more meetings, with everyone chiming in about how to shore up this constituency or how to appeal more directly to that bloc of voters. Some of the long-time political workers loved strategizing for the sake of strategizing. Others wanted to curry favor with me no matter what I said. And still others, like Thelma, Gail, and the Bergmans all just wanted to help and were willing to offer suggestions, but at least they understood that spending too much time on some pointless issues would be unproductive. Over the months leading up to the election, I became both more cynical about people's motives and more confident that I wanted to be me, not just a well-groomed political name.

Speaking of grooming, eventually Ben had two women from the party visit me to go over my wardrobe, hairstyle, and makeup. I resented their presence before they even showed up, but I tried to be polite about it. The wardrobe specialist didn't mind most of my clothes choices, but she also recommended, like Gail, that I get them taken in a bit. "You have a good figure, Susan. You should show it off better."

I grimaced. "I want to look good," I said. "I don't want to be a sex object."

Finally I agreed to get some tighter slacks.

The hair-stylist/aesthetician made some minor recommendations. "I know you'll be on the go a lot," she said, "especially after you win. Let's keep it simple. Basically, what you're doing is fine, but here's a simple concealer I recommend for touch-ups between your various meetings."

By the end of their visit, my resentment was gone, and I thanked them for their help.

I decided early in the campaign that I would **not** do any campaigning on September tenth through the twelfth. I wanted to spend those days by myself and with our children, reflecting about Fred, our lives with Fred, everything we had cherished about Fred, and everything we had gone through over the past year. It was a good time to take stock, and I hoped everyone involved with the campaign would understand. I wouldn't answer the phone then; instead I forwarded all the calls to the campaign office with a brief message that I was unavailable for those few days.

As the campaigning intensified, the children and I struggled to re-adapt to our new lives. We still had regular breakfasts together most days, and we still had dinner together three or four times a week, and we always set aside Sundays up until mid-afternoon just for us. But there were constant intrusions -- phone calls at breakfast, last minute dinner invitations that didn't include the children, people stopping by, and campaign trips out of town.

At one point, we talked about how crazy our lives were, especially with the spur-of-the-moment intrusions and changes of plans.

"Mom, I'm okay with it so far," said Timothy, "I'm still finding it pretty exciting. And in some ways, I think the increased independence we have is helping us grow up."

Liz added, "I'm okay with it, too. I think, like, it helps that we're all in the same school now, and so we have plenty of time to, like, be together."

She paused before going on. "Mom, I think watching you handle things has, like, been one of the best educations we could get. You are so cool and so careful. Like, this is all so worth it."

Timothy had wanted to give up soccer and Liz had wanted to give up Spanish Choir, so they could campaign more, but I wouldn't let them.

"I know that being a part of the campaign is fun and interesting and will certainly be a valuable part of your lives, but your studies and school activities are much too important for you to be taking time away from them. You can help in the office sometimes, and you can help with trips and events on weekends if you don't have other things planned for yourselves. But you must keep up with your schoolwork and your after-school groups."

As an afterthought, I added, "Timothy instead of coming to the office to help out, I want you to take driving lessons. You need to get your license as soon as you can. If something were to happen to me, we'd need a driver in the family. And it would be a big help if you could drive when you, Liz, and your friends want to do something together."

We all worked hard, and the stress overwhelmed us sometimes. One day in October, Liz and Timothy were bickering about who had to clean up what in the games room. Even though I knew teen sibling bickering was normal and that they had bickered plenty in the past, I stopped them and said, "We have to get ready for more tension and stress. If I win this, and it's looking as if I will, our lives will be like this, only more so, for the next six years. This is what we signed up for. We'll have to keep working at everything, now."

"Don't worry, Mom," Liz replied, "We're in it all the way. We'll try to work things out without making a big deal about it all."

And then she exclaimed, "Group hug!"

And the three of us hugged each other.

- - -

I love autumn. I met Fred in the late autumn at Kansas State, and we both liked the song, "September in the Rain" – "The leaves of brown came tumbling down…"

We put in numerous appearances at high school and college football games that fall. I wore my almost-Cornhusker-red blazer to the University of Nebraska homecoming game in Lincoln and set it off with some new, snug white pants.

It was then that I became aware of men looking at me, "that way". I was flattered that they found me attractive, but I wanted to be thought as a capable, caring person and not a sex symbol.

- - -

In late October the campaign committee wanted me to go back out west for one last push. They scheduled me go to harvest parties and celebrations in about ten different places over two full days of visits. That meant I'd have to leave Friday afternoon and wouldn't be able to return until late Sunday night. The children had their own activities planned that weekend, and wouldn't want to go with me.

Thelma said, "I have to stay home that weekend, and I know your children will be happy to stay with us. Maybe you should invite Jeremy to go with you…" and she gave me a knowing half-smile.

"Great idea!" I said very matter-of-factly. "I think I will. How do you think the others in the campaign will react?"

"Get separate rooms, and make sure they look as if they've both been slept in. And don't talk about it in public."

"Okay, and don't book us into the homes of supporters!" I said with a wink.

I didn't email the invitation to Jeremy. Instead I called him and said, "We need to have coffee together.

We went to a small boutique-type coffee place. After we got our coffees and were seated, I looked at Jeremy and asked, "Would you like to join me on the trip out west next weekend? Thelma can't go and the children have their own social events, and so I thought I'd invite you."

It was a mixed signal for sure. He seemed and acted confused.

"I don't want to go on those trips by myself," I explained. "I'll be too tired to drive all over the place, keep up appearances, make speeches and everything. I'd love to have you with me. We'll have to get separate rooms, of course, for the sake appearances, but I want to spend those two nights with you."

He just stared at me. "Wow! You sure are clear about what you want."

"I am. For now. I want to be with you this coming weekend. I want it to be hard work and romantic and fun. I have no idea whether we're a good match, and for this weekend I don't care. I just know that it seems right to do this now."

"I want all that and more," he said. "It must be clear to you by now that I am hopelessly smitten with you."

"Well, until that wears off," I said very matter-of-factly, "let's have fun together. But we have to be careful, too. I see no reason to arouse concerns or get tongues wagging until after the election."

The next day, Ben was on the phone to me. "Susan, I hear that you and Jeremy are going on the western tour together. Even if you two are seeing each other, be careful. The last thing you need right now is any kind of scandal or disruption to the campaign."

We were very careful. When I booked the rooms at a hotel in North Platte, I was offered the Governor's Suite. The desk clerk said, "It has a very large conference room for meetings, with a large bedroom for the Governor on one side and a second bedroom for his assistant on the other side; both have full en suites and are quite private".

The suite was perfect. We scheduled two early breakfast meetings in the conference room to make sure everyone got the picture that we were there to work on the campaign and had separate and separated bedrooms. With those arrangements, it was easy to be careful and still have a good time privately.

We were both looking forward to the weekend, but before we left, I said to Jeremy, "Would you mind doing most of the driving this weekend? I'll need all the rest I can get, which is why I wanted someone to come along. And I can imagine we'll both need some rest when we get back …" and we both smiled.

"Something else. I went off the pill after Fred died. You'd better stock up on condoms."

I had never expected anything like it, but on the way there I stroked his leg … a lot. We were both unbearably ready, but we had a late "Meet the Candidate" party to attend at the home of a local campaign supporter. We checked in at the hotel, and when we went to the suite, we spent at least five minutes passionately kissing and fondling each other.

"I want a quickie right now," I said, "But I don't, too. Let's wait until we get back from the party and have time to relax together."

We skipped dinner, though, because we couldn't resist each other. It was passionate, crazy, and wonderful, and then we showered quickly, soaping each other luxuriously.

"I can't wait until the party is over," I said, kissing his chest in the shower. "I want to do this some more!"

The weekend was a great success in more ways than one. Having sex again was wonderful, and having a lot of sex with Jeremy that weekend was really nice. I liked him even more after the weekend was over.

My only concern was that he had too many expectations about me and about us. On the drive home, I opened up the topic. "Jeremy, I hope you know I like you … a lot! And the weekend with you was so good in so many ways."

"But?" He sensed it coming.

"I can't get involved long-term. I don't want to, and I know my children aren't ready for it. They both like you a lot, too, and are happy that we're seeing each other, but they come first. Way first. Do you understand?"

"I'm not sure," he said. "Are you saying you want to have an open relationship with me and be free to date and sleep with others, too?"

"Good grief, no!" I exclaimed. "And if you want a relationship like that, let's just agree that we had a wonderful weekend together and not date any more. I'm monogamous by nature."

"So am I," he said. "I guess this means we're secretly going steady? Like high school?"

I smiled, leaned over the console, and kissed his cheek. "Okay. We're going steady, but just for now; and if either of us wants to end it, let's both feel free to do so. I've gone through so much in the past year, I have no idea what I want or where I'll be long-term."

Part 4: Senator Susan Young

Chapter 39 – A Foregone Conclusion

The pre-election polls were indicating that I had a substantial lead over my opponent, and in the final tally, I received 65.3% of the vote, which I'm told is an impressive landslide.

Thelma booked a huge set of banquet rooms at the downtown Omaha Hilton for our post-election party. She insisted on a bevy of well-tended cash bars, with snacks set out everywhere. The polls closed at 8pm, and the major media sources were declaring me a winner by 8:30.

Jeremy was in his element, firing out press releases and meeting with other members of the media. I was happy and I was celebrating, but I still felt a twinge of cynicism, watching all the politicos shaking hands, hugging each other, congratulating each other. I vowed to do my best to avoid being sucked in by all the "politicking" that I would have to face.

Party loyalists kicked off the speeches at 8:30, thanking everyone and announcing that the major media sources had already declared, "Susan Young is the next Senator representing Nebraska!" followed by wild cheers that rocked the entire hotel.

At 9:15 my Democratic opponent paid our celebration a visit to concede victory to me. He was gracious and charming -- I could easily imagine that in different circumstances, he would have won the seat handily.

By the time he finished speaking, over a thousand people were in the combined banquet rooms, offering congratulations and celebrating. Finally, Ben and Cindy found me in the crowd, among the well-wishers. "It's time for your acceptance speech," said Ben.

He had done a wonderful job of running the campaign, and Thelma had done a terrific job of organizing the events. I looked at Ben, Cindy, Thelma, and Jeremy, and felt an overwhelming sense of gratitude, maybe even love. We were a close, efficient team.

I located the children near the food tables, as expected, along with their friends. I took their hands, and we walked together to the platform; I wanted them by my side, and they were basking in the limelight.

As we went up the stairs to the speaker's dais, I saw Ben put a large photo of Fred in front of it.

The photo filled me with different of emotions. Mostly as I looked at the picture of Fred, I felt wistful. I missed him and I wished he were there with me. I knew that without his death and notoriety, and without his money enabling me to do all I had done in the past year, no one would have known who I was; and certainly no one would have suggested I run for anything other than maybe president of the PTA.

I also felt a bit of guilt, looking at Fred's photo because less than three weeks earlier, I had spent a weekend with Jeremy Hall. It wasn't the same as being with Fred, and I was glad that weekend had happened, but it felt strange just then, thinking about having been with Jeremy and looking at Fred's photo with all the love and devotion that I truly felt.

I wondered if having the photo there was a bit too much, but it didn't matter: the election was over and I would no longer be trading on Fred's name and tragic death, not even implicitly.

I made sure the children stood on each side of me. I had Ben, Cindy, Thelma, and Jeremy stand behind me, with the Party officials off to the sides of those four people.

After thanking everyone for their support and thanking my opponent for such an upbeat, positive, above-board campaign, I began my acceptance speech by singling out every person on the platform and saying a few words about each of them, and when I got to the children, their friends let out enormous whoops and cheers.

During my speech, I made reference to Fred.

> We all know that my husband, Fred Young, is here with us in spirit as we celebrate. But one thing many of you don't know but probably suspected is that beginning over a year ago, the children and I have worn some of Fred's neckties to various events, especially during the campaign. We wanted to make sure that Fred was with us on the campaign trail.

I was interrupted by huge cheers.

> But now we must look forward to the future. Our country is embroiled

in new challenges that no one seems able to deal with reasonably or quickly. We promise we will work to change that as we prepare for our move to Washington, D.C.

My family and I will always maintain our home here in Omaha. This is where we live. But with Fred gone, I also need to have my children with me so we can share our love and lives together. We will soon be looking for accommodations in Georgetown, and the children will transfer schools at the end of the semester.

Jeremy wanted the two of us to celebrate together, but I declined. I told him, "This celebration has to be for more than just the two of us, Jeremy; it has to include my friends and the children."

I then shocked myself when I said to him, fortunately out of earshot of anyone else, "Cold showers can be very sexy, you know…"

The children and I left the party a little after midnight, "The children have school tomorrow," I announced frequently as we said our "good-byes" to everyone on our way out.

At home, the momentousness of the occasion hit all three of us.

"So, like, this is it!" said Liz. "You won, and we are, like, actually moving. This is so exciting. It'll be so hard concentrating in school now, for sure!"

"I'm excited, too," said Timothy, "but I'm a bit nervous, too. These are big changes. At least the Hazeltons will be there, so we'll have some good friends to start with."

We had to be in Washington to take office, on January 3rd. We had less than two months to find accommodations, get the children into new schools, and get moved. I thought the campaigning was hectic, but the next two months were even more hectic.

With the help of lawyers, we used some of my investment funds to create a real estate corporation that would buy two houses and then rent the houses to us and to the Hazeltons. The next evening, we had the Hazeltons over for dinner to go over the plans for moving to Washington.

"Thelma, I'd love it if we could live near each other there, the way we do here, but I also don't want to set up anything where we might intrude on each other's spaces or expect too much from each other."

"Whew." Both she and Dale were pleased.

"I know," I agreed, "but I hope we can be close enough to socialize and maybe so the children can go to the same school."

Beginning that very Thursday, we took a long four-day weekend with all four children and the three of us adults to fly to Washington, leaving late on Thursday afternoon.

It was a tense and chaotic, visit. Thelma and I had meeting after meeting, all arranged for us to get to know Senator Tansky and his staff and to have the ins and outs of the Senate explained to us. Fortunately, Ben, Jeremy, and Barry Jones of the Nebraska Republicans had prepared us about the various people we would meet, but we quickly learned that we had to scan the various dossiers and documents for the more salient points.

On Friday morning, Dale began his tour with the four children. Over the previous two months, we had gone through dozens of housing listings and information about schools. We settled on contacting The Field School, a private school with an excellent and growing reputation to see about enrolling the children there. That was their first stop, where the children met with admissions counselors and took some basic placement tests. The school was pleased that we had selected it for our children; it was always a feather in the cap of any private school when the children of the Members of Congress enrolled in the school, and here were four students coming to their school.

The administrators there did everything they could to make the transition from Burke School to Field School go smoothly for the children. During the next two weeks, Field teachers got in touch with the teachers at Burke to make sure they knew which courses the students needed to take at Field to dovetail with their courses at Burke. It wasn't completely seamless, but overall the change in schools went quite smoothly for the children.

While the children were busy with the admission testing and interviews that morning, Dale took the opportunity to meet with some of his business people who were based in DC; then in the afternoon he and the children traveled around in a minivan with a real estate agent to look at houses within a mile of the school.

Our eyes popped when we saw the prices of the houses. I told Dale and Thelma, "Don't worry. The corporation will rent you whatever place you settle on, and then as I told Thelma, we'll sell it probably for some outlandish capital gain when you're ready to leave."

I said, 'When *you're* ready to leave,' because even though I hoped they would stay in Washington the whole time I was there, I knew things could change, and I didn't want them to feel obligated to stay more than a year or two. After that, I could probably adjust without Thelma and Dale and so I tried to use subtle language just to let them know I'd be okay if they didn't stay all six or more years.

The real estate agent was practically drooling when Dale got in touch with her. Not only would she be selling a house to an incoming senator, she'd be selling two houses and earn a year's worth of commissions.

All afternoon Friday and all day Saturday, Dale and the children looked at places we might consider living in. They collected flyers and ads for each place they hadn't ruled out and brought them back to the hotel in the evening. The more we looked at the ads and the more we thought about trying to maintain homes both in Omaha and in DC, the better condo living sounded to both families, as long as we could find places near each other that were spacious and modern enough.

Seth said, "If we don't have a guest bedroom and don't have a basement, we should be okay, since we'll still have our house in Omaha to store most of our stuff."

Aaron agreed, "We won't be bringing all our stuff with us. Three bedrooms and two bathrooms should be good for us."

Thelma and I were in a massive spin from all the meetings we had 'taken' and from all the information we had tried to process, and so we pretty much let Dale and the children decide on a short list of condos. They settled on some condos that were down near the Potomac River and the Georgetown Reservoir, within about a mile of The Field School.

As we looked through the information that night, we settled on similar units that were just a block apart. Both condo units had what we were looking for, including dishwashers and all the major appliances, in-unit laundry rooms, and kitchen-dining-living room areas that were quite open. I bought them, sight unseen, trusting Dale and the children. That felt so strange. I had never delegated such a big personal decision before, but I decided, "It's only for now, and I actually trust Dale and the children."

We took possession of our condos on December 15th, which meant we'd have to plan our move to take place around the Christmas holidays. I wanted to spend the holidays in Omaha with our friends there, and so did Thelma, but we knew we'd have to move before the New Year.

"No New Year's Eve party this year," we told the children. "We'll be in DC by then." They were all disappointed and yet excited, too.

Everyone in Omaha wanted a piece of us, a slice of our time, "just a few minutes" or more. We had over a dozen invitations to have Thanksgiving dinner with various people. The invitations from friends and neighbors were hard to turn down, but I was actually relieved to turn down the invitations from political folks: "That is so kind of you to think of us! But we already have plans. Thank you so much!"

For Thanksgiving, we had just the Bergmans from next door and the Plagges from behind us over for dinner. Thelma and I talked about having a group dinner, but the minute we thought about the teenagers, we realized the dinner would get out of hand if we tried to invite all the girlfriends and their parents. "How about I invite them all for the 'Holiday Party' this year?"

We agreed to that plan, and then I reminded the Bergmans that I wanted to hold the neighborhood party before we moved to Washington.

"Are you sure you'll have time to do it?" asked Kathy.

"We'll make sure we have time," I said. "We really want to have the party this year before we leave for DC."

"I'm glad you'll be able to do it,' said Kathy. "And would it be okay for me to bring some Jewish snacks?"

"I'd love it!" I enthused, "and I know the children would, too."

As we planned the Holiday Party, we tried to limit the guest list to include just the neighbors who had been coming to the parties for years. Guest list! I was beginning to feel like the socialite I never really wanted to become, and yet it was inevitable.

We did our best to limit the guest list, but we wanted to invite Sandra, Becky, and their parents; and I wanted to invite Ben and Cindy, and Jeremy, too. Limiting the guest list beyond that was difficult, but I was learning; I had never faced issues like these before I became a politician.

"Before I became a politician"? I can't believe I thought, much less just wrote, that phrase. I didn't want to admit that I was really a politician even though I knew I was one. As I reflected on it, I realized I had always tended to behave like a politician.

When I was a teenager working at the family hardware store in Salina, Kansas, I quickly learned how to be polite to all the customers, even the ones who had complaints. My parents began to treat me as the designated public relations officer for the store because I handled things reasonably well there.

Also, waiting tables in Brookville serving chicken dinners at the hotel involved another, slightly different type of work with the public, especially with guests who didn't quite understand what it meant to have chicken dinners served 'family style'. And of course, all my work with Arkero Foods involved acting like a politician, both within the firm as I did my best to keep office politics under control, and then again as a consultant working directly on public relations projects for the firm. And then I remembered how shocked I was by how much I sounded like a politician when I held the press conferences the previous fall, long before anyone suggested I run for the Senate.

After the election, scheduling became even more difficult than it had been during the campaign; everyone wanted to have us over to congratulate us and to say 'good-bye'. The children had their usual social and school activities, but everything felt more pressured after I was elected and while we were planning our move.

I had kept the Monday evening after Thanksgiving clear, and everyone who had worked on the campaign and who still had access to my calendar knew it. So I wasn't surprised when, on Thanksgiving Friday, Jeremy Hall invited me to "come over for dinner on Monday evening…" a clear euphemism for spending some time together again.

I eagerly accepted; after all, that was why I had kept that evening free. "Why don't I pick up some food to bring?" I suggested.

He objected at first but relented when I pointed out that he had taken me to dinner during the summer. I suggested Chinese food; we had eaten cartons and cartons of Chinese take-out at the campaign office, and so I had a pretty good idea of what he liked.

Thelma called me fifteen minutes later.

"I see you've blocked off Monday evening for 'personal time'," she said. I could hear the teasing in her voice.

"Yes, Jeremy has invited me to dinner."

"Uh huh." She sounded just slightly sarcastic.

"But I'm not sure how much food we'll be eating…" and we both laughed.

"Whoa, girl! Sounds exciting!"

When I told the children they'd have to fend for themselves for supper that night, there was no hint of what my plans were. But as I went out the door, Liz giggled just a bit and said, "Remember, Mom, you have to be home by midnight!"

I liked being with Jeremy. I hoped we would be able to spend some time together outside of work while we were in Washington. I was realistic enough to understand, though, that we might not have a permanent relationship, and that evening I insisted we talk about it.

"You know I've been going through a lot of changes since Fred was killed," I said to him while we were cuddling, "and I have no idea what the future holds. Jeremy, I am really enjoying whatever it is that we have in our moments together, but we have to be free to change, to grow, or whatever it's called."

He was clearly disappointed and maybe even hurt. "I think you are the most amazing woman I've ever met," he said, and then he added somewhat tentatively "I want you in my life, and I want to be in your life."

I leaned over him and kissed him.

"Jeremy, I'll give you what little I can … for now … but we both must be prepared that whatever we have now will change. You've been through it before, so you know. Things change. All I ask is that we continue to care for each other and be kind to each other, no matter what."

I added, "You are a brilliant, savvy journalist. Even if things don't work out between us romantically, I sure hope we can hold our working relationship together."

Jeremy tried to agree, but he was clearly reluctant and disappointed. He went on, "I don't like the feeling of being in limbo or part-time," he said. "I want to be with you more, not less."

"I understand," I said as I caressed his ear. "It's just that I don't want to give you any false expectations. I love being with you, but I've been through so many changes in the past year that I have to expect there will be more, and so do you. For now, though, I'm enjoying you in every way."

He looked at me and asked, "So this means we're still going steady?"

"Of course, Silly," and I kissed him again.

I had never thought of myself as a live-for-the-moment type of person; I had always planned and saved and prepared for the future. Fred's death left me quite unsettled, though, and I surprised myself by being so open to having the type of relationship that Jeremy and I were having. One thing I knew for sure was that I was going to be careful about committing to anything more than 'going steady' at that point.

Chapter 40 – Christmas, 2002

We arranged with the Hazeltons that we would all drive to Washington the day after Christmas in separate cars, us in our family sedan, and the Hazeltons in their minivan. We figured it would take us about twenty hours of driving time to get there, and so to make sure we didn't rush, we planned to make the trip over three days, leaving late in the morning on the day after Christmas and then spending the second night in a motel just outside Washington. We'd arrive at our condos on the morning of the 28th and have a few days to get settled before I was formally sworn in.

"We're not taking **any** furniture or linens or dishes or anything," Thelma and I agreed. "We'll buy or rent things there. And that way, we will still have everything here, ready and waiting for us in Omaha whenever we come back for visits, like at Spring Break, Easter, Memorial Day, and summer vacations."

With those plans in mind, Thelma and I flew to Washington in early December for a massive two-day shopping spree. Our first stop was at our condos, where we arranged for the condo managers to take delivery of the things we were planning to buy and ship. We spent almost the entire remainder of our time at Hecht's Department Store buying beds, mattresses, dining room sets, living room furniture, towels, sheets, dishes, dinnerware, and some basic household supplies, specifying that we wanted delivery on or after December 16th and further specifying that we would pay extra, if necessary, to have the furniture assembled and set up in the appropriate rooms. Neither of us wanted to spend a lot of money on everything, and we reassured each other that if we bought something but realized later that we really couldn't stand it, it wouldn't hurt too much if we didn't spend too much on it in the first place.

"It only has to last six years," I opined.

Thelma looked at me sharply.

"You've already decided you won't run for re-election?" she asked.

"Well, not really. It's just that who knows whether I'll be re-electable after people learn more about my views and my votes."

The Holiday Party at our home in Omaha was a tremendous success. We had fancy canapés set out everywhere throughout the main floor of the house; in the basement games room we had mini hotdogs, veggies and dip, and pizza pockets; and, of course, we made a big point of serving only 'bloody plonk' as the wine offering, much to the amusement of everyone, especially Maggie Nelson. Timothy and Liz even printed up labels for the bottles: "Red Bloody Plonk" and "White Bloody Plonk".

When the Bergmans arrived, they had three platters of Yiddish appetizers.

"I'm tempted to hide these so we can have them all to ourselves," I laughingly told Kathy, "but I think we'll put them right here on the kitchen table, where everyone can get at them."

Kathy immediately replied, "Okay, but how about we combine them differently so I can take one platter, something of a sampler, down for the youngsters in the basement."

Even though it was supposed to be a Holiday Party, it was also a congratulations-farewell party, too. Those who wanted to talk about policy issues didn't get much of our time, but our truly good neighbors and good friends had the decency to avoid political hot buttons , making the entire party fun and heart-warming.

In addition to our usual decorations, the children insisted that we hang mistletoe in the front hallway. Everybody was kissing everybody; it was almost like a giant love fest. The children and their partners all kissed dramatically under the mistletoe, and they eagerly waited and watched when Jeremy arrived to see what would happen. I wasn't about to put on a show for everyone, and so we quick-kissed. The children all cheered because we kissed but booed because it was so impassionate, but their boos quickly turned into laughter as everyone hugged everyone.

As people left the party, they all said their good-byes and even shed a few tears. Both Thelma and I reassured everyone that we'd be back in Omaha frequently. "I'll be back," I said in what was probably the worst fake Schwarzenegger accent ever attempted.

"What are you giving Jeremy for Christmas?" Liz asked when the party was over.

"I have no idea," I answered. "Any suggestions?"

"Maybe a CD?" suggested Timothy. "Or maybe a book?"

"I don't know… I'd like to give him something a bit more personal."

"If he has mentioned a particular album or book that he really would like, that could be quite personal," Timothy countered.

"How about a shirt? A sweater?" suggested Liz.

I hesitated. "I don't know …"

"Okay, Mom … a thong!" Said Liz, laughing at me.

"Maybe …" I joked back. "What would be a good color?"

I considered buying him a gold chain. A tasteful, not-too-garish one -- nothing like the ones you see on pro athletes. I had no idea, though, whether that would be appropriate. My feeling was that it was something he had never worn but that he might like, as a symbol of something vague between us. It seemed a bit too much, though. I didn't want to provide him or anyone else with misleading signals.

Instead, I took him to a tailor and had some custom shirts made for him.

Christmas that year was *so* different from Christmas the previous year. A few months after Fred was killed, we were feeling sorry for ourselves, and there was a sense that we lacked direction. We didn't know what to expect in the future, and I'm sure that if anyone had told us then what we would be going through in the ensuing year, we'd have laughed at them.

But there we were, a year later, looking forward to so much that was new – jobs, homes, friends, publicity … there was so much that was so different from what we had imagined.

Going to church for the Christmas service on the Sunday before Christmas was quite an operation – confused but joyful.

Jeremy wanted to go to the service with us, but I told him that I wanted to sit next to my children again, the way I had the year before. I suggested that he come along and sit with others and then join us afterward at our house for cocoa, along with the Hazeltons, Sandra and her parents, and Becky and her parents.

The post-church cocoa party was turning into quite a huge affair, much to the delight of everyone. I hoped I'd be back in Omaha every year at

Christmas time so we could continue having it.

As she had the year before, Liz arranged to have dinner with the Hazeltons. At the same time, Rodney Blair and Lanny Overhill (Sandra's parents) had Timothy and me over to their place for a light supper before the church service. One difference was that this year, Rodney and Lanny went to the service with us, but in their own car so that they could drive themselves home after having cocoa at our house.

After the gigantic cocoa party, and after everyone else had left, Jeremy took my hand and pulled me into the living room. "Susan," he said as he took a small box from his pocket, "I know this is very teen-agery, but I want to give you your Christmas present now, away from the others."

When I saw that it was a small box, I almost recoiled in fear. I hoped he wasn't proposing to me. If he was, I would be blunt in saying "no" but at the same time I didn't want to send him away.

I shouldn't have worried, not even fleetingly; I could tell from the size of the box that it probably wasn't a ring, and I relaxed. His gift was a fifty-dollar prepaid magnetic striped Metro Pass for the DC transportation system! It seemed so mundane and yet so thoughtful. I loved it. I didn't want to use it ever. I wanted to frame it so I could save it the way I had saved the ceramic cat Fred gave me shortly after we met.

"When I was in DC looking for an apartment, it occurred to me that even though Senators have chauffeured cars, you might want one of these for when you're not traveling on business. It's more of a symbol of change than anything else, I guess, but I wanted to get you something unique."

I kissed him.

"You're so thoughtful!" I said, and I kissed him again.

"I'm *so* thoughtful," he replied, "that I bought passes for Timothy and Liz, too. I have no idea what your kids will be doing in DC while you're working, and I know the DC cab system is pretty efficient, but this way they'll have another, prepaid way to get around."

I knew I would either use a Senate-provided driver or take a cab myself nearly all the time, but I wasn't about to tell him that because I appreciated his gift ... mostly ... .

I could see what he was doing, though: he wanted me to ride the Metro so he could take photos of 'A Day In The Life' and make me look like 'one of the people'. I resented the subtle pressure to be political, and I resented the idea that everything involving me was geared toward politics and appearances. And at the same time, I resented my paranoia.

I didn't let on to Jeremy about my various resentments. After all, my resentment was about being on display and having to pay attention to political angles every minute; it wasn't toward Jeremy at all.

Well, not much. I knew Jeremy wanted me to be more aware of the political angles for everything, and I knew he was eager for me to be a full-time politician in everything I did, and I resisted that pressure when I could in ways that I hoped wouldn't confront or hurt him.

All-in-all, I was grateful for the passes. I knew the children would love having the passes, just so they and I could go exploring. What is more, I knew that my buying tailor-made shirts for Jeremy was really no different: I was giving him a gift that I thought would be helpful in his career, and that's what he was doing with the Metro Passes for me and the children.

And then I surprised him with another little gift box.

"Hey!" he objected, "You've already bought me some very nice, custom-fit shirts. You're not supposed to do this…"

I kissed him again and murmured into his ear, "Be quiet and open it."

He burst in to laughter as he pulled out three luggage ID tags and a key fob that all said, "Omaha, Nebraska" on them.

"One for your suitcase, one for your laptop case, and one for your backpack," I said. "I don't want you to forget where you're from."

He caught on right away and added, "And it will be great identification for us, too. We should buy a boxful of these things for everyone in the office."

"I already did," I laughed. "In fact, I ordered several hundred and had them sent to my new office in DC. I would especially like to have the key fobs on hand to give to the other senators, the office staff, and some of the visitors we'll have there."

Jeremy chuckled. "So, you *do* think in terms of politics now and then!

Anyway, it's a great idea, but I wonder whether you ordered enough…"

"I think so. I'm guessing that most visitors from Nebraska would like souvenirs related to Washington, D.C., not Nebraska, when they visit. These first few hundred will be for the other senators and other people who will need reminding that I'll be a Senator from Nebraska. The remaining key fobs are for long-time lobbyists and other visitors who aren't from Nebraska. They'll need constant reminding, too."

"I see what's going on. You'll do this to promote the fact that you're representing Nebraska, not yourself, and so these will be non-political gifts for everyone. It's a nice thing to do and still take the high road."

I winced slightly because he had said that in such a political-manipulation tone of voice. I knew that what he had said was probably in the back of my mind as well, but I didn't like thinking or talking about it that way, not even with close friends and political strategists.

I hesitated and spoke in a political half-truth mode I was beginning to resent in myself. "I suppose so, but let's not think of that way. Let's think of it as a nice thing to do for people that will help promote Nebraska."

For Christmas Eve, we did exactly the same things the children and I had done the year before. We had hot dogs, coleslaw, and potato chips, we sang Christmas carols, we watched TV specials, and we wrapped gifts. At 9:30 we said good night to each other and went upstairs, where the children filled my stocking and I filled theirs.

When Timothy and Liz rushed into my bedroom on Christmas morning and climbed onto the bed, I smiled at them and said, "It's real, isn't it. We're moving to Washington – tomorrow! – you're changing schools, and I'm going to be a senator. Who would have imagined this a year ago!?"

All of the stocking gifts that year were related to travel, to moving, and to living in Washington, DC. The children got underwear again: Timothy's had a picture of the Washington Monument strategically placed over the fly, and Liz's had a picture of Susan B. Anthony. We all had a good laugh about those, and then I pulled out the underwear they had chosen for me: red lacy bikini panties.

"Oooh lah lah!" said Liz in fake surprise. "I guess Santa knows if you're being naughty or nice!"

I actually was embarrassed that the children would think about my sex life. I blushed, and we all laughed as Liz added, "Wow, Mom, your face is almost the same color as your panties!"

My main gifts to the children were laptop computers. I knew they would want to keep in touch with their friends in Omaha, and I knew I would want my own laptop for my own use. They loved them!

We spent the rest of the day taking down the Christmas decorations and packing up all the things we had set out that we wanted to take with us but hadn't already shipped. Timothy insisted on spending the afternoon with Sandra. "I'm packed, Mom, and I really want to be with her to say goodbye."

The move to Washington was flawless. We left Omaha at about ten o'clock the next morning in a two-vehicle caravan with the Hazeltons, and we pulled into DC at nine o'clock on the morning of the 28th. We were brimming with curiosity about what the units would look like since we had pretty much left the furniture arranging to the condo managers.

Our condo looked like a long-term-stay-for-executives type of place. The dining room and living room looked nice, aside from the lack of suitable area rugs in the living room and the bare walls. In the kitchen, the counter was stacked with boxes of what Liz called "kitchenry", trying to make it sound mysterious, like wizardry or witchery.

"Let's make a list," I said. "Even before we begin to unpack, we need to think about things we'll need soon. Soap, shampoo, dish soap, dishwasher detergent, flour, butter, milk, juice, what else?"

"Mom, the freezer in this fridge isn't huge, and we're going to want to have lots of frozen meals on hand," said Liz.

"Right," I answered, "So let's not buy too much frozen food at first, but let's see if we can find a place to put a small freezer, too."

Timothy started our shopping list and put "freezer" at the top of it. As we unpacked our suitcases, we'd call out things we wanted added to the list.

"Tampons," called out Liz.

I think she was trying to tease and embarrass Timothy, but he called back very matter-of-factly, "Which brand and which style?"

The shopping list was huge by the time we had our suitcases unpacked.

Some of the boxes we had mailed early had already arrived, and the condo manager had put them in the closets. We had a lot of work ahead of us, and I was glad we had the rest of that day and the next to ourselves, with no meetings and no social events.

"Where are the internet connections?" asked Timothy. "I want to write to Sandra."

"I think we'll need to get something installed," I said. "Isn't there some way you can 'text' each other using your phones?"

"Mom, have you ever actually tried to use your cell phone to send a text? It isn't easy pressing different numbers different numbers of times to get each letter. And Sandra doesn't have a cell phone anyway. Most teenagers don't, you know."

"Oh yeah. Well, maybe you can check with the condo management to see what we have to do to get the internet here with jacks in each bedroom and in the kitchen?"

Timothy got right on it. ... After he used some of his cell phone allowance to call Sandra.

"That's not fair!" cried Liz in a fake-whine. "He gets to call his girlfriend, but I can't call Seth because he and Aaron don't have cell phones yet and we don't know their home number here."

I said, "Why not see if you can call Thelma's cell phone and ask if you can speak to Seth?"

"Do you really think that would be okay? I mean, this is personal, not business."

"I'll call her and ask," I offered.

Thelma was bubbling over with excitement when I called her.

"Everything is going so beautifully!" she said. "Thank you so much for everything you have done to make this work for us!"

"Enough already. What are you doing about the internet there?"

"That's one of the things that is going so well here. The super in the building says the cable company has this thing called wi-fi that we can use, and we won't need to have jacks or cords. We can all use the same wi-fi at the same time anywhere in the unit."

"That sounds like exactly we need, too! Hold on…" I called to Timothy and explained it to him, asking him to look into it with our condo manager.

Thelma went on, "I don't know about your family, but we need two things: lunch, and a bucketload of groceries. How about we go out to some plaza together? Call your driver and tell him to expect seven people…" Thelma laughed, and then she quickly added, "Seriously, we'll probably need to take both cars."

We ended up at a pizza place over on Wisconsin Avenue and then at the Safeway across the street from it. Liz was so happy to be seeing Seth again that afternoon that she forgot I had made the call so she could talk with him.

Chapter 41 – Finding Our Way

Long before we arrived in Washington, we had several different invitations to New Year's Eve parties. One was from Agbrakan, the farm lobby group, and I turned it down immediately. Apparently, lobbyists make a lot of pitches and don't always expect a high success rate.

We ended up accepting the invitation from Senator Tansky, whose Senate seat I would be filling on January 3rd. It turned out to be a combination farewell/New Year's Eve/welcome party, and we were among the honored guests.

All eight of us, including Jeremy, went to the party, and all eight of us were impressed by the food and the atmosphere. Thelma, Dale, and I had agreed that if the children were offered champagne at midnight, they could each have a small glass of it, but we naively hadn't expected there to be nearly 300 people at the party and that we couldn't really monitor the children. I quickly changed the plan and told the children, "No alcohol. Not tonight. Not here. We'll talk more about alcohol and what's reasonable for you tomorrow."

As the party wore on, the children were constantly amazed and impressed, both positively and negatively, about the high life in political circles. I wasn't at all sure I liked it. I was happy they would be exposed to new foods and new lifestyles, but I was concerned that they might go through their teen years expecting people to fawn over them.

"Mom, is this caviar?" Liz asked. "It tastes salty and fishy. I don't understand why people like it. I'd be just as happy with fish sticks."

"It's a symbol," offered Dale. "It's a symbol of money and influence. I don't see the point either, but it's fun to be able to try it."

Of the 300 people at the party, at least 100 were there primarily to meet me and, if possible, have a word or two with me. I did my best to redirect the conversations to be congratulations to Senator Tansky, away from us and away from politics. It was his party, and I didn't want to divert the attention away from him. Also, I dreaded having to deal with all the political talk. I just wanted to relax, enjoy myself, and get to know people.

Thelma and Dale ran interference informally by hovering near me. As people approached, Thelma or Dale would smile at them, introduce themselves, and engage them in conversation. I don't know if they planned that strategy, but I loved it, and we employed it often after that.

There were about fifteen or twenty other teenagers there, and our four children mingled with them, trying to learn what life would be like in the nation's capital. They got quite an introduction that evening.

Timothy later said, "I felt as if the other kids there was trying to play a mind game with me. I'm sure glad the Hazeltons are here so that we have some genuine friends. I liked Andy Petry, though. He's a senior at The Field School, and plays soccer; his sister goes there, too. It was good meeting someone else who goes to that school before we actually start there ourselves."

"He seemed nice," said Liz, "but his sister is a vamp. She's got her eyes on you, Timothy. Be careful," she warned in a teasing voice.

Seth joined in, "He did seem nice. But most of the others? It's like they're all trying to outdo each other and make sure they outdo us. Well, I for one will be happy to let them. I have no idea how to play these social games, so I just stand back and watch."

Aaron contributed, "I watched you, Seth. You were good. Whenever you were challenged by someone, you turned things around and asked them more about themselves and their schools. I learned very quickly from you, big bro, and did the same thing."

Liz agreed. "There were basically two types of girls. Some continued to try to make me feel small and ignorant with snotty put-downs, but others stopped the mind games, and we actually talked back and forth. It was easy to pick out who might be real and who was probably fake."

Meanwhile, Jeremy was in his element, glad-handing everyone, making sure everyone knew who I was and, of course, who he was.

When the midnight countdown began, Jeremy staked out a position next to me making sure he'd be the one to kiss me first. I had encouraged Jeremy to keep his distance from me during the party, but at midnight we had a good kiss, and during the post-kiss hug, I murmured in his ear, "Soon, I hope. Soon." I kissed his neck, leaned back while still holding him, smiled, and then kissed his neck again before breaking away.

During the countdown, I noticed out of the corner of my eye that Liz led Seth off away from the others and buried herself in his chest. Later she said,

"I wasn't going to kiss all those other kids. I don't even know them."

Timothy was overwhelmed, though, with 'interest' by the young (and not-so-young) women there, all wanting to kiss him and wish him a Happy New Year. I think that evening was the first time in his life that Timothy began to realize that he had something that girls found attractive. He was clearly surprised, but pleased, and he seemed to enjoy going along with all of them.

Meanwhile, Aaron managed to get in on a lot of the kissing action himself, much to his delight and much to the amusement of his parents.

Later Thelma told me that Aaron and Becky had been boyfriend-girlfriend mostly out of convenience. "They were more friends than romantically involved," she said.

"You know," I replied, "being good friends may lead to a healthier, longer-lasting relationship than any of the others will have."

At midnight Dale and Thelma kissed each other and the few people around them, but then they made their way to Jeremy and me for midnight kisses as well. I was glad they had. Their presence kept many of the others at bay.

"Geez, girl," said Thelma, "You should sell tickets!"

I laughed, but inside I wasn't amused. I felt as if everyone in the room wanted a piece of me for one thing or another.

Thelma and I agreed that our families should spend New Year's Day 2003 apart, just to make sure we didn't begin to rely on each other too much.
... Well, the best-laid plans... et cetera.

Liz had already invited Seth to come to our place to watch Oklahoma and Washington State in the Rose Bowl, and I had already invited Jeremy to come over for the game, too.

Meanwhile, Timothy had been invited to go to Andy Petry's. That left Aaron, Thelma, and Dale and so I said, "I know this isn't working out the way we planned, but why don't you three come over to our place for the game. We'll have something to eat at half-time, and then after the game we can call the Schultzes and Bergmans and use our phones to join in singing 'Auld Lang Syne' in the street with all the neighbors."

Jeremy hadn't been with us the year before when Dale got all the neighbors to hold hands and sing together out in the street. He wasn't sure what to expect, but we eagerly filled him in.

During the game, Dale called the Bergmans and I called the Schultzes to set it all up, and then right at thirty minutes after the game was over, we called them. They were ready for us, along with about twenty-five of our neighbors, standing in front of the Bergmans' house in the street, and we all sang the song at least three times, followed by wishes of "Happy New Year" shouted in chorus and all sorts of offerings of best wishes and protestations about how much we all missed each other already.

When we were alone in the kitchen, Jeremy hinted that he'd like to spend the night.

"Where? On our couch?" I asked. "I'm not ready to have you spend the night here when the children are here."

He looked crestfallen.

"Jeremy, we'll travel together at times, and we'll have some late work nights now and then. As I said last night, 'Soon, I hope. Very soon'."

"Okay," he agreed reluctantly.

And then he grinned widely, "What about some phone sex then?"

I burst into laughter. There was no way I was going to have phone sex with anyone, but the thought of it was fun.

Just then Thelma came into the kitchen.

"Alright, you two, what's the joke?"

Jeremy blushed, and I just laughed harder.

"I'll tell you later," I said, and I had to wipe the tears out of my eyes from laughing.

I don't think Jeremy was nearly so amused as I was, but to mollify him I grabbed his behind when I reached up and kissed him. I wanted him to know that in my mind we were still "an item" even though I wouldn't spend the night with him in my home with the children there ... not yet, anyway.

Timothy got home two hours later, after everyone else had left, even though the Petrys lived only a few blocks away.

"How was it?" I asked.

"Mom," you were right. Life in DC is *so* different from life in Omaha."

"How so?"

Liz was very eager to hear what he had to say, and he didn't hold back. I don't know how they developed such a trusting relationship with each other, but I'm certain it helped them both get through the next few years.

"Lots of people were there, like some of the parties we used to have in the basement back home, only bigger. The fridge was stocked with white wine and beer, and all the kids were drinking. Mom, I wasn't prepared for that …"

Oh, Oh. I regretted not having prepared them better.

"And…?"

"I had some beer. I didn't much like it, though. Some of the kids there had way too much to drink and got falling down stupid and were throwing up in the bathroom. That wasn't much fun."

"I had hoped to introduce you two to alcohol myself, here at home," I said. "I'm sorry I didn't do that sooner. But I'm glad you're okay."

"Andy's sister, Vicki, is a junior at Field and is really into acting and theatre and all that stuff. …"

It seemed he wanted to be encouraged to say more, and so I did.

"What's she like?"

"Well, she's very dramatic, and she really came on to me."

"What'd I tell you, Timothy!" taunted Liz.

"What does that mean, Timothy?" I asked.

"She kept hanging around me, draping her arm over my shoulder, smiling at me. She called me her 'handsome friend' and announced that she was claiming me as her own. It was embarrassing, and everyone was watching or half snickering, waiting to see what I would do."

"And ...?"

"I took her aside and told her, 'You seem really nice, but I have to tell you that I have a girlfriend back home.' Do you know what she said? She said, 'That's okay. She can have you when you're home, but I want to have you when you're here.' And then she kissed me. Mom, the kissing was exciting, but I had to break away. It didn't feel right."

"Wow, Timothy," said Liz. "I thought she might be like that when I met that Vicki person at the New Year's Eve party last night."

"This is all so different for me." He said. "So fast. I'm scared about it all, but I really have to admit that I liked it, too."

Liz was shocked. "What about Sandra?"

"I'm staying true to her," replied Timothy, "but kissing Vicki was pretty exciting, ... Does that make sense? Is it okay?"

Liz was outraged.

"It makes sense that you aren't staying true to Sandra. Timothy, how could you? We haven't even been away for a week!"

Timothy wasn't stopped by Liz's outrage. Instead he said, "Sandra is very special to me. She brought me out of my shell and awakened me in ways that I'll always be grateful for. But I'm just being honest, Lizzy ..."

His calling her Lizzy so condescendingly didn't help much.

"I'm not sure I want to hear this, Timmy," she replied, emphasizing 'Timmy' in as sarcastic a tone as she could muster.

"I'm sorry, Liz. But let me try to be honest with you and Mom. And I'll try to be honest with Sandra, too. Being kissed by all those girls last night at the party, and being desired by another girl made me feel good."

"How will you feel if Sandra starts kissing other boys?" asked Liz.

"I don't know. ... " He hesitated.

"What am I saying? I know." He was embarrassed. "I'll hate it. I'm not even sure I want to know about it. And the hard thing is that I think she probably kissed other boys herself last night at some party. Mom, I need some help here …"

I wasn't at all ready for this. Off the cuff, I tried to help.

"Being admired and desired physically can be great. For us women, sometimes it isn't so great, too, if it leads to unwanted attention and suggestive comments, believe me. But in this case, it's almost as if Vicki was the one giving the unwanted attention and making the comments?"

"The thing is, Mom, I don't think I didn't want it. Does that make sense? When she came on to me with her suggestive smiles and touching me, I was actually pleased. I was even aroused, Mom."

"Being physically aroused when someone shows interest in you is normal. The thing you'll have to deal with is, 'what do you do about it?'"

"I know, Mom. I think I'm still in love with Sandra, but I want to do things with Vicki, too. Is that wrong?"

Liz was beside herself. "Timothy! What if Sandra called you right now and told you the same thing? Huh? What if she said, "I love you Timothy, but I'm going to make out with other boys while you're gone, and I might even have sex with them'? Huh? How would you feel?"

"I'd be devastated… I know I would. But I think that's likely to happen anyway. So just let me say that when it happens, and I know it will, I *will* be devastated. Does that change things for me?"

I waded in. "Do you want to talk about it with her before it happens?"

"How, Mom? It would be like breaking up. I know it would end up with us breaking up. And I don't want to break up with Sandra."

And then he added, somewhat speculatively, "I think maybe Vicki's coming on to me was part of a ritual or hazing. Everyone there was watching. It was as if they had all been through this with her and with each other dozens of times, and I was the new kid being inducted into some group. When I got that feeling, I said, 'Well, I think I'd better head out now. We have some family things planned for early tomorrow.' I know that was a lie, but I didn't want to stay after that.

"Mom, I really liked the physical contact with Vicki, but I didn't like the feeling of being on display and being tested."

"Welcome to Washington, D.C." I muttered. "What have I gotten us into?"

Then Timothy got a coy smile I hadn't seen him use before.

"You know what? As I was leaving, Vicki kissed me again and said, 'Maybe next time you can spend the night.' Mom, I don't even know her!"

"Whoa!" said Liz. "I'm sure glad Seth wasn't at that party! Mom, is that what our lives will be like here?"

"They don't have to be. You can choose what you want. Timothy chose to leave when he became uncomfortable, and I know you would, too."

"There's more, Mom," Timothy added. "As I was walking home, one of the other girls from the party, I think her name was Paula, came running after me and actually took my hand. 'Vicki's like that,' she said. 'Be careful.' And when we got here, she said, 'I want to kiss you, too, but I'm not going to because I barely know you.' She smiled and said, 'See you in school.'"

"Mom!" said Liz, "Timothy is becoming quite the Romeo. I sure am glad Seth wasn't there and I'm not going through all this."

"You will, my dear little innocent one," I thought to myself. "You will."

I cautioned her, "Liz, you have no idea what's in store for you. Those same girls will go after Seth, too. I'll be surprised if there isn't some contest among them to see who can do what first with the new boys. And let me warn you right now: some of the boys here might also have a contest to see who can do what with you, too. There might even be a pool… Be prepared; just be straight and be honest."

Chapter 42 -- **Initiation**

That night I had another long talk with Fred.

"Fred, what have I done?" I was nearly crying. "I almost wish I hadn't run for the Senate and moved here. ... What have I done?"

"You've introduced the kids to new lifestyles," he said. "You've shown them more than they would ever see or experience in Omaha."

"But they're so young! So inexperienced!"

"They're going to have experiences we never imagined," Fred said. "I'd be scared, too, if I were there with you. But let's hope the grounding we've given them will see them through everything."

"Oh, that's all good and well to *say*," I said in an exasperated tone. "How do I get them through all this safely?"

"I know you'll be busy," Fred answered, "but make sure you keep talking with them and asking them things. And don't let them get off with evasive answers you don't like. Let them explore; let them develop; let them grow. Let them make mistakes, even. But keep talking with them."

It was one of the best imaginary conversations I'd had with Fred since the first conversation we had after 9-11. It was just what I needed. It helped me relax, and it reminded me of just how much I had to trust that the children would be okay, no matter what they went through.

I put Fred's photo on my dresser when we moved into our condo. I was glad I did. I still loved Fred, and I really missed him, especially when I was dealing with teen issues. I cried some more as I kissed the photo... and then I laughed at myself as I wiped the lipstick smear off the glass covering the photo.

The next morning, Thursday, I had the Senate car picked me up at 7:30, and we stopped along the way to pick up Thelma and then Jeremy, whose apartment was in Georgetown. That became standard for us.

We went to the Hart Senate Office Building to meet with our staff again, and to meet with the old guard of the Senate. Most of the other senators were quite condescending in their attempts to be helpful while keeping me "in my place" – at least that was how it felt. It was a different set of initiation rites than the children would go through but it was no less unpleasant. I wanted to be on the Senate Foreign Affairs Committee, but so did everyone else; I was both a rookie and a woman, and so there wasn't a hope. Because I was from Nebraska, I was made junior member of the Nutrition and Agricultural Development subcommittee of the Senate Committee on Agriculture, Nutrition, and Forestry. And because I was a woman, I was put on the Children and Families subcommittee of the Health and Welfare Committee.

I didn't mind the committee appointments. I knew that seniority was important in the Senate, and Ben Gruvel had prepared me. In fact, given my education, my work, and my volunteer background, those two committees were perfect for me. I wasn't out of my depth and I had some working knowledge of the issues we would be dealing with.

Neither Ben nor Barry Jones was bothered by those committee appointments because they understood the realities of Washington, but Jeremy was upset. "You're too smart and too good to be on those committees," he said. It was then that I realized how ambitious he was. He wanted me to be on more important committees so that he could have more influence himself as my press secretary. I loved his ambition and yet I was wary of it.

When we arrived at the office on January 2nd, the staff had all submitted their resignations. I had to accept a few of them, but I did so reluctantly. I wanted Thelma as my personal assistant and Jeremy as my press secretary. But because I was a rookie with fewer committee assignments, I had to let some of the junior research staff members go as well. We had pretty much let them know about it all a month earlier, and they all understood the way things worked. Fortunately they had all found other positions, so it wasn't terribly traumatic for anyone.

Senator Tansky had already abandoned his office and Washington a week before Christmas; he was looking forward to retiring to his farm in Nebraska, and so when we arrived on January 2nd, we were ready to move in.

My own inner office had a small parlor-type sitting area, a study with a massive desk, an en suite, and a small sleeping alcove.

"How often did Senator Tansky sleep here?" I asked Bill Ashford, my Chief Legislative Assistant.

Everyone in the office burst into laughter.

Thelma, Jeremy, and I were confused.

"What's the joke?" asked Jeremy.

Betty Elsbury, the office manager, laughed some more and said, "Oh he used that bed a lot, but I don't think he ever slept there…"

"Welcome to Washington," I thought, but I wouldn't look at either Thelma or Jeremy, knowing full well what they were thinking about how much use that bed might get.

"Oh," I said, and added with a very straight face, "I guess he took a lot of short rests there then?"

Thelma couldn't control her laughing. "Stop, girl! I'm gonna wet myself."

Betty looked at me with a very serious look and said exactly what I had said to myself, "Welcome to Washington, Senator."

The children's school didn't begin until the following Monday, and so while Thelma and I were at the office, they were on their own. My imaginary talk with Fred the night before settled me down, but I was still quite curious about what they would do that Thursday.

I needn't have worried.

The children stayed home in the morning, waiting for the cable guy to show up and install the equipment for wi-fi in both condos. Once that was ready, they were in immediate contact with each other via Hotmail. Then they met at a deli on MacArthur Boulevard for lunch and walked up to Field School together, just to check out the school some more, along with the neighborhood between our condos and the school.

"Mom," Liz exclaimed later, "there are **so many** people here in DC, and the houses are so much closer together than they are back in Omaha."

"We walked up to the school," said Timothy. "It's about the same distance as our walk to Burke School back home, but Mom it's a really high-class school. I'm not sure we'll fit in."

"Of course you will," I said. "You'll see. You're the new students, and everyone will want to get to know you."

I didn't add, but I thought, "Also, you're the children of a Senator. You'll fit in," and even thinking like that embarrassed me. I didn't like that part of what was happening to me.

Timothy continued, "Mom, you should see the soccer field behind the school. It's beautiful. I can't wait for soccer practice to begin. Andy says official practices don't start 'til the end of February but he and some of the team will get together there this Saturday afternoon if it's not raining to run through some drills and kick the ball around. They've invited me to join them. I'm really looking forward to this!"

"After we walked around the school grounds and the soccer field," Liz chimed in, "we kept going up Foxhall Road, just a few blocks until we came to some paths in a park. Mom, the paths all connect around there, and we were able to walk through beautiful parkland practically all the way back home. It was so special, just the four of us walking, running, shouting, singing, and laughing, and all the trees! There were no leaves on them, and that made them even more beautiful in a way. And there's a paved tunnel, all lit up inside for people to walk through, going under the canal next to the river. Oh Mom, it was wonderful."

Well, apparently the concerns of the day before were long gone.

"Tomorrow is a big day," I said. "I take the oath of office at the Capitol building. I've made arrangements so that you two can be there with me. The ceremony is at ten, but we'll try to get to the office by eight-thirty so you can meet everyone in the office."

"Mom, I still can't believe this," said Liz. "It's like a fairy tale."

"Yes, it is **like** a fairy tale," I said, emphasizing 'like'. "Liz, what happened? You don't use the word 'like' in every sentence anymore."

"You noticed! I decided it didn't sound grown up, so I've made a real effort to get rid of it. Seth noticed it, too, and he approves."

She was beaming, "I'm almost fifteen now. I don't need to talk like a wannabe valley girl."

I said, "Let's celebrate tonight. And you know how we'll celebrate? **Not** by going out for dinner but by cooking a nice meal here at home. I have no idea how often we'll be able to do this, so let's call this a celebration.

About ten minutes later, Timothy came out of his bedroom. He looked crestfallen.

"Well, we all knew it would happen," he said, and he left us hanging.

Liz picked up right away. "Sandra is dating someone else, right?"

Timothy nodded, stoically holding back his tears.

"I think the talking we did yesterday really helped prepare me. That plus the talks we had all last year, and believe it or not those books on teen relationships helped too. She wrote that she's going to a Creighton basketball game with Louie Peterson. He was always following her around, so I guess that doesn't surprise me. But it still hurts."

He started crying. Liz and I both went to him and hugged him.

"I knew all along that this would probably happen. I just didn't expect it this soon. She says she still loves me and she doesn't have romantic feelings for Louie at all, but that doesn't matter. I think she's gone from me, if not with Louie then eventually with someone else."

"Do you want to call her and talk about it?" I asked.

"Maybe. I don't know. I need to let this sink in."

"While it's sinking in, just remember everything that happened last night and everything you said about it, Timothy," said Liz. She could be brutally honest.

"I know," said Timothy. "I know. I've already thought about that. I'm just so confused. In some ways, I wish we hadn't left Omaha and come here."

My heart sank.

"Don't worry, Mom" he rushed to reassure me. "I know this had to happen. Remember I said last spring that I figured Sandra is probably not my forever girlfriend … at least I don't think she is. I don't know, maybe we need to date other people to find out. Still it doesn't take away the hurt."

We sat on the couch together with Timothy between us. So much for fixing dinner at home as a celebratory thing. Instead, we watched some television and ordered pizza.

I wondered if there were any other single-parent members of Congress with teenagers. I'd have to ask Betty Elsbury in the morning.

The senate car picked up the children and me at 8:30 on Friday morning and drove us to my office at the Hart Building. After showing the children around the office and introducing them to the staff, I took them down to the underground subway that takes Senators back and forth between Hart and the Capitol building. It's only a two-block walk between the two buildings but the subway was more helpful than most people might think; it not only protected us from the cold or rain or heat, but it also protected us from lobbyists. I quickly discovered that if I tried to make the two-block walk on my own, I would more than likely be approached by a lobbyist with some position to 'explain'.

I came to love the subway, but that morning the children and I were just plain intrigued and impressed with it. We'd been on subways as tourists in London and Paris, but this one was so different; it was clean and quiet, and it wasn't crowded.

I was one of thirty-three Senators being sworn in on Friday, January 3rd. Of those thirty-three, twenty-one had been re-elected but there were twelve newcomers, and I was the only female among the newcomers.

"Where are all the other senators?" asked Timothy.

"They're working," answered Bill Ashford, my legislative assistant.

Timothy and Liz were both confused.

"I thought being here in the Senate was what Senators did," said Timothy.

"This is just where everything is formalized," Bill replied. "Nearly all the **real** work of the Senate is done in subcommittees, committees, private meetings, restaurants, bars, and hotel rooms. And when they're not in meetings, the Senators are usually in their offices reading the reams of material that everyone wants them to look at or else they're drafting letters, responses, policy positions, or maybe even possible legislation. Your mother will very likely spend no more than a few hours each week here on the Senate floor. Most of her work will be behind the scenes, which is far less glamorous but also far more important."

He added, "And many Senators aren't back from the long Christmas and New Year's break. There are a few committees trying to get some work done now, but most of them won't be reconvening until next Tuesday."

Jeremy took dozens of photos during the swearing-in ceremony and had access to quite a few more from official sources. As soon as he had any prints that he liked, he faxed them off immediately to all the major media sources in Omaha, along with brief stories he had written to go along with the photos. At that point, he seemed more like a publicist than a press secretary. He wasn't really helping me deal with the press and their questions so much; rather, he was busy promoting me as Senator every chance he had.

"I know what grunt reporting is like," he told me. "Reporters have more assignments than they can handle. I know what editors are like, too; they have more stories to cover than reporters to cover them. So anytime someone like me sends them a fully-written piece that might be of interest to their readers, it's likely to be published."

And so Jeremy wrote lots of stories for and about me. One of them about my first day as a Senator said, in part:

> Today marked a breakthrough in Nebraska politics as Susan Young was sworn in as the first woman elected to serve a full term as the state's senator. Senator Young, who was elected in a landslide vote in November, took the oath of office on the floor of the Senate on Friday morning, along with thirty-two other Senators.
>
> Senator Young's background in agriculture and food led to her immediate appointment to several important Senate committees and subcommittees that deal with agricultural policies, nutrition, and the family.
>
> When asked about the appointments, Senator Young said, "My studies in college emphasized food and nutrition, and my ongoing work with Arkero Foods built on that background. I look forward to helping shape the nation's policies in these areas."
>
> The Senator went on to say, "As most people know, my husband, Fred Young, was actively involved with the agriculture sector of the economy, particularly the financial aspects, and particularly in

Nebraska. Because he and I were so close, I learned a great deal through his work that will help me while I'm here in Washington, working for Nebraskans and all Americans."

Jeremy had written my words. He was becoming my speechwriter, but I insisted on approving everything that went out over my name.

The fax of that story was accompanied by photos of me taking the oath of office and posing with Timothy and Liz.

When we got back to the office, the staff all congratulated me, and then Bill Ashford handed me a small, neatly wrapped, book-sized box. "We all chipped in and bought you a present," he said.

But before I could gush and finishing saying, "Oh you shouldn't have," Betty Elsbury piped up, "Nonsense! We paid for it out of your office expense fund, but you'll be glad we did."

I opened it, and it looked like some sort of combination of a cellphone, walkie-talkie, and microcomputer.

"It's a Blackberry 6210," said Bill. "It's a pre-release model we were able to get our hands on. It's a cellphone that you can send and receive texts on, **and** you can send and receive emails with it, too!"

"And the best part," added Betty, "is that communications with a Blackberry are extremely secure."

It looked big and bulky, and I could see there was no way I'd be touch typing on it.

"Why?" I asked.

"Well," said Betty. First, you don't want to have your personal cellphone tied up with Senate business all the time. You want to be able to confine your Senate business to just one phone with a different number.

"Second, we're going to want to communicate with you a lot, and you won't always want to talk on a cellphone with us, but we can still text and email if you have one of these."

"I get that," I said. "I'll change my personal cellphone number and give it out to family and friends but give everyone in the office this number."

"Many Senators have three or four cellphones," laughed Betty. "That's the only reason they carry briefcases... to hold all their cellphones!"

"I don't want anyone calling me on Senate business except a few people in this office," I emphasized. "Please do not give out either of my cellphone numbers to anyone. No matter how important someone else might think something is, have them go through this office, okay?"

"Exactly!" said Bill. "That's the way most Senators operate."

The afternoon was all business for me, meeting with other senators who were in town and spending more time getting to know my assistants and staff members. Meanwhile the children explored the Capitol building itself, using their visitor passes to wander the halls and ride the congressional subway back and forth to the different buildings.

Chapter 43 – **Trying to Settle In**

No matter how hard I tried to organize myself, there weren't enough hours in the day to do my job and still have all the time I wanted for Timothy and Liz. I felt as if I was shirking all my responsibilities all the time: I couldn't attend all the meetings, Senate floor votes, official functions and have any time left to read the briefs, reports, draft legislation, etc., much less spend time with the children. I quickly realized why each Senator had such a large staff – just to help them sift through and prioritize everything.

Thelma and I debriefed in the car on the way to the office. I told her what I needed to get done that day, and she would fill me in on appointments, meetings, hearings, and political obligations. But after only three days of that routine and barely seeing my children, I said to Thelma, "This isn't working. I have to block off at least two, preferably four, hours every day after school to be with my children and have supper with them. If some sub-sub-subcommittee holds hearings or meetings during those times, I'm not available. We'll have to send a staffer."

"I wondered how you'd handle it all, girl," she replied. "I think the staff are prepared to take on many of the committee meetings and do much of the report reading. Bill has them well-organized by specialties for reading reports and draft legislation so they can give you executive reports and help you organize everything you have to juggle."

"I guess I have to let my guard down a bit and trust them, don't I?"

Thelma added, "I know you like to have your finger on things, but look what you did with the Foundation! You turned it all over to me to run. You can do that with a lot of your other work here in the Senate, too."

I lowered my voice because I didn't want the driver to overhear me.

"I could do that because I know you, Thelma, and I trust you. But how much can I trust the staffers to feed me summaries that are unbiased?"

I stopped myself and chuckled a bit. "Let me rephrase that. How much can I trust Bill and the staffers to feed me summaries and priorities that are consistent with my own biases?"

"I don't know," replied Thelma. "Already I have the sense that Bill likes political maneuvering – everything that you have always not liked."

"That can be good, in a way, can't it? I can leave all that stuff to him and concentrate on what I think is important?" Yes, I ended that with a question mark. I wasn't sure.

Thelma said, "The major problem is that Bill might be under the sway of the farm lobbyists, and you don't want to be there. You'll have to get a feeling for yourself, but you'll also have to make it clear to him what your views are."

"Okay. Can you help by keeping your ears and eyes open to see how important that difference is? And can you keep an eye out for a replacement for him among the staffers, someone who might be more inclined toward skepticism when it comes to the farm programs?"

"Sure. There are several staffers that he seems to underutilize. I'll try to figure out whether that's because they aren't as good as the others or because they have different leanings."

"Good. But let's keep in mind that for the most part I agreed with Senator Tansky on most policies, and so I imagine we should be okay with the staff… for now, at least. We just have to be careful."

And then I added almost woefully, "I don't have time for everything. One thing is clear, though. I need to move my children up on the priority list. I don't know how other Senators see their families, but I must see mine. So, I think I'd like to schedule no more than two breakfast meetings per week, preferably on weekends when the children are sleeping in; and no more than one dinner meeting per week. Otherwise early mornings, late afternoons, and dinners have to be for my children. I'll work in the evenings after eight, if I have to, but I don't want to leave them on their own very much."

Thelma sighed a sigh of relief. "Whew! With Dale not around so much we were struggling to keep the family together and sane at our place, too. For the sake of both families, I'll make sure this happens."

- - -

"How are Seth and Aaron doing? How's school going for them?"

"So far so good. They both say the classes aren't very hard yet, mostly just continuing on from things they already studied at Burke High School in Omaha. But their social lives are in upheaval."

"Aaron is loving it all so far," she continued. "'Mom,' he said. He was almost bubbling with excitement! 'Here at Field School, it's considered an honor to be in the Chess and Go Club!' And I think he is overwhelmed by the attention he's getting from many of the girls."

"So is Timothy," I grimaced. "I'm afraid the girls here are much more 'advanced' than I'd like. He's already been invited to spend the night by one girl, and who knows how many others are in line. I'm not keen on this, and that's one reason I want to be there for the children more."

Thelma laughed. "Yeah, Seth has told me about it. According to Seth, Timothy is taking it all in calmly and not giving in too quickly to all the temptations."

"The girls must be after Seth, too," I suggested.

"Oh, I think so." She dragged that out a bit as she said it. "He doesn't want to talk about it much, but Aaron says Seth and Timothy are viewed as the two prize catches of the month. He said, 'Mom, you should hear how the girls talk about those two, especially when Liz isn't around. I think the only reason they talk to me is cuz I'm Seth's brother.'"

That afternoon, I met with the senior staffers and told them, "I can see how much I have to rely on all of you for getting everything done. At the same time, I have some serious obligations to my teen-aged children, and so I've asked Thelma, and I'm asking all of you, not to schedule any meetings for me between 4pm and 8pm. I'll be happy to return to the office after 8 for any meetings, and I am willing to meet for early morning breakfasts on Saturdays and Sundays. There will, of course, be some exceptions, but let's try to stick to this as much as possible."

I continued, "I'm not sure I can adhere to this schedule myself, but in the meantime this means that we'll be asking many of you to fill in for me at various meetings and public hearings. As a result, I will be dependent on all of you, as well as the junior staffers, to help deal with the paperwork and to help explain and interpret all the goings-on here."

They actually seemed pleased that they would be doing what they saw as important background work for me.

- - -

I asked Bill to stay behind in the meeting room. "Bill, I think you know my positions on most issues. Do you agree with them?"

He was surprised to have been put on the spot so abruptly.

"I think so. Let's see: Abortion is legal, but you are personally ambivalent about it, so leave it to the states or private parties to fund. We need to be cautious about Afghanistan, and President Bush had better be very certain about the facts before taking on any more middle eastern wars. Poverty programs must have built-in schemes to help people get off welfare. Okay so far?"

"Perfect. All that sabre-rattling in the President's administration really worries me. Surely we don't need to take on Saddam Hussein in addition to the Taliban. And now for the toughies."

Bill looked surprised.

"Bill, I have two other major concerns about national politics. First, the deficit. I will not support any budget that doesn't reduce the deficit. We're saddling future generations with too much debt. I know the arguments about investing in the future, but the high government debt is soaking up too many of the funds that should be available for private investors, and all the government borrowing is pushing up the interest rates too much. We have to make hard choices. We won't like it, but we can't keep running up the deficits the way we have been."

"I'm fine with that position," said Bill. "As the session continues, we'll have to make hard choices ourselves, here in this office, about what spending cuts we will encourage or support and what spending to increase or at least not cut. The decisions you make about these trade-offs will affect how people perceive you back in Nebraska."

"Good. I'm glad we agree on that. But the one area where we are spending too much and really endangering the health of the economy is the agriculture sector. Bill, I know you have good friends among the agriculture lobbyists, and they will pressure you incessantly, but we have to try to phase out most of those programs gradually."

"Is it okay if I sit down?" he asked.

His request puzzled me, but then I realized that in a way he was treating me like royalty. I gestured to the chair without saying anything.

"The farm lobby is huge," Bill said. "They'll have your scalp. They'll withdraw all the funding for your campaign over the next six years. Are you sure you want to do this?"

"So be it. They're costing the taxpayers billions of dollars and hurting the economy. I have to be true to myself."

"But what about the party? Don't you care about keeping this seat in the hands of Republicans?"

I pondered that for a moment – a long moment. I think the long silence made Bill uncomfortable; that and the stare I gave him.

"I'll tell you what," I said. "I'll keep these views to myself for now. And initially I'll try to work with the farm lobby on programs that will help them but that will not add to the deficit. I'll make it clear that I find the tariff and trade protections we have for sugar and cotton unacceptable, but I won't say anything ... yet ... about farm price supports and the myriad other programs that need to be dismantled."

"The trade protection for sugar has done wonders for corn producers," Bill said. The high price of sugar has dramatically increased the demand for HFC, that's high-fructose corn syrup, and bolstered the price of corn."

"I know what HFC is, Bill, and I know how the sugar protection has pushed up the demand for HFC. However, as a nutritionist let me tell you, the explosive use of HFC appalls me. It's more addictive than sugar and it's a major contributor to obesity. I won't back off from that view."

Bill's face sank.

"Bill, I will not go around saying things like that right now. The problem I want to address right now is whether you want to stay on as my legislative assistant, given my views. I need to be able to trust you and trust the reports and information you and the staff provide for me. I have no reason not to trust you at this point, but I have to know if you're willing to work with me in spite of these positions."

Bill started to answer but I stopped him.

"Let me be clear, Bill. ... Good grief, that sounds like the introduction to a political speech, and I hate those so much. ... Bill, I have no desire to hurt the Republican Party. Within two years, I will likely have made my views known, and I will almost surely have upset the state hierarchy and political machine with some of my policy positions. If the rest of the voters aren't persuaded that I'm the right person for this office, I will make it clear long before I'm up for re-election that I won't run again. Then the party can find a candidate more suitable to the farm lobbies and you can probably keep your friends among the lobbyists."

I hoped I hadn't sounded sarcastic because I meant it.

"Senator," Bill said. ...

It was difficult for me to get used to being addressed as 'Senator' by people in the office. When I asked Betty to call me 'Susan', she said, "We won't do that, Senator. Not even at parties or if we meet on the street. People who work here know that calling you anything other than 'Senator' would be highly inappropriate. We have already spoken with Ms. Hazelton and Mr. Hall, and I think they understand that at least here in the office you are to be referred to as 'Senator'."

I smiled and told her, "I'm drawing the line at my children. Even in the office, they may call me 'Mom'."

"Senator," said Bill, "I quite appreciate your positions. Perhaps the farm lobbyists have swayed me unduly in the past, but that was consistent with Senator Tansky's positions. I have every expectation of being loyal to you, not to the lobbyists. However, if you don't object, I would like to keep all this quiet for now and let it seep out slowly as your speeches and votes on various bills are noted. Is that alright with you?"

"It certainly is. I have no desire to stir up controversy at this point."

- - -

I didn't know Bill, and I didn't know if I could trust him. He could very easily have said those things to me and in the meantime told the lobbyists, "Don't worry; we'll bring her around." The world of politics made me feel as if I was living in some sort of spy novel. Who could I believe? Who could I trust?

I wanted to talk with Thelma and Jeremy about my doubts, but if there were manipulative games being played, I didn't want to reveal that I was suspicious or even slightly skeptical.

I wanted to call Ben Gruvel and talk with him, but I knew he had maneuvered in the background to get me to run for the Senate, and so I didn't completely trust him either. I hated the suspicion and lack of trust, but I felt as if there was no way out of it.

Chapter 44 – Striking a Balance

I spent both Thursday and Friday evenings of the next week at home with the children. We prepared meals together and we talked about what was happening in their lives. I had missed doing that with them, and I was determined not to let go of it.

"Who's the most interesting of your new friends?" I asked.

Liz hesitated some and then said, "Mom, I don't really have any new friends here yet. I spend most of my time with Seth."

And then she quickly added, "And Timothy and Aaron, too. Actually, I guess at school I spend more time with Aaron than I do with Seth or Timothy since he and I are in the same classes."

She continued, "You know, it's really strange, Mom, being in such small classes. We can't hide. We have to have our homework done or it's really obvious to everyone that we've been slacking off. That makes it harder, but I think it's good. Back at Burke, you could get by for days, just sliding along, but here the teachers know right away if you're not keeping up."

Liz had deftly changed the subject away from friends toward schoolwork. I went back to classmates, though: "Well, have you met any interesting class mates?"

"They're so different from our friends back home. They have money and they're sophisticated. They all seem to have traveled quite a bit, too. One of them, named Luanne, seems different from the others, and that makes her a bit more interesting, I guess."

"How so?"

"Well, the others are all cookie cutter versions of each other; at least that's how they seem right now. But Luanne stands out. She wears her hair shorter than anyone else, and she proudly announces that she buys all her clothes at Goodwill. She's intriguing just because she's different."

"What about you, Timothy?"

"I like Andy Petry and the guys who play soccer. I think I'll fit in okay with them. The drills we had to do back at Burke trained me pretty well. But," he continued, "the girls here are something else."

I repeated the question I had asked Liz: "How so?"

"When Sandra first started talking to me last year, I thought she was being maybe a bit forward, but she was nothing like these girls. They ask me to sit with them at lunch, the ask me to walk home with them. I don't know what to make of it. In some ways, I want to go full-blown Casanova just for all the contact, sex, and fun, but it's so new to me that I'm holding back for now."

"Mom," said Liz with a fake shocked tone of voice, "Put condoms on the weekly shopping list!"

It was a faked tone of voice, but she did seem shocked. I certainly was.

Timothy seemed a bit in shock, too. "Mom, how can I figure out what's real and what's just point-scoring?"

"Point-scoring?"

"I think there's some sort of contest among the girls to see who can get the new boys in bed first."

I dreaded hearing that.

"I knew it!" said Liz a little too loudly. "They all hush up when I'm around, but I know they're all after both you and Seth. Oh, Mom, this is so scary. What if I'm not good enough for Seth? What if he wants more and gives in to their advances? I'll be destroyed!"

"Talk to him about it!" I said. "You need to talk about it."

"What about you, Liz?" asked Timothy. "From what I overhear, there's a contest among the boys to see who can get to you first, too."

"No," she responded very quietly, shaking her head. "No. I am **not** just a piece of meat to be fought over."

I was pleased and a bit relieved that they both could be so open with me, and I was glad I had resolved to spend more time with them. And although I was actually shocked by their revelations about what was going on at the school, I knew it was typical of the social interactions in many schools, especially expensive prep schools.

My sense was that Timothy was interested in joining the social life at Field School but that he was confused about what was real and what was just talk, sex, and game-playing. I was glad he was holding back as he tried to figure things out and find his own comfort zone.

My sense also was that Liz was in for a rough time. Seth would be a target for the girls at the school, and they would do anything they could to break up the relationship between him and Liz. I hoped that whatever they might go through, they would all emerge from it as healthier young adults. … It really was clear to me at that moment that I had to stop thinking of them as children and start thinking of them as young adults.

The next Saturday, the children and I went exploring using the Metro cards Jeremy had given us for Christmas. We had been on subways in other cities, but we quite liked the Metro. I think we rode every inch of it that day, enjoying the street musicians at the different stops and exploring some of the neighborhoods. At one stop, there was a group of fabulous baroque or renaissance musicians playing different gigues and dances. We watched and listened to them for nearly half an hour and even attempted some minor dancing, tipping them generously before we finally moved on.

Out in public, I hadn't been recognized as 'Senator' yet, and it was a relief just to be out with my children, anonymously, exploring and being together. We made sure we re-visited the three major monuments (Lincoln, Washington, and Jefferson), but unlike our previous visits when the family was traveling on vacation, we took our time and just relaxed together. Also, the children were free from the social pressures at school and could put all their tensions and concerns aside. When we got home late that afternoon, I asked them what they enjoyed the most.

"For me," I said, "It was the buskers, especially the baroque ensemble. They were really good. We never would have heard them if we hadn't been on an outing today."

"They were good, Mom," said Timothy, "but I think my favorite was the Lincoln Memorial. It was so awesome to be there, just the three of us. I felt as if Lincoln was actually present."

Timothy was looking for some grounding, a sense of integrity and fighting off his desire to be more cavalier than suited him.

"I liked the street vendors," said Liz. "We can't buy food on the streets in Omaha, and it was so much fun buying a hot dog one place and huge soft pretzels at another place."

Timothy added, "I liked the Jefferson Memorial, too. It was so calming, being there by the river and with so few other people around. I may declare it to be my private place to go to think."

"I liked it, too," said Liz. "Fewer people helped make it so nice, and I liked being near the river, too. ... And," she added pensively, "I liked the reflecting pools. I guess I'm a bit of a water freak…"

- - -

"Mom," asked Timothy, "why are so many people down on Jefferson and not on Washington? They were both slave owners, weren't they?"

"Yes, they were. I think part of the difference was that Washington freed his slaves in his will, and Martha Washington freed hers before she died. But Jefferson didn't free many of his own slaves, and he had some children by at least one of his slaves. I think that gives Jefferson a bit of a bad rap, though, because he also fought to ban the import of slaves and he often wrote about gradually abolishing slavery."

"How could people ever think it was okay to own other people?" asked Liz.

"It was part of history. Conquering armies took slaves more often than not. But the slave trade from Africa really sank us, as humans, to new depths. The disturbing thing about slavery is that it wasn't until just two or three hundred years ago that a substantial number of people here and in Britain began to talk about abolition."

- - -

That evening, the three of us made garlic-cheesy toast and trout for dinner. I expected we would then sit and watch television together after dinner, but I should have known those days were pretty much gone.
Timothy went into his bedroom and was using some sort of 'chat' feature to type messages back and forth with different people. Liz, meanwhile, was being tortured by her thoughts about Seth and all the girls at their school.

"Mom, he's being invited to all sorts of things by the other students, and they don't include me very often. I get that I'm a lot younger than they are, but I have no idea what goes on at those parties … or after them either. I don't know what to do…"

She was sobbing. "Mom, help me, please."

"Okay, let's start with some questions, okay?"

"Okay," she gulped.

"Does Seth show any interest in the other girls? I mean is he friendlier with them than he was with other girls back in Omaha?"

"I think so, but I'm not sure. Some of it's just because we're the new kids, and we're all being a bit more friendly. He doesn't seem to be flirting with them, and I don't see much of a response from him to their rather obvious approaches to him."

"Let's turn the tables for a minute. How are you reacting to all the approaches from the other boys at school?"

Silence. And then, "I see what you mean. I like the attention, and I do respond to it in a very minorly flirty way myself."

"Have the two of you talked about this at all?"

She seemed embarrassed.

"Yes. We've both said we didn't like seeing the other one flirting. Mom, I don't even like seeing him talking with or even looking at those girls now that I know what's going on. But I don't want to say much about it because I don't want to be a nag or a suspicious girlfriend. Mom, I want to trust what we have. I want us to be solid together."

"Do you think the solidness between you two is gone? Or going?"

"I just don't know!" she wailed.

"I'm guessing he doesn't know either."

"You're probably right. He sees me talking with other boys and then other girls come on to him, he probably thinks, 'well if she's going to, I will too.'"

"You two really need to talk this out. Don't just let it happen."

And then I remembered the time in high school that probably hurt me the most. "When I was in high school, Tommy DeYoung and I were really close, or at least I thought we were. Then for a week or so I felt as if he was pulling away from me but I was afraid to ask him about it. Then he showed up at the next dance with someone else. I was really hurt. I should have asked him about it when I first felt it. We'd have been okay as friends if we had talked about it, but I really hated him for a long time after that, all because we didn't talk about it when we needed to."

Liz was straight-forward. "Mom, I don't want things to end between Seth and me, and I'm afraid they will if I ask him."

"I may be wrong," I replied, "but if asking him would lead to a breakup, then not asking him will just lead to even more heartbreak later. You *have* to talk with him."

"Okay. Can I call him and invite him over?"

"Sure. I have reams of papers to go through, so I'll hide out in the bedroom and work."

- - -

Five minutes later, Liz knocked on my bedroom door.

"The Hazeltons were out all day, too! They just got home. When I said I really wanted to talk with him, he said he really wants to talk with me, too, so he'll be over in a few minutes."

I don't know what they talked about or how they resolved things. There were long periods of quiet talk, interspersed with laughter, shouts, and screaming.

After Seth left, Liz came into my bedroom and lay down next to me.

"Thanks, Mom. I don't know what's going to happen between us, but I think I can handle whatever it might be now. I've known Seth ever since we were little kids, and we've always been good friends. I'm going to make sure we never lose that. But gosh, I sure do love him."

"I know." I patted her hand and said, "and I think he loves you, too."

Just as she hugged me, Timothy knocked on the door.

"I heard you two talking and wanted to join in, okay?"

"Sure," said Liz. "and thanks for not barging into the living room while Seth was here."

"I almost wish I had. You know, Liz, Seth gets lots of teasing from the other guys at school. He gets teased for dating a ninth-grader, and he gets teased for not going out with all the girls who are after him. You know what he says? He tells them, 'Liz and I fell in love after being friends for 13 years. I'm not going to ruin that.'"

"He said the same thing to me tonight! And I love him for that."

"But?"

"But when I told him how 'interested' you were in the advances from Vicki and the others, he said, 'I understand that. Even though we're a couple, I gotta admit that it feels good to be sought after by other girls.'

"I wanted to slap him. But then I remembered that it feels good to me to be sought after by other boys. We talked about it, and I still worry that eventually he'll find someone else, but I think the strength of our friendship will be good."

And then she got a funny look on her face. "What were you doing on your computer all evening, anyway, Timothy?"

"I started out chatting with Sandra. But then she had to leave to go to the basketball game. She and I are pretty close, I think, but nothing like you and Seth."

"*Started out* chatting with Sandra?" Liz was relentless.

"Then I think I must have answered chats from at least six or seven girls from school. Most of them just wanted to flirt and not talk about much, not really. But Paula still seems pretty nice. She and I were online for close to an hour."

"An hour!?," exclaimed Liz. "What did you talk about for an hour? I'll bet your typing speed has really improved!"

Before Timothy could say more than "We just...", Liz interrupted. "You weren't having chat-sex, were you?"

That really embarrassed Timothy. "No. In fact that didn't even seem likely with Paula ..."

"But?" Liz took two syllables to say the word.

"Vicki suggested it. It was fun chatting about it, but I told her I need more time. About ten minutes later, she chatted back, 'There! Is that enough time?'"

Timothy's embarrassment spilled over into laughter. It was infectious, and we all laughed.

- - -

After the children went to bed, I called Jeremy.

"Have you ever heard of chat sex?"

"What's that? Is it like phone sex but using online chatting instead of talking to each other?"

"I guess. But I have no idea. That's why I'm asking you."

"I'm just guessing, but I don't quite understand how you can do anything while you're typing. Along those same lines, Susan, when are we going to try out that sleeping alcove in your office?"

I had already decided.

"We aren't. I don't want to be constrained when we're together that way, and I don't want too many people raising their eyebrows about us. But when's the next evening that we're both free? I need to spend some time with you at your place ... going over some press releases."

Jeremy laughed. "I'll make time tomorrow evening. Will that work?"

"I think so. I'll check my schedule in the morning and let you know."

"Wait," he said. "I can check it right now. Remember most of us know what's on your schedule. ... There's nothing on for you tomorrow evening. I'll block off the evening for ... what shall we call it?"

"A press policy briefing?" I quietly smiled to myself.

"Sure. And if we're holding that briefing at my place, I will have to work from home much of tomorrow just to get the place straightened up a bit, so don't have your driver stop for me in the morning."

Chapter 45 – The Shifting Landscape

Jeremy and I had infrequent "press briefings" over the next few months. I think the other staffers suspected we might have been in a relationship, but we were quite circumspect, especially at the office. Even when we met alone in my private inner office, we were quiet and didn't spend inordinate amounts of time together, even after those two or three late-night meetings when, contrary to my prior instincts, we did "try out" the sleeping alcove.

Over those few months, though, I felt as if Jeremy was drifting away from me. In truth I was feeling the same way, and so I wasn't terribly upset about the development. But remembering my advice to Liz and Timothy, I confronted Jeremy after one of our late evening meetings.

"Jeremy, I feel as if we're drifting apart. What do you think?"

"I still have a very high regard for you, Susan," he said, "and I love being with you when we're together. However, you are a **very** busy woman. I would like more from a relationship, but I have known from the beginning that I am more committed to 'us' than you are. I'm beginning to see that there is no future for the 'us' that I hoped for."

I wanted to mutter some sarcastic put-downs to him. I had always known that he wanted more from me than I was willing to give. I controlled myself, though.

"Jeremy, I hope I never misled you."

"What has misled me is the kindness, the caring, dare I say the 'love' you have shown me at times, your enthusiasm for my work, and your enthusiasm in bed. But I do want more than you are willing to give, and I feel frustrated by that."

"I know. And Jeremy, no matter what, I don't want to lose you as a press secretary. You're quick, and perceptive, even brilliant. If we decide to break up as lovers, I certainly want you to stay on here at the office."

I waited. And waited some more.

Finally he said, "I guess I'm glad you raised all this. I am still smitten with you, but it is very difficult for me to continue our relationship the way it has been. If I have seemed a bit distant, it's because I'm trying to maintain my own identity, apart from yours, despite wanting to be more of a unit with you. I have to admit to myself that what I want with you is not attainable, and so I'm feeling sort of alone right now."

"I must have been picking up on those feelings in you. Good grief, I wish I'd been this perceptive with Fred. Maybe I could have understood what was happening when he seemed to be pulling away."

I shook my head. I actually tapped my right thigh slightly the way Fred used to whenever he wanted to stop unpleasant thoughts.

"That's past, though. This is present. If we can't agree on what type of relationship we should have, what should we do?" I asked.

"I need some time to think about what I want and what I can live with."

"About everything?" I asked tentatively.

"Yes, I think so. I'm not sure I can stay on as your press secretary if we are not involved as lovers."

I felt a sense of panic, but I hoped I controlled it.

"Let's try it, please," I said. "We've been mostly platonic here in the office anyway and have worked together very well, or so I thought. It shouldn't be much different."

"I don't know," he said. "Every minute that I'm working with you, I'm also wanting to make love with you. I want to go to dinner with you, just you. I want to go off to the mountains for a long weekend with you, just you."

"I have wanted those things, too, Jeremy, but you know everything else that I have to worry about and think about. I just can't. Not now."

"I know, and that's what has made it so hard here, working with you."

"Jeremy, think back to what you saw in me before we became lovers. Do you want to work with that person? Do I have enough to offer you as a Senator, as someone who wants to make changes for the better, to keep you here, as if we had never been lovers?"

He smiled and said, "If we had never been lovers, I would be trying to become your lover, for sure."

He continued, "Susan, this is ridiculous. Of course, I want to work for you, even if you're a politician!"

Hunh! I knew it was *because* I was a politician that he wanted to stay on. I didn't completely trust him because of his ambition, and yet that was the very thing I wanted to count on, too... More sources of inner conflict.

- - -

The sources of outer conflict in my life became much more apparent, though during those first few months. Through various votes, briefings, presentations, and meetings, it had become increasingly clear to the farm lobbyists that I was not their friend. The lobbyists began a campaign to get me removed – they used the term 'reassigned' – from the agriculture committees I was on.

At first it was subtle, as they tried to get me appointed to other committees, thus increasing my workload to the extent that I could not devote so much attention to agricultural issues. That strategy was doomed from the start, though, because I simply assigned the work for the other committees to my staffers and continued to focus my own time and energies on agriculture.

Another strategy included a series of letter-writing campaigns. As the letters, many of them verbatim copies of the lobbyists' positions, came pouring in, Bill said, "Don't worry, we've seen this sort of thing before. Even though we read each letter, most of that work is done by junior staffers, and they quickly learn which letters are part of letter-writing campaigns supported by the lobbyists and which ones are genuine."

In truth, I saw fewer than one-half of one percent of all the letters written to me about farm policies. We did, however, keep a list of who sent letters and emails, and it was Bill's idea that we categorize each message in a giant spreadsheet for future reference.

A third strategy involved pressuring my big supporters to get them to call me about farm policies. Barry Jones, as head of the Nebraska Republican Party, was concerned about keeping farm support, and he was on the phone to my office at least three or four times each week, worrying "what on earth are you trying to do to us?"

Eventually I instructed Betty Elsbury to limit the number of calls she put through from Barry. I realized he had nothing new to say to me; he was just responding to pressure from the farm lobby.

The most difficult calls were from our old friend, Ben Gruvel.

"Susan, when Senator Tansky announced he would not seek re-election, the party was concerned about finding an electable candidate. I knew you could be elected, but I had no idea how much damage your views on agricultural price supports would cause the party and the state."

"Ben, I never made my views a secret to you or to Barry Jones. I think the big talkers from the Agbrakan and their crony lobbyist groups have made more of my views than they should."

"They're up in arms, Susan! You need to do something to appease them."

"Let me ask you something, Ben. What has been happening to the prices of farms in Nebraska ever since I was elected? What has been happening to the prices, especially of farm **land** compared with other commercial real estate land in Nebraska?"

I had done my homework, and I was prepared to fight back. Despite dire warnings from Agbrakan, farmland was selling at all-time high prices. People who had their feet on the ground and were voting with their investment dollars had little fear that I would destroy their farm investment values.

"Okay, okay," Ben replied, "I know farm land prices aren't tanking the way Agbrakan says they will, but you and I both know that's because most farmers and investors think that your views won't carry the day in the Senate. If your views gain some traction, we'll have another farm finance crisis on our hands."

"And hurt all you farm mortgage companies," I cynically thought to myself. "Ben, if people are buying farmland, and if your firm and others are granting mortgages, all speculating that federal government policies to prop up prices will be perpetuated, why should taxpayers bail out you out if the policies change? People have been speculating about government policy, and they have won big over the past sixty or more years. It's time to slow that process if not reverse it."

The Gruvels and the Youngs were clearly more than drifting apart. I knew that Timothy and Liz would always think of them as Uncle Ben and Aunt Cindy, but the closeness that I had felt with them was in jeopardy.

The next day I fired off an email to Ben at Klein-Staily:

> Ben, it was good talking with you yesterday. I hope you understand my views. I've seen too much money flowing from taxpayers to farmers in the past and we have to slow that down.
>
> More importantly, I'm concerned about the high prices resulting from many farm price-support policies. These higher food prices have a serious impact on the lives of especially lower-income families. Gradually changing these policies will most surely be important for improving the economic conditions of lower-income families; but changing these policies will also have an impact on the nutritional health of the nation.
>
> I know that farmers and farm lenders have concerns about my views. I hope I have made it clear to you that I would never advocate a wholesale immediate removal of our agriculture policies. I will, however, continue to work for a gradual reduction in those aspects of the policies that affect taxpayers and consumers most negatively. I anticipate that even if I had my way, farmland prices would not suffer dramatically. The most likely scenario over the long haul would be that they might not keep pace with the prices of other commercial real estate.
>
> I do have another related issue that must be dealt with: I will advocate strongly for scaling back our "food for peace" programs. By sending our surplus food to less developed countries we are killing their own agricultural sectors. As Republicans, we must stay true to our view of encouraging self-help, and we're not doing it. But again, let me reassure you that even if I have my way on this topic, I will argue for a gradual shift in policy. We owe that to the consumers in the developing countries, where local prices will surely rise without the influx of so much food from the United States; and we owe it to the farmers and lenders here at home if for no other reason than to allow our farmers time to adjust.
>
> As always,
> With deep love and affection for both you and Cindy

My letter gave Ben some minor ammunition for fighting back against the lobbyists. He could now tell them I wasn't a slash-and-burn type of person and I would not do anything drastic, even in the areas where I had particularly strong views in opposition to those of the farm lobbyists.

I copied my letter to Jeremy, Bill, Thelma, and several of the senior staff members, warning them that it was confidential. I was prepared to face the onslaught if the letter leaked out, but I didn't want to do that if I didn't have to. I preferred that Ben and Jeremy handle things slowly, if possible.

Jeremy lived up to my expectations, handling Agbrakan and others aggressively, yet adroitly. He often fired back at them with questions like, "Don't you care about low-income consumers?" or "Where has Senator Young said anything about eliminating agricultural policies?" or "Did you even read carefully what she has written about her nutritional concerns and HFC?" or "How much farm land do *you* own?" and "How much do you personally stand to gain from continued farm subsidies?"

He also continued issuing press releases: on average three or four each **day**. Most of them had to do with photos of visitors – photos of me watching Timothy play soccer, photos of me with Timothy and Liz on the Metro (I knew he'd had that in mind at Christmas!), photos of me meeting with farm lobbyists and others, photos of me with President Bush and Colin Powell. Every chance he had, Jeremy turned something into a photo-op. Fortunately, he was an early adopter of digital technology, and so our photos were plentiful, inexpensive, and timely.

Jeremy also hired a staffer to deal with the new internet social media outlets like Myspace, Facebook, blogging, and website updates; the staffer was also tasked, of necessity, with dealing with computer security.

My views on the Middle East probably caused me more problems than my views about agriculture policies. In the early spring, I was called to the White House to meet with President Bush and Vice-President Cheney, where they quietly but forcefully explained the administration's position that we needed to stop Saddam Hussein before he could develop and use weapons of mass destruction.

My response was, "We need more evidence before we upset the delicate balance in the Middle East. You know the Shias are eagerly waiting for us to help them get rid of Hussein and remove the Sunnis from power."

Next they scheduled a meeting for me with Donald Rumsfeld and Colin Powell. They tried to set it for four o'clock on Thursday afternoon, but I balked, wanting to spend the time with my children. "That won't work."

"What???" screamed their appointments secretary. "What could be more important than the security of your country?"

I groaned. "If the security of the country is so important have them come to my office tomorrow morning at nine o'clock."

I didn't care if I offended anyone about it, and I hated being bullied.

There was a massive intake of air at the other end, but before they could speak, I said, "Seriously, I'll move or cancel most other appointments that I have coming up in the next week, but I won't meet between four and eight pm most days. Hold on for a moment and let me have Ms. Hazelton join me. She's my personal assistant and looks after my appointments. We can work this out in less than five minutes, I'm sure."

I buzzed Betty and asked her to have Thelma come into my office. I was smiling, but Thelma was concerned.

"Someone is trying to set up an appointment for me with Secretaries Rumsfeld and Powell to try to persuade me to change my views on Iraq," I said. "Let's put them on speaker phone so we can work out something."
Thelma could tell from my manner that someone had tried to push me around and that I was pushing back. Within less than a minute we negotiated a seven o'clock breakfast meeting the following Saturday.

"There. That was easy, wasn't it," I said into the phone.

- - -

When we met on Saturday, we had coffee. No muffins, no eggs, no bacon; nothing else. I couldn't resist, "I thought we were meeting for breakfast."

Secretary Rumsfeld said, "There must have been some misunderstanding. It's a pre-breakfast meeting."

I smiled. "I guess it is now," thinking to myself, "What a jerk!"

We had Jeremy take some photos, and then all their staffers were told to leave the room. I assumed the room was miked, though.

The meeting was nothing more than a rehash of General Powell's pathetic presentation to the United Nations. He seemed like a strong, intelligent man who had somehow been emasculated.

I felt sad. Sad for him and sad for the nation.

"General," I said, not using his title of 'Secretary', "Your presentation both at the UN and here has been terribly unpersuasive. So, some hired guns may or may not have told lies about Hussein? Some skillful photographers may or may not have taken photos of something that may or may not be suspicious, or the photos may or may not have been doctored? We're talking about the possible loss of thousands or even tens of thousands of human lives, and we're talking about upsetting the balance in the Mideast in ways we cannot imagine. Are we prepared to go to war to support the Kurds in Iran, Syria, and Turkey? Are we prepared to let the Shia overrun the Sunnis in Iraq and possibly elsewhere? How many wars can we fight? Didn't the lessons from Vietnam mean anything? I expected more and better."

They answered by repeating their case. It was nothing new. And it was unconvincing.

Then Secretary Rumsfeld opened some negotiations I should have expected. "We really need you onside with this, Senator Young. What can we do to bring you on board?"

"What do you mean?" I asked, feigning innocence.

To his credit, General Powell left the room. He clearly wanted no part of what was about to happen. Or maybe he just wanted 'plausible deniability'. For all I knew, he might also have left the room to signal someone to turn on a recorder. That's how suspicious I had become.

Rumsfeld called in two staffers and then left the room himself, saying to them, "See what you can do…"

He didn't even bother to introduce them.

"You know," said the first one, "not all the children of Senators receive full scholarships or even admission to the college of their choice. We can make sure your children do."

I just looked at her blankly.

She continued, "We can also do the same thing for the children of your personal assistant, Ms. Hazelton."

No response from me. I might have blinked a bit, though, since doing something like that for the Hazeltons sounded pretty nice. But the fact that she knew my personal assistant's name and that they had children who might be going to college soon bothered me. I wondered, "How much do these guys know about me? And how do they get all this information?"

The second staffer added, "We can also arrange a lucrative speaking tour for you, if you like, and we can guarantee you a rewarding consultancy, along with the directorships of several major corporations, if and when you choose to leave the Senate."

I stood up and said, "No thank you."

When I returned to the office, I sat there for a long time, shaking. It was 8am by the time I calmed myself; and when I finally felt settled, I called the children.

"Do either of you have anything you can't get out of this weekend?"

"Not really," said Timothy. "I was going to an informal soccer practice, but I don't have to."

"I'm feeling the urge to explore the area, so pack some overnight bags. I'm leaving the office in half an hour, and we'll go somewhere and spend the night. We'll talk about where when I get home."

Next I called Thelma. "Thelma, I've been leaned on ..." and I hesitated. If someone was listening in on my phone calls, I didn't want to say anything that would reveal my situation. "... over the past few days about my agriculture policy views," I lied, "and I don't like it."

"Part of the job, girl. Time to stay tough."

"I'm not sure I can, though. Cancel my appointments until Monday afternoon, okay? If anyone asks, tell them I have serious PMS."

"What???"

"Joke, Thelma. Just say I'm unavailable and you don't know where I am. I don't even know where I'm going, but the three of us are running away."

"I'm jealous. Can we come with you?"

I adopted a serious tone of voice.

"Not. This. Time." I said. "I'll fill you in next week."

Instead of waiting half an hour, I completely turned off my Blackberry and left the office right then. I had lied to Thelma in case her phone or my phone was bugged. It was a weak deception at best, but it was all I could think of on the spur of the moment.

I didn't use a Senate driver to go home; instead I took a cab to a local car rental agency and rented a non-descript car that I parked around the corner from our condo building. I took the back way into the building, rushed into our unit, and threw a few things into an overnight bag.

"What's going on, Mom? Where are we going?" asked Liz.

I put my finger to my lips and shaking my head 'no' said, "We're going to Europe for the weekend," I had no idea who might have bugged what, and who might be following me. The morning encounter really frightened me.

I led the children to the rental car, and when we got moving, I took some unusual turns, hoping we could see if we were being followed. The children were concerned and excited, but I just kept putting my finger to my lips and shaking my head.

Finally, I pulled into a church parking lot.

"Mom," said Timothy, "This is it? The only reason we slunk away was to go to a different church?" and he laughed nervously. "What happened, Mom? Why the cloak and dagger? Why the back entrance to the building? Why the rental car? What's going on?"

I turned off the engine, and had us all get out of the car.

"I had a very unpleasant meeting this morning. I was bullied, and some people said some things that made me feel very uncomfortable. I don't trust them, and I don't want them to know where we are right now. There is probably no reason to be concerned, but I want to get away and put the experience out of my mind for the next two days if I can. So... Where would you like to go?"

"How about the mountains west of here?" asked Liz.

"Yes! And let's do some walking or hiking," enthused Timothy.

I was hungry, not having gotten the promised breakfast, and the children hadn't eaten yet either, and so we picked up McMuffin combos from McDonalds, a breakfast treat that went over well with the children.

It was a great trip out to western Virginia. We ended up at a small bed and breakfast in Warm Springs, and then spent the afternoon exploring along the river. In the evening we played some old board games in the lounge of the B&B, sitting in front of a warm fireplace. It was idyllic, and it was just what I needed.

The next morning, while the children were sleeping and before breakfast, I drove to a pay phone over in the next village and called Thelma collect.

"What's with the collect call, girl? And where's your Blackberry?"

"I shut it off and I left it in our condo back in DC," I said. "I don't want anyone to find me right now."

"That was probably a good idea. We've been getting all sorts of inquiries about your whereabouts from the White House, the Defense Department, the State Department, the FBI…. I don't know what's going on, Susan, but you're in **BIG** demand this weekend, and it's not from the Ag-lobby."

"Well, as you might have guessed, given my views, I've alienated a lot of people in DC. I needed to get away from the pressures they were trying to apply. You wouldn't believe it all," I said, "… the stupidity on one hand and the brazen pushiness on the other."

"Like what?"

"I don't think I'd better go into it right now," I said. "Let's just say that being a Senator is not a good job for a weak person or for a person with no personal savings."

"You need to write a book, girl!"

"I'm thinking about it. … Meanwhile, if people ask, tell them I've gone camping over in the mountains."

"But where are you, really?"

I hesitated.

"Okay," I lied. "We're down in Norfolk, looking at the shipyards."

"Really?"

"Yes, but don't tell anyone, please. We came here because we figure it'd be the last place anyone would look for us."

Chapter 46 – Coping with Paranoia

On Monday morning, I wrote out notes for Thelma and Jeremy by hand and slipped the notes to each of them as secretly as I could.

> *Confidential! Do not show this to **ANYONE**!!*
>
> *Meet me tonight at 9:30 at the SouthEast Motel 6, just beyond Temple Hills. I will text you a number late this afternoon.*
>
> *Add nine to the number I will text you, and that will be the room. Come separately.*

They each looked confused and concerned when I slipped them the notes in private. I shook my head almost imperceptibly, and then smiled, hoping to reassure them.

I went to the Motel 6 by taxicab at 3:30, booked a room under the pseudonym 'Jaylie Gordon', and paid an extra two hundred dollars in cash to cover any unanticipated expenses, just to preserve my anonymity. I certainly didn't want to give my real name or use my credit card to pay for the room. They didn't seem perplexed; in fact, I assumed they were used to this type of behavior from all sorts of people.

They assigned me room 207, and I immediately texted "198" to Thelma and Jeremy. It was a very basic, smallish standard two-bed room with about a foot between the two beds, a desk in the corner, an all-plastic bathroom, and a small television set on the desk. Then I took a taxi back to the Hart Senate Building, where I had the senate driver take me home.

At 8:30, I told the children I had to go to a meeting and might be late. I had done that plenty of times before, but because of our get-away on the weekend, the children were a bit concerned.

"I know. After our weekend, this seems odd. But I'll be fine tonight. It's just a private, off-the-record meeting with Thelma and Jeremy."

When Jeremy and Thelma arrived, I turned up the TV volume, and had us sit on the two beds facing each other so we could speak softly.

"What's going on?" asked Thelma? "Why the secrecy and sneaking around?"

"I was offered a substantial bribe by people I assume are staffers for Rumsfeld, Powell, and Cheney."

Neither of them seemed as shocked or upset as I was. I wondered if I was over-reacting.

"They offered me a LOT to, as they put it, 'come on board' with the second Iraq War. A LOT! I'm sure there's a great deal of money at stake for the military-industrial complex. ... And the way it was offered made me fear for the lives, health and everything else of my family, my friends, and me. I may be over-reacting, but I needed to talk with you two and let you know what's going on, if nothing else."

Thelma just sat there, across from me, and very softly said, "Wow, girl. That's a toughie!"

Jeremy put his arm around my shoulder, trying to comfort me, but it was just a macho move. I remained rigid, and he got the message. After he removed his arm, I turned to him, sitting next to me on the bed, and asked him very seriously, "What do you think about it all, Jeremy?"

"Well, from everything I've ever read or heard, those guys play hardball all the time. I have to wonder what the big hawks here in Washington have on Colin Powell that they could get him to make that pathetic presentation before the UN ..."

"I wonder that, too," I said, "but right now I need input from each of you. What should I do, if anything? And who in the office can I trust? For now, I'm trusting no one other than you two. I'm assuming they are monitoring everything: my phone calls listened to, my office and home bugged, my car with a tracker on it, everything."

"Did you record the conversation with them?" asked Thelma.

"No, I didn't. Worse, I was afraid they'd have killed me to get it back if they thought I had. That's how worried I've become. As I said, for the past three days, I've been assuming the worst of everything and everyone."

Jeremy thought for a moment and then said, "You know, Susan, I don't want to minimize what you're going through, but I cannot think of any senator who has ever been killed under suspicious circumstances..."

I retorted. "But maybe that's because they all caved in to the pressure."

I was afraid I was becoming almost silly about it all, and yet I was worried about potential threats involving the children. I also let them know I was worried about possible threats to Jeremy, Thelma, or Thelma's family – those would upset me just as much.

"I would say something to the anti-corruption department of the FBI," I added, "but I'm not even sure I can trust them!" and I broke down in tears.

At that point I let both of them comfort me.

Thelma had a good suggestion. "Maybe you could call the Senate Security group and tell them you're concerned about some of the pressure being applied by lobbyists. Would that work?"

Jeremy added, "If there are threats, you're entitled to protection ..."

"But I have no proof of any threats," I said.

"Here's another thought," I offered. "Jeremy, can you find a good security firm with no involvement with the departments of state, agriculture, or defense? I'd like a private security firm to check my home, car, and office for bugs, but I don't really trust any government agency to do it since they could well be under the thumb of the military-industrial complex."

Thelma jumped in. "Better yet, get Senate Security to do it and then have the private firm come in afterward to see what they missed.

Much to my relief, the Senate Security sweep of my offices found no indication that anything was being bugged. Much to my even greater relief, the private security firm that Jeremy brought in a week later also found nothing in my office, car, or home.

My office was so clean, I was suspicious. That's how worried I had become. I said to Jeremy, "Use a different phone than your own. Find some security firm in Houston or Dallas and get them to do the sweeps next week."

He looked at me in disbelief. "Susan, how far are you going with this?"

"Jeremy, I care about you, Thelma, and our children. I have to know."

Meanwhile, of course, Bill, Betty, and the other staffers were becoming equally concerned when we had the office checked for bugs and microphones.

"Do you really think people would bug a Senator's office?" asked Betty.

"If you knew and heard some of the tactics being used to influence me," I said, "You'd want the office swept for bugs once every hour."

That same day, Jeremy's media staffer was told to hire a consultant to make sure our computers were safe from snoops.

I wasn't sure who to trust or what to believe, but after all the investigations and safeguards, I felt better about doing my job as Senator. In the end, I had no evidence that anyone had ever tried to bug my office or my home; and I received no threats, veiled or otherwise, involving the children, Thelma, Thelma's family, or any of the staff members.

I was embarrassed but relieved. And I could almost return to normalcy. Almost.

Chapter 47 – Returning to Normalcy?

The United States and its allies went to war in Iraq again, despite my misgivings. I made sure I was absent from the Senate chambers any time there was a vote or debate about Iraq2 just because I realized that whatever I might say would have absolutely no influence on the outcome of Senate deliberations, and I saw no reason to use up my miniscule portion of good will by speaking out against the new war.

Meanwhile Timothy and Liz were going through the usual teenage things – school, after-school activities, acne, and the rest of the standard teen traumas.

Timothy finally gave in and "spent some time" with Vicki Petry.

"It was good," he said, "but I liked being with Sandra better because of the emotional closeness I had with her. Vicki does some rather exciting things, but I don't feel close to her. I certainly don't love her."

And then he continued as if he was pondering something.

"I do sort of like Paula, though. She and I are pretty different, but there's a freshness and a sense of honesty about her and between us. Vicki is furious about it, but that doesn't bother me because she wants to own me, not be in a relationship. Even though I had sex with Vicki, I think it's more like I'm going with Paula. We do a lot together at school, and we hang out after school quite a bit, too."

"How are things with Sandra?" Liz asked.

"I miss her. I know she's dating other guys, but we both talk as if we'll get together again over Easter break when we're back home. I have to say, though, that I like Paula a lot, too."

"How are things with you and Seth?" I asked Liz.

"We love each other, Mom, but I don't like the feeling of desperate love that I seem to have more and more. I liked it better when it was more like 'we grew up together and realized we liked each other so much it was like love.' Now I'm more scared than happy."

"What are you afraid of?"

She looked down at her hands. "I'm afraid he'll find someone else."

"What makes you say that?"

"He is always talking with other girls… the older ones who are juniors and seniors. I'm sure he'd like to go out with them, but I don't want him to!"

"Do you want to go out with other boys?"

"Mom, we've talked about this before. I'm intrigued. And I know Seth is intrigued by the idea of going out with other girls."

Timothy chimed in, "Liz, you know he goes to senior parties where there are lots of other girls. I think he's getting a good sense of what the others are like just from those parties and from all the locker-room-type talk among the guys. It's like he's going out with other girls, but he isn't really. Doesn't that happen with you and all the freshman parties?"

"Sort of," and then she smiled coyly, "but it's not the freshman boys who intrigue me. It's the junior and senior boys …"

"What if you both decided to date other people? Would that work?"

"No!" Liz exclaimed. "I'm intrigued by the thoughts of dating others, but I can't imagine I'll ever meet anyone so right for me as Seth."

Wow! That was more strength of feeling than I was prepared for. It sounded too desperate, exactly what she had been worried about.

I was saved from saying that when Timothy interjected, "How do you know, Liz, until you date others?"

"I just can't bear the thought of Seth dating other girls," she conceded.

"And that's the crux of the matter, isn't it," stated Timothy, more bluntly than I expected. "It's not that you don't want to date others; it's that you don't want *him* to date others. Right?"

- - -

Easter was late in 2003 – April 20th. We were all excited about going back to Omaha for the Easter break, and we were looking forward to seeing our friends back home. The school holiday included Good Friday and Easter Monday, but Thelma and I agreed we would leave for Omaha on Wednesday evening and return to Washington on Tuesday evening. We notified the school, and it turned out we weren't the only ones who extended the holiday from a four-day weekend to a six-day weekend.

"What if something comes up in the Senate that I need to be here for?" I asked Bill Ashford. "Bill, you've been here long enough to have a good read on what's important."

"For the most part, you can miss votes and committee meetings and it won't matter. Many senators take the Easter weekend to visit their constituencies. Things might be different with the Iraq war going on, but if there's anything that comes up for which you might be the swing vote, I'll let you know right away, and you can be here in just a few hours."

So the Hazeltons and we flew home Wednesday evening.

Dale met us at the Omaha airport to drive us home. "Where's Jeremy?" he asked. "I wasn't sure we could fit all eight of us in the van, but I thought he was coming with you."

"He might come later," I replied, "but he wants to stay back in DC to finish up some of the projects he is working on."

Thelma glanced at me sharply. We both had the sense that one of the 'projects' Jeremy was working on was a female staffer for one of the Congresswomen from Florida.

I sighed quietly. I had essentially driven him away, but I was missing the contact with him, and I was concerned that I might lose him as press secretary as well. However, I also knew that I could cope without him.

Our house was in excellent shape. It helped that Dale often stayed in their home and looked in on ours, too, just to monitor the situation. The agency we had hired to look after things not only kept it clean and well-protected, but they had put out pots of Easter lilies in each of the main floor rooms.

I spent Thursday morning meeting with people in the constituency office in Omaha and Thursday afternoon at the constituency office in Lincoln. In both places I came under serious scrutiny for my opposition to the Iraq War, but I held strong in my views. I continued to point out that (a) there was essentially no evidence of weapons of mass destruction, and (b) the

Shias were already licking their lips in eager anticipation of driving the Sunnis out of power.

My positions on agriculture policies had not become clear to everyone yet, but there were questions about those, too. I emphasized my opposition to tariffs and other import restrictions for cotton and sugar, and made clear that nutritionally I had strong views about how unhealthy HFC was. But we managed to steer clear of my general views on agriculture subsidies.

Most of my time in the offices, though, was spent dealing with constituency issues: war veteran issues, people whose overseas relatives needed visas, and complaints about the airlines and the major telecommunication firms.

Ben was with me in the Omaha office. We had an uneasy truce between us, in that he knew I was still very popular with the electorate, and he wasn't about to challenge that popularity; and yet he also knew that my views on farm policies would be unpopular in Nebraska as they became known. He kept trying to nudge me or even push me in the direction of the Agbrakan views, and I had to stop him at one point.

"Ben, please stop this. I feel as you are trying to wear me down with all your convoluted arguments. I don't accept them."

"Susan," he said, "you were elected to serve the people of Nebraska. You aren't doing that with your opposition to the farm programs. You're...."

"Stop!" I said firmly. "Enough."

"But listen Susan, ..." he persisted...

"No! Ben, you listen. I know very well why and how I was elected. I also know how and why my name even came up as a possible candidate. You and your friends got together and encouraged me to run because you all knew I'd win in a landslide because of two things: Fred's death in 9/11, and the way I handled myself and the press in the eight months after that. It had nothing to do with my views on anything."

"Susan, I've known you for years..."

I interrupted again. "Yes, and you should know I resent it when people try to push me around. That's what's happening now, so stop, please."

Ben was fuming. When Barry Jones picked me up to drive me to the Lincoln office, Ben was conveniently gone from the office, not having said 'goodbye'. It hurt, but I didn't care. I did, however, begin to wonder whether I should have our savings managed by someone else. I'd have to think about it and meet with him if possible.

Barry Jones wasn't much better. He, too, was worried about the eventual loss of support from the farm communities and all the urban districts where people still had emotional and financial attachments to farming. I told him what I had told Bill Ashford, "Within two years everyone in the country will know my views on the major issues, and if, after four years, it looks as if I will be unelectable for a second term, I'll give you two year's notice that I won't run for re-election. That will leave you plenty of time to find a different candidate."

I think he was appeased, at least a bit, when I told him that.

I didn't get back home until after 8pm Thursday evening. Meanwhile, all four children had decided to visit Burke High School to see their friends.

"It was strange, Mom," said Timothy, "walking through the halls with no classes to attend. We weren't quite sure what to do with ourselves."

"Yeah," said Liz, "and the teachers didn't want us roaming the halls while classes were in session, so we hung out in the school office and library until lunch and then we ate with our friends. That was fun, and they were happy to see us and all, but I sorta felt out of it, too."

"The guys on the soccer team were glad to see me. They asked coach if I could play in the game tomorrow afternoon! He said that since I'm not a student there any more, he really couldn't let me play for the school. But he invited me to their workouts."

"Mom, you should have seen Aaron!" said Liz. "I think all the changes he's had at Field School have really affected him. He was chatting up all the girls and had an air of confidence about him I'd never seen."

"How did Becky take all that?"

"Oh, I think she loved it and hated it. She loved seeing him as a stronger, more confident person, but I think she was jealous and hurt, too."

"Did she talk to you about it?"

"Sorta. But I think she and he had pretty much drifted apart anyway. I'm not even sure if they'll go out while we're back here. She might be dating someone else, but I'm not sure."

And then she went on in a very different, somber tone, "Mom, I think things have changed here; it's more like Field School now."

"Oh? How?"

"The girls are much more aggressive here than I remember. Lots of them came up to Seth and Timothy and gushed all over them. I hated them."

"Your anger and jealousy will drive him away from you if you're not careful," I told her.

"I *know*, Mom," she wailed, "but I can't help myself."

"Well, you had better learn to cope with it all somehow. Seth is a decent, friendly, young man. He will always be attractive to other girls now and other women later. If you try to constrain him or if you show your jealousy, he will surely come to resent it *and* you."

She started crying.

"Mom, I can't help my feelings. I just can't help having them."

"I know," and I repeated what I had told her before. "It's what you do with your feelings that counts, though, Liz."

Timothy stepped in at that point, with his usual approach.

"Liz, did you realize how much interest the guys on the soccer team had in you? There were times I felt as if they were talking to me but looking at you. Weren't you a bit pleased by all that interest in you?"

"I didn't even notice," she pouted.

And then she smiled and said, "Who am I kidding? Of course I noticed, and of course I liked it."

"I need to tell you two about a couple I knew at Kansas State," I said. "Allen and Zoe. They had been high school sweethearts, and they went to K-State together. During their last year of college, something happened between them, but nobody understood what it was. When I asked Zoe about it, she told me, 'We just needed to get away from each other and experience more.' And then she confided, 'I went on a date with someone else last night, and I had no idea what it meant to date someone or to go out with someone. I think Allen felt the same way. We're still good friends, though.'"

"Mom…" Liz started to interrupt.

"I'm not through with the story. Ten years after we moved to Omaha, I saw Allen and Zoe together with three children at The Westroads Mall. They were happily married. Allen said, 'About two years after we decided to split up, I was partying on the beach in Daytona. I looked out over the ocean and was overcome with a sense of longing. I realized right then … why then I'll never know … but I realized right then that I wanted to spend the rest of my life with Zoe. I called her and told her that, and here we are.'"

Liz was starting to tear up again. "Oh, Mom, that's a such a lovely story. I hope you're not making it up to make me feel better."

"No, I'm not. But Liz, you have to know that it doesn't always turn out that way. I'm not saying that will happen if you and Seth begin to see other people, and maybe a more important and valuable story would be about all the people who didn't stay together, and both found someone with whom they were better-suited. But when I see you two together, I know there's something special between you that will always be there, no matter what."

I turned to Timothy.

"Did you see Sandra? How are things between you two?"

He looked around and seemed a bit embarrassed.

"We talked some at lunch, and while we were talking, Louie Peterson came over and put his arm across her shoulder as if he was claiming her for his own. Hunh. He should have known better. She won't be owned, that's for sure. Later when I saw her in the hallway, she gave me a hug and slipped a note into my hand."

Liz was excited, and I had to admit I was a bit more than just curious.

"What did it say? What did it say?" Liz badgered him. "I'll bet you saved it. Show it to us!"

Timothy pulled out the note and opened it for us to see.

> Timothy, my dear handsome man, I will always love you. Please don't let Louie put you off. I go out with him because you're not here, but you are in my heart. Call me tonight. I want to spend the day with you tomorrow.

"Mom, that's not like her. She has a romantic side, but not like that, at least this is new to me."

Liz interrupted, "Do you like that side? Do you like what she wrote?"

Timothy was deep in thought. Finally, he said, "I just don't know. I loved her, for sure, and I still do in many ways. But I think I'm falling for Paula, too, back in DC. And I don't think it's fair to either of them."

Liz was relentless. "So? What are you going to do?"

And she got a sassy leer. "Are you going to go spend the day in bed with her tomorrow, Timothy?"

"I don't know. I'll call her for sure. And I really do want to spend the day with her."

And he got an equally sassy look, "But I think we'll talk a lot first."

"Well, ask her if she's told Louie she still loves you."

"That's pretty direct, and I can bet she hasn't told him that. Otherwise, he wouldn't have tried to act so possessive at school. But you can be sure I'll tell her about Vicki and Paula and the others at Field School. I'll try to keep it vague, but she's smart. She'll get the drift."

And then he looked at me, "Mom, I don't get it. What does she see in me? Why is she trying to hang onto me? I'm not here, and she knows I hang out with other girls. What's going on?"

"I don't want to overdo this," I said, "but I expect she misses you. She has dated other boys and she realizes she'd rather be with you."

"But what if I've dated other girls and realized I'd rather be with them?"

"If that's what has happened, you have to come to terms with it."

That night I called Jeremy, hoping he was home ... and alone.

First we rehashed all the meetings I'd had to endure and he offered his condolences and insights. And then he asked about the children.

I told him briefly about the turmoil in their love lives.

He interrupted me, "Susan, I don't want to hear about turmoil in love lives."

"Jeremy," I said, "I miss you terribly."

"I miss you, too, Susan."

I barely stopped myself from telling him I loved him. Instead, I said, "Come to Omaha. We'll make time to be together."

"That is *so* tempting," he said. "But I have too many other things I need to get done here in Washington this weekend."

I suspected either that he was seeing someone else or, it occurred to me, that he couldn't easily shell out whatever it would cost for a last-minute flight to Omaha over the Easter weekend. I bit my tongue and didn't offer to pay for the flight. If things were ever going to work between us, it couldn't be because I paid.

"Susan," he went on, "I am still smitten with you. I still want to be your lover. But I can't get away right now."

"Let's make more time for each other when I get back, then," I smiled.

- - -

Thelma looked refreshed and lovely. Coming home to our own homes and our neighbors had really boosted her morale. So had being home with Dale. I envied their closeness, and I missed both Fred and Jeremy.

That was an odd sensation, missing both my late husband and my on-and-off lover. I'd never experienced anything remotely resembling dual loyalties, and I felt as if I was betraying them both by missing them both.

I sometimes wonder if feeling that sensation helped me understand what the children, especially Timothy, were going through.

Seth and Liz had spent the day together down by the Missouri River, just walking and talking. I knew they were close, and I knew that the more they talked, the closer they would be; but I also expected they would eventually split up. Liz's desperation and jealousy would be too much for their relationship.

On Good Friday evening, the Schultzes held a big neighborhood party. We barbecued on their deck overlooking the reservoir and drank wine and beer and had a wonderful time. Timothy joined the party late, bringing Sandra with him. He was quiet, and she was a bit more chatty than usual. I sensed things may not have been going well between them, but I also wondered why he had brought her to the party if they weren't getting along well.

Aaron was becoming… well, not the life of the party but someone who could command a presence with his wit and his charm. There was a side of Aaron emerging that none of us had anticipated, not even his parents – a confident, engaging side. It looked as if the move to Washington had been good for him.

Harry Schultz said, "Hey, everybody, let's sing some Easter carols!" We all laughed as he put on some Easter music like "Peter Cottontail" and "Easter Bonnet", but then we couldn't think of any others that we wouldn't be singing in church on Sunday. Someone laughingly suggested the hymn, "Put Your Hand in the Nail-Scarred Hand," but that was shouted down pretty quickly.

Kathy Bergman offered, "I Don't Know How to Love Him", and we were all pleasantly surprised by her suggestion and that she had made it.

Then she looked around, threw her hands out and in her best Yiddish accent, said, "Vaht? You think a nice Jewish girl vouldn't know any Christian songs? You vould prefer, maybe 'Another Vun Bites The Dust?"

I think some of the neighbors were surprised by her sense of humor, but the children thought it was funny, and I liked it, too – a nice, light touch of irreverence. I was liking her more and more.

Chapter 48 – **Returning to Hecticity**

As we were walking back up the hill from the Schultzes, I asked Seth about his plans for the next year since he would be graduating from the Field School that spring.

Everyone stopped. We all wanted to hear what he had to say, and no one had discussed it openly it seemed.

"Well, Ms. Young, I was so wrapped up in all the action and everything last fall that I never got around to signing up for the SATs or applying to any colleges…"

He hesitated just a bit and put his arm around Liz.

"To tell the truth, I don't really like the thought of going off and leaving Liz, and so I was thinking I might just work for a year or two. But our math teacher, Mr. Hayden, said I should go to college. He told me, 'You're a good, serious student, Hazleton. Don't lose that. Go to college somewhere in the District next year and then transfer to a better school if you want to.'"

"So I sent in a late application to a couple of colleges in the District. I'll live at home where it'll be cheaper, Liz and I will still be able to see each other quite a bit, and I'll just take the bus or Metro, depending on where I end up going."

Liz put her arms around him and hugged him tightly, right there in the middle of the street, in front of everyone. I think that was the kind of commitment she was looking for.

Seth continued, "Mr. Hayden says that George Mason University, over in Fairfax, is an up-and-coming place and that the commute from home would be okay since I'd be going against the major flow of commuters."

Then Thelma turned to Timothy and asked, "What about you, Timothy? You'll be graduating in a year. Have you given any thought to what you'd like to do?"

"I expect I'll go to college somewhere. I always figured I would just go to Lincoln and carry on from there, but now I'm not so sure."

"Why not?" asked Dale.

"I don't know. I have no idea what I want to do with my life, and I don't want to waste time and money going to college if I'm not ready to buckle down and learn a lot there."

That night we talked more about Timothy's uncertainties.

"Mom, I enjoy school, and I know I'm doing well in my courses, but I really don't have a clue what I want to do. What do you think?"

"I think two things," I said, mentally kicking myself for sounding like a lecturing politician.

I tried to mellow what I was saying.

"I'm sure the Field School has good counseling services," I said "with the entire battery of tests they can provide. They should be able give you vocational interest tests, personality tests, and aptitude tests. Let's see what they can do for you, and if they don't have the facilities to do this kind of counseling, we'll find a place that will do it."

"Okay. I think I missed out on that testing last year at Burke High. Do you think it will help?"

I laughed, "Maybe. When I took the interest tests, I rigged my answers to say I should be something like a church leader or social worker, but I knew I was rigging the answers and so I didn't pay much attention to the results. But... just taking the tests and rigging the answers helped me understand more about what I wanted, though."

"The second thing," I added, "is don't slack off now. Your performances in high school will determine a lot for you later in life."

The long Easter weekend was good for us in so many ways. Liz was becoming more reassured and less desperate in her relationship with Seth, Timothy was maturing and learning about so many difficult aspects of life, Thelma positively radiated after having a lot of quality time with Dale in their own home, and Aaron blossomed even more with his new-found confidence. And me? I was beginning to learn more about the nuances of political life. There were so many conflicts and challenges, and even though I had tried to anticipate them all, I had clearly been less than successful.

While the conflicts about my views on agricultural policies were tense, I was pretty well prepared for them. I wasn't prepared, though, for having a falling out with Ben Gruvel over my views. I had loved and respected that man, and it saddened me that he was trying to bully me – that was the only word for it. I visited him and Cindy again on Saturday morning, along with the children, just to try to make things better between us.

Ben was unapologetically apologetic. He said nice things, and I replied with nice things. We renewed our commitment to work together, and we hugged each other as we all said our good-byes, but it was evident to all of us that Ben was forcing his niceties. I knew he felt that with my views on agriculture policies, I was letting him down or worse.

The other aspect of being a senator for which I had not fully prepared myself was having to do so much socially with all the supporters, loyal party workers, and hangers-on. They had all worked very hard to help me win the nomination and the election, and I couldn't just ignore them all. And so on Saturday afternoon, we held a huge reception for the workers in Lincoln and all points west; then Saturday evening we held another huge reception for all the Omaha workers and supporters.

For both receptions we'd had cork-based coasters with

From the Desk of
Senator Susan Young
2003

printed on them to give out as thank-you favors. We went through over a thousand coasters and could have given away hundreds more.

Thelma and I kept in touch on Saturday with our Blackberries, but I was determined to try not to intrude on her family life over the Easter weekend. I went to the constituency office receptions by myself, and it was an odd feeling. I missed Ben; I missed Jeremy; I missed having Thelma around; I missed my children; and, of course, I missed Fred. I was on my own, as a politician, and it all felt horribly unreal.

On Sunday we went to the Easter Sunrise Service at the church. The reception was different from most of our after-church receptions simply because I, the Senator from Nebraska, was there. Most of the worshipers just looked at us and smiled; but others wanted say a few words to us. Often the words were "It's nice to see you," or "How are things going for you?" Some wanted to let me know that they agreed with me about Iraq2, and their support was very reassuring.

The children and I spent the rest of the day together… at least most of the time. Of course, with cell phones and laptops, we all had connections with other people some of the time, too.

After church, we all changed and went for a very long walk up around the Candlewood Reservoir. For me the walk was like trying to re-establish roots for all of us: me with Fred, the children with their father and with their home community.

"Timothy," I asked, "how are things? With you and Sandra and Paula?"

"Sandra and I sort of broke up."

"Sort of?"

"Well, we both know we're dating other people. She was not at all happy that I was dating other girls, but she understood or at least pretended to accept it. In the end she said, 'Timothy, I want you to know that you're the one for me,' and she started singing a very slow, sad version of Olivia Newton-John's song from Grease, 'You're the One That I Want.'"

Liz groaned, "how corny! That doesn't sound like Sandra!"

"I know," said Timothy. "She always seemed so rational and cool and avant-garde and… I don't know. I started crying when she sang," and he started crying again.

"Mom, Sandra always seemed so … I don't know … fun-loving, for sure, but in control. And now she seems desperate to keep me, and that's something I never expected. I thought she would just say 'Have a good life' or something like that. I don't get it. And it confuses me even more."

"Did you tell her you'd slept with Vicki?" Liz asked.

"No, I couldn't be that explicit. I did tell her I had become 'involved' with several girls," and he used air quotes when he said "involved".

"I don't think she wanted to know the truth about my actions with Vicki and my feelings about Paula. And I don't know how I feel about Paula now, after being with Sandra and hearing her pour her heart out to me."

"Mom, Sandra is smart and she's usually very tough. I just don't know what to make of it."

"So why did you sort of break up?" I asked.

"She insisted on it. She said she wants me to see other girls and then come back to her. Oh, Mom, this is so difficult."

I had always liked Sandra, and she went up in my estimation with that revelation. I didn't look at Liz, but I hoped she could say something similar to Seth if that situation ever arose between them.

The silly thing was that even though I admired Sandra for her attitude, and I wanted Liz to be able to say things like that if necessary, I didn't feel that way myself. I laughed at myself because even though I didn't want to commit to Jeremy, I didn't really want him to see other women.

"Why are you laughing, Mom?" asked Timothy. "This isn't funny at all!"

I was really embarrassed.

"Oh, Timothy, I'm so sorry. I honestly wasn't laughing at you or about your situation. I was laughing at myself as I realized that even though I don't want to commit to Jeremy, I also don't want him to date other women. That's so hypocritical and unfair of me, and I was laughing at myself for that."

"I get that," said Liz. "It's like my being intrigued by other boys but not wanting Seth to be intrigued by other girls."

"Maybe a bit like that," said Timothy, "But it's different, too, because you and Seth are committed to each other; Mom and Jeremy aren't, and neither are Sandra and I."

"Another difference," I added, "is that I don't have much interest in dating other men. Most of the men who show an interest in me are philanderers, losers, adulterers, and/or lobbyists who are after my political influence and don't give a hoot about me."

"But one similar thing," I went on, "is that I expect my life and Jeremy's life to diverge over time. He's a superb writer and journalist. I'm sure he will want to move on to bigger and better things eventually, and I don't want either of us to have to deal with that when it happens."

Liz smirked, "Oh, I get it. You're in it for a good time, not a long time."

I groaned slightly and then replied, "Maybe. I'm not sure that's wrong or bad, though, if we both agree to it. Yes, we care about each other, but I won't be tied down and I don't want to tie him down either, even though in my heart I do want to tie him down."

"Do you love him, Mom?" asked Timothy.

"I don't know. I certainly don't feel about him the way I felt about your father. But I do care for him, and quite deeply in many ways. Just not enough, I guess, to commit to him in any significant way."

And then I laughed some more.

"Did you know that we actually agreed to 'go steady' last fall?"

The children stopped and looked at me with wide eyes.

"Really, Mom!" said Liz. "Do people do that anymore?"

"I don't know, but I think we both wanted to have some sense of a partial or temporary commitment, if nothing else."

I looked out at the reservoir and felt a touch of sadness.

"I think we sort of broke up last month." I said and smiled at Timothy, emphasizing 'sort of'. "Jeremy wanted us to be together more, but I didn't want to take time away from you two or from the Senate. I know it was the right thing to do, but it still makes me sad. ... I don't know if he's dating anyone else; really and truly I hope he isn't and yet really and truly I hope he is. ... Oh, what a mess!"

"Mom," said Liz, "You got it worse than either of us. I hope you'll keep us up to date because I really need to learn from you about all this stuff."

"Well there's one more thing," I added. "I have no idea what my perfect match would be. And I have no idea how long I'd have to wait and date to find a better match than Jeremy. But this is where I'm different from you two – I don't need or want a life partner; I've had one, your father. We weren't a perfect match, but we were a *good* match, and we always worked together to provide a good home for all of us."

"Mom," asked Liz, "what happened to Dad the last few years of his life? Was it just that financial thing? Or was there something else?"

The children had picked up on it too…

"I'm not sure," I replied. "I honestly don't know. But you're right, Liz. He did seem more distant sometimes. Not always, but every once in a while, he seemed more … contemplative might be a good word … thinking about things and keeping his thoughts private. I wish I knew."

That evening the children held a sort of reunion party down in the games room with all their friends. It was like old times in that Aaron was with Becky, Timothy was with Sandra, and of course Liz was with Seth; and the rest of the old gang was there, too. But I was alone up in the kitchen. I had plenty of work to catch up on, and so I didn't mind the time alone but I did mind the loneliness. I missed having someone in my life now and then, and I especially missed it now that we were back in our home in Omaha. And yet … Oh, I was so confused.

- - -

Jeremy made a point of meeting us all at Dulles Airport on Tuesday afternoon with two cars from the Senate car service. I wasn't sure he had the authority to commandeer two cars, but I assumed he had worked out something, and I most definitely appreciated his meeting us.

Everyone else watched eagerly as he and I greeted each other, and I'm sure I disappointed them by not grabbing him and kissing him. I wanted to; actually, I wanted to go to bed with him. But I also didn't think it appropriate for a Senator to have major public displays of affection. Once we were in the car, though, I had him sit next to me in the back and gave him a big hug and kiss, much to the delight of Timothy and Liz.

I had the driver drop the children at our condo but then drive Jeremy and me to my office. It was after quitting time, but Bill was still there. The three of us spent a half hour confirming things we had corresponded about with our Blackberries, and then Bill left.

I sat behind my desk and looked at Jeremy. He sat in the chair across the desk from me. We just sat there and smiled at each other. After a very long three minutes, I asked, "Do you think we've waited long enough?"

"Let's give it another few minutes," Jeremy said, but he was already on his feet, coming around the desk. ...

- - -

Timothy and Paula had talked on the phone briefly and had e-chatted a great deal while we were in Omaha. He was torturing himself in a situation I had thought most young men would love – at least two girls after him in two different cities. In his confusion, and maybe to help end it, Timothy was extremely eager to spend some time with Paula, and so he went to visit her at her home that evening.

We talked when he got home from her house.

"Mom, this is all so hard! Paula doesn't seem as right for me as Sandra, but there's something about her that I absolutely love. We don't agree on music or sports or politics, and yet I love talking with her and being with her. Is it possible to be soul-mates even if you don't have anything in common?"

"What is it about her?" I asked.

"She's nice. She's kind to other people. She's smart, too. She knows stuff I never thought about. And I really like how much she seems to like me."

"Well," piped up Liz, "You'd better stop sleeping with both of them until you decide..."

Timothy was visibly upset, indignant even.

"I didn't have sex with Sandra while we were home, and I haven't had sex with Paula. I love them both, but in such different ways. I told Paula about Sandra. She just reached out and touched my arm gently and said, 'Timothy, you are lovely. I want to be your girlfriend, but if you don't want to commit to that, I understand.'"

"So, where do things stand?" I asked.

"I can't commit to Paula. Not after seeing and being swept away by the romantic side of Sandra. I just can't."

I repeated, "So where do things stand?"

"We didn't say things this way, but I think I'll hang out with Paula while I'm here, sort of as if we're boyfriend and girlfriend ... that is, if that's okay with her. I'll even hug her and maybe kiss her. But I won't have sex with her. Then I'll see how things are with Sandra this summer."

Then he suddenly changed gears.

"Say! In the car, you and Jeremy certainly seemed back together for a couple that had just 'sort of' broken up. ..."

Chapter 49 – Striving for a Sense of Normalcy

Over the next month and a half, things seemed almost normal. The children were active socially and did **very** well in school. Burke High in Omaha had prepared them well for the Field School. Timothy was selected captain of the soccer team, and Seth was voted Prom King.

"It's okay, Mom," said Liz. "He just has to dance with the Prom Queen for that one dance, and that's okay. The rest of the night he's mine!"

Meanwhile, Jeremy's time in my office became obvious to all the staffers. We had become an item in their eyes despite trying to be discreet, and I told Betty and Bill that we had been seeing each other since the previous summer. Having it out in the open made it so much easier.

Also, during those two months, Thelma made at least two trips to Omaha, and Dale spent more time in DC. Everything seemed to be going well for us all.

Of course, things weren't perfect. I still wondered when, not if, Jeremy would leave me, either romantically or professionally, and I tried to prepare myself for it. Mostly my preparation was to try to enjoy the time as it was, but I really wasn't cut out for the "live for now" mentality.

Because of the Iraq War, there was no major official summer recess for the Senate until August, but we all planned and took substantial breaks from Washington to go back to our homes.

That made things awkward for the both Hazeltons and us.

We all wanted to be back in Omaha for the summer, but we knew that Thelma and I would still have things to do in Washington in July. Also, I wasn't at all keen on leaving the children in our home in Omaha or in the condo in DC on their own for long stretches.

Arrangements became considerably easier when the Senate took a ten-day recess from June 27th until July 7th.

Bill Ashford volunteered, "Senator Tansky always went home for the summers, and if they needed him in the Senate for anything, Agbrakan would fly him back on a private jet. I'm guessing that won't be a viable solution for you, right?"

I just smiled. "Well, after the children's school ends in mid-June, I plan to spend as much time as I can then and in July with my children in Omaha. I hope you and the staffers can figure out a way to give me at least an eight-hour notice if you think I might be needed back here."

We agreed that unless there was pressing business, Thelma and I would be in DC from late Monday night until mid-afternoon on Thursdays, at the most; and we'd maybe not get back to DC until sometime on Tuesdays if possible, spending five nights a week in Omaha with our families and only two nights a week – Tuesdays and Wednesdays –in DC.

I wasn't at all thrilled about leaving the children on their own for two or three nights each week, and I certainly didn't want to impose on Dale to look after them. The Bergmans, Schultzes, and Plagges all offered to help out, though, and that eased my mind a bit, knowing that each week a different family would be checking up on Timothy and Liz.

The children were, for the most part, pleased with the arrangements. They both readily found summer jobs because, after all, who wouldn't hire a Senator's children? Timothy was hired by Quality Meats to work on the production line, and Liz got a snack bar job at the golf course.

Timothy's job was gruesome, and it involved some seriously heavy lifting, too. He toughed it out, though, and was developing more upper body muscles than I thought we'd ever see in him. Liz had to be toned down just a bit at the snack bar because she had a tendency to get sarcastic if customers weren't polite. Those were good learning experiences for both of them.

Meanwhile, Jeremy and I spent two nights a week together in the condo in Washington, and it was great. We got to know each other better, as we fought, loved, disagreed, and worked things out together.

The summer was difficult for the children socially, though. They had developed new friends in Washington, and their friends in Omaha had changed. The standard get-togethers of 16-22 teen-agers in the basement games room no longer had the same appeal, and with them all working, socializing wasn't as easy as it had been when they were in school together.

Timothy and Sandra hung out together some, when they had time, and they seemed to grow together over the summer; they even began talking seriously about where to go to college... together! I felt sorry for Paula, though, as it became clearer that Timothy preferred being with Sandra when he could. He and Paula had a spark of something between them, but it just wasn't enough.

Liz and Seth were something else, though. After being so close for so long, they broke up that summer. I don't know whether it was boredom with each other or if one of them did something to offend the other, but they decided to stop seeing each other as boyfriend and girlfriend. Liz went out with some different boys, including a caddy from the golf course, but she didn't flaunt it around Seth. And Thelma told me that Seth was dating other girls "just for the summer" but again he tried to be careful not to hurt Liz's feelings.

As a result of the changes that summer, we did fewer things together as families. But we all still seemed to get along okay. The only real difficulty that emerged, and it was fairly minor, was when Aaron asked Liz to go to a movie with him.

"Mom, I can't date the brother of my former boyfriend. Seth and I were too close. It just doesn't feel right."

"Then don't," I advised. "Let's just all be friends."

Through July, and especially in August, my overly busy schedule slowed considerably, but I still met with constituents; and finally I bit the bullet and held a series of meetings with the farm organizations. Those discussions were tense, even fierce, as the lobbyists expressed their dissatisfaction with my positions on agriculture policy. I reassured them that I had no intention of ever supporting, much less proposing immediate elimination of farm price supports; in fact, I told them I was confident that price supports would *never* be eliminated no matter what I thought. That explanation helped some, but they knew that I would always oppose the import restrictions for sugar and cotton, that I wouldn't support continuation of the ethanol program, and that I would always oppose having the federal government buy up 'surplus' grain to send to developing countries.

The result of the meetings was a very fragile truce, with both me and the farm lobbyists hoping that none of the issues would become important on the Senate agenda.

In early August, Jeremy came to Omaha for a visit. He and I both assumed he would stay with us… with me… in our house… in my bedroom.

"Are you children okay with it if Jeremy visits us and stays here?" I asked.

"Sure. Why not?" asked Timothy.

"Mah-ahm," said Liz, again stretching "Mom" into two syllables, "we know you two have been sleeping together for a long time. He's nice; so as long as you're happy, it's fine with me."

Jeremy stayed for a week, and during that time we continued working on policy positions, especially my concerns about incentive-based poverty programs and about Iraq2. We also made sure that the four of us did things together several times instead of going our separate ways or hanging out at home each evening.

Thelma spent a lot of the time in July and August working on the scholarship program for the Fredrick Robert Young Foundation and trying to make sure that my political schedule took me near places where I could meet with some of the new scholarship recipients. And somehow I managed to fit in a few meetings with LOST that summer.

Over the Labor Day weekend, the two families drove back to our condos in DC together. When we reached our condos, Thelma and I watched with curiosity as we all said good-bye to each other, wondering especially how Liz, Seth, and Aaron would handle the situation.

Liz was perfect. She hugged all four of the Hazeltons, telling each one of them that she loved them, wishing Seth good luck at George Mason University and arranging to walk to Field School with Aaron and Timothy on the Tuesday after Labor Day.

Jeremy was waiting for us at our condo building, and he and I made no secret of how much we had missed each other since his visit to Omaha.

On Labor Day itself, I was expected to attend several different picnics and political events. It was difficult for me to go to these things because I knew most labor unions strongly supported the Democrats, not the Republicans, and so when I spoke with people at the events, I tried to emphasize my concern for poor people and my dissatisfaction with policies like ethanol and agricultural tariffs that made prices higher for the poor.

Jeremy attended those events with me, and we thoroughly enjoyed eating picnic food and watching the kites and balloons. Meanwhile the Hazeltons took their family, along with Liz and Timothy to Mount Vernon, George Washington's plantation in northern Virginia along the Potomac River.

When they returned, Liz was beside herself with happiness.

"Mom, while everyone else was going through Washington's house and looking at his wooden false teeth, Seth took my hand and led me down to the riverside. He told me he loved me, Mom, and it was beautiful."

Timothy was surprised by the development. "So where do things stand with you and him? Will you be able to date boys at Field School, or will you be left out? Will he start dating girls at George Mason?"

"I'll tell you in a minute," she said, "But where do things stand with you and Sandra and Paula?"

"I'm pretty much committed to Sandra," he said. "I'll go to parties and things, but probably without a date. I sure do like Paula, but we're just so different. It feels strange to say I love Paula, too, but not at all the way I love Sandra. I think Paula and I will always be best friends, though."

And then he looked at Liz and said, "You know, Liz, we could go to some things together when Seth isn't around. And we could go with Aaron and some others in a group. We don't have to have dates for everything."

"I've thought about that, too," said Liz. "There aren't many things I really need a date for. It'll be fun to go to things with you and Aaron and others from school and just hang out as friends. Besides, Seth will still be living at home; he and I will be seeing each other some on weekends, and maybe we'll even have study dates together now and then."

I wanted to ask Liz what had happened with them during the summer, but I didn't have to.

She told us. "Seth told me that going out with other girls was okay, but every time he was out, he was imagining he was with me. The more he was with other girls, the more he realized he wanted to be with me. I told him the same thing happened to me. It was fun being with different boys, but every time I thought about it, I realized I'd rather be with him."

"Mom, is this what you meant?"

Chapter 50 – Beginning to See the Light

I was reluctant to completely reassure Liz that dating a few other people for a month or so during the summer would mean they had experienced enough to know they were right for each other, but I was happy for them both that they had had some experience dating others. And I was happy for Liz that she seemed less worried, less desperate about her relationship with Seth.

Things didn't go so well for me that fall between Jeremy and me. One evening in early October, he stopped by our condo to tell me he had been offered a senior reporting position with the Washington Post and that he wanted to take it.

"I'm not surprised you were offered that job," I said, trying to hide my sense of loss. "As I've been saying all along, you are good – very good – and I have dreaded this moment since before the time I asked you to work with me over a year ago. I'll find someone else to be my press secretary, I'm sure, but I'll miss your talent and your insights."

And then I looked down. I couldn't look at him without crying. I added, "and I'll miss *you*. I know we won't be able to see much of each other from now on, and I know you'll want to be careful about even the possible appearance of any potential conflicts of interest..." and I began to tear up anyway.

"Tell me not to go," he said. He was crying, too.

I knew what he was asking, but I just couldn't do it.

"I can't, Jeremy. You're too good and too ambitious. You need to do this. If I asked you to stay, you'd always wonder what might have been."

As I sent him home that night, I hugged him closely and we both cried some more. "Just so you know," I said, "I do and did love you."

It felt as if I had done the right thing: I didn't want a life partner; at least I didn't want one at that stage in my life. Still, I knew that I would be lonely without Jeremy in my life would miss him terribly.

Over the three-day Columbus Day weekend, Sandra came to visit us. There was no question about it; she slept in Timothy's room with him. I shook my head and wondered in amazement about how much things had changed during the past twenty-five years.

That Saturday night, Timothy took Sandra to a party hosted by Andy and Vicki Petry. It was a Columbus Day themed party, and everyone was to show up in a costume related to Columbus Day. I gather most of the others were dressed as sailors, conquistadors, or Caribbean Indians, but Sandra and Timothy covered themselves in red stick-on dots.

"We're going as smallpox," announced Timothy, "one Columbus's gifts to the new world."

Where did he get that? Anyway, I was glad to see he was questioning the standard history taught in most schools.

They left the party early and were half laughing and half crying when they came in the door.

"Ms. Young," said Sandra, "those friends of Timothy's are so *different*!"

"How so?" I smiled as I asked my usual stock question.

"Well, for one thing, all the drinking. Sure, we drink a bit at some of our parties in Omaha, but not like that! And all the overt flirting and sex talk. It's exciting, in a way, but I'm not sure I want to leave Timothy here without me anymore," she laughed.

"Can you guess how Vicki treated her?" Timothy laughed.

"Tell me. I don't think I want to guess."

"She said, 'Oh, you're *cute*! No wonder my boyfriend likes you. How about a threesome?' Just like that!"

"Mom, she actually referred to me as her boyfriend! I was so embarrassed."

"It's okay, lover-boy," laughed Sandra. "After meeting her, I'm not so concerned about you."

And then she got a serious tone of voice.

"I *am* a bit concerned about *her*, though. She's more than just a little weird. I think she's going to have some seriously rough times in life."

"Was Paula there?" asked Liz.

Again Timothy was a bit embarrassed, and said, "Yes, she was."

Sandra said, "She was one of the nicest people at the party. I can see why you like to spend time with her. If I lost you to her, I'd understand it. I'm so glad we had those two and a half months together this summer to work on our relationship, though," and she leaned over, touched his shoulder, kissed him, and took his hand, leading him into the bedroom.

Sandra and Timothy spent the rest of the weekend discussing where to go to college the next year. Money wasn't a problem for either of them since Timothy had an educational trust fund, and the universities where Sandra's parents taught both had scholarship funds for children.

Through their discussions, they realized that neither of them had a very good idea of what they wanted to do after college or what they wanted to study. They had both gone through batteries of tests designed to help them decide what they wanted, but the results were so vague that neither of them felt very confident about where to go or what to study.

"Go to as good a school as you can," I said, "because the credential of coming from a good school will serve you well later in life."

They agreed they didn't want to go to a big-name Ivy school and they didn't want to go to a huge state university even though they did talk about some pretty good ones for a while. In the end they agreed to look at top-rated small midwestern liberal arts colleges like Oberlin, Grinnell, and Carleton as their potential first choices. Then they also agreed to look at other similar schools in case they didn't get into one of their top choices, and so they looked at Monmouth, Knox, and Coe Colleges.

"You need to think about the next part very carefully," I cautioned them. "I know you are both very smart and very good students, but what if one of you gets admitted to a top school and the other doesn't? Or what if you're only admitted to different schools?"
They hadn't thought about it. And they didn't want to think about it. But I pushed just a bit.

"Let me offer an option," I said. "If you don't both get accepted together at one of your first-choice colleges, then each of you should go to the best college you can, separately, and work very hard so that you can get good enough grades to transfer after your first year. Now that I've been out in the world again, I can see that being from a good school is very important.

People don't ask, 'What were your grades in college?' They ask, 'Where did you go to college?'"

During that autumn, Dale Hazelton arranged with his firm to spend much more time working in Washington. He still commuted to Omaha for some of his work, and while he was there he continued to monitor the firm we had hired to look after both our houses. I was relieved that Dale had been able to make that arrangement with his work because it meant it was much less likely that Thelma would leave in the near future. With Jeremy gone, I didn't want to lose her, too.

With Jeremy out of my life, I became more interested in the social life of Washington DC. Well, maybe not so much 'more interested in' as 'more involved in'. I went to more parties, and I actually started accepting dinner-date invitations from other men. The social life was fun, and so was the dating, but it all felt terribly ... well, I guess 'political' is the best word to describe it. I was on my guard all the time, asking myself, "What does she want? Why did she invite me to this party? What does he want? Which lobby group is he with?"

Most of the time it was obvious what people wanted, and that made the situations much easier for me to deal with:

- The wives of several Members of Congress wanted to set me up with friends of theirs.
- Several different farm lobbyists took me to dinner, allegedly to try to get to know me better as a person.
- Representatives from Planned Parenthood wanted to speak with me about my ambivalence on abortion.
- And I couldn't count the number of mid-level executives from all the war corporations who tried to meet me socially, one way or another.

I had kept my slimmer shape by watching my diet and trying to keep up with exercise, and that quite clearly attracted some of the men. I tried to make sure I said goodnight to those men at the front door of the condo or in their limos so I wouldn't have to get rid of them later. I missed having sex with Jeremy, but I wasn't about to hop into bed with the next available man.

Seth was taking a night course on Tuesdays at George Mason, and Liz took the bus over there after her school to meet with him those days. They studied together and had fast food together for supper, and then she did homework in the library. When his class was finished, the two of them took the bus back home together.

At least that's what Liz told me initially.

Later I learned that actually she was sitting in on his history class with him and absolutely loving it.

"Mom, my own school work is really easy. I get it done at school and on the bus. And this is so cool. I actually get what's going on in the course, and Seth and I get to talk about it, too. I just love this! We're not just studying names and dates; we're learning why things happened."

"Thelma," I said in late October, "Let's book off a noon and afternoon for you and me to go to lunch over across the bay bridge at one of the places on Kent Island."

"I'd love it! There are several great-sounding places over there where we can have a private lunch for just the two of us so we can catch up."

Thelma booked us a quiet corner table on a Tuesday at the Kentmorr Crab House, and it was perfect. We practically had the place to ourselves, and the wait staff not only didn't recognize me, but they seemed to understand that they should not hover around us while we talked. I just hoped our eating space hadn't been bugged; I still had some residual paranoia.

After we ordered some wine, I didn't hesitate to get into the problems I was feeling.

"Thelma, I hate this job."
"Then quit, girl!"

"I can't. I committed to so many people that I would serve out the term, but you can bet I won't run for re-election. When we're home for Thanksgiving, I want to meet with Ben Gruvel and Barry Jones to let them know.

"I haven't been here even a year," I continued, "and I can see I'm not cut out for this life. I was much more content back home, working with a few charities, and spending more time with my children and our friends."

"I thought I could do some good here. I thought I could help make people's lives better. But all I'm doing is fighting, fighting, resisting, and resisting. It's like a high-stakes board game for most people here, but it's not a game for me, and I hate the lack of trust I feel constantly."

"You're all over the place, girl! What's the problem? Or should I ask 'What, specifically, are the problems?'"

"You're right," I said. "Let me try to organize my thoughts a bit better.

"First there is all the time pressure. My children are growing up, and I need to be a bigger part of their lives."

Thelma hesitated before responding.

"I know. In addition to being your personal assistant, I'm managing the FRY scholarship program. It ain't easy. I know I don't have to read all the drek that crosses your desk, and I don't have to go to all those meetings, so it's easier here for me. Also, I have Dale here, too, and he's a big help with all the details of life you have to handle on your own. If you're really going to serve out your term, we should talk about things you can do and that we can help you do to reduce the time pressures."

"Thanks, Thelma."

"The other thing is that your kids are pretty active and pretty responsible…" and then she smirked a bit. "I wouldn't let my son date your daughter if they weren't!"

I just smiled. I wasn't in the mood for this type of banter.

Thelma picked up on it right away.

"Listen, girl, what would you do if you had more time to spend with your kids? Huh? They have their own lives to live, and you're home with them over the supper hour most nights. You've done a good job of rearranging your schedule so you can do that."

"Maybe. I asked others how Representative Glennson handles her time. You know she's a single mother of teenagers, too, and do you know what she does? She ships her children off to boarding school! They don't even come home for Thanksgiving! Well I'm not doing that!"

"Maybe you can rely on the staffers to do more reading and screening for you? I know you're up 'til all hours reading briefings and draft legislation. Can you farm out more of that?"

"Oh, Thelma, I'd love to, and I really want to, but I just don't know who I can trust in the office."

"Well, girl, you'll have to trust a few more people, or else you'll drive yourself crazy. Especially I think you can trust Bill Ashford with more. I've picked up on a few things he has said that indicate he's happy to be supporting you and your views on most things."

We sat quietly sipping our wine as our meals were delivered.

"Trust. You nailed it! That's the second thing about the job that's getting to me. Trust and suspicion. I've never been in situations like this where I have to be wary of everyone and everything around me. That's so hard!"

"It's hard because it matters more now," Thelma replied. "We have all the same tensions back in Omaha; it's just that they don't matter much, so we just trust and let things go. But here, you're making all sorts of important decisions; you can't just trust everyone."

"Here's a suggestion, then. How about I try relying on Bill and Betty even more in the office? How about I try trusting them more. If I ever find out they're not in line with my views on something, maybe I can shift that portion of work to a junior staffer? Will that work?"

"Now you're thinking!"

We ate in silence for a few moments. Finally she looked up at me and said, "Susan…," It was unusual for her to call me 'Susan' instead of 'girl', and so I knew something else was on her mind.

"What?"

"How much of this is due to Jeremy's resignation and your break up with him?"

Without hesitation, I answered, "Some, I'm sure. I miss him. But not only did I expect us to break up, I actually forced it. When he told me about his job offer from the Washington Post, he also said, 'Tell me to stay'. Thelma, he was asking me to agree to a long-term relationship with him, and I couldn't. Instead, I said the same thing to him that Timothy said to me about running for the Senate – 'you'll never know if you don't try it, and you'll be wondering "what if" for the rest of your life.' I couldn't live with him if I thought I had kept him from a major dream position in journalism."

"So, you're saying, 'yes, the break up with Jeremy is part of my problem."

I held up my fork as if I was about to flick some crab meat at her.

"Yes," I admitted, "and no. I knew this would happen, and I even tried to prepare my mind for it. And yes, I do miss him."

"Is there any way you two can keep seeing each other?"

"Not really. Dating a politician is sure way to ruin one's career as a journalist. And dating a journalist is not always great for a politician."

Chapter 51 – **Breaking the News**

In mid-November, Jeremy called me. He said it was just to talk and catch up, and he spent a lot of time asking me about the children and about the Hazeltons. He said his job was going as well as expected.

"What a pressure cooker!" he exclaimed. "I feel under the gun to produce newsworthy columns all the time, and I love it!"

When he talked about the pressure, I had faint hopes that the job wasn't working out for him and that he'd want to work with me again in the future. But when he added, "I love it!" that dashed my hopes … for the moment.

But just for the moment.

"Susan," he went on, "I miss you. I know better than to ask for more than going steady, but I want to go steady with you again."

"I miss you, too, Jeremy. But how can you date me and do your job with integrity?"

He snorted, "I think at least half the people working here are dating or seeing or living with politicians or lobbyists or someone involved with government policy. I wish I had known that from the outset. If they tried to restrict dating and partnerships here, they'd have trouble keeping a full staff of writers and editors."

"Come over!" I implored him. "Right now!"

And he did.

- - -

Dale returned to Omaha on the Tuesday before Thanksgiving, and the rest of us flew home on Wednesday afternoon. Thelma had arranged a meeting with Ben Gruvel and Barry Jones for that evening, and I asked her to be a part of it, too.

We met at my Omaha constituency office as soon as we landed.

"Ben, Barry," I said almost as soon as I went into the conference room, "I will not be running for re-election. I will serve out my term, doing my very best for everyone, but I don't like this life."

"Why don't you resign now if you don't like it?" asked Barry Jones, altogether too eagerly.

I knew the state Republicans couldn't wait to replace me with someone more amenable to the wishes of the farm lobby.

"I promised the people of Nebraska that I would serve a full term. I would never be able to live with myself if I dabbled and quit. Ben, you know I'm not that type of person."

"Also," I added, "I'm actively involved in a great deal of important work in the Senate right now. I want to do what I can to see it through."

Ben had remained stone-faced through the discussion, but then he spoke. "Susan, you and I have had our clashes, our serious disagreements, but I am confident that you would be re-electable if you want to run again in five years, despite your views on farm policy. The voters of Nebraska love you and love your cautious views on war and welfare and foreign policy and you name it. Please don't be hasty."

I hadn't anticipated that response from Ben. He had been merciless in his attempts to bully me about farm policy. And yet, there he was, pushing me to reconsider.

"Why, Ben? Why are you not jumping for joy?"

"Susan, you're a tough fighter and a tough opponent. I respect that about you. I more than respect it; I admire it. Also, you have a stronger sense of integrity than I have seen from any other politician. I may vehemently oppose your views on farm policy, but I have so much respect for you as a person and as a politician, I can't help but want you to run again."

I actually got up from my chair and hugged him. "Thank you, Ben!"

And then he turned to Barry Jones and said, "Listen, Barry, no matter how much the farm lobby might be concerned about Susan, they know she's easily re-electable. They know she can win re-election even without their support. They may not come on board, but they won't necessarily come out strongly for the Democrats either. And let's admit to ourselves that having Susan re-elected would be good for the Republican Party, both here in Nebraska and nationally."

The four of us – Ben, Barry, Thelma, and I – went out to dinner that evening to patch things up, to celebrate, and generally to enjoy life.

Timothy went to dinner Wednesday night at Sandra's home. Her parents had similar advice as mine about colleges, but they also stressed the importance of 'brand recognition' from the top Ivy League schools. Timothy and Sandra began to rethink their choices after that discussion.

Lannie, Sandra's mother told them, "You have nothing to worry about from the other students at the Ivy schools, some of whom might be elite snobs. Timothy, your mother is a Senator, and Susan your parents are university professors. You might be surprised how accepting everyone would be there. Give it some thought."

That evening, Liz was on her own ... but not for long. She called Becky, Seth, and Aaron and invited them over to the games room.

"Mom! Things are *so* different now! Instead of playing games and having belching contests, we sat around and talked about history and the evolution of people and everything. It's *so* different and *so* cool!"

"How were Aaron and Becky?" I asked.

"They were cool, too! They are good friends. They're both dating other people, but they are still very good friends. I've never seen anything quite like it, and it was wonderful. Oh, Mom! Life is so wonderful!"

On Thursday morning, we had a leisurely breakfast at home. I told the children that I had informed Ben and Barry that I wouldn't be seeking re-election.

"I just don't like the job and the working conditions," I smiled.

They were both disappointed.

"But Mom, you must be good at what you do. I know you'd win again," said Liz, brimming with confidence.

"Uncle Ben thinks I'd win, too," I agreed, "but winning isn't the only thing I want in life. I want serenity. Oh, I know serenity is supposed to come from within me, but it can't so long as I'm a Senator. By the time 2008 rolls around, Timothy you'll be finishing college, probably, and Liz you'll be well into your college education..."

Timothy interrupted, "That's right, Mom, and so you'd have more time to fight for what you believe in without having to worry about us!"

"You're right, I replied. "But I don't like it. I don't like the fighting, the resisting, the plotting, and scheming, the suspicion, or the paranoia. I'll try to stand up for all that I believe in for the next five years; that was my commitment to the voters; but I can't do it any longer than that."

"We'll see, Mom!" said Liz with a smirk, "You're very good and you might just get used to it."

That afternoon we were invited to the Schultzes to watch the Thanksgiving NFL football games and to stay for Thanksgiving dinner. It was pleasant and relaxing. I was sure that part of the reason I felt so relaxed was that I had come to terms with my job. Another part of the reason, I'm sure, was that Jeremy and I were back together.

"How about we sing some Thanksgiving carols?" suggested Harry Schultz, and we all laughed, remembering the big party the previous spring, when Harry had suggested we all sing 'Easter carols'.

"Okay," laughed Gail, "but who knows the words to any Thanksgiving songs?"

"No problem," said Harry, and I took a very brief, quiet moment for reflection.

"No problem" had been one of Fred's stock phrases; that and "No prob, Bob". I hated the phrases back then but after two years, I missed them.

"I put together a CD-mix of songs. We can just sing along every once in a while, when we know the words."

I always liked, "Over the River and Through the Woods," and we all knew some or most of the words for it; and even though we all knew we'd be singing "We Gather Together" in church on Sunday, we sang along with it, too. I didn't know any of the other songs; I didn't even recognize snatches of them. The children all did, though, and sang along with the ones they knew.

That evening Liz tentatively asked if Seth could sleep over.

I gulped. "It's okay with me, but somehow I feel as if I should discuss this with Thelma. Would that be okay?"

"Mah ahm… she knows. We've slept over before at their place."

My mind said "WHAT??" but I controlled myself. I tried to act fake upset.

"Really! And she didn't bother to discuss it with me! Well, at least you know she respects your privacy. … I'm calling her to chew her out for not letting me know …"

"Oh, for crying out loud, Mom! What would you have done if you had known? Grounded me?"

I just laughed. "You're probably right, Liz. And, yes, it's alright to have him over. But I want him to sleep in the spare bedroom, or better yet, in the games room."

She was horrified that maybe I had misunderstood.

And then we both burst into laughter.

Teen sex. I was never going to adjust to it.

Chapter 52 – **Not Announcing Announcements**

The Gruvels invited us over for dinner on Saturday evening. Ben was planning to barbecue steaks, and Cindy was going to look after everything else; they didn't want us to bring a thing.

"Cindy," I said when she called with the invitation, "The children are in pretty close relationships now. Timothy and Sandra are talking about where to go to college together, and Liz and Seth attend some classes at George Mason together. Is it okay if they bring their 'partners'?"

I laughed at myself and asked, "Cindy, what's the right word for a boyfriend or a girlfriend that you've been seeing for a long time?"

"I don't know, Susan. 'Partner' works for me. And yes, it'll be great to have all of you here if you can all make it. Ben will just have to put more steaks on the barbecue."

When I told the children we'd been invited to dinner Saturday at Uncle Ben's and Aunt Cindy's they were okay with it, but not ecstatic; however, when I told them they could bring Seth and Susan, they became quite enthusiastic.

"That'll be great," said Liz. "Wait 'til Seth sees that mansion they live in!"

Shortly after we went in, Cindy said, "Why don't I show you young people around while Ben and Susan pow-wow out on the patio?"

Ah, so it was going to be part business, part pleasure.

"Cindy said you wanted me to 'pow-wow' with you out here, Ben," I said as I walked out to the patio. It was cold out there, but it was private.

"Well, I wouldn't put it that way, Susan. I just wanted to let you know again that I am confident you will be re-elected if you decide to run again. But I also want to let you know that I will respect your decision, if you choose not to seek re-election."

In other words, he had rethought everything, and he would be just as happy if I didn't run again. At least that was how I read it in my guarded, cynical frame of mind.

"Thanks, Ben," I said, masking my cynicism. "I'll always value your support and advice."

And then, just to get a better read on how he really felt, I tried to gauge his reaction as I asked in a serious, maybe beseeching tone of voice, "Ben, honestly, what do you think I should do?"

His pause made it clear to me that he and Barry had decided that it would be best for the party if I didn't run, but I let him try to talk his way around that. He did, and he was good.

"Susan, I've learned from our past struggles that trying to tell you what to do is a fool's game. I hope you understand that I will back you solidly whatever you decide."

"I know, Ben, and I'm so grateful. For now, let's just keep everything quiet so I can get my work done in the Senate without being treated like a five-year lame duck. If anyone asks any of us if or when I'll announce my decision, we should all agree that I'm not thinking about re-election now but I'm trying to focus on my work in the Senate. We can announce it maybe a year and a half before the election, but please not until then."

I had always loved Ben and Cindy, and I knew we would always be friends, but our split on agriculture policy eroded a corner of our friendship.

We hadn't gotten together with the Hazeltons the entire time we had been home for Thanksgiving, at least not as just our two families. I wasn't sure it could happen that year, but I wanted it to. I wanted to recapture some of the old feelings of neighborliness and friendship, and so during dinner at the Gruvels, I excused myself to text Thelma on her Blackberry while I was in the bathroom. I couldn't believe I did it, but I knew it was almost standard procedure for people with Blackberries.

"Would your family like to do something with our family tomorrow? I would," I texted.

I immediately turned off my Blackberry so the beep announcing her reply wouldn't disrupt our dinner with the Gruvels.

When we got home, though, I turned the phone back on and found a message, "We want to fly your family to Paris next weekend for breakfast, okay?"

I laughed out loud, and showed the messages to Timothy and Liz.

"That's gotta be Aaron," said Liz. "He's been pranking people's phones at school, too. One day Ms. Collier left her phone out, and Aaron used it to order pizza for the entire class. Fortunately, the pizza place called to confirm the order. Ms. Collier was definitely not pleased, but I think deep down she was amused."

I called Thelma on our regular cellphones, "Thelma, did you get my message?"

"What message?... Aaron!!!???!!! ... What have you done??" followed by screams, giggles, laughter.

When Thelma came back on the phone, she said in a nasally voice, "We regret to inform you that you had only five minutes to confirm your acceptance of that promotional offer, and it is no longer available. Would your family settle for a McDonalds breakfast tomorrow instead?"

"I'd love it! That way we can do something fun together and still have a few hours to repack before we fly back to DC."

Sandra came along to McDonalds. Eight people for breakfast at McDonalds. That sounded pretty good to me; in fact, it was a symbol of something significant for me. I was fed up with pretentious parties and expensive meals.

That afternoon before we left, I called Jeremy. After we got past all the romantic stuff about missing each other, I said, "Jeremy, I want to put on a massive McDonalds party for my staff. Will you join us if I do?"

He laughed and said, "Senator, 'whither thou goest, I will follow.'"

When we got back to DC, Thelma chartered two buses for my staff members and their families for what we told them would be 'The Most Unusual, Unpretentious Holiday Party Ever'" We set the party for early afternoon on Saturday, December 6th, and I made arrangements with a local McDonalds to have extra staff members on hand to deal with us all.

At first no one believed it when we pulled into.... McDonalds??? Really?

And then everyone started laughing and cheering. It was, indeed, the most unusual, unpretentious holiday party ever, as everyone pigged out on double quarter-pounders, Happy Meals, Big Macs, shakes, McFlurries, fries, the whole menu. And while we were waiting for the food orders to be ready, I made one of my shortest speeches:

> I don't know about you folks, but this suits me at least as much as afternoon tea at The Ritz. I hope you'll all have fun.

Then I walked around and gave each family a Christmas card with a $25 McDonalds and a $25 Wendy's gift card. I remembered how much we had appreciated the pizza gift card from Betty LeDuc right after Fred was killed, and I hoped my staff members and their families would have fun with these cards.

We also made sure that each of the children got happy meal toys and books that we had brought especially for them and that were a bit nicer than the standard happy meal toys and books.

The party went off without a hitch; everyone said they had a better time than they would have at a standard Christmas party, and I think they meant it. And of course Jeremy was there, taking photos for an article in the Washington Post, "Senator Entertains at McDonalds". Later, he told me the editor wanted a headline "Senator Entertains on the Cheap" but he finally persuaded them to use the more neutral headline when he pointed out how much had been spent on gift cards and toys and books.

"Jeremy, I worry. You're not my publicist. You're not even my press secretary anymore. You can't do this, can you?"

"Probably not, at least not on any regular basis," he said. "It'd be way too obvious if I do it too often since people know I used to work for you. But that's how most of the writers there get their stories – from and about people they know or used to work for. I'll be okay; don't worry."

- - -

We spent Christmas back in Omaha, and Jeremy came with us.

On Christmas Eve, after everyone had sung carols and filled stockings, Jeremy gave me a small box. I half-hoped it was a ring. I knew I wanted to marry him.

It wasn't an engagement ring, though. It was a rubber O-ring, like the gaskets you used to find in a faucet.

I was puzzled, but I knew there had to be a story along with it, and so I smiled and asked him, "Okay, Jeremy, what does this mean?"

"The O-ring is a gasket. It stops leaks – sort of a stop-gap measure. In our case, though, it means I have a real ring waiting for you when you're ready."

"Do you have it with you?" I asked eagerly.

He was stunned. "No," he stammered. "It's in my apartment back in Washington…"

"Then the engagement is off," I laughed, but I quickly added, "No, no! I mean Yes, Yes! I mean … well you know what I mean. Just don't go flying back to DC to get it!"

I loved Jeremy, and I wanted to figure out how we could spend the rest of our lives together.

"Do me a favor," I said, "and get something here so you can propose to me on New Year's Day, in front of the children and the neighbors. I want them all to be a part of it. It doesn't have to be fancy, but something to make sure we get formally engaged that night."

"That'll work," he said. "The ring in Washington is on approval, so I can return it with no hassles. Let's go choose something tomorrow."

In the meantime, I wore the O-ring on my ring finger. And later I saved it, along with the ceramic cat that Fred had given me. I cherish those two gifts more than any of the other gifts I ever received from Fred or Jeremy.

Our times apart and all our struggles had led both Jeremy and me to conclude we wanted to be together. We didn't know where our careers were going to take us, but we knew we wanted to be a couple anyway, even if we couldn't always be together physically.

I was so excited that I couldn't keep the news from the children or from Thelma, and Thelma couldn't hold it in either. She told her family about it the next morning, and by noon their friends and our friends all knew about it; I was sure the whole town knew about it by mid-afternoon. When Ben heard the news, he wrote a brief email:

> Congratulations and best wishes to you both. Get a pre-nup and make new wills.

Get a pre-nuptial agreement.

I knew he was right, but the advice did put a bit of a damper on our warm bubbly feelings about the engagement. Jeremy, bless him, agreed with Ben.

I don't know how people negotiate pre-nuptial agreements. It's like negotiating a divorce before you get married; marriage is supposed to be loving, caring, and giving, not adversarial. But Jeremy was an angel about it. I suggested he might want to take a walk up around the reservoir and spend some time thinking about it.

"Sure… If you'll come with me," he smiled.

We walked; we talked; we held hands. We scowled; we frowned; we smiled. We had been together enough to know we wanted to commit to each other, but Ben's message had really bothered us.

Finally, I suggested, "Let's get engaged now, but let's leave the date for some long time in the future. That way we can back out if we want, but we can still play house for now. We can talk about the pre-nup later."

By the time we got to the Schultz's house for the annual neighborhood New Year's Day party, everyone was excited because they all knew Jeremy was going to propose. At 11:30, Gail got everyone's attention and Jeremy got down on one knee to propose. Everyone cheered as I accepted, and it all felt both good and anti-climactic. It was good to share the moment with our family, friends, and neighbors, even though he had essentially proposed to me on Christmas Eve.

On the way home, once again we all stood in the street in front of the Bergman's house, held hands in a giant circle, and sang a couple of choruses of "Auld Lang Syne". It was the third year in a row we had done that, and we all vowed to do it every year, by cellphone if we couldn't be there in person, as we had done from Washington the year before. The tradition is still going on there now, many years later!

Chapter 53 – **The More Things Changed...**

Jeremy never moved in on a permanent basis. He kept some clothes and some personal effects at my condo, but we never could face the struggles of combining our lives and households completely. It was probably better that way because the engagement meant we were committed to each other; but not completely moving in together meant we were still independent, and I needed that strong sense of independence at that point in my life.

Jeremy wasn't entirely happy with our arrangement. He wanted to move in with us, but at the same time he could see that there truly wasn't room for all of us and for all of our activities, at least not the way we wanted to engage in them. We exchanged keys, though, and Jeremy spent several nights a week with us.

In January, Timothy and Sandra received and accepted early admission offers from Princeton University, where they had applied following her parents' advice. I was thrilled beyond belief that they would be only a short train ride from Washington. And in the spring, Liz negotiated with Field School to get credit through a special program for a course in European Civilization that she and Seth took together at George Mason.

Meanwhile, in the Senate I continued my work trying to convince other senators to balance the federal budget and step back from our military operations. I met with veterans, who seemed to despair about our chances of wrapping things up quickly in either Afghanistan or Iraq. "It's easy to drop bombs," I said in one speech from the Senate floor. "It's not so easy to defeat the opposition or to bring about stability in those countries." I repeated my earlier question, 'Did we learn nothing from Vietnam?'"

And with the on-going US involvements in military operations, the budget deficits soared.

Letters from my constituents indicated that they still had major concerns about my opposition to agricultural price supports, but they strongly supported my efforts to reduce budget deficits. Their take on our foreign-military policy was mixed: they wanted the wars to be over, but they wanted to support the troops. Through my public appearances and various policy statements, I tried to make a distinction between supporting our soldiers and supporting the military-industrial complex. I'm not sure I was ever entirely successful.

In the fall of 2004, Seth re-enrolled at George Mason University. "Ms.

Young," he told me, "they have some really fascinating professors; I am really enjoying myself there. I am so glad in so many ways that I didn't go away to college," and he took Liz's hand.

"Me, too," smiled Liz. "And it has really worked out well for me to take courses for credit there. Field School has been great about that, Mom."

With Timothy and Sandra at Princeton and Seth at George Mason, Liz and Aaron started spending more time together, walking to and from school most days, even going to parties together sometimes. Finally, I asked Liz whether that was at all awkward.

"Not really," she said. "Aaron knows that Seth and I are an item, and he helps make sure the boys at school know it, too. Besides, he's dating some ninth grader now, and he seems happy with that."

And then she added, "but I'm not so sure his girlfriend is okay with our friendship. I tried to explain it to her once, but she just said, 'Yeah, like, whatever.' That's so rude! I was trying to be nice and maybe even friendly with her, but she just got all huffy. Oh well, Aaron will let her know... or more likely, he'll dump her. My guess is that before long he'll be dating Paula's sister, Michelle. She's in our class, and she and Paula are both really nice."

"But Aaron is one of my best friends," Liz continued. "I feel so lucky to have such a good friend who is a boy but not a boyfriend. The other girls in school don't understand that. For them it's impossible to be good friends with a boy without becoming boyfriend and girlfriend. I get that ... for them ... but this is perfect for me."

In the spring of 2007, I announced that I would not be seeking re-election the following year. We held a press conference in Omaha, with Ben Gruvel and Barry Jones and other state officials present, at which I read the following press release:

> I have decided not to seek re-election in 2008. I want to thank the voters of Nebraska and my friends for all your support during the past four and half years. You have all been marvelous. Thank you.
>
> Over the years that I have been in the Senate, I have done my best to help check runaway spending and to try to rein in our country's increasing military activities. I've been far from successful, but I hope my work has helped our nation along these lines.

In other areas, we have helped try to make lives better for lower-income Americans by working toward freer trade agreements with Canada and Mexico and by encouraging more incentive-based welfare programs.

There is so much more to do, but I must pass the torch to others. The reasons are many:

First, I want to spend more time working with the Frederick Robert Young Foundation, where we are now helping nearly thirty students with their college educations each year.

Second, I feel it is important to rekindle my work with LOST, an important organization devoted to helping young people who have suddenly lost a parent.

I would be remiss if I didn't mention all the staff members who have been so helpful, teaching the tortuous political ropes to this rookie politician. I especially want to thank Bill Ashford, my legislative assistant, and Thelma Hazelton, my personal assistant and good friend for over twenty years now. I couldn't have made it without you, Thelma!

And finally, I owe special thanks to Jeremy Hall, my former press secretary and my fiancé. He has added a dimension to my life that I didn't know I was missing.

The next winter while I was still trying to do what I could as a lame duck senator, Jeremy was offered an upward, diagonal promotion to become an associate editor at The Boston Globe.

"Take it!" I urged him. "We'll still commute to see each other. We can make this work."

"Okay," he agreed reluctantly, "but eventually we need to end up together, Susan."

I agreed, but I liked my life as it was, too, and I wanted to return to Omaha. I didn't want to live in Boston or Washington DC or anywhere other than Candlewood after I left the Senate. To be honest, I was tired ... but not too tired to commute to be with Jeremy frequently.

We all went back to Omaha for Easter in 2008. The Schultzes had just come back from their family winter-break vacation with a slightly unsettling story about an incident that occurred on their recent trip to Jacksonville, Florida.

"We went into a convenience store to buy some snacks, and we were waited on by a guy who reminded us all of Fred, in a way," said Harry.

"He was a lot skinnier than Fred, and his head and beard were completely shaved, and his voice wasn't exactly the same," said Gail cautiously.

"But still," Harry continued, "there was something about him that somehow reminded us all of Fred. Maybe it was his eyes? We actually argued about it in the car for a few minutes, and to check him out some more, I went back in and asked for directions to the football stadium. He looked right at me, and there was something about him that seemed eerily like Fred, but at the same time I knew it couldn't have been Fred. It was just such a weird sensation."

As we expected, I sold the two condos in Washington for much more than I had paid for them, and the corporation we had created to buy them did very well from the capital gains, despite losing money on paper while renting the units to my family and to the Hazeltons.

Moving back to Omaha and living there full-time was harder than I thought it would be. The neighborhood had changed; some people had moved out and others moved in, and all the young people our children's ages were moving away and building their own lives. Timothy and Sandra were planning to move to the west coast with new jobs; Seth and Liz were both working part time in Washington while Seth studied for his Law Degree and Liz finished her undergraduate degree. None of them could get away very often to come home to visit, and so I traveled to visit all of them, Jeremy included, several times a year.

One day in March, a couple of months after we had re-settled in Omaha, Thelma came over for coffee.

"You know, it's so different being back here after all the hustle and bustle of Washington DC," she said, "but ever since we knew you weren't returning to the Senate, I have been receiving some very attractive job offers both here and in Washington…"

She was struggling to keep it in.

"And…?" I couldn't help but smile as I encouraged her to tell me about it.

"Believe it or not, Agbrakan offered me an assistant vice presidency at an astronomical salary."

"You wouldn't, would you?" I was quite upset.

She laughed, "No, of course not! Get a grip, girl. That was only one of the job offers."

I breathed a sigh of relief.

"Actually, the vice-president for public affairs at Mutual of Omaha asked me to be his personal assistant."

"That sounds pretty exciting!" I said, "Public affairs, huh? Does that mean lobbying?"

"It sure does, girl; that, and media relations. I'd be his assistant, much the way I was your assistant in DC, but with more to look after than his appointments. And you know what?"

I didn't know what to expect, so I just said, "Tell me!"

"I told him I wanted the title of Assistant Vice President for Public Affairs, and I wanted at least double what you were paying me in salary. You know what he said?"

She didn't wait for me to ask, "What?"

"He said, 'I won't tell anyone what you just said if you don't. Here's the job offer: I was ready to give the job title change after six months, but there's no reason for you not to have it now. And the full job offer is for triple what you were making in Washington plus benefits, plus an unlimited expense account."

"Wow!" was all I could say at first, but then I added, "That is absolutely wonderful! You deserve it, Thelma!"

"So the very first thing we're doing is you and I are going to Le Voltaire again for lunch today, my treat, on my brand new corporate credit card!"

Thelma thrived in her new job, and Dale was able to shift much of his work back to Omaha. They seemed so happy together.

Meanwhile I was lonely. My children were gone, and Jeremy was in Boston. I built up thousands of frequent-flyer miles, visiting them all so often, but I still missed them, and so during my first year back in Omaha, we all learned to use Skype and keep in close contact.

I threw myself back into my other work. I took over the management of the FRY Foundation when Thelma went to work for Mutual of Omaha, and I re-established my working relationship with LOST. Once again, the church, the United Way, the Civilian Police Review Board, and many other groups asked me to be a board member, but I turned them all down. I wanted to do things on a more national or international scale, and so I became a partner with Liberty International Consulting of Chicago, where we promoted the reduction of trade barriers in agriculture and everything else, and we continued exploring my own skepticism about America's military involvements overseas. It was quite a relief to be working with an organization I felt a part of, and I enjoyed it. What's more, through them I made sure to travel more frequently to Boston, Washington DC, and the west coast, spending more time with the children and with Jeremy.

Nevertheless, rattling around in my big house in Candlewood felt different. There were no children in the games room anymore, no big get-togethers with the Hazeltons or any of the other neighbors. We still had our neighborhood Holiday Party in different homes, and we still got together at the Schultzes on New Year's Day. But on a daily basis the house felt empty – except when Jeremy or the children came to visit. We had big get-togethers for those occasions.

I considered selling the house because it was too big for just me. And yet I treasured the memories of what used to be, raising our family there, of the joy and happiness I had with Fred and then again even after he died; and I also remembered my thoughts shortly after he died when I told Kathy Bergman that I wanted to provide a base for my children and their children to visit, a base for them to call home, and a place for them to store things, and a place for them to reflect on their own happy memories.

And so I'm still here ... for now, anyway.

The End

About the Author:

John P. Palmer was born and raised in Muskegon Michigan. He attended Carleton College (Northfield, Minnesota) where nominally he majored in economics and minored in math and religion, but, he says, "The truth is that I majored in the identity crisis, minored in bridge, and barely graduated." From there, he attended The Chicago Theological seminary, took economics courses at The University of Chicago, and earned a PhD in economics at Iowa State University.

He moved to Canada in 1971, and he currently lives in London, Ontario with his wife. He has three children, seven grandchildren, and two great grandchildren. He is a professor emeritus in the economics department at The University of Western Ontario. His hobbies include music, theatre, sports, and photography. He remains active doing economics as well, having recently presented a paper on homelessness to the UN-funded Urban Economy Forum.

Susan's Story emerged in his mind as he was completing his first novel, **2605**. Reading both novels gives some insight into the minds of both Fred Young and Susan Young.

He gratefully acknowledges the suggestions and input from

> Jack Allingham,
> Bev Early,
> Lissa Kuzych,
> Dale Tassi, and
> Carolle Trembley.

Other books by John P. Palmer available on Amazon:
- **2605**
- **Three Murder Mysteries**
- **Murder at the Office Christmas Party**

Made in the USA
Columbia, SC
22 June 2020